ASTRONAUT ACADEMY
RE-ENTRY

WRITTEN AND ILLUSTRATED BY

DAVE ROMAN

COLOR BY FRED C. STRESING

:01

First Second
NEW YORK

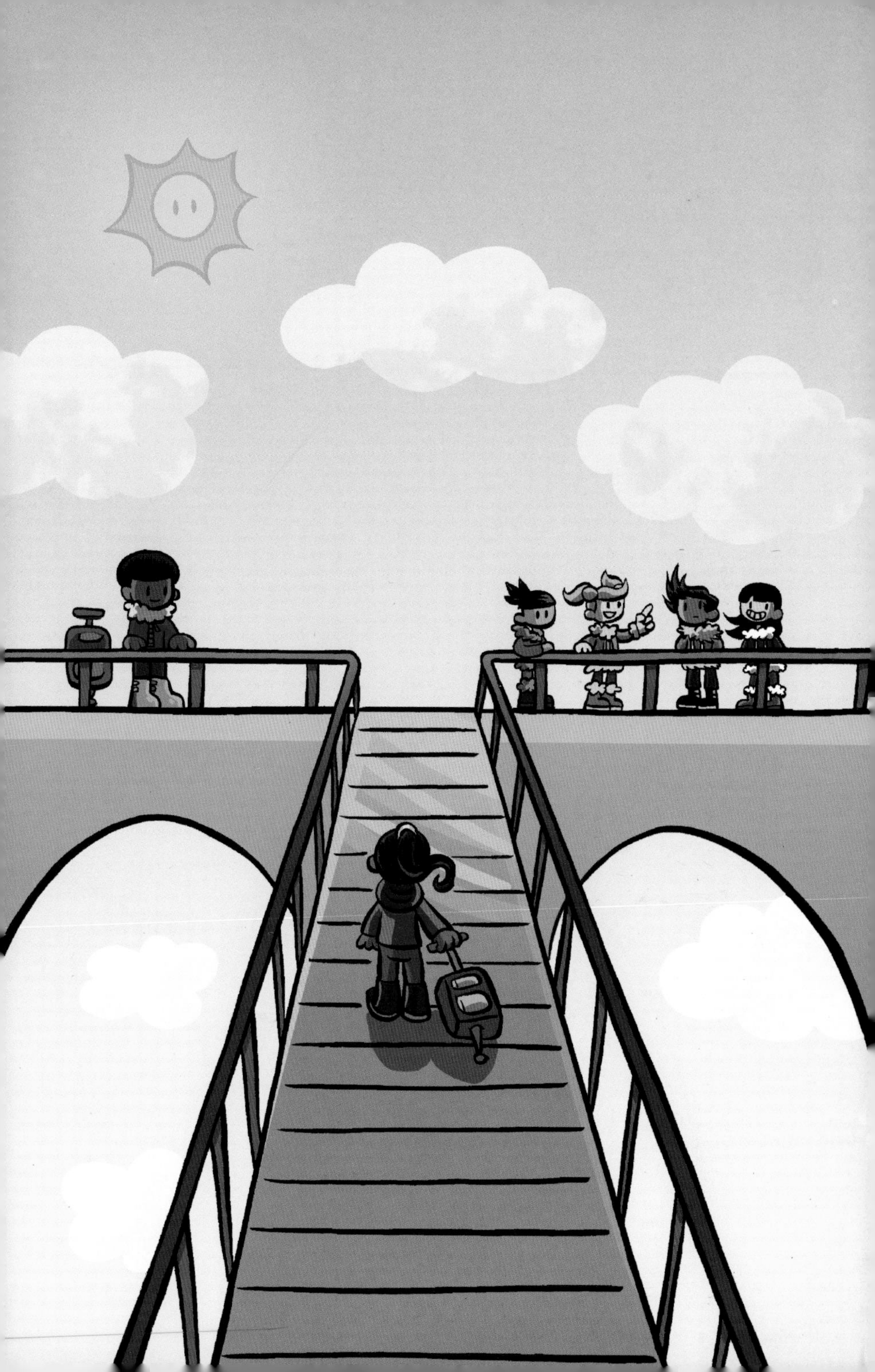

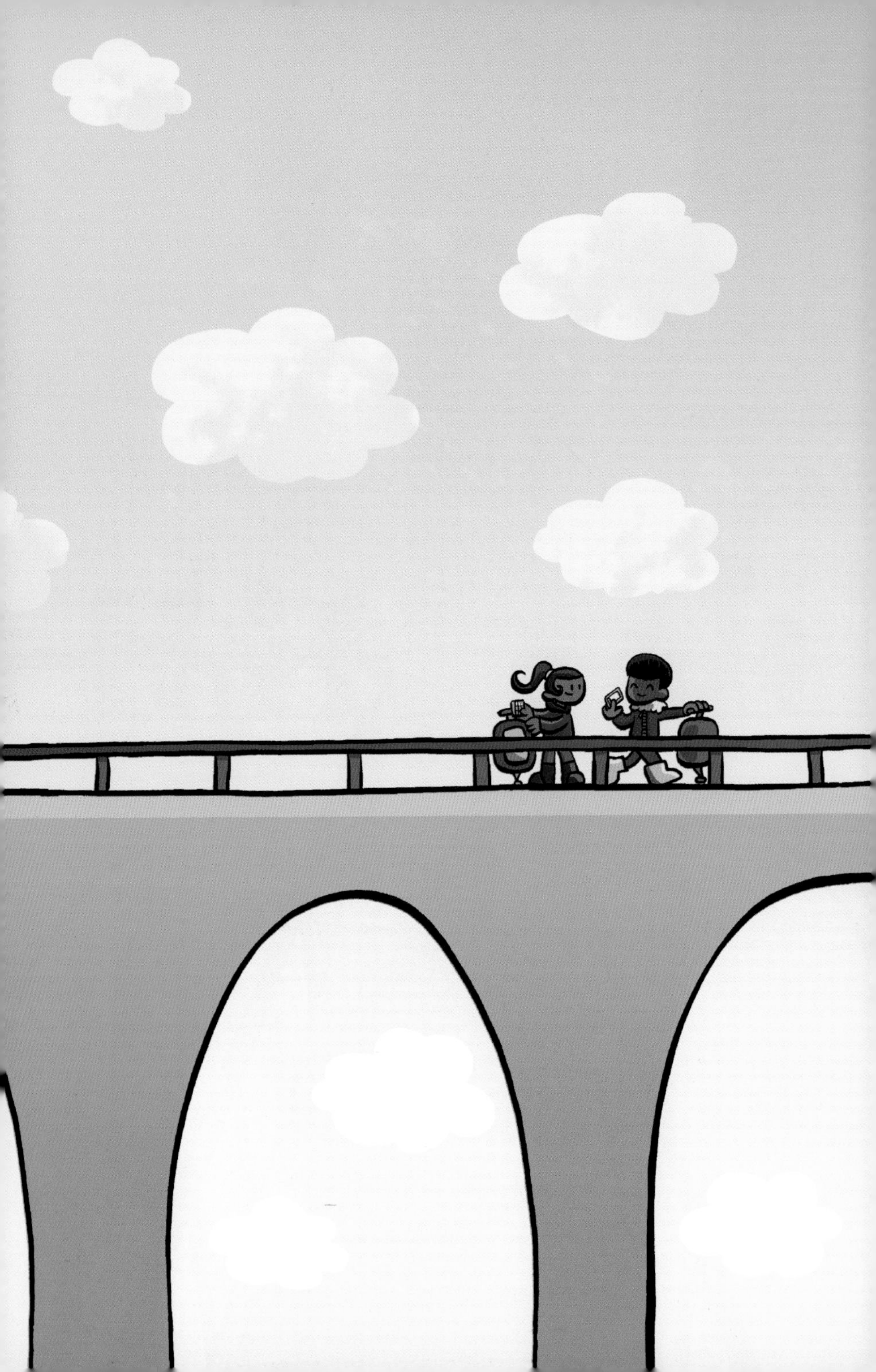

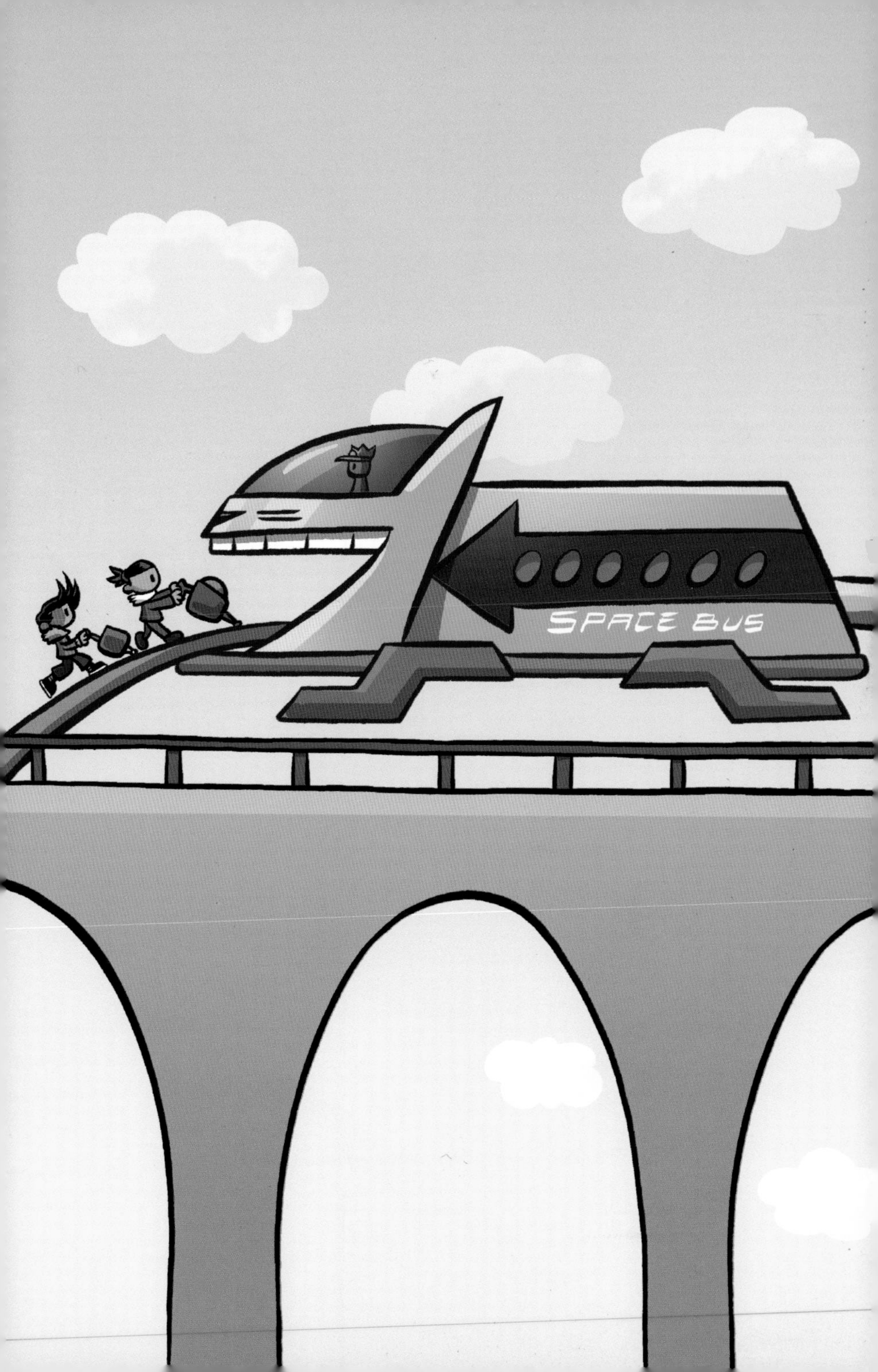
SPACE BUS

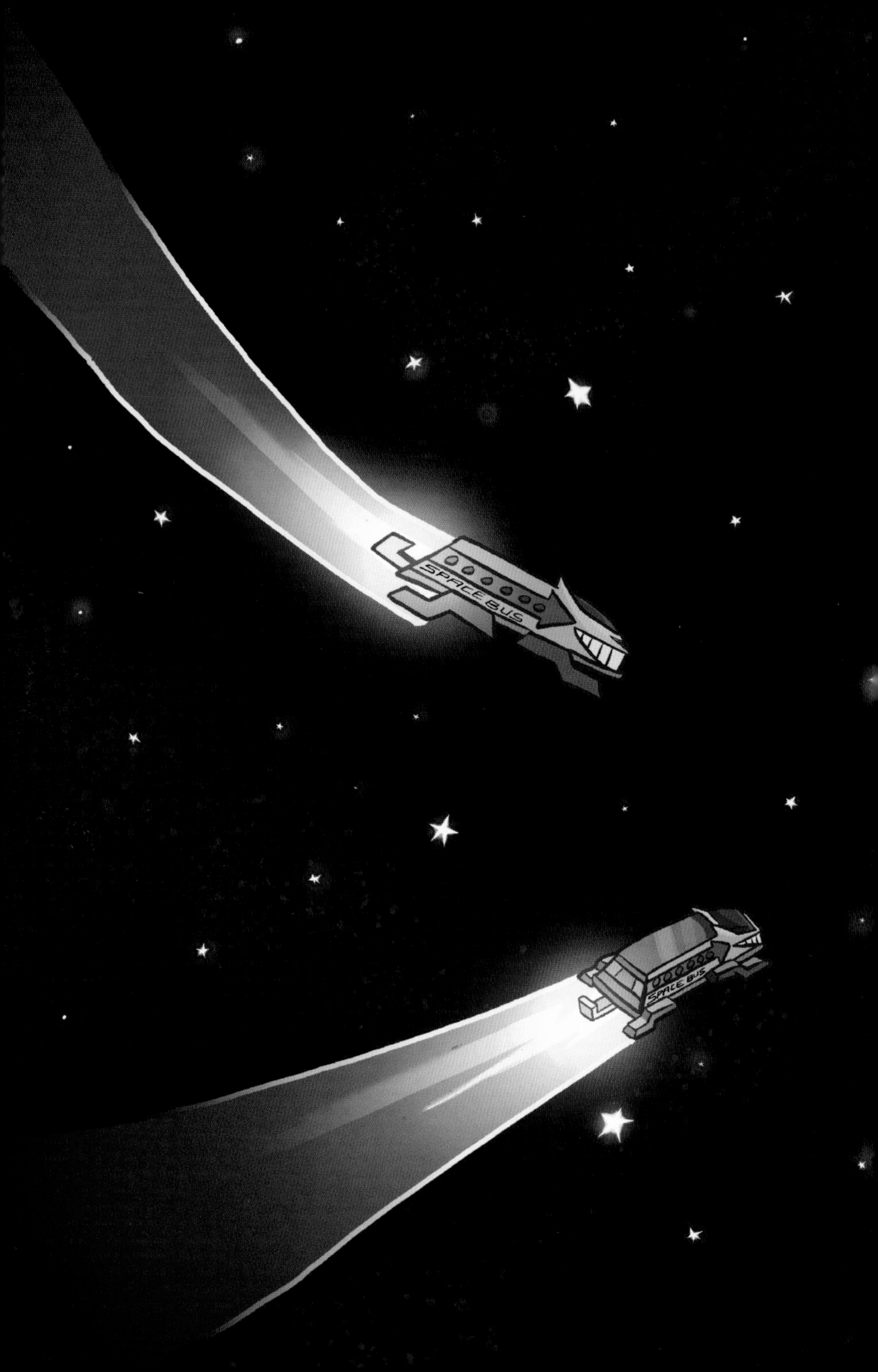
SPACE BUS
SPACE BUS

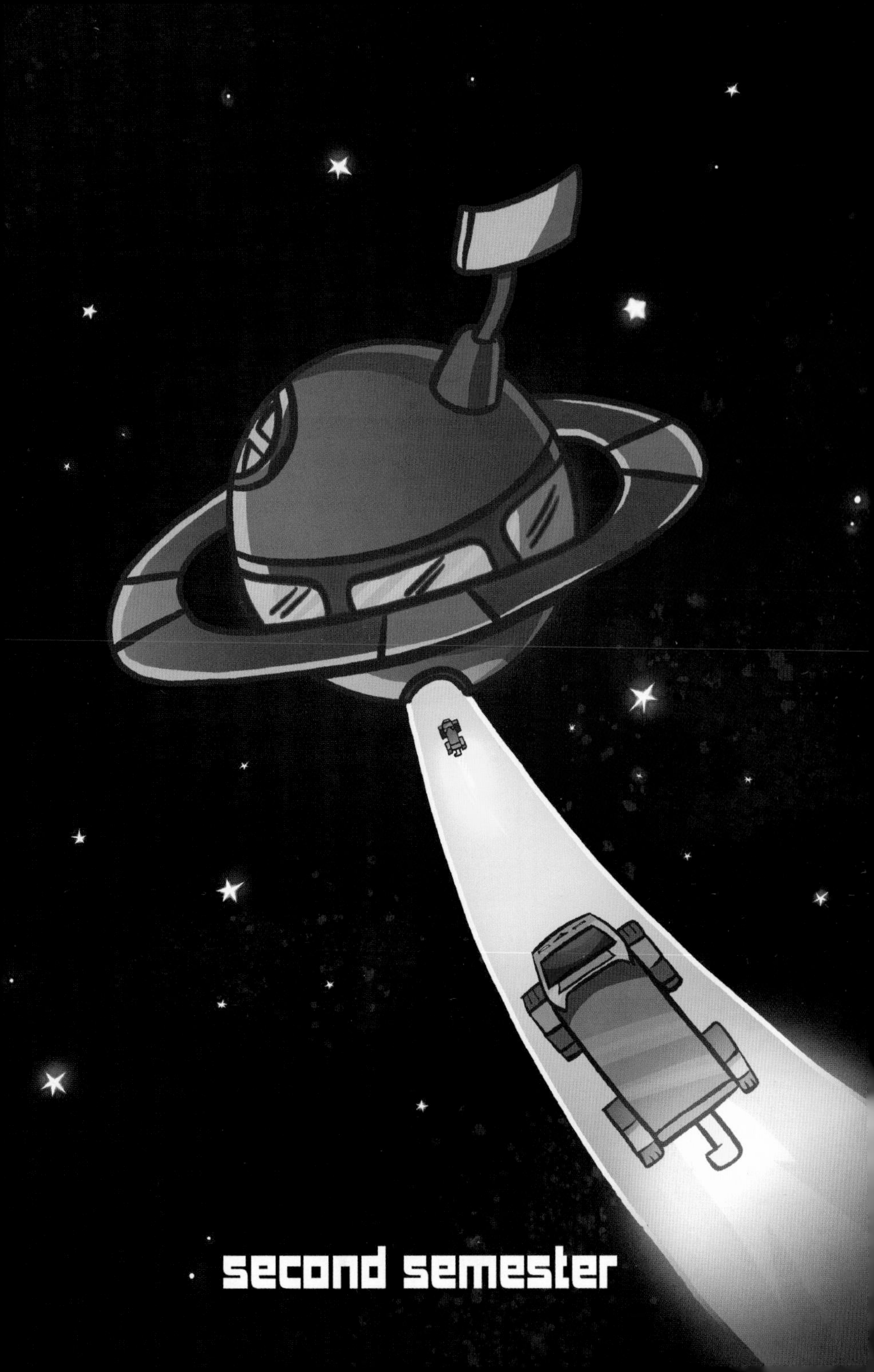
second semester

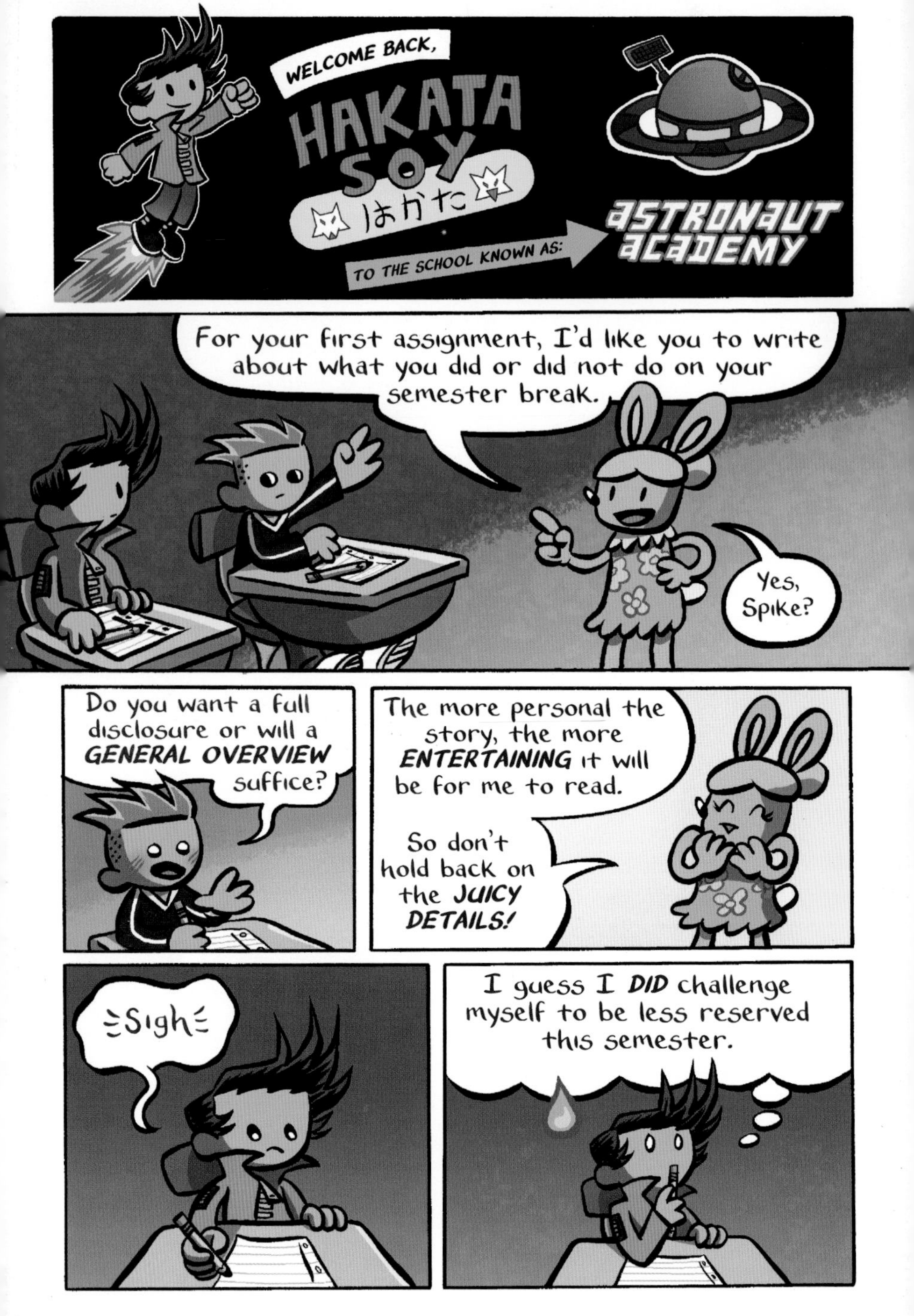
WELCOME BACK,
HAKATA SOY
はかた
TO THE SCHOOL KNOWN AS:
ASTRONAUT ACADEMY
For your first assignment, I'd like you to write about what you did or did not do on your semester break.
Yes, Spike?
Do you want a full disclosure or will a GENERAL OVERVIEW suffice?
The more personal the story, the more ENTERTAINING it will be for me to read.
So don't hold back on the JUICY DETAILS!
Sigh
I guess I DID challenge myself to be less reserved this semester.

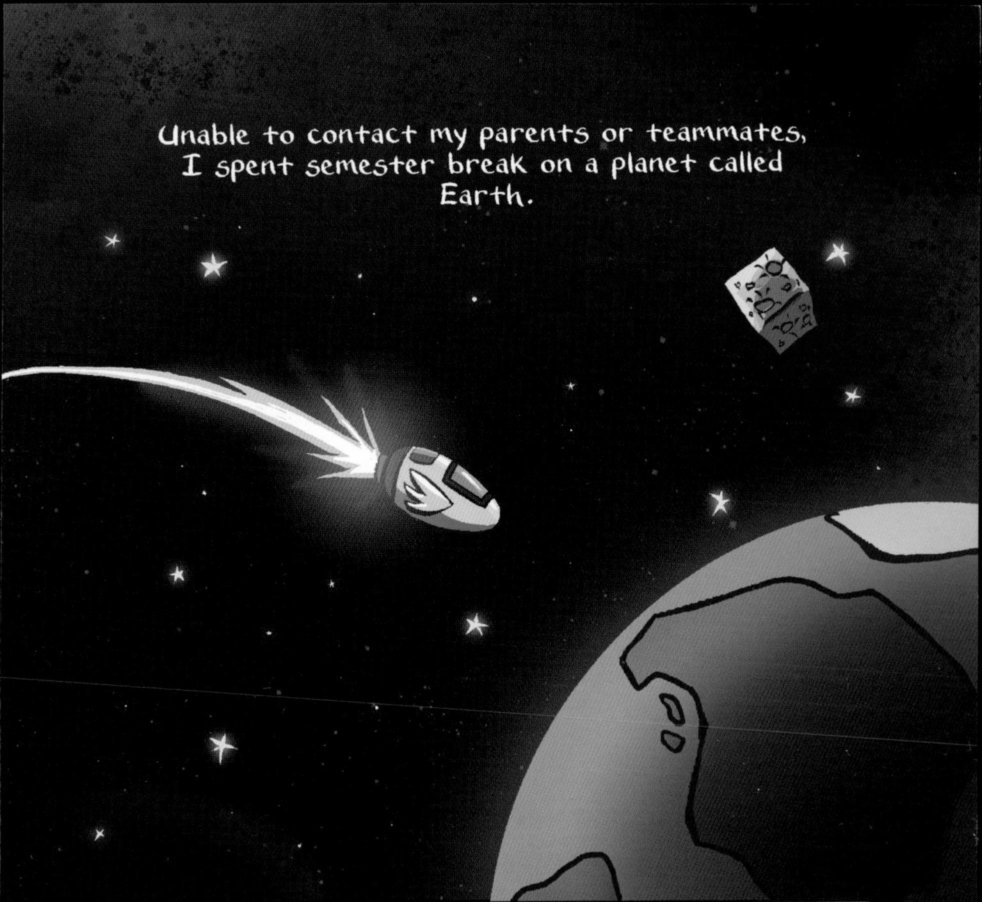
Unable to contact my parents or teammates, I spent semester break on a planet called Earth.

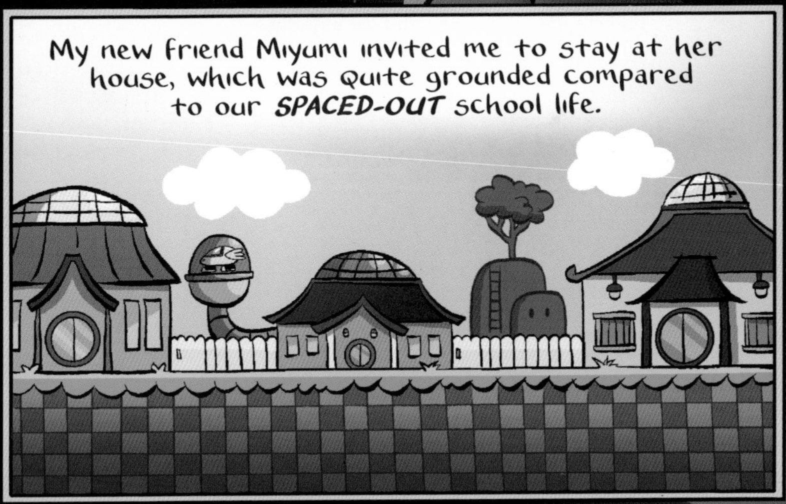
My new friend Miyumi invited me to stay at her house, which was quite grounded compared to our *SPACED-OUT* school life.

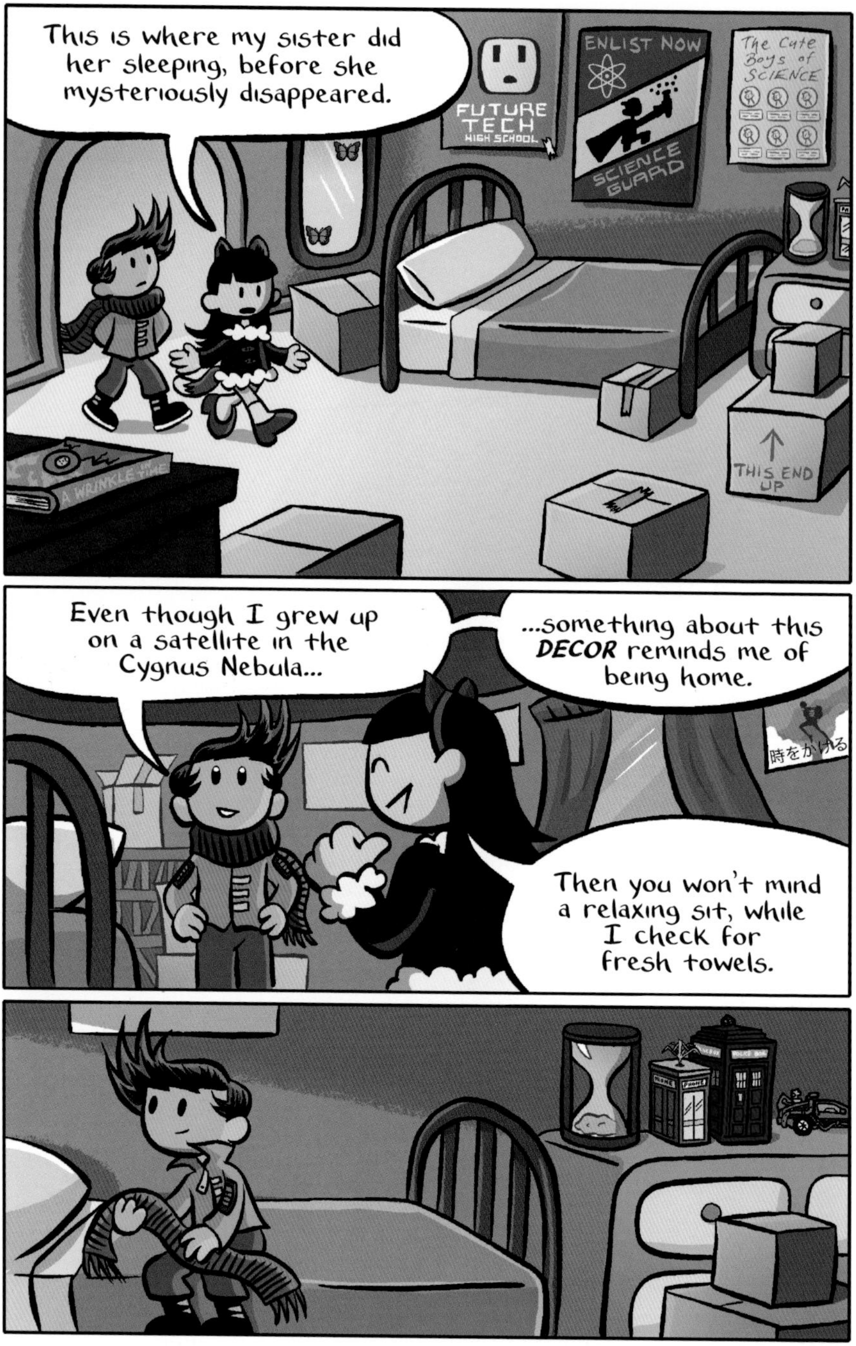
This is where my sister did her sleeping, before she mysteriously disappeared.
FUTURE TECH HIGH SCHOOL
ENLIST NOW
SCIENCE GUARD
The Cute Boys of SCIENCE
A WRINKLE IN TIME
THIS END UP
Even though I grew up on a satellite in the Cygnus Nebula...
...something about this ***DECOR*** reminds me of being home.
時をかける
Then you won't mind a relaxing sit, while I check for fresh towels.

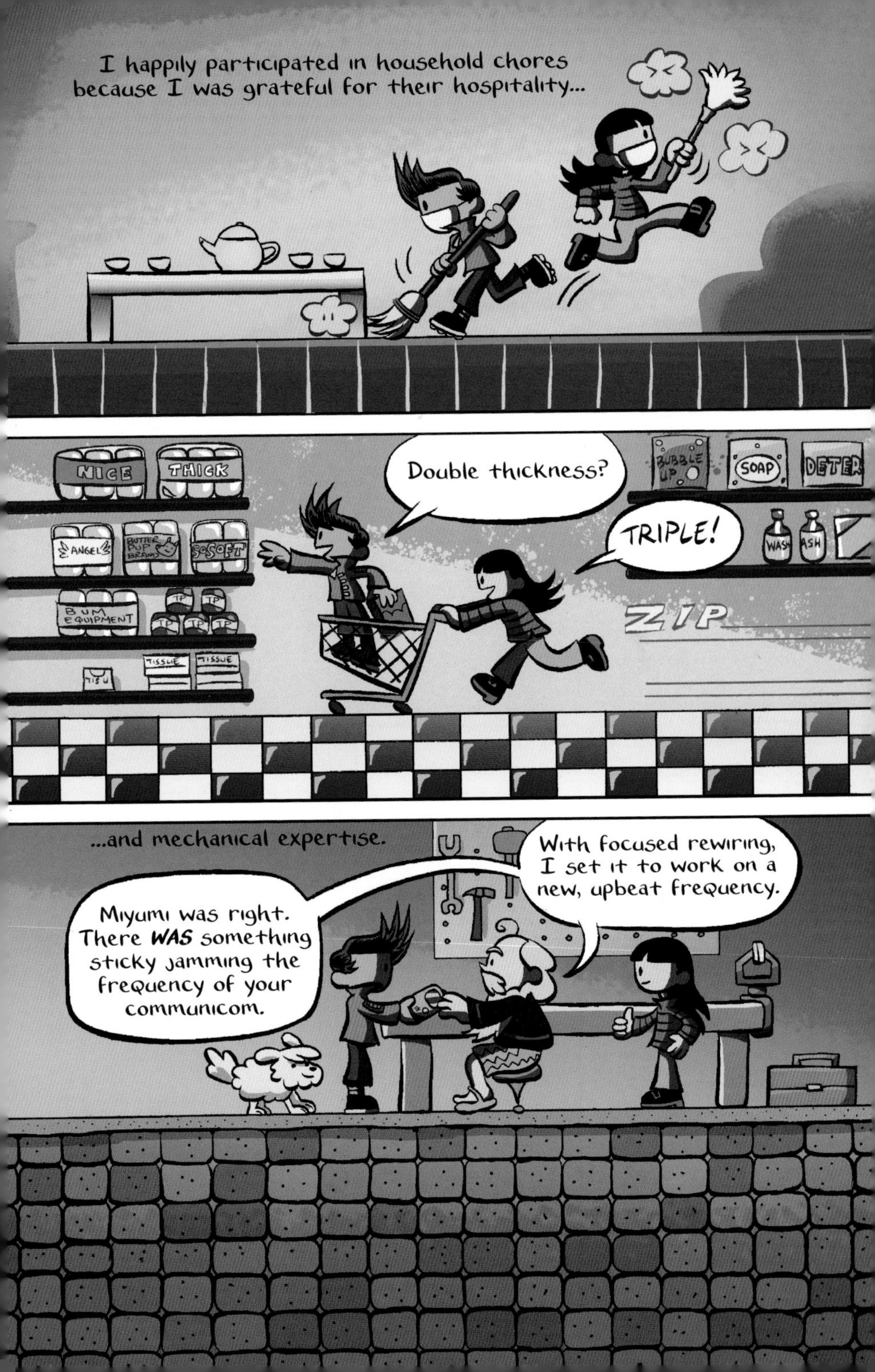
I happily participated in household chores because I was grateful for their hospitality...
NICE
THICK
ANGEL
BUTTER PUP BRAND
SOSOFT
BUM EQUIPMENT
TP
TISSUE
TISSUE
TISU
Double thickness?
BUBBLE UP
SOAP
DETER
WASH
ASH
TRIPLE!
ZIP
...and mechanical expertise.
Miyumi was right. There **WAS** something sticky jamming the frequency of your communicom.
With focused rewiring, I set it to work on a new, upbeat frequency.

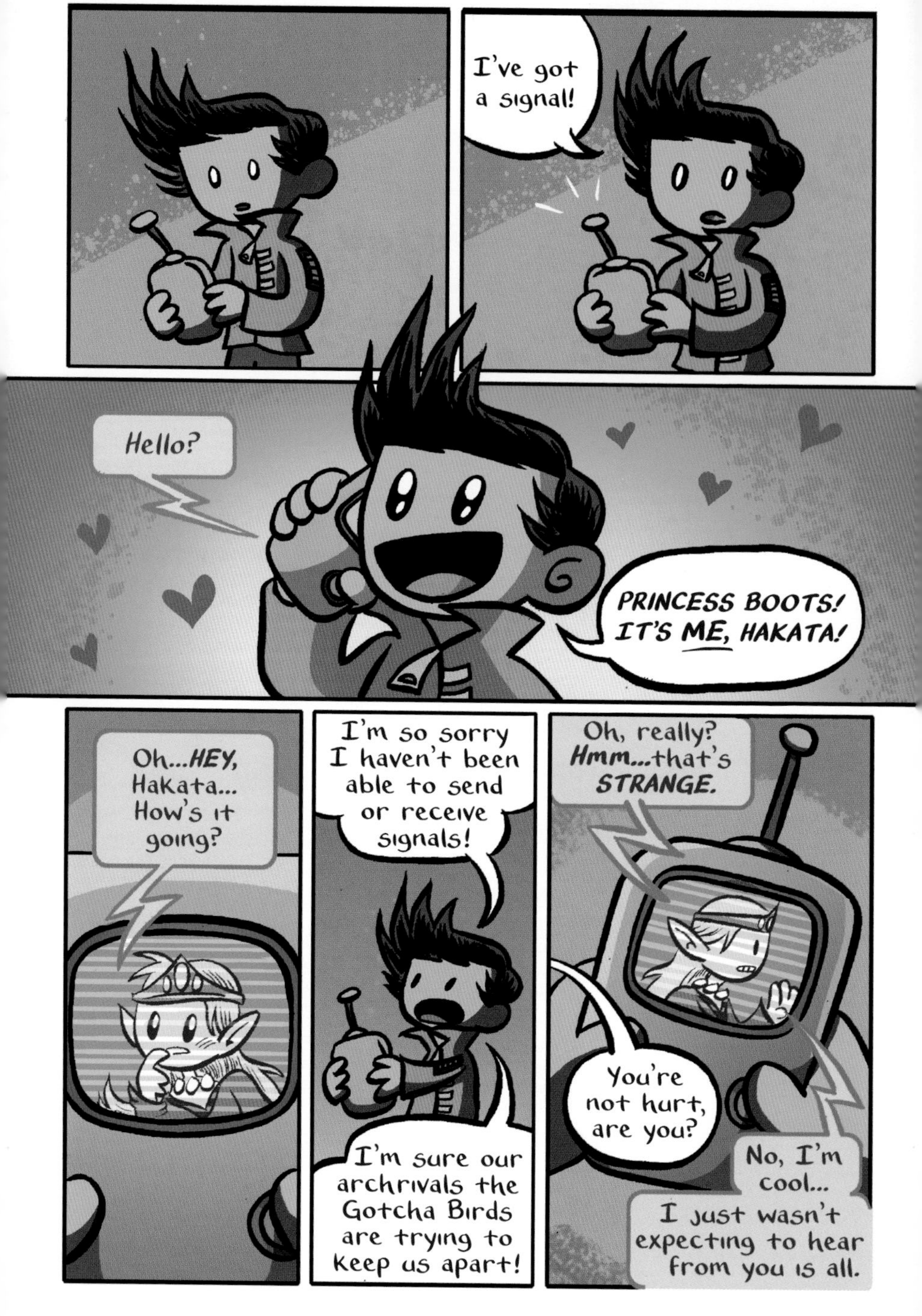
I've got a signal!
Hello?
PRINCESS BOOTS! IT'S ME, HAKATA!
Oh...HEY, Hakata... How's it going?
I'm so sorry I haven't been able to send or receive signals!
I'm sure our archrivals the Gotcha Birds are trying to keep us apart!
Oh, really? Hmm...that's STRANGE.
You're not hurt, are you?
No, I'm cool...
I just wasn't expecting to hear from you is all.

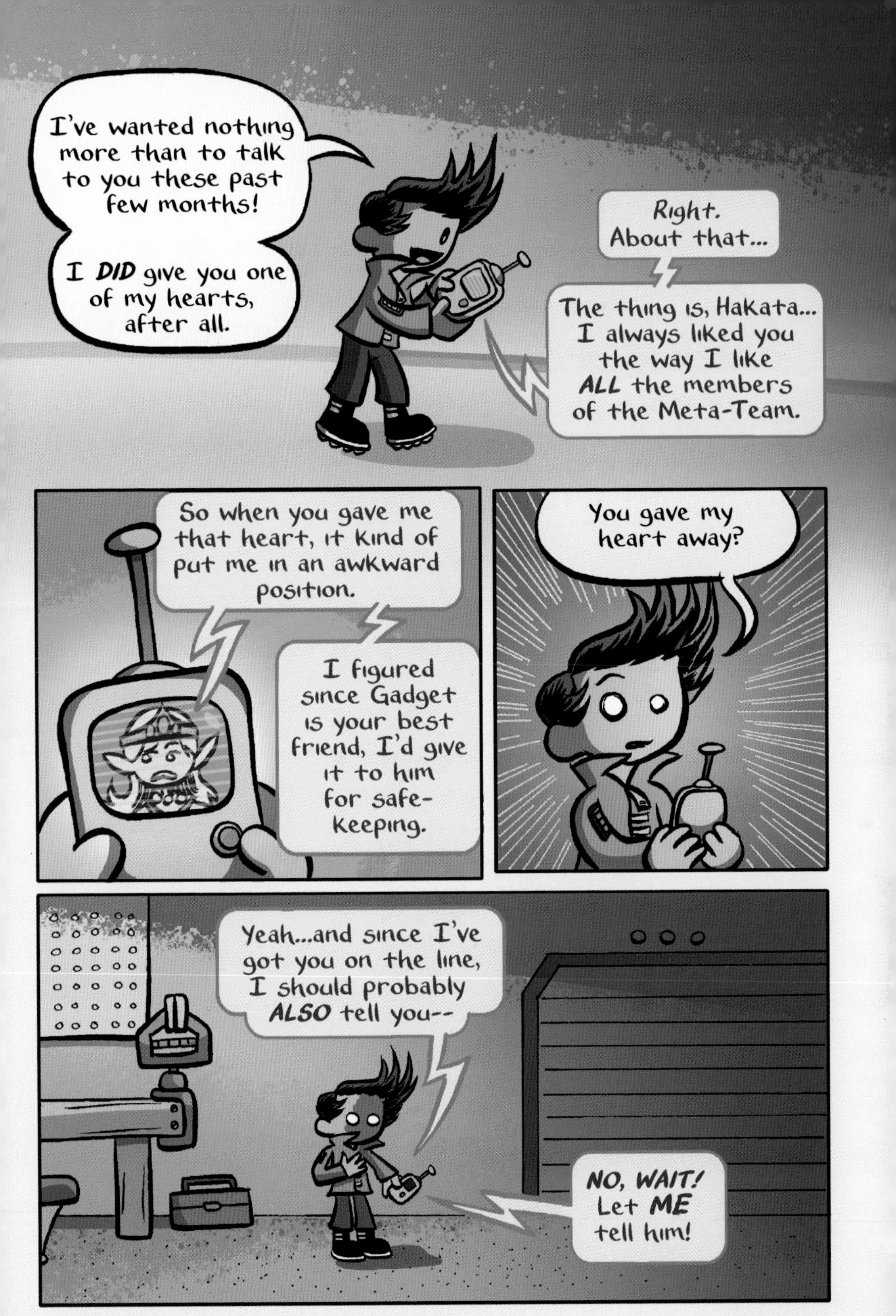
I've wanted nothing more than to talk to you these past few months!
I **DID** give you one of my hearts, after all.
Right. About that...
The thing is, Hakata... I always liked you the way I like **ALL** the members of the Meta-Team.
So when you gave me that heart, it kind of put me in an awkward position.
I figured since Gadget is your best friend, I'd give it to him for safe-keeping.
You gave my heart away?
Yeah...and since I've got you on the line, I should probably **ALSO** tell you--
NO, WAIT! Let **ME** tell him!

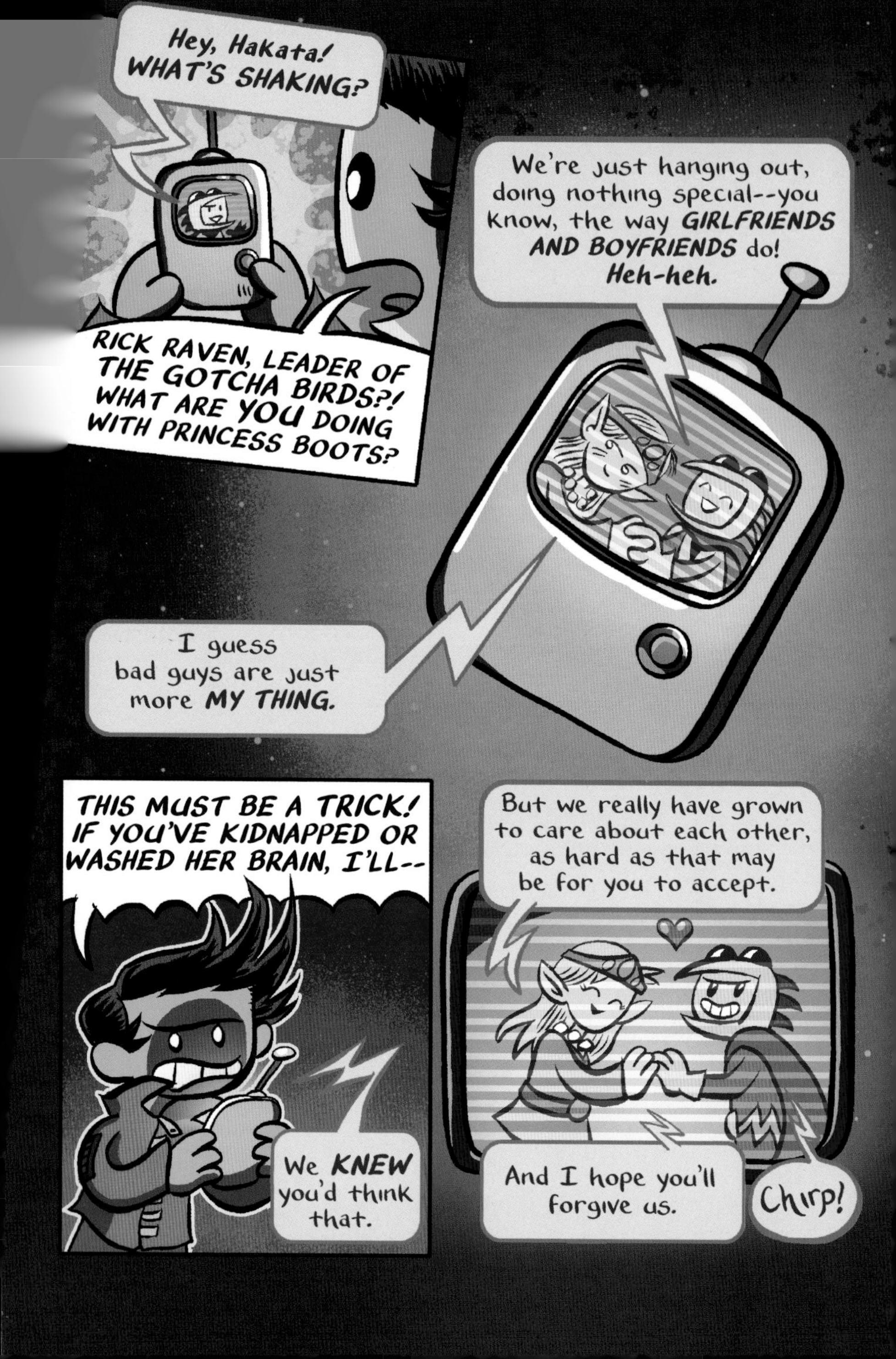
Hey, Hakata! WHAT'S SHAKING?
RICK RAVEN, LEADER OF THE GOTCHA BIRDS?! WHAT ARE YOU DOING WITH PRINCESS BOOTS?
We're just hanging out, doing nothing special--you know, the way GIRLFRIENDS AND BOYFRIENDS do! Heh-heh.
I guess bad guys are just more MY THING.
THIS MUST BE A TRICK! IF YOU'VE KIDNAPPED OR WASHED HER BRAIN, I'LL--
We KNEW you'd think that.
But we really have grown to care about each other, as hard as that may be for you to accept.
And I hope you'll forgive us.
Chirp!

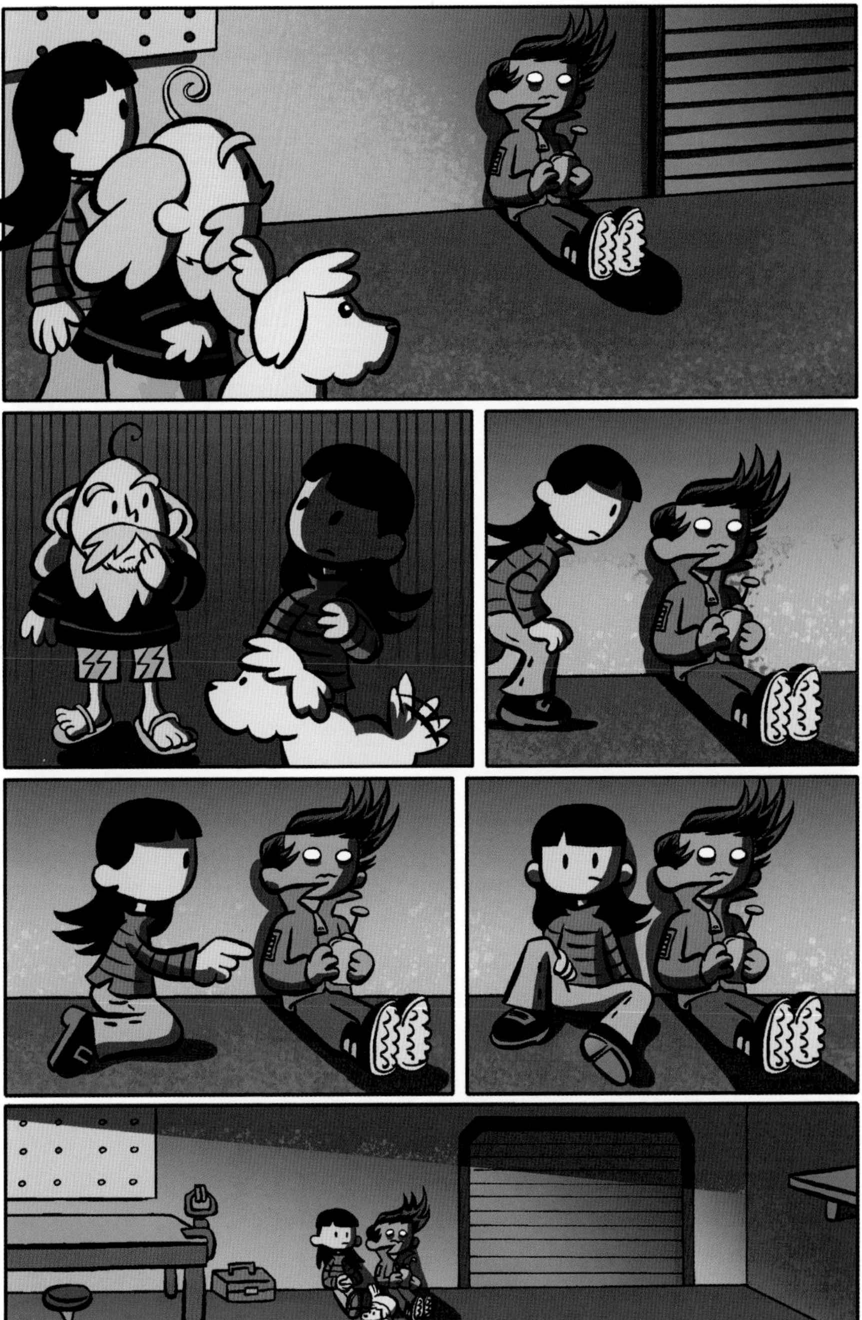

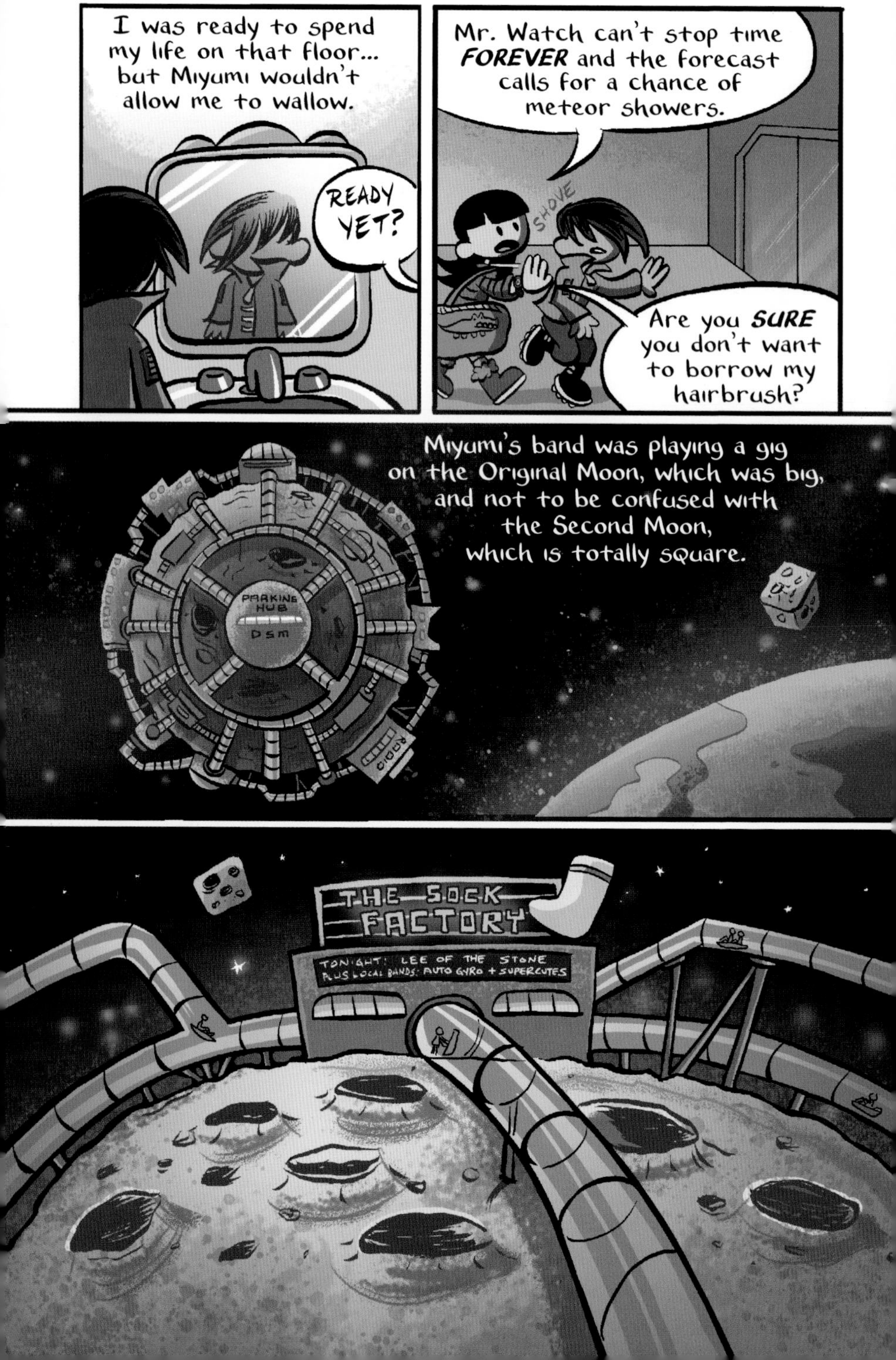
I was ready to spend my life on that floor... but Miyumi wouldn't allow me to wallow.
READY YET?
Mr. Watch can't stop time **FOREVER** and the forecast calls for a chance of meteor showers.
SHOVE
Are you **SURE** you don't want to borrow my hairbrush?
Miyumi's band was playing a gig on the Original Moon, which was big, and not to be confused with the Second Moon, which is totally square.
PARKING HUB
DSM
RADIO
THE SOCK FACTORY
TONIGHT! LEE OF THE STONE
PLUS LOCAL BANDS: AUTO GYRO + SUPERCUTES

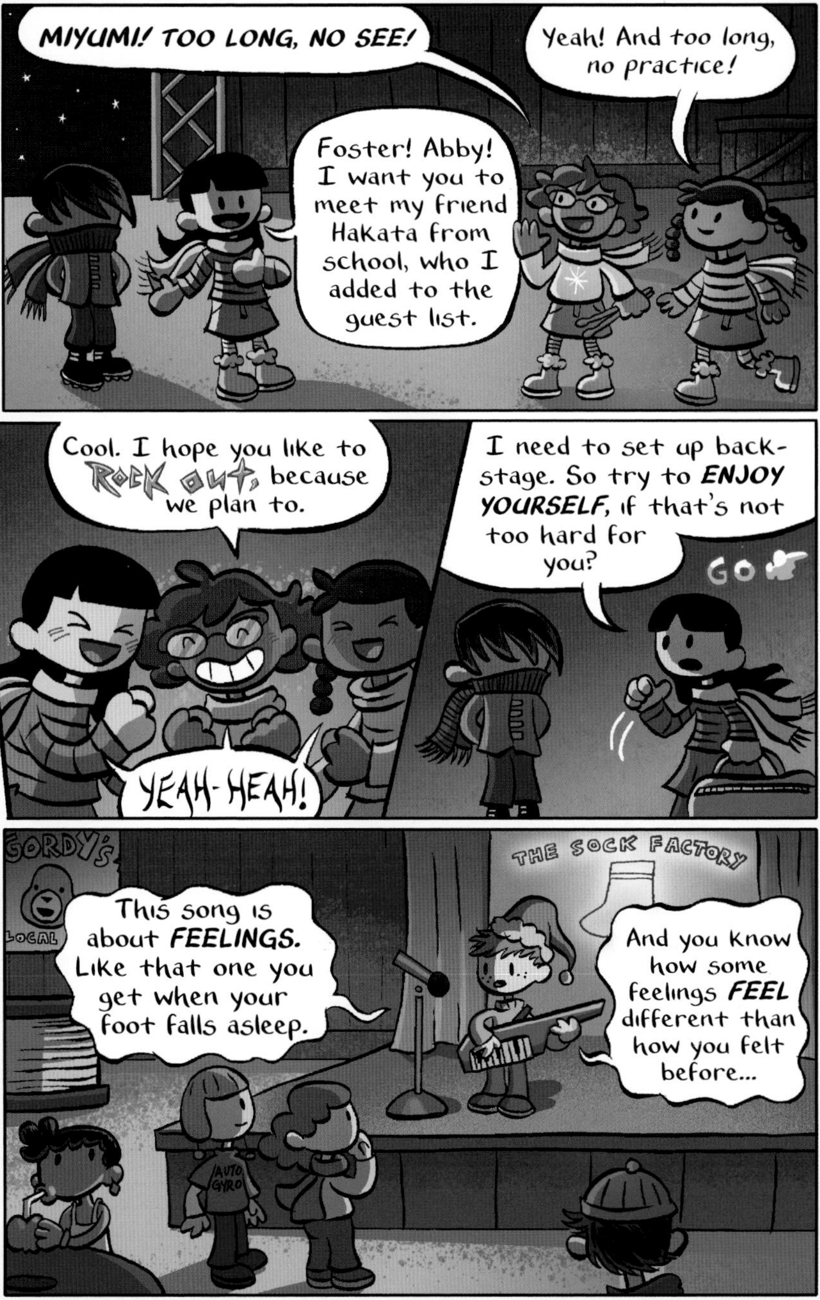
MIYUMI! TOO LONG, NO SEE!
Yeah! And too long, no practice!
Foster! Abby! I want you to meet my friend Hakata from school, who I added to the guest list.
Cool. I hope you like to ROCK OUT, because we plan to.
YEAH-HEAH!
I need to set up back-stage. So try to ENJOY YOURSELF, if that's not too hard for you?
GO
GORDY'S
LOCAL
THE SOCK FACTORY
This song is about FEELINGS. Like that one you get when your foot falls asleep.
And you know how some feelings FEEL different than how you felt before...
AUTO GYRO

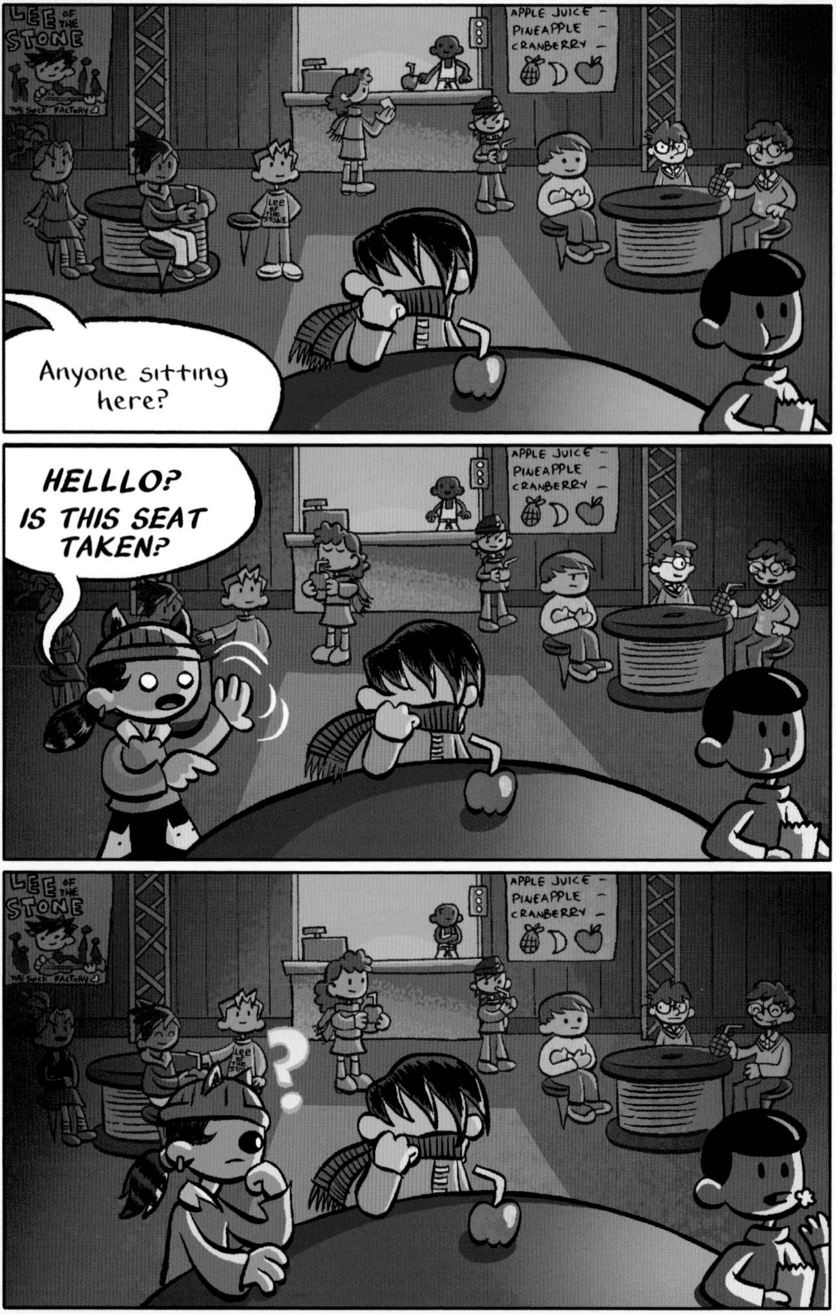
LEE OF THE STONE
THE SOCK FACTORY
APPLE JUICE
PINEAPPLE
CRANBERRY
Anyone sitting here?
HELLLO? IS THIS SEAT TAKEN?
?

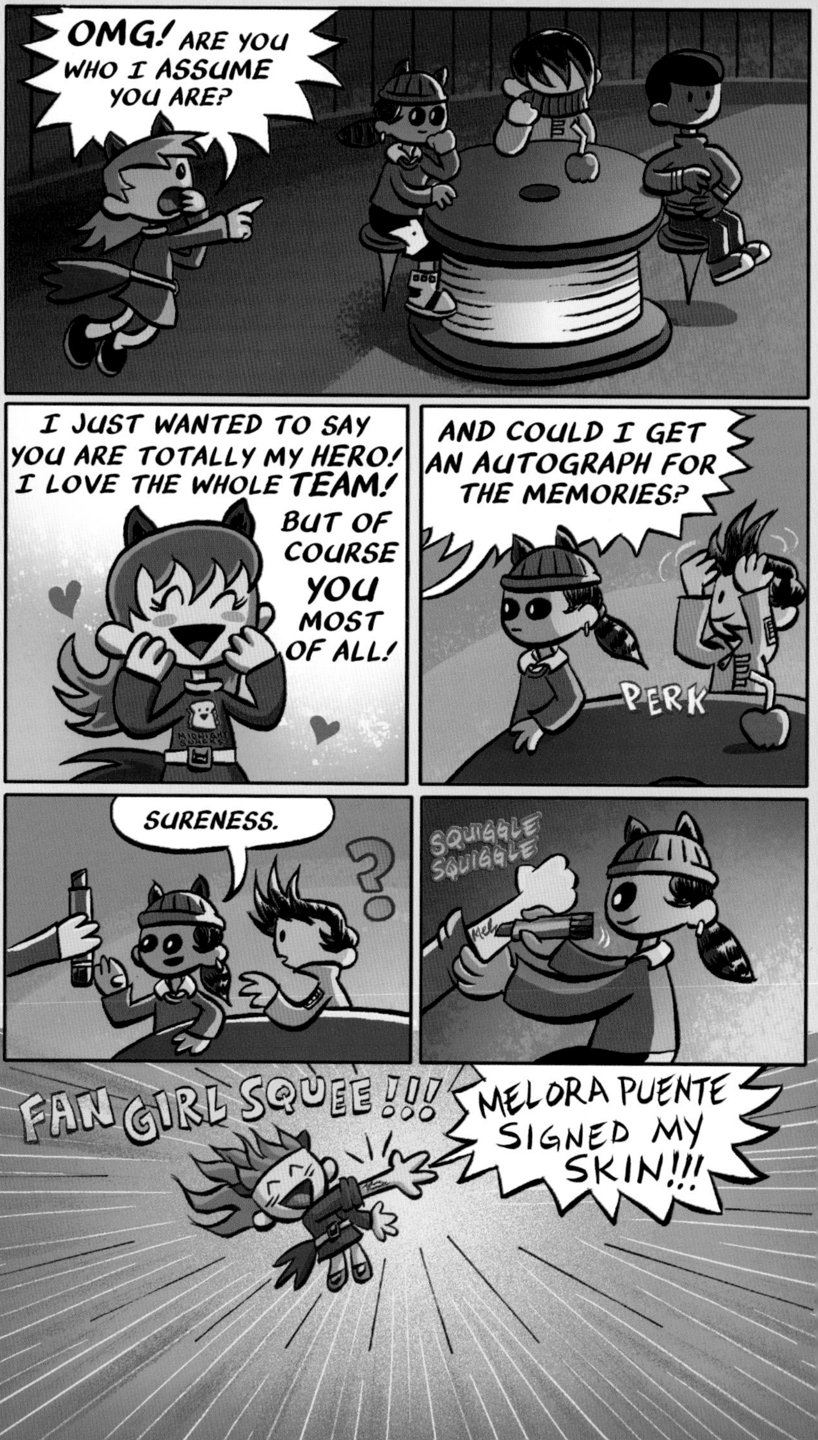
OMG! ARE YOU WHO I ASSUME YOU ARE?
I JUST WANTED TO SAY YOU ARE TOTALLY MY HERO! I LOVE THE WHOLE TEAM!
BUT OF COURSE YOU MOST OF ALL!
MIDNIGHT SNACKS
AND COULD I GET AN AUTOGRAPH FOR THE MEMORIES?
PERK
SURENESS.
?
SQUIGGLE SQUIGGLE
Mel
FAN GIRL SQUEE!!!
MELORA PUENTE SIGNED MY SKIN!!!

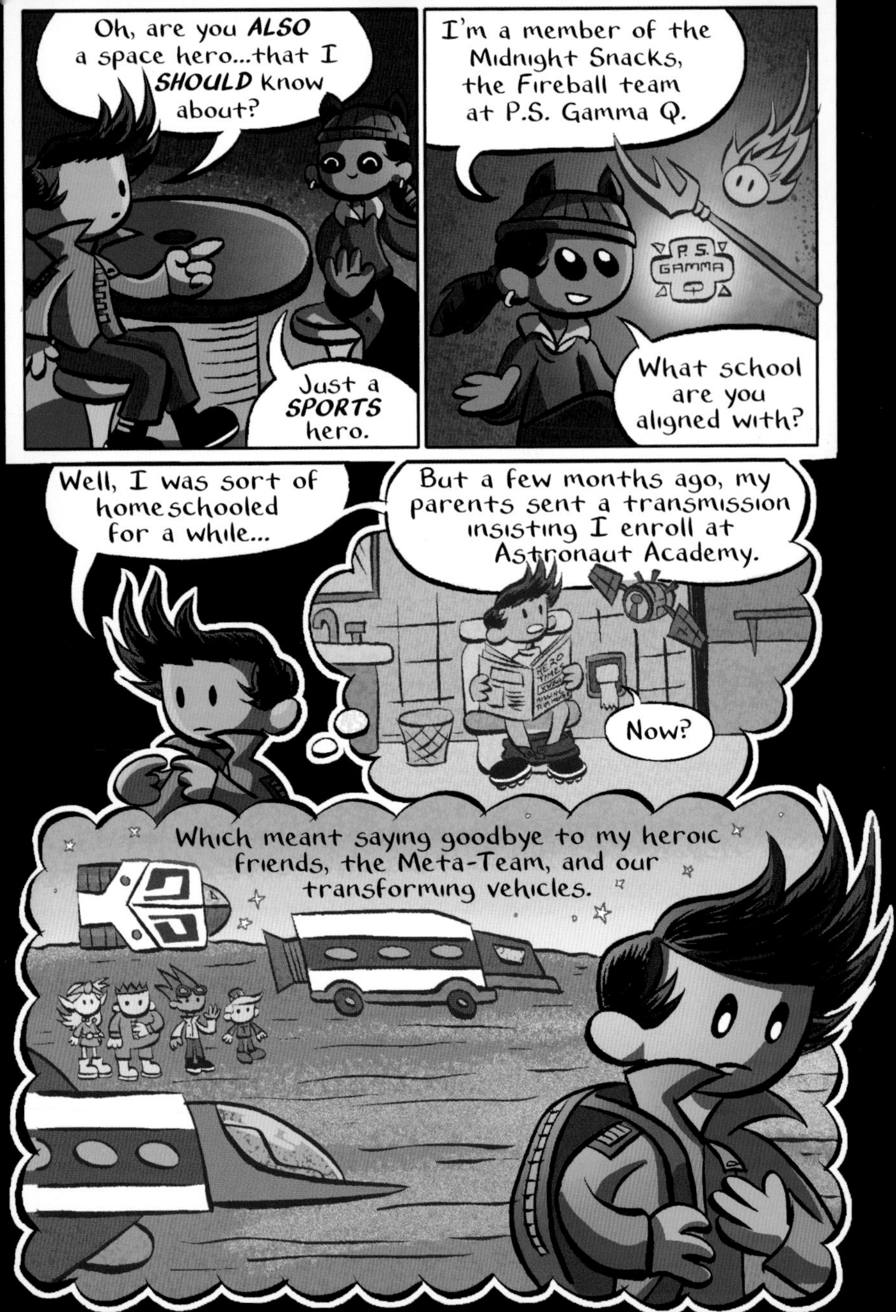

Oh, are you ALSO a space hero...that I SHOULD know about?
Just a SPORTS hero.
I'm a member of the Midnight Snacks, the Fireball team at P.S. Gamma Q.
P.S. GAMMA
What school are you aligned with?
Well, I was sort of homeschooled for a while...
But a few months ago, my parents sent a transmission insisting I enroll at Astronaut Academy.
Now?
Which meant saying goodbye to my heroic friends, the Meta-Team, and our transforming vehicles.

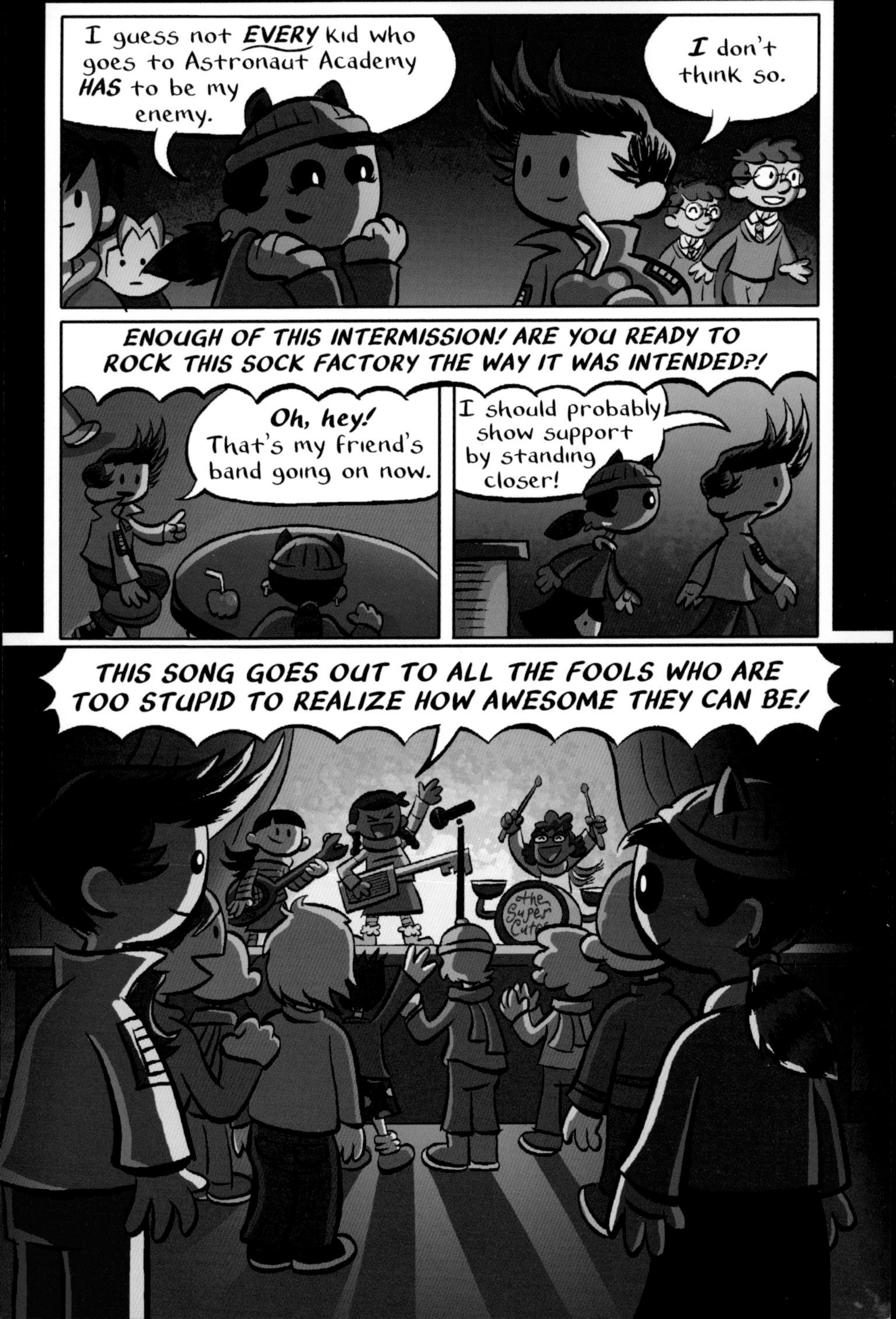
I guess not EVERY kid who goes to Astronaut Academy HAS to be my enemy.
I don't think so.
ENOUGH OF THIS INTERMISSION! ARE YOU READY TO ROCK THIS SOCK FACTORY THE WAY IT WAS INTENDED?!
Oh, hey! That's my friend's band going on now.
I should probably show support by standing closer!
THIS SONG GOES OUT TO ALL THE FOOLS WHO ARE TOO STUPID TO REALIZE HOW AWESOME THEY CAN BE!
the Super Cutes

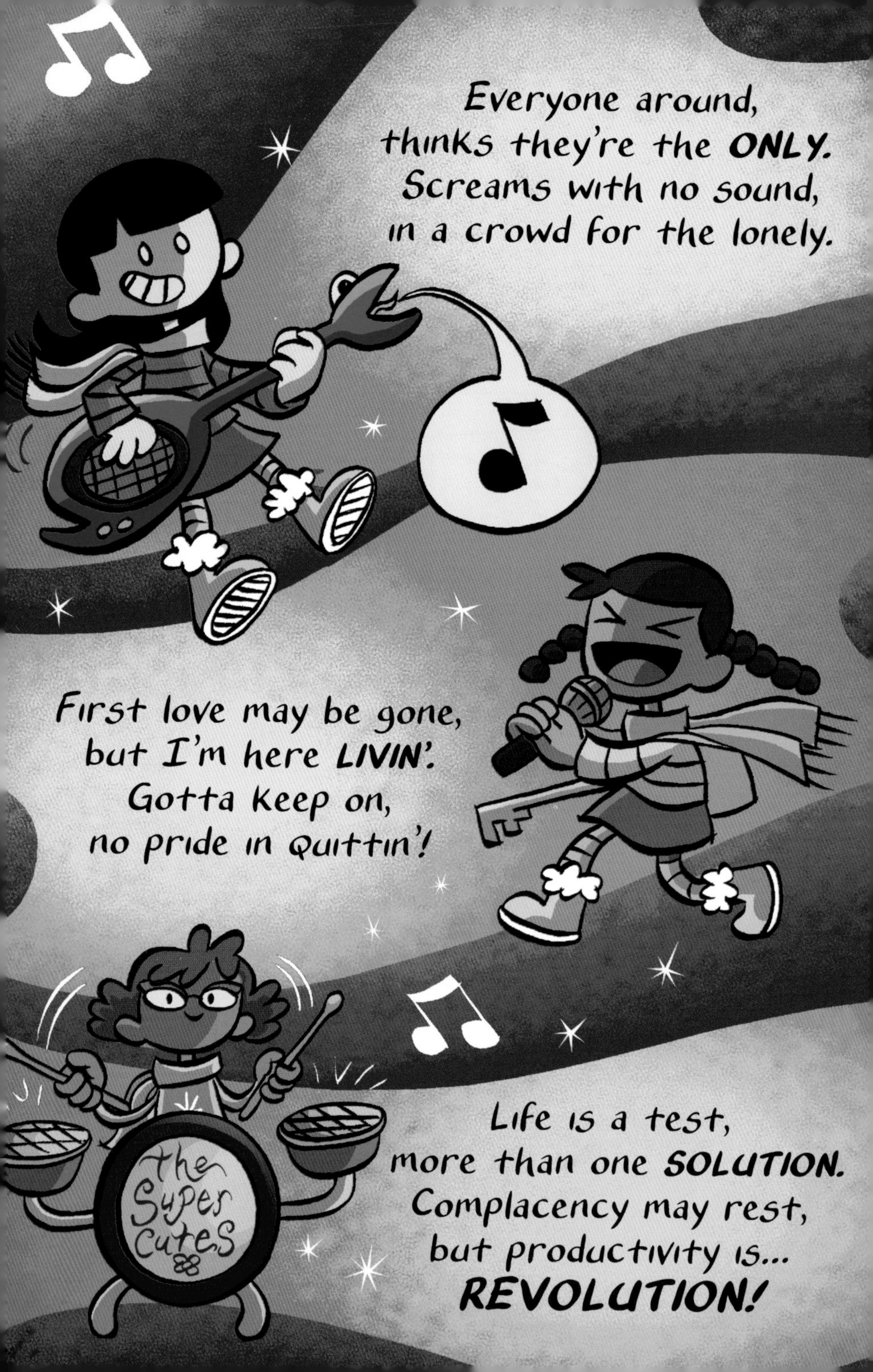
Everyone around,
thinks they're the ONLY.
Screams with no sound,
in a crowd for the lonely.
First love may be gone,
but I'm here LIVIN'.
Gotta keep on,
no pride in quittin'!
The Super Cutes
Life is a test,
more than one SOLUTION.
Complacency may rest,
but productivity is...
REVOLUTION!

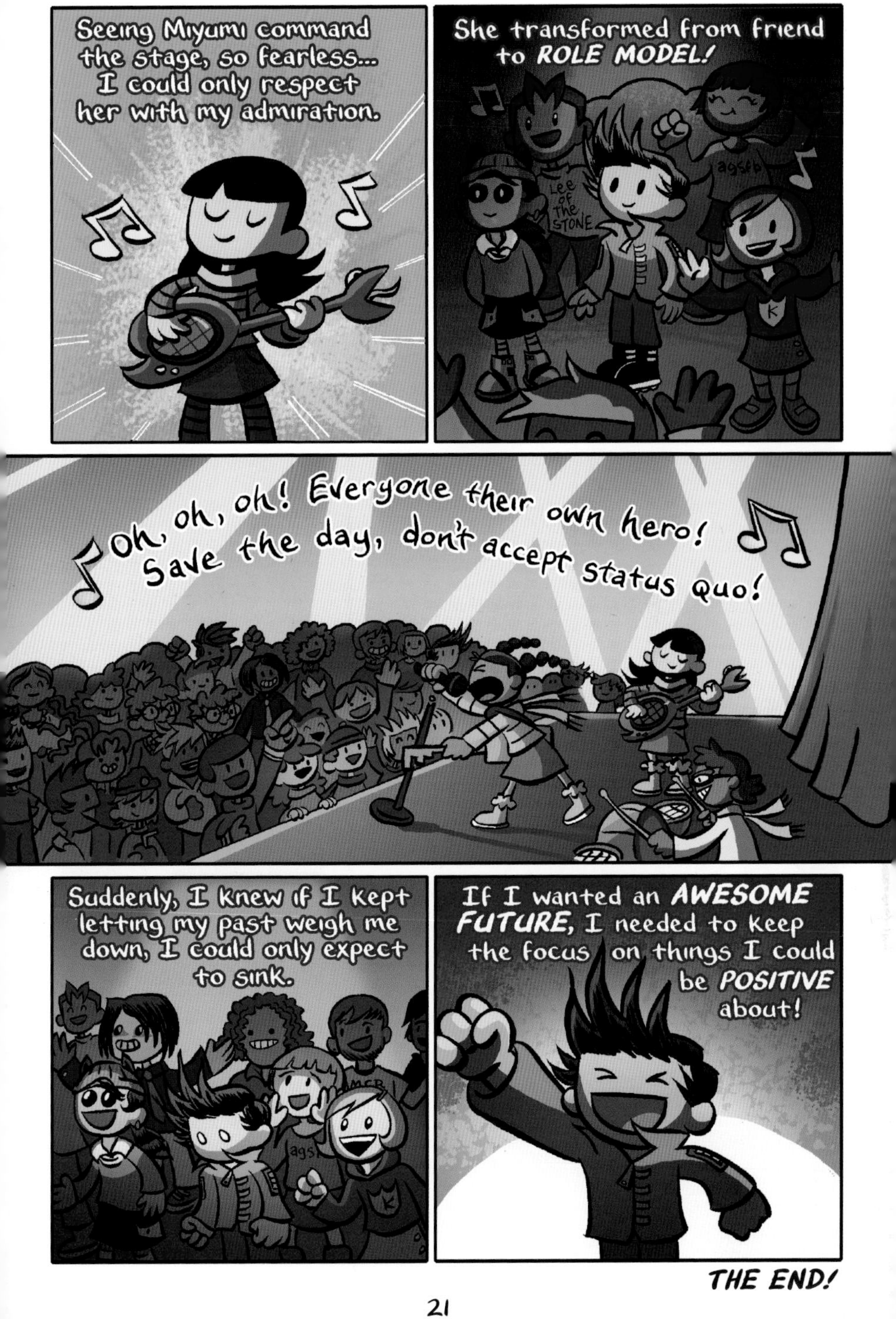
Seeing Miyumi command the stage, so fearless... I could only respect her with my admiration.
She transformed from friend to ROLE MODEL!
LEE OF THE STONE
agsfb
K
Oh, oh, oh! Everyone their own hero! Save the day, don't accept status quo!
Suddenly, I knew if I kept letting my past weigh me down, I could only expect to sink.
MCR
ags
K
If I wanted an AWESOME FUTURE, I needed to keep the focus on things I could be POSITIVE about!

THE END!

MY name is:

MARIBELLE
MELLONBELLY

And I am the richest and most Pretty girl in all of:

ASTRONAUT ACADEMY

IT PAYS TO BE THE BE$T

What did I do over my holiday break?

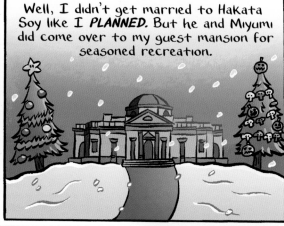

Well, I didn't get married to Hakata Soy like I **PLANNED.** But he and Miyumi did come over to my guest mansion for seasoned recreation.

Miyumi and I tried to relive our glory days but some things just don't bounce like they used to.

Hoot!

Ha!

Heh.

FSSS

FFPH

But before all that...

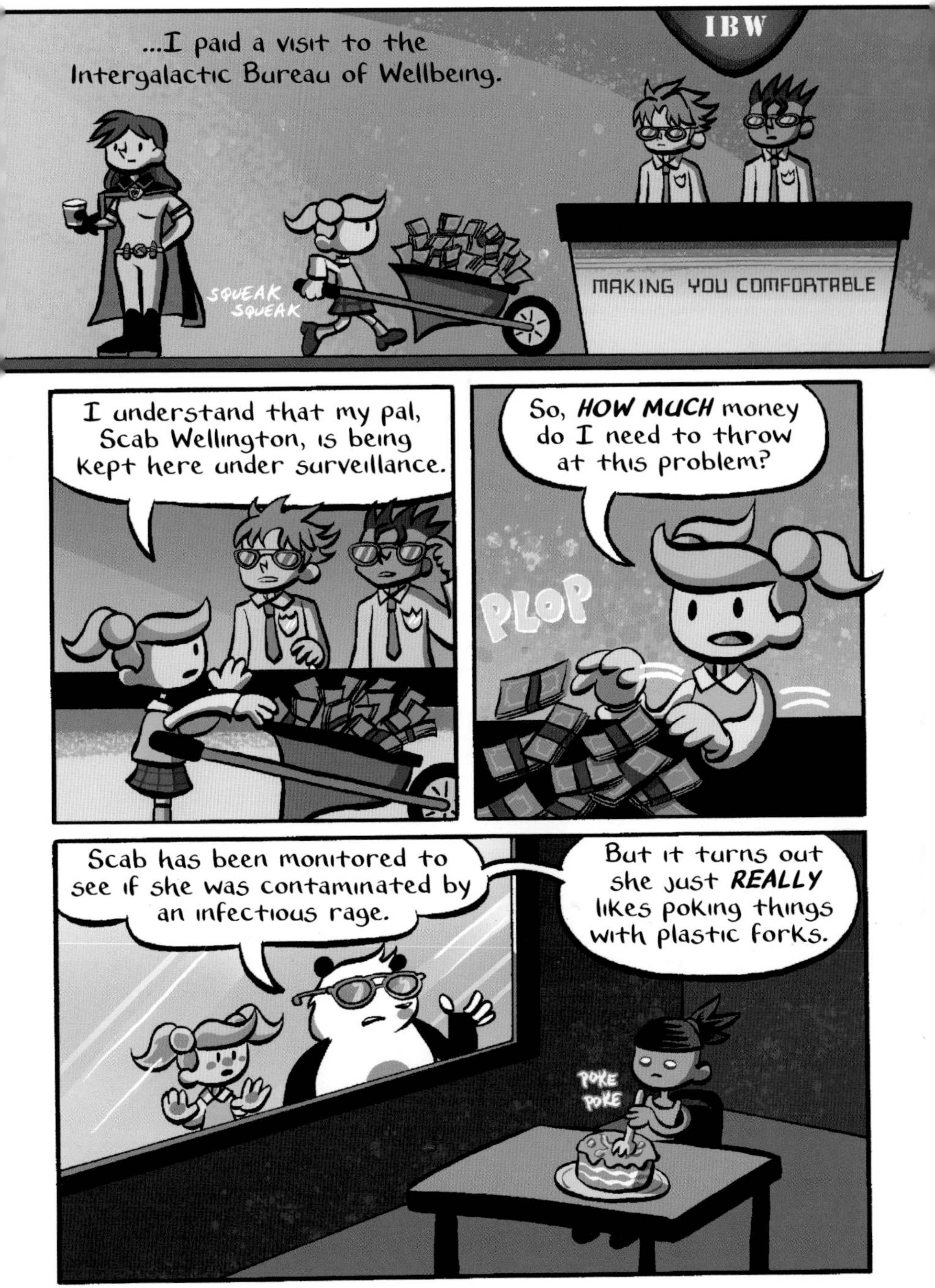

...I paid a visit to the Intergalactic Bureau of Wellbeing.
IBW
MAKING YOU COMFORTABLE
SQUEAK SQUEAK
I understand that my pal, Scab Wellington, is being kept here under surveillance.
So, HOW MUCH money do I need to throw at this problem?
PLOP
Scab has been monitored to see if she was contaminated by an infectious rage.
But it turns out she just REALLY likes poking things with plastic forks.
POKE POKE

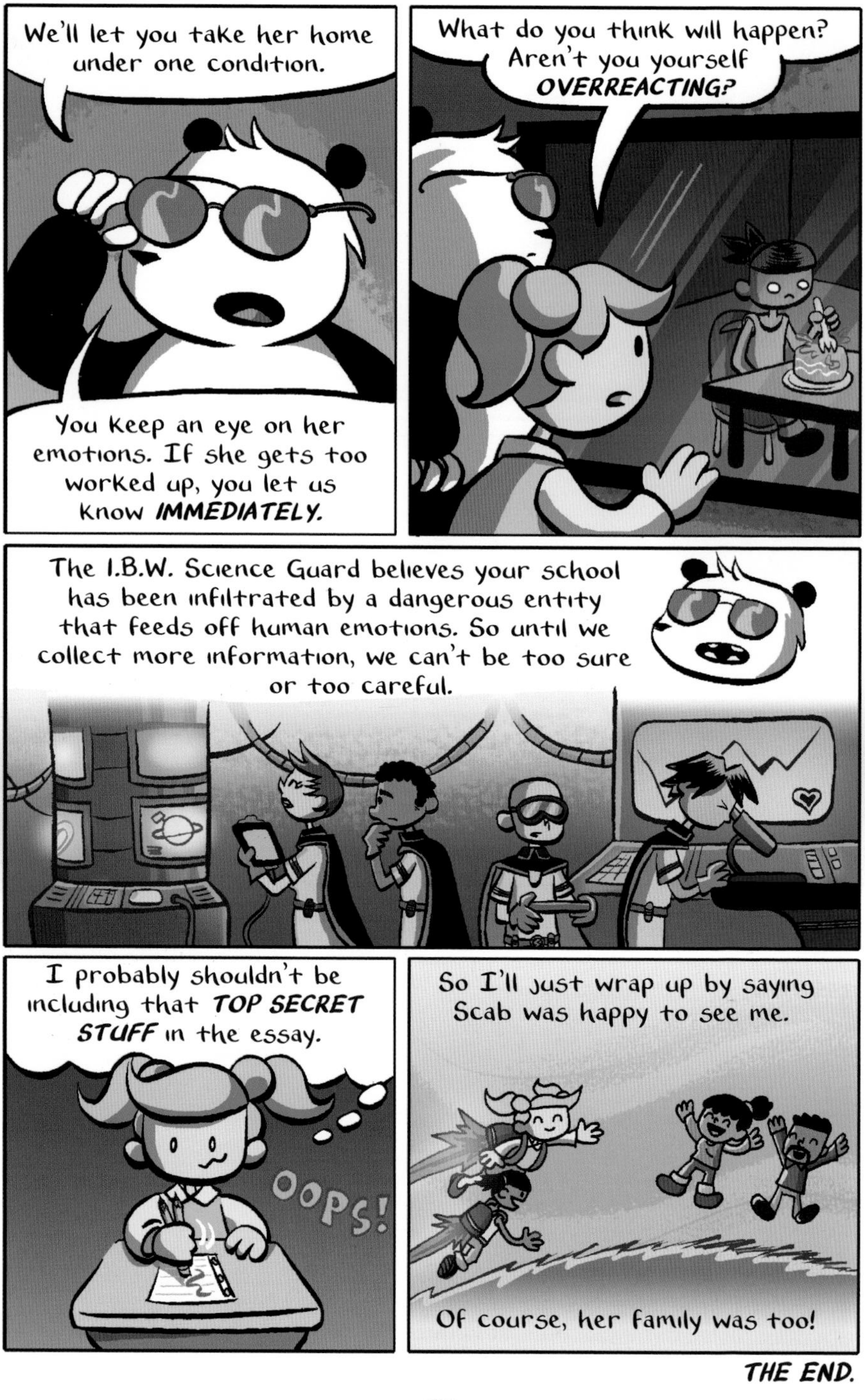
We'll let you take her home under one condition.
You keep an eye on her emotions. If she gets too worked up, you let us know IMMEDIATELY.
What do you think will happen? Aren't you yourself OVERREACTING?
The I.B.W. Science Guard believes your school has been infiltrated by a dangerous entity that feeds off human emotions. So until we collect more information, we can't be too sure or too careful.
I probably shouldn't be including that TOP SECRET STUFF in the essay.
OOPS!
So I'll just wrap up by saying Scab was happy to see me.
Of course, her family was too!

THE END.

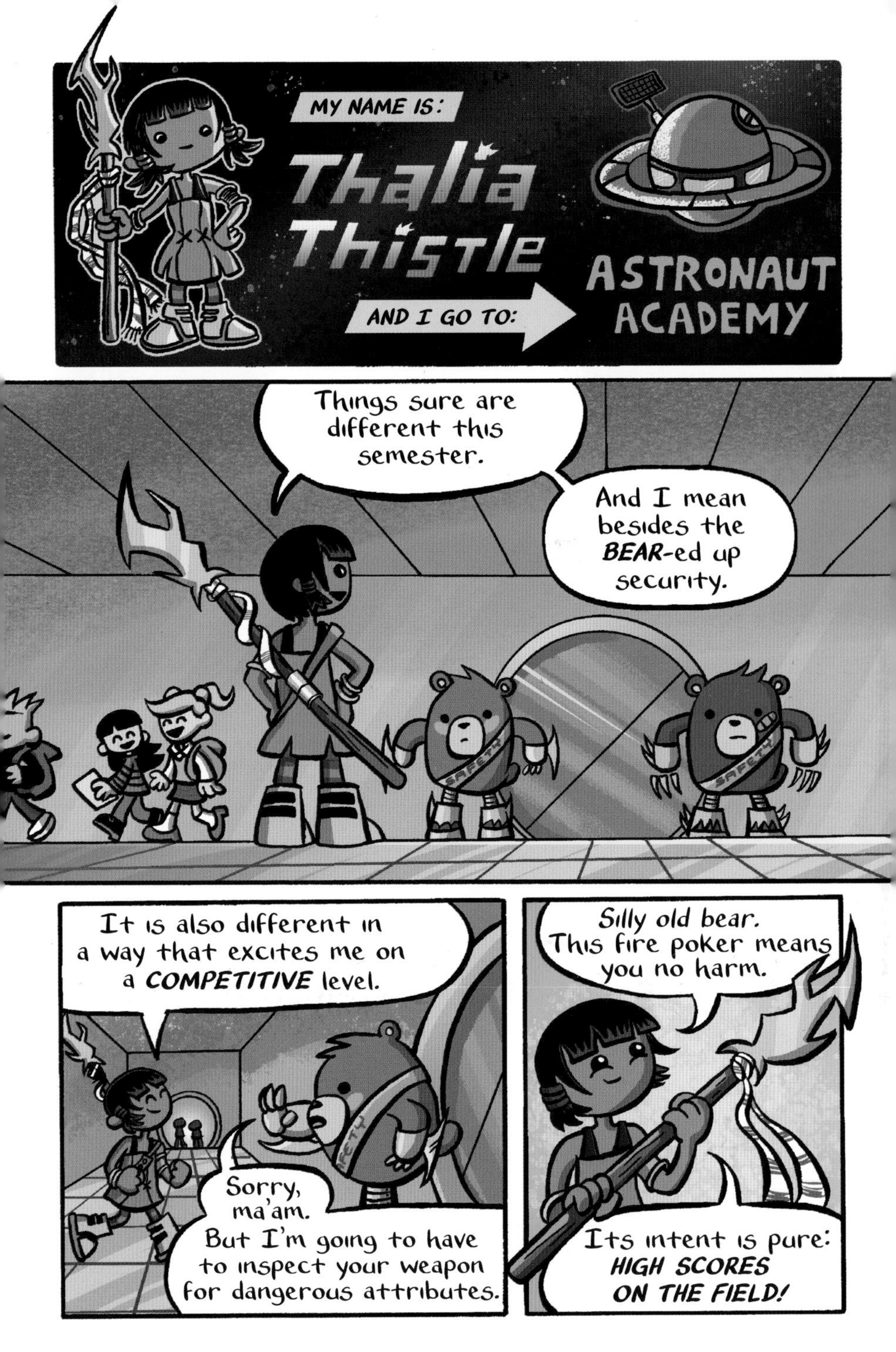
MY NAME IS:
Thalia Thistle
AND I GO TO:
ASTRONAUT ACADEMY
Things sure are different this semester.
And I mean besides the BEAR-ed up security.
SAFETY
SAFETY
It is also different in a way that excites me on a COMPETITIVE level.
Sorry, ma'am. But I'm going to have to inspect your weapon for dangerous attributes.
Silly old bear. This fire poker means you no harm.
Its intent is pure: HIGH SCORES ON THE FIELD!

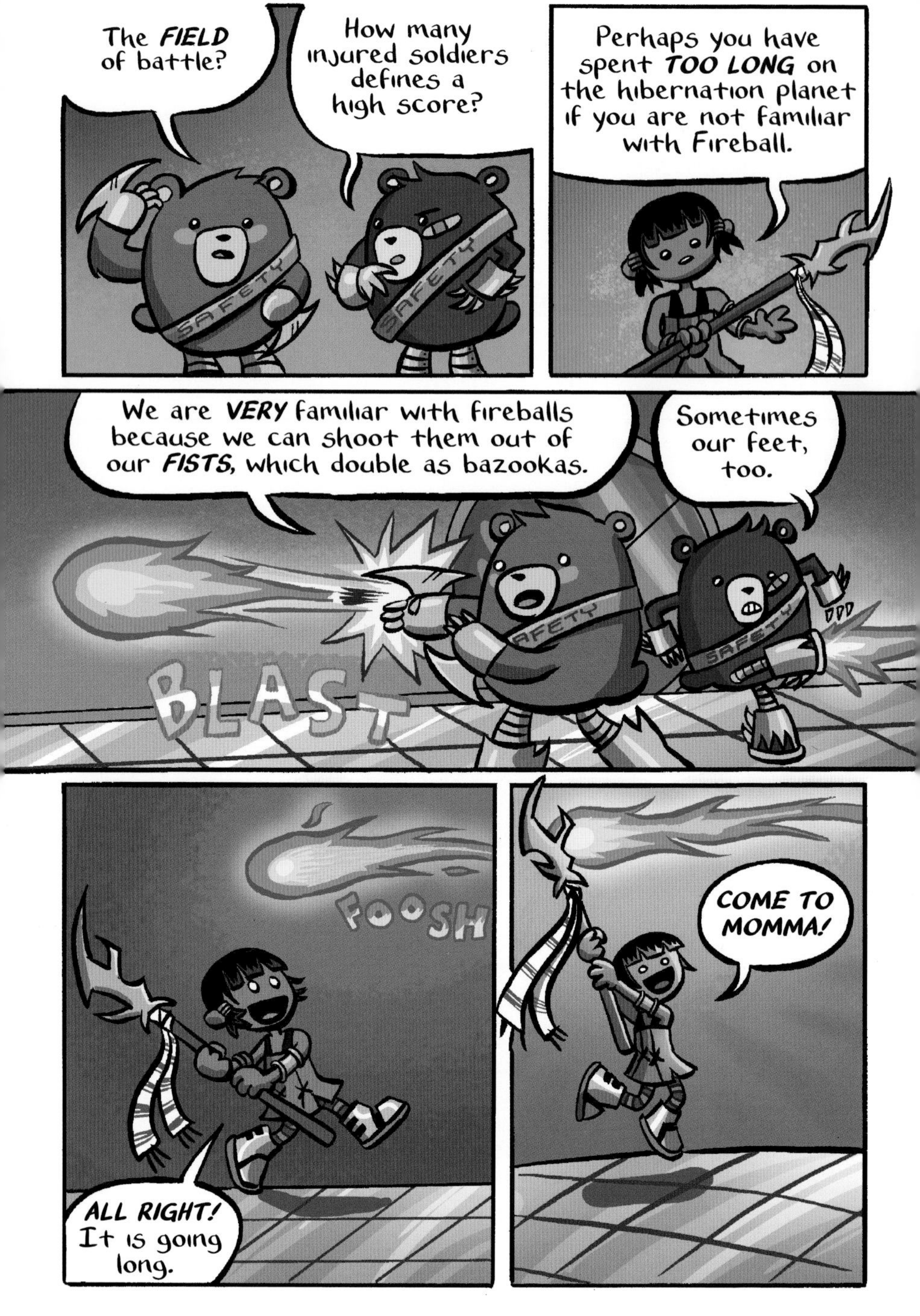
The FIELD of battle?
How many injured soldiers defines a high score?
Perhaps you have spent TOO LONG on the hibernation planet if you are not familiar with Fireball.
SAFETY
SAFETY
We are VERY familiar with fireballs because we can shoot them out of our FISTS, which double as bazookas.
Sometimes our feet, too.
BLAST
SAFETY
SAFETY
FOOSH
ALL RIGHT! It is going long.
COME TO MOMMA!

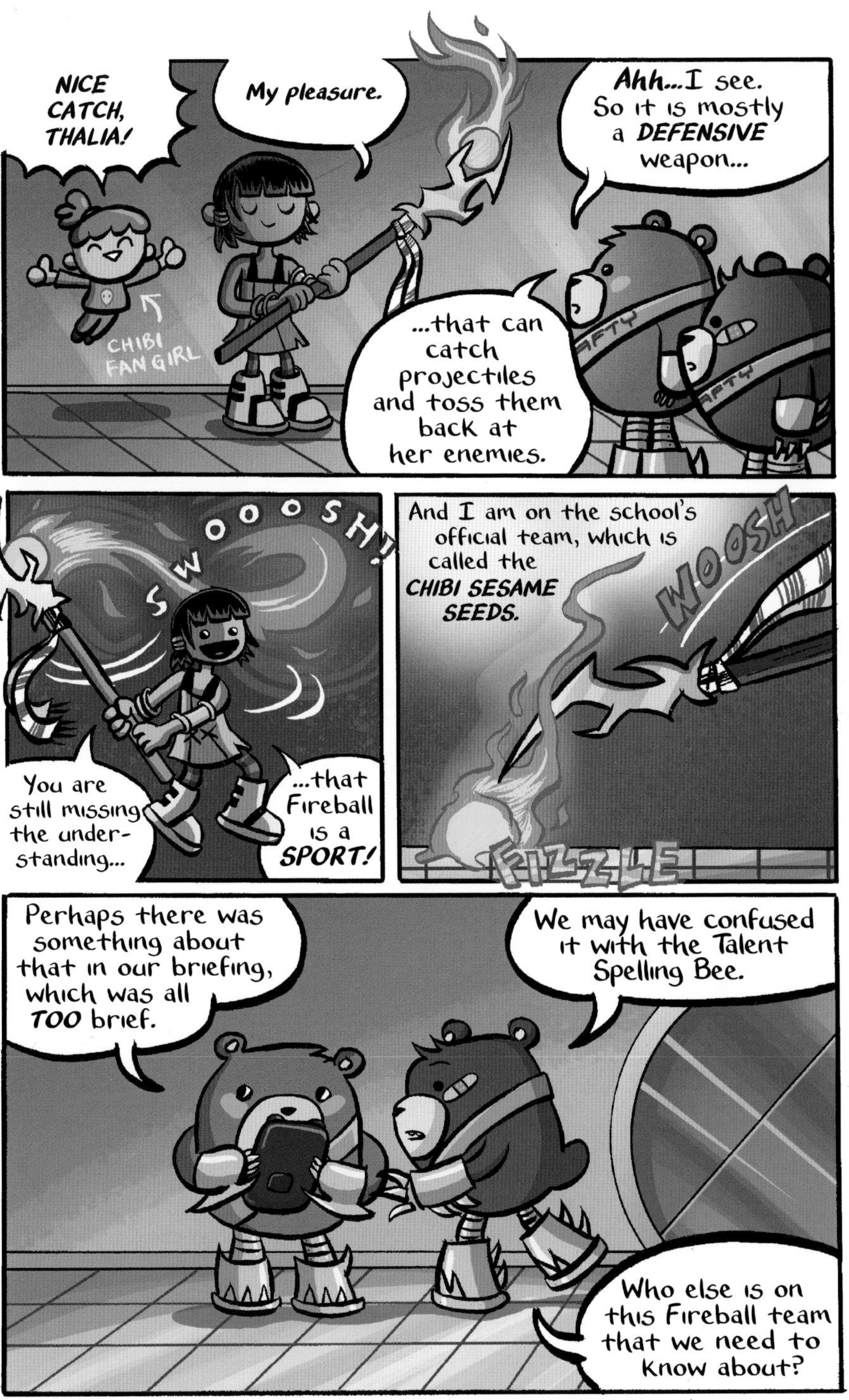
NICE CATCH, THALIA!
My pleasure.
Ahh...I see. So it is mostly a DEFENSIVE weapon...
CHIBI FAN GIRL
...that can catch projectiles and toss them back at her enemies.
SWOOOOSH!
You are still missing the understanding...
...that Fireball is a SPORT!
And I am on the school's official team, which is called the CHIBI SESAME SEEDS.
WOOSH
FIZZLE
Perhaps there was something about that in our briefing, which was all TOO brief.
We may have confused it with the Talent Spelling Bee.
Who else is on this Fireball team that we need to know about?

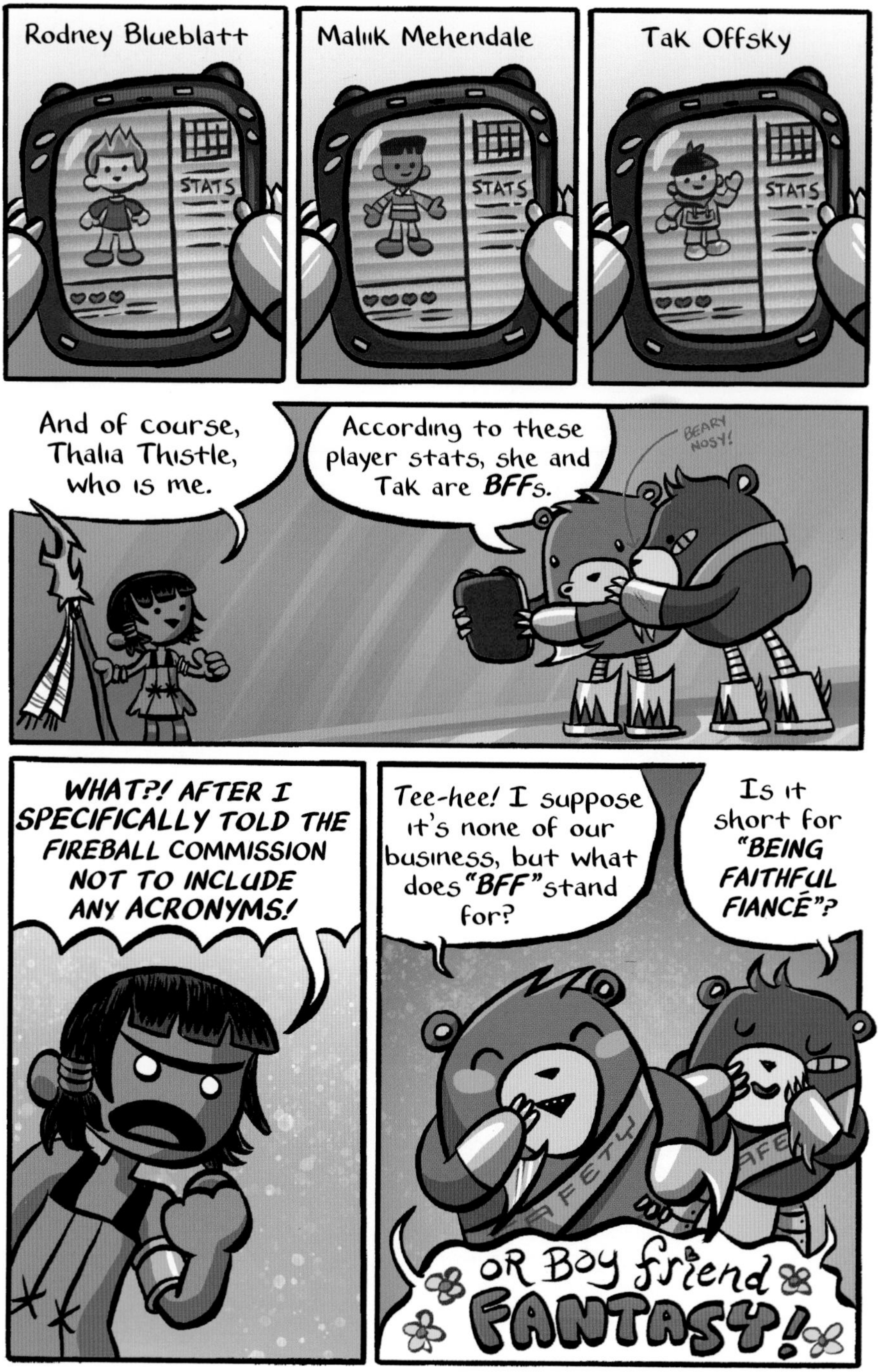
Rodney Blueblatt
STATS
Malik Mehendale
STATS
Tak Offsky
STATS
And of course, Thalia Thistle, who is me.
According to these player stats, she and Tak are *BFF*s.
BEARY NOSY!
WHAT?! AFTER I SPECIFICALLY TOLD THE FIREBALL COMMISSION NOT TO INCLUDE ANY ACRONYMS!
Tee-hee! I suppose it's none of our business, but what does "*BFF*" stand for?
Is it short for "*BEING FAITHFUL FIANCÉ*"?
OR Boy friend FANTASY!

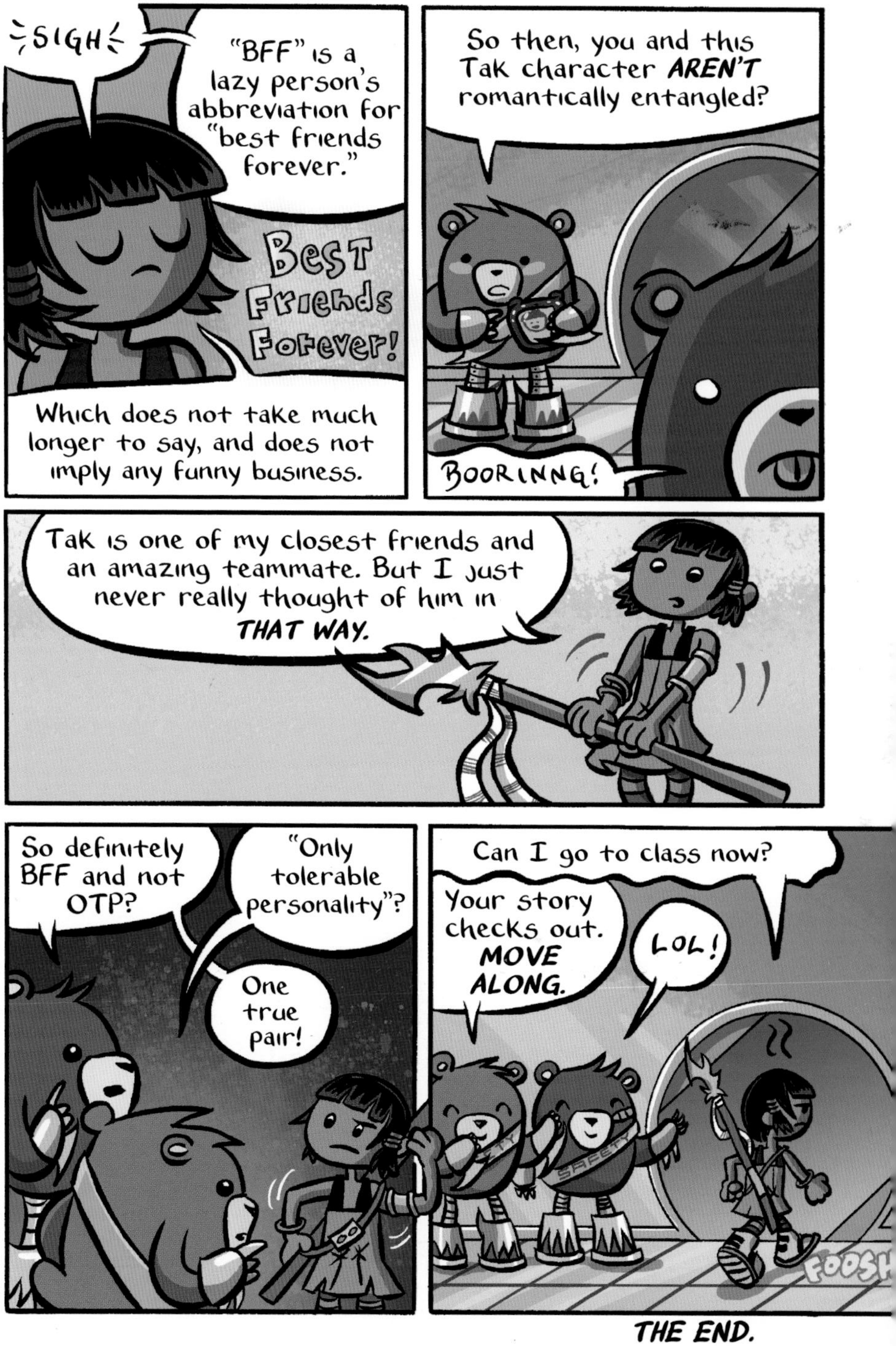
SIGH
"BFF" is a lazy person's abbreviation for "best friends forever."
Best Friends Forever!
Which does not take much longer to say, and does not imply any funny business.
So then, you and this Tak character **AREN'T** romantically entangled?
BOORINNG!
Tak is one of my closest friends and an amazing teammate. But I just never really thought of him in **THAT WAY.**
So definitely BFF and not OTP?
"Only tolerable personality"?
One true pair!
Can I go to class now?
Your story checks out. **MOVE ALONG.**
LOL!
SAFETY
FOOSH

THE END.

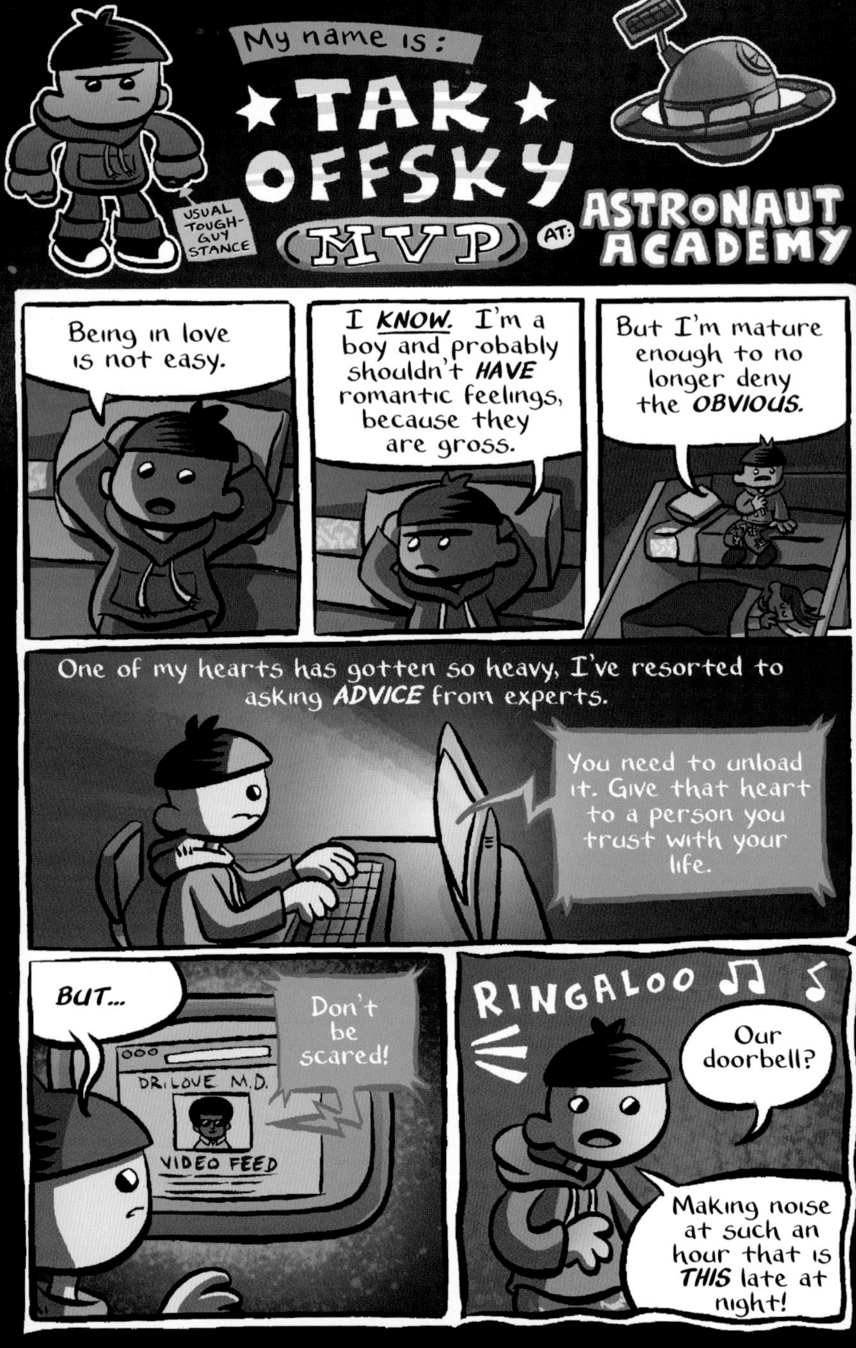
My name is:
TAK OFFSKY
USUAL TOUGH-GUY STANCE
MVP
AT:
ASTRONAUT ACADEMY
Being in love is not easy.
I KNOW. I'm a boy and probably shouldn't HAVE romantic feelings, because they are gross.
But I'm mature enough to no longer deny the OBVIOUS.
One of my hearts has gotten so heavy, I've resorted to asking ADVICE from experts.
You need to unload it. Give that heart to a person you trust with your life.
BUT...
Don't be scared!
DR. LOVE M.D.
VIDEO FEED
RINGALOO
Our doorbell?
Making noise at such an hour that is THIS late at night!

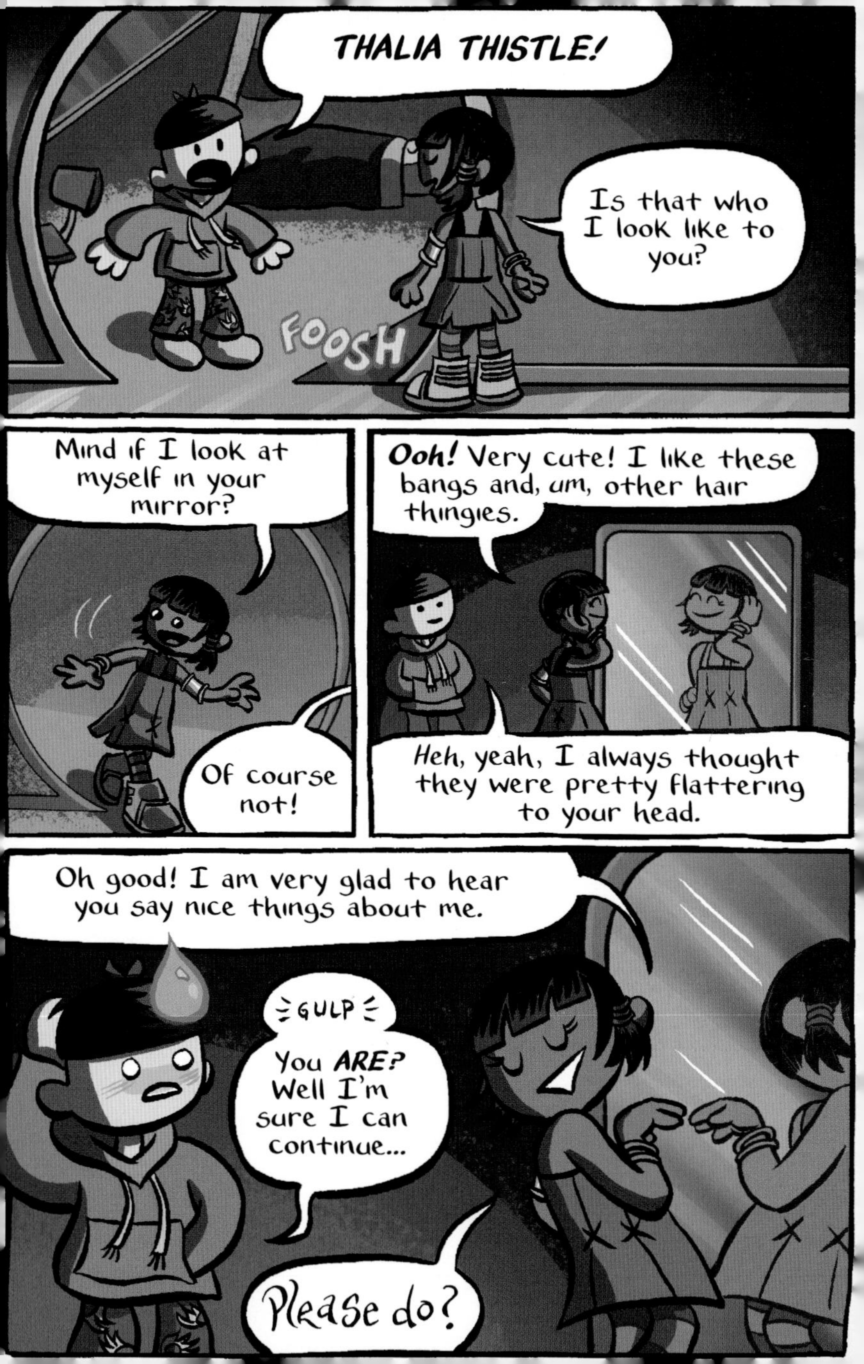
THALIA THISTLE!
Is that who I look like to you?
FOOSH
Mind if I look at myself in your mirror?
Of course not!
Ooh! Very cute! I like these bangs and, um, other hair thingies.
Heh, yeah, I always thought they were pretty flattering to your head.
Oh good! I am very glad to hear you say nice things about me.
GULP
You ARE? Well I'm sure I can continue...
Please do?

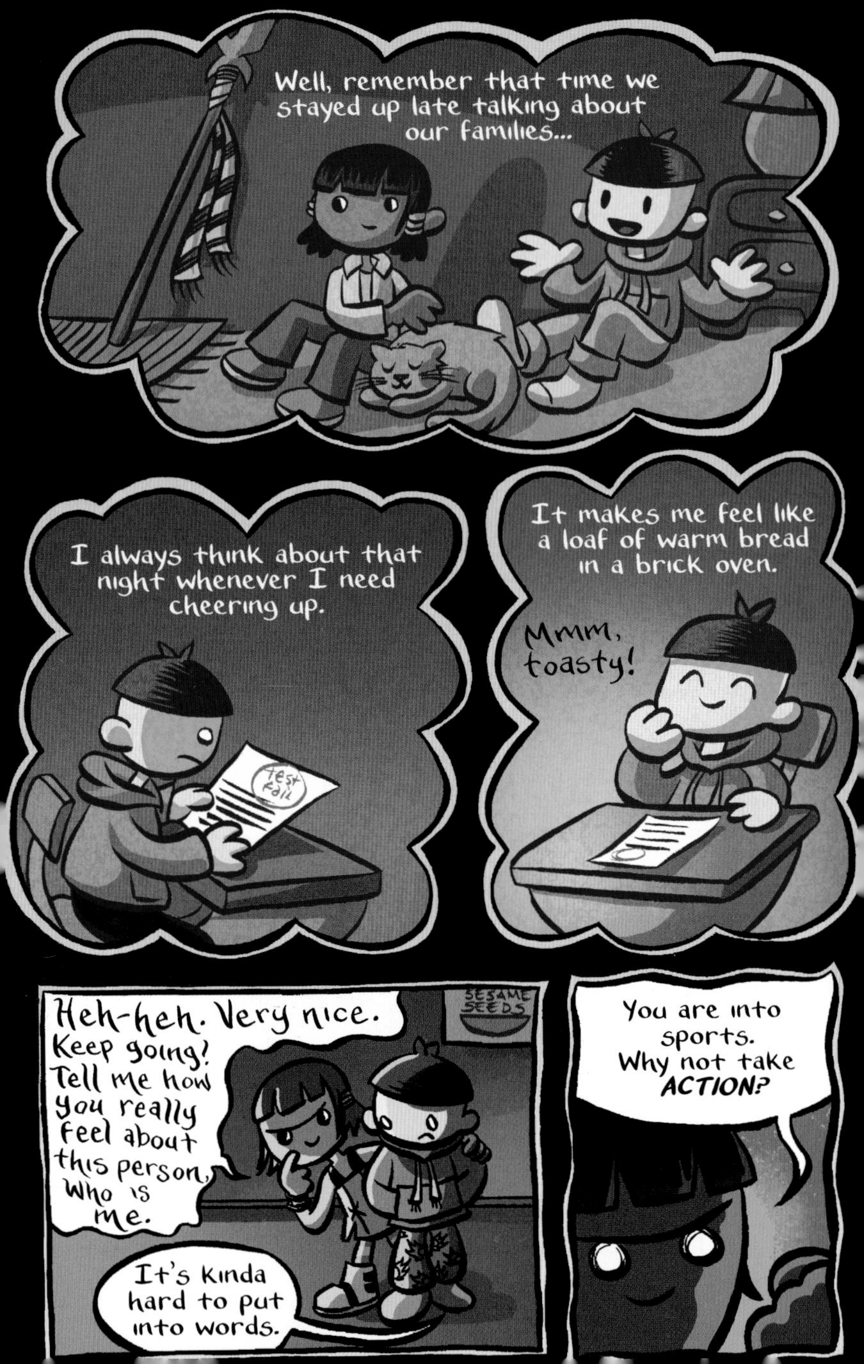

Well, remember that time we stayed up late talking about our families...
I always think about that night whenever I need cheering up.
test fail
It makes me feel like a loaf of warm bread in a brick oven.
Mmm, toasty!
SESAME SEEDS
Heh-heh. Very nice. Keep going! Tell me how you really feel about this person, who is me.
It's kinda hard to put into words.
You are into sports. Why not take ACTION?

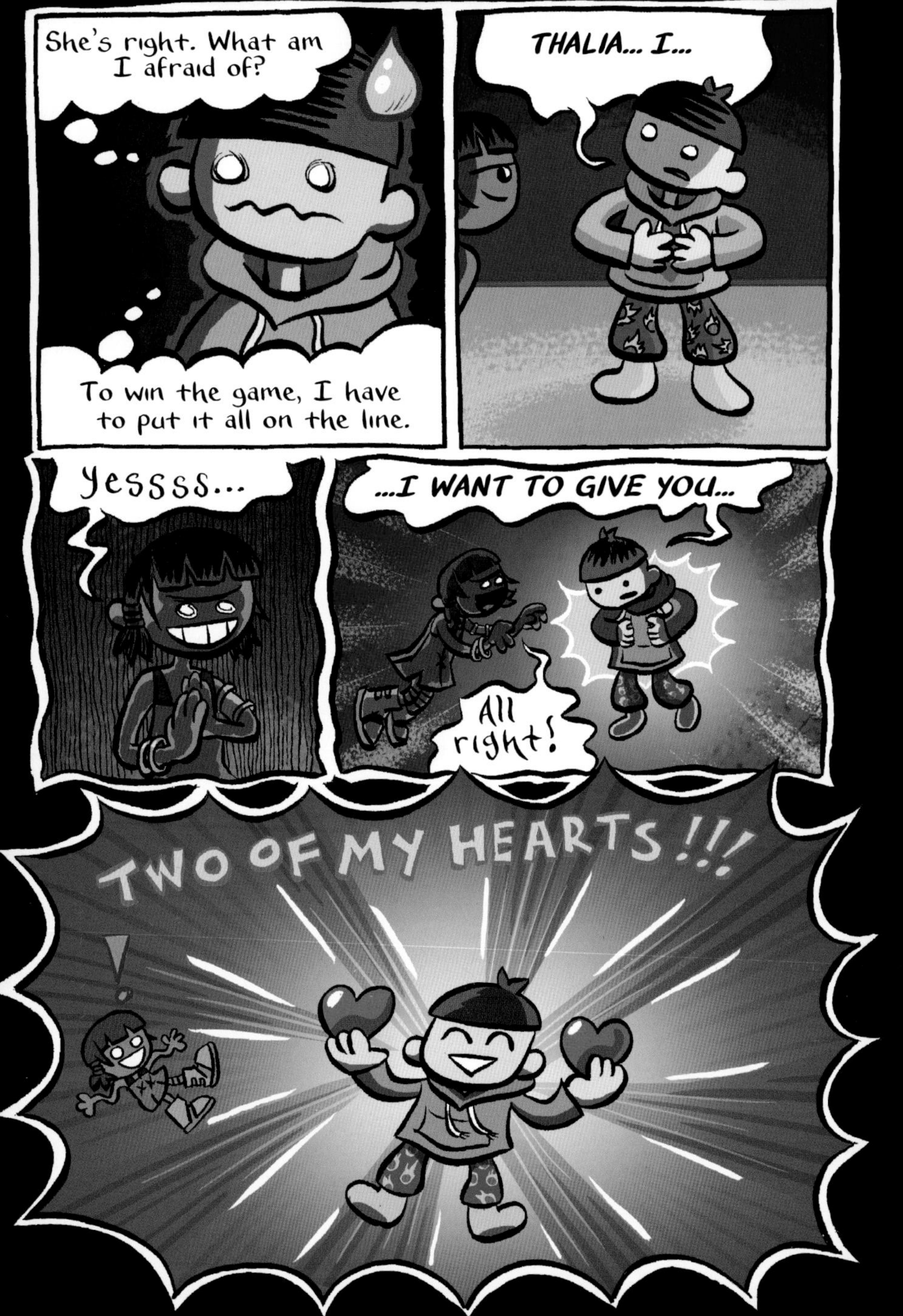
She's right. What am I afraid of?
To win the game, I have to put it all on the line.
THALIA... I...
Yessss...
...I WANT TO GIVE YOU...
All right!
TWO OF MY HEARTS!!!

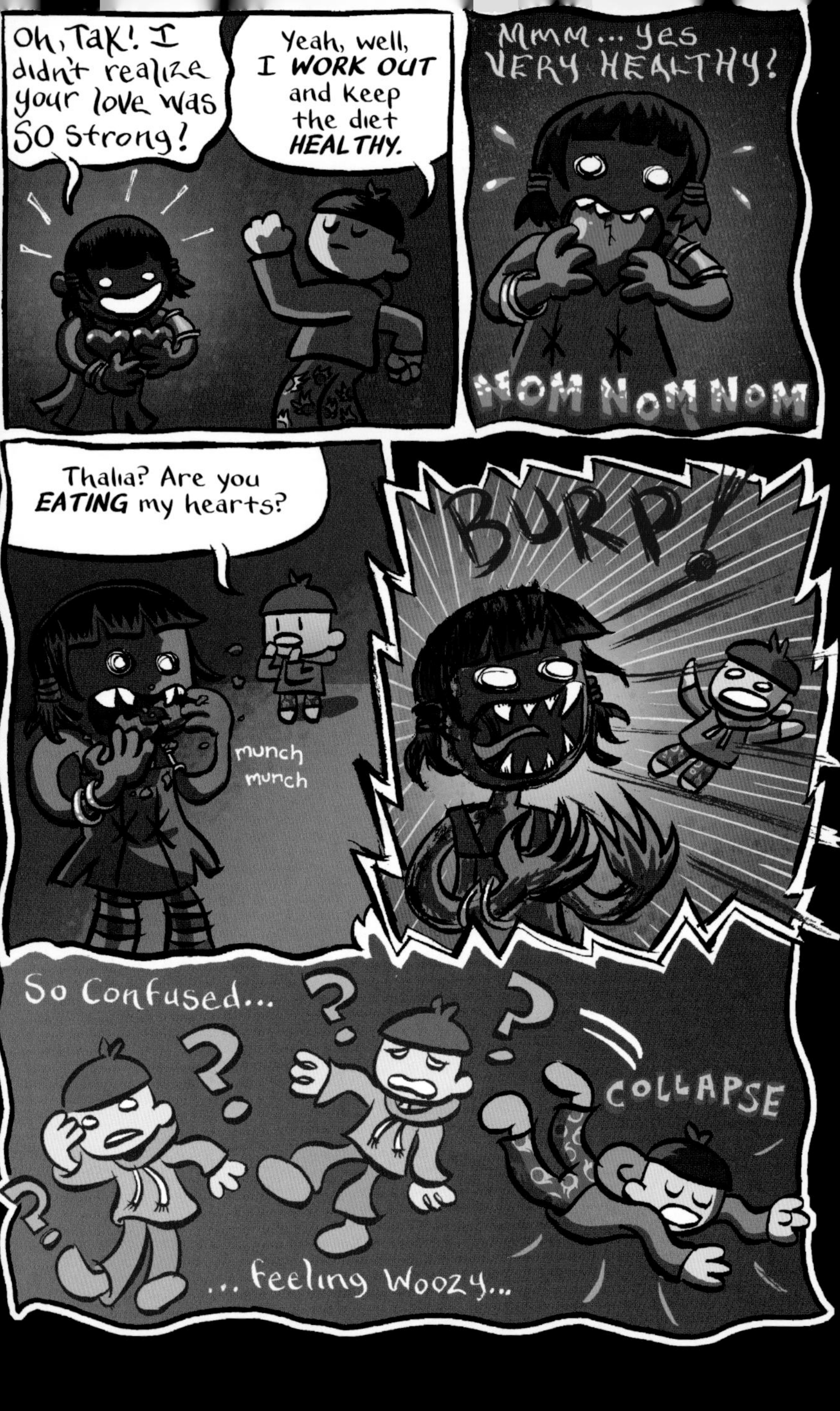

Oh, TAK! I didn't realize your love was SO strong!
Yeah, well, I **WORK OUT** and keep the diet ***HEALTHY.***
Mmm... yes VERY HEALTHY?
NOM NOM NOM
Thalia? Are you ***EATING*** my hearts?
munch munch
BURP!
So Confused...
COLLAPSE
...feeling Woozy...

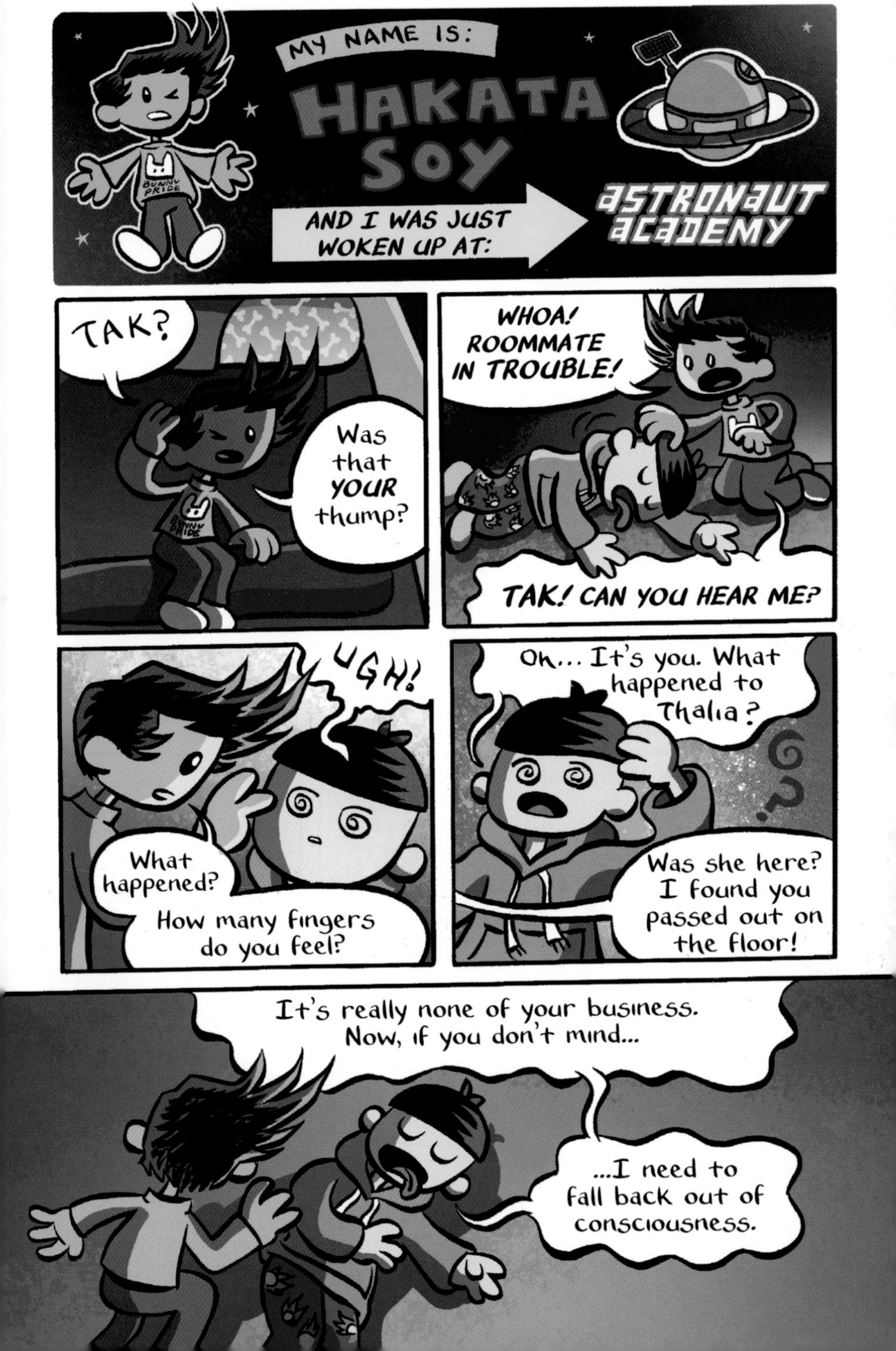
MY NAME IS:
HAKATA SOY
AND I WAS JUST WOKEN UP AT:
ASTRONAUT ACADEMY
TAK?
Was that YOUR thump?
WHOA! ROOMMATE IN TROUBLE!
TAK! CAN YOU HEAR ME?
UGH!
What happened?
How many fingers do you feel?
Oh... It's you. What happened to Thalia?
Was she here? I found you passed out on the floor!
It's really none of your business. Now, if you don't mind...
...I need to fall back out of consciousness.

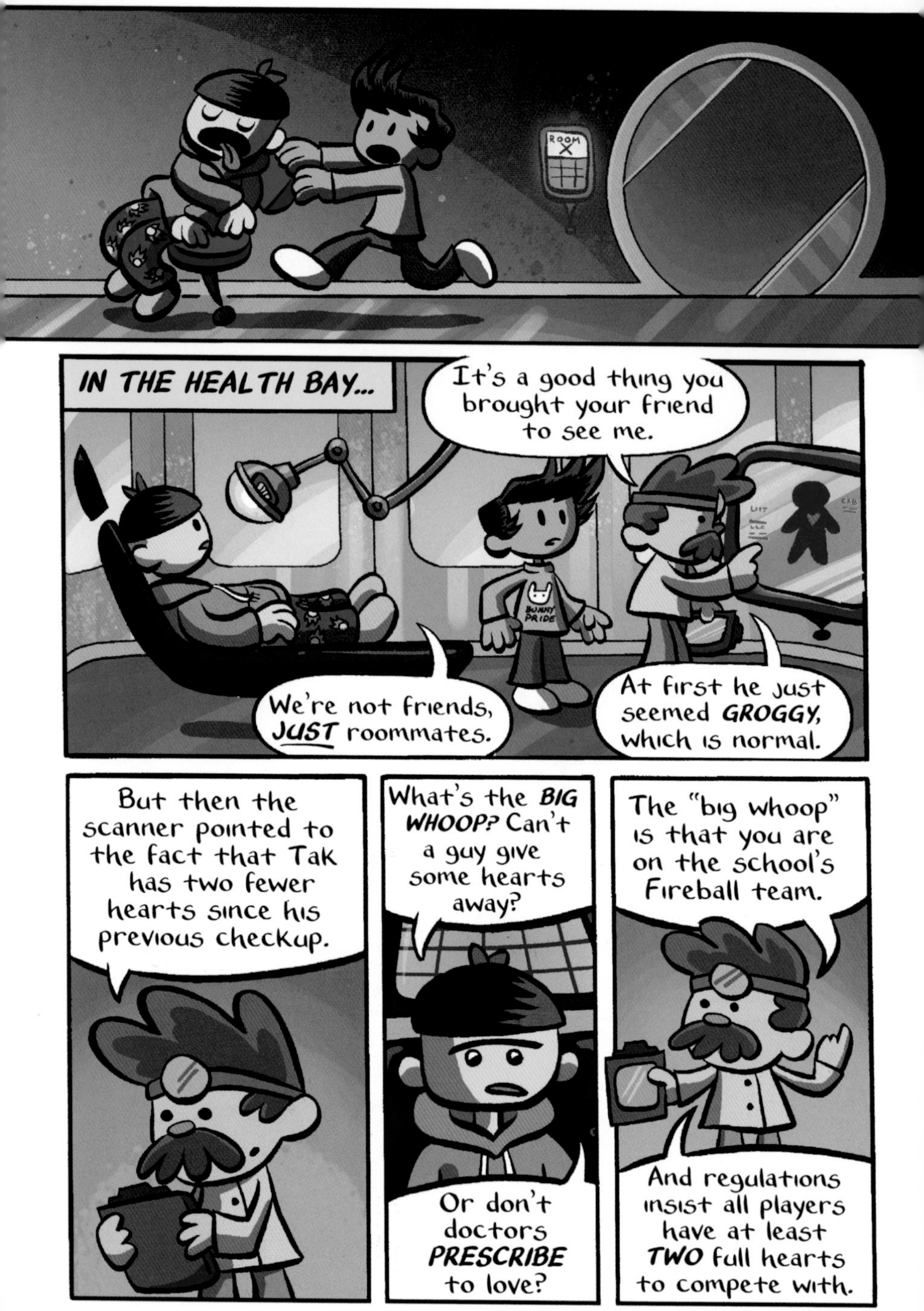
ROOM X
IN THE HEALTH BAY...
It's a good thing you brought your friend to see me.
We're not friends, JUST roommates.
BUNNY PRIDE
At first he just seemed GROGGY, which is normal.
But then the scanner pointed to the fact that Tak has two fewer hearts since his previous checkup.
What's the BIG WHOOP? Can't a guy give some hearts away?
Or don't doctors PRESCRIBE to love?
The "big whoop" is that you are on the school's Fireball team.
And regulations insist all players have at least TWO full hearts to compete with.

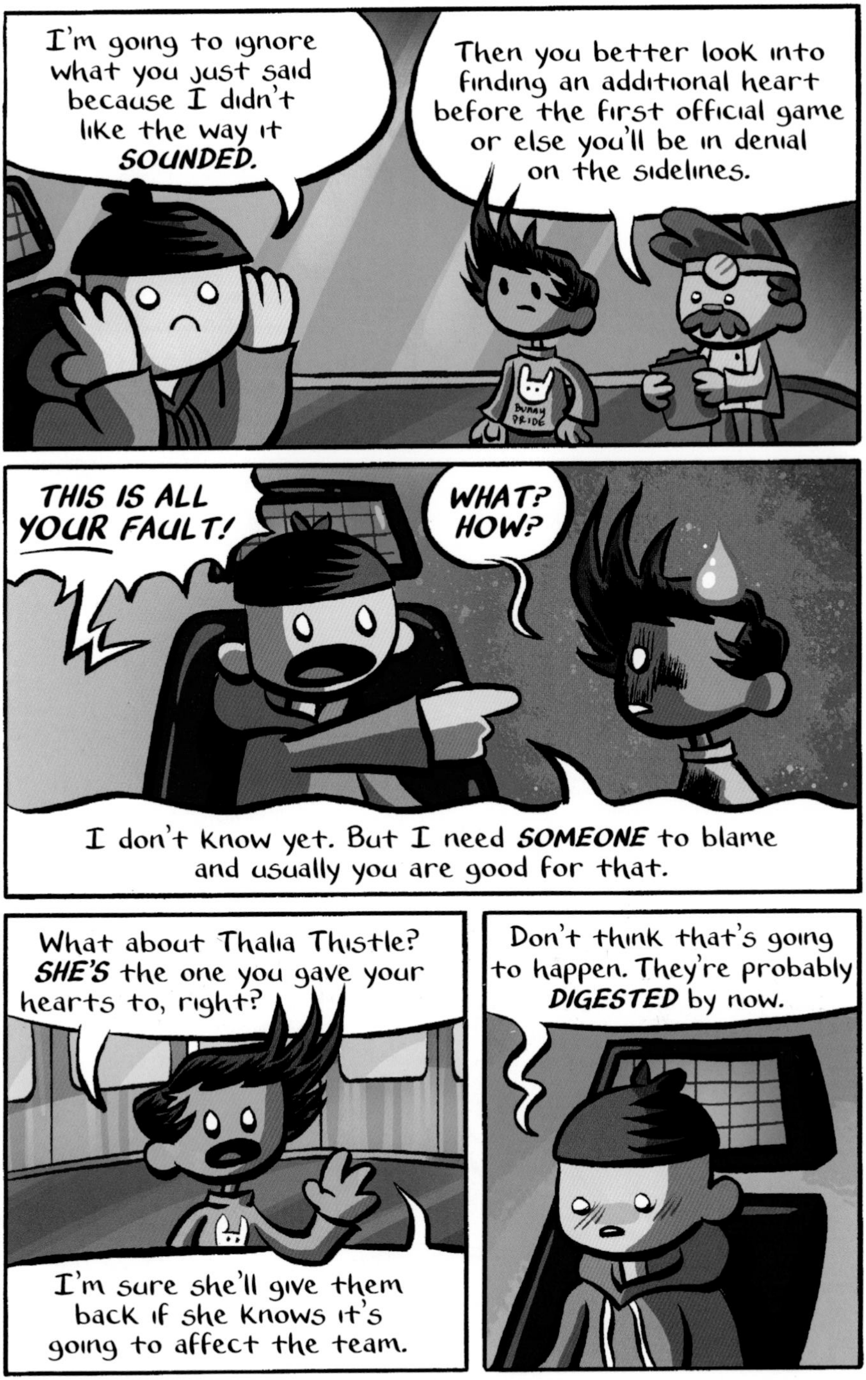
I'm going to ignore what you just said because I didn't like the way it SOUNDED.
Then you better look into finding an additional heart before the first official game or else you'll be in denial on the sidelines.
BUNNY PRIDE
THIS IS ALL YOUR FAULT!
WHAT? HOW?
I don't know yet. But I need SOMEONE to blame and usually you are good for that.
What about Thalia Thistle? SHE'S the one you gave your hearts to, right?
I'm sure she'll give them back if she knows it's going to affect the team.
Don't think that's going to happen. They're probably DIGESTED by now.

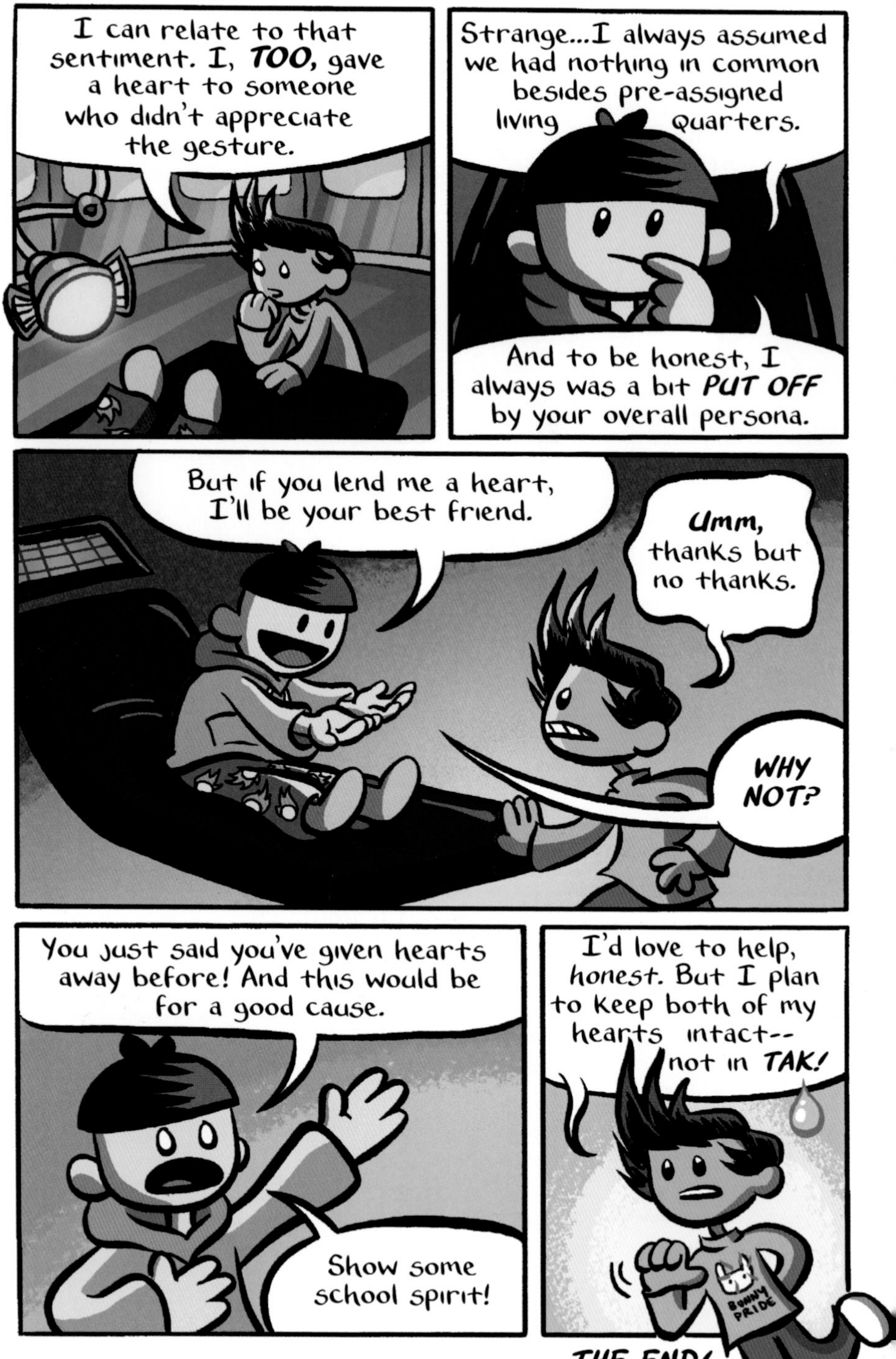
I can relate to that sentiment. I, TOO, gave a heart to someone who didn't appreciate the gesture.
Strange...I always assumed we had nothing in common besides pre-assigned living quarters.
And to be honest, I always was a bit PUT OFF by your overall persona.
But if you lend me a heart, I'll be your best friend.
Umm, thanks but no thanks.
WHY NOT?
You just said you've given hearts away before! And this would be for a good cause.
Show some school spirit!
I'd love to help, honest. But I plan to keep both of my hearts intact--not in TAK!
BONNY PRIDE
THE END!

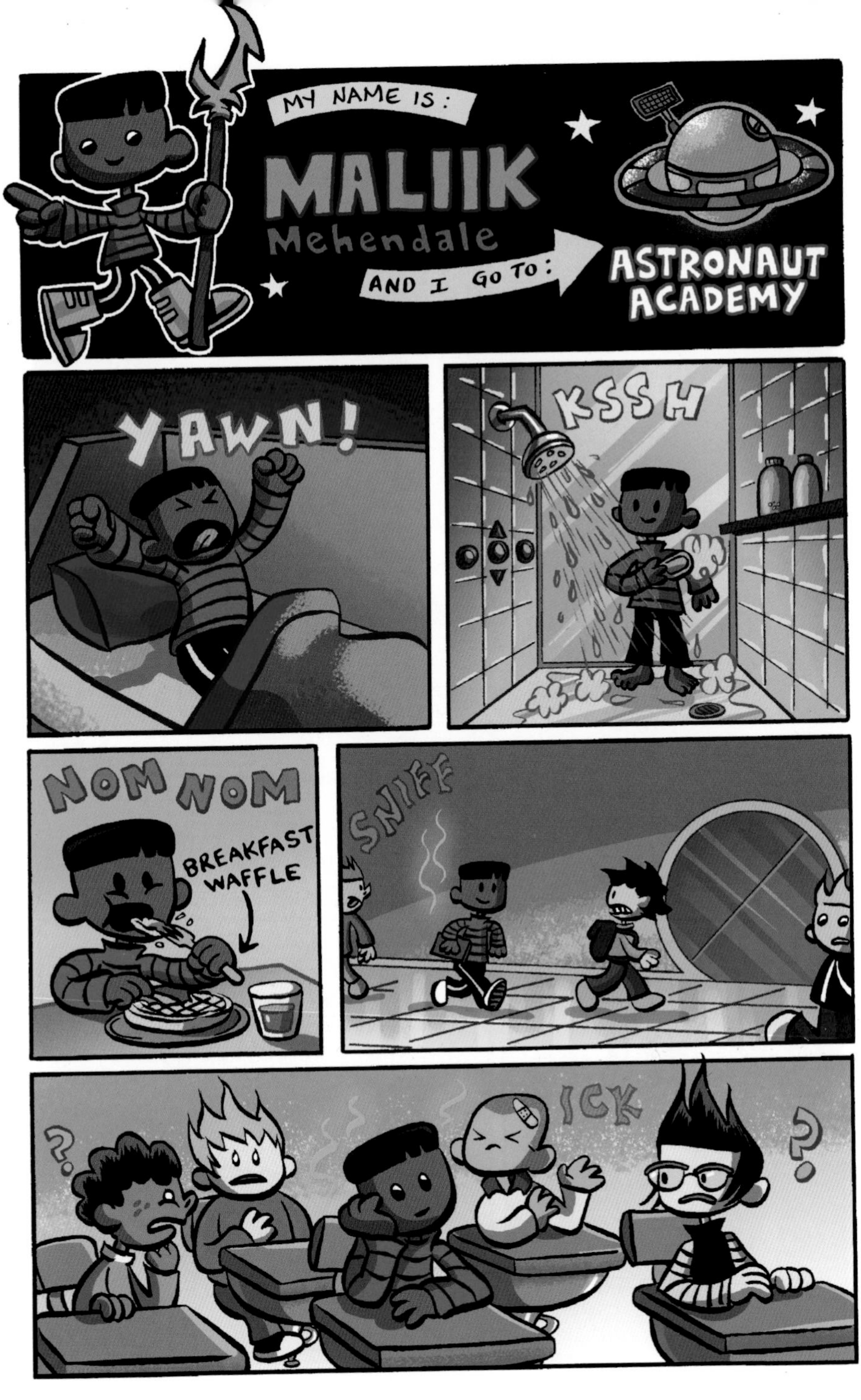
MY NAME IS:
MALIIK
Mehendale
AND I GO TO:
ASTRONAUT ACADEMY
YAWN!
KSSH
NOM NOM
BREAKFAST WAFFLE
SNIFF
?
ICK
?

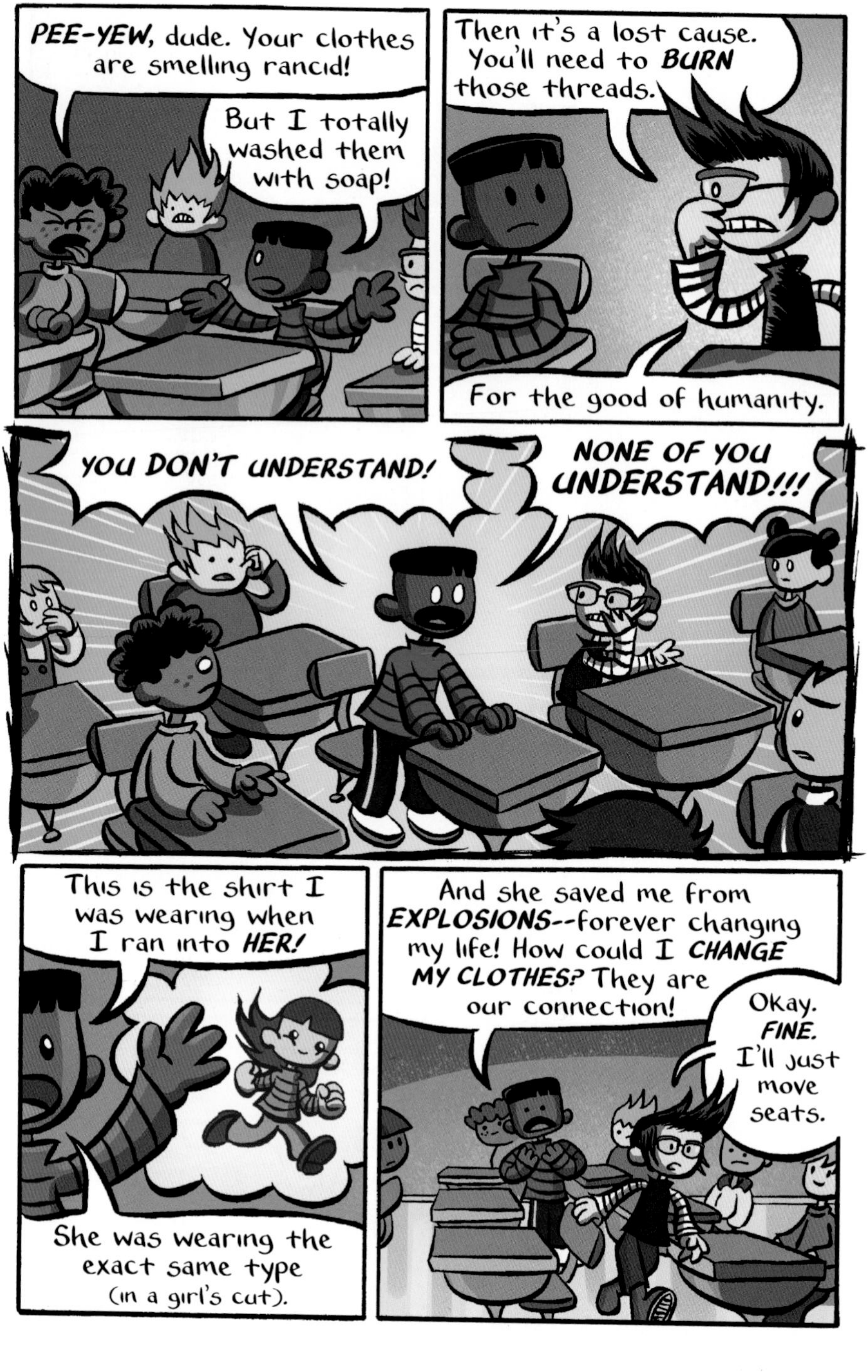
PEE-YEW, dude. Your clothes are smelling rancid!
But I totally washed them with soap!
Then it's a lost cause. You'll need to BURN those threads.
For the good of humanity.
YOU DON'T UNDERSTAND!
NONE OF YOU UNDERSTAND!!!
This is the shirt I was wearing when I ran into HER!
She was wearing the exact same type (in a girl's cut).
And she saved me from EXPLOSIONS--forever changing my life! How could I CHANGE MY CLOTHES? They are our connection!
Okay. FINE. I'll just move seats.

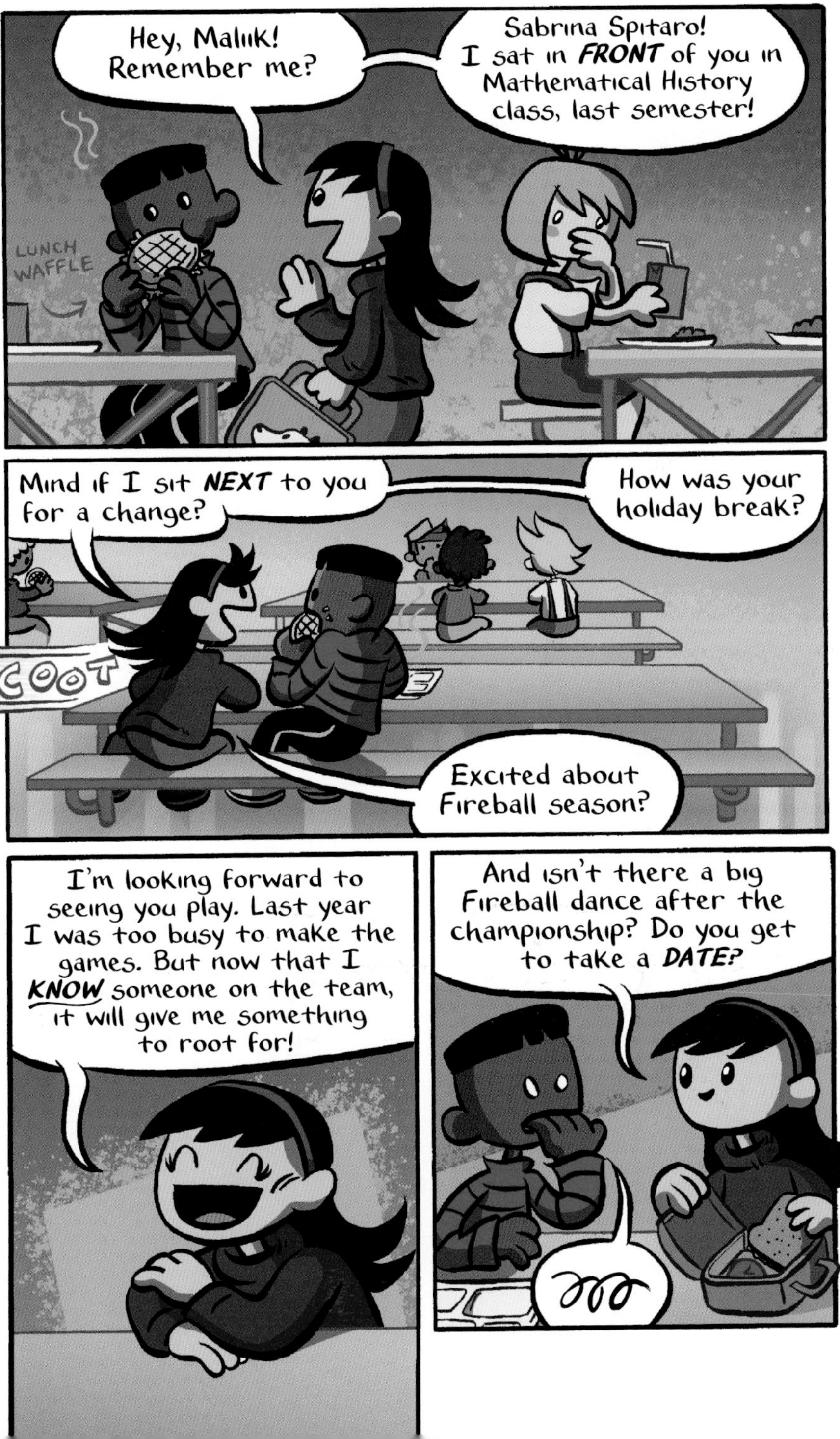

Hey, Malik! Remember me?
Sabrina Spitaro! I sat in FRONT of you in Mathematical History class, last semester!
LUNCH WAFFLE
Mind if I sit NEXT to you for a change?
How was your holiday break?
SCOOT
Excited about Fireball season?
I'm looking forward to seeing you play. Last year I was too busy to make the games. But now that I KNOW someone on the team, it will give me something to root for!
And isn't there a big Fireball dance after the championship? Do you get to take a DATE?

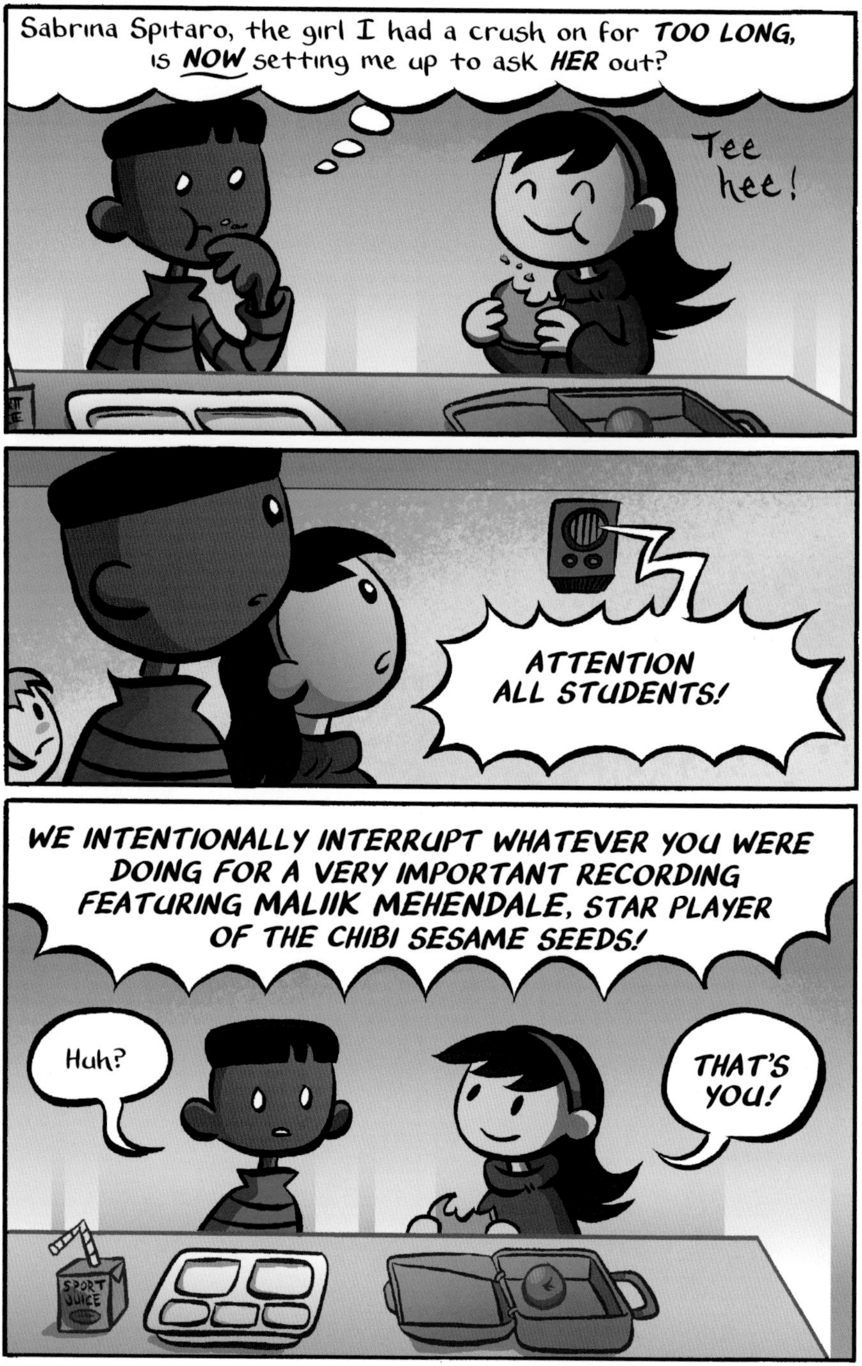
Sabrina Spitaro, the girl I had a crush on for TOO LONG, is NOW setting me up to ask HER out?
Tee hee!
ATTENTION ALL STUDENTS!
WE INTENTIONALLY INTERRUPT WHATEVER YOU WERE DOING FOR A VERY IMPORTANT RECORDING FEATURING MALIIK MEHENDALE, STAR PLAYER OF THE CHIBI SESAME SEEDS!
Huh?
THAT'S YOU!
SPORT JUICE

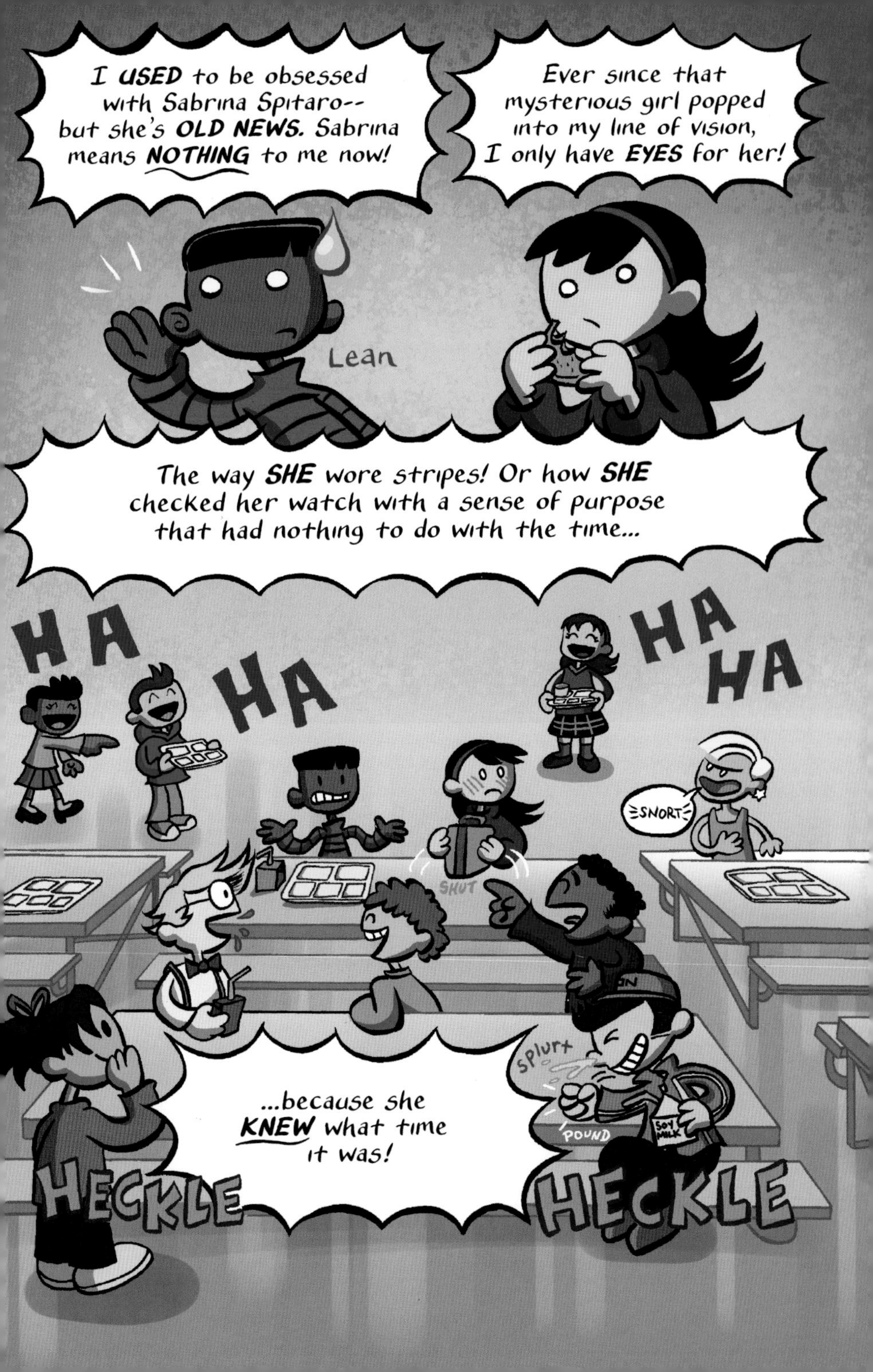

I USED to be obsessed with Sabrina Spitaro-- but she's OLD NEWS. Sabrina means NOTHING to me now!
Ever since that mysterious girl popped into my line of vision, I only have EYES for her!
Lean
The way SHE wore stripes! Or how SHE checked her watch with a sense of purpose that had nothing to do with the time...
HA
HA
HA
HA
SNORT
SHUT
splurt
POUND
SOY MILK
...because she KNEW what time it was!
HECKLE
HECKLE

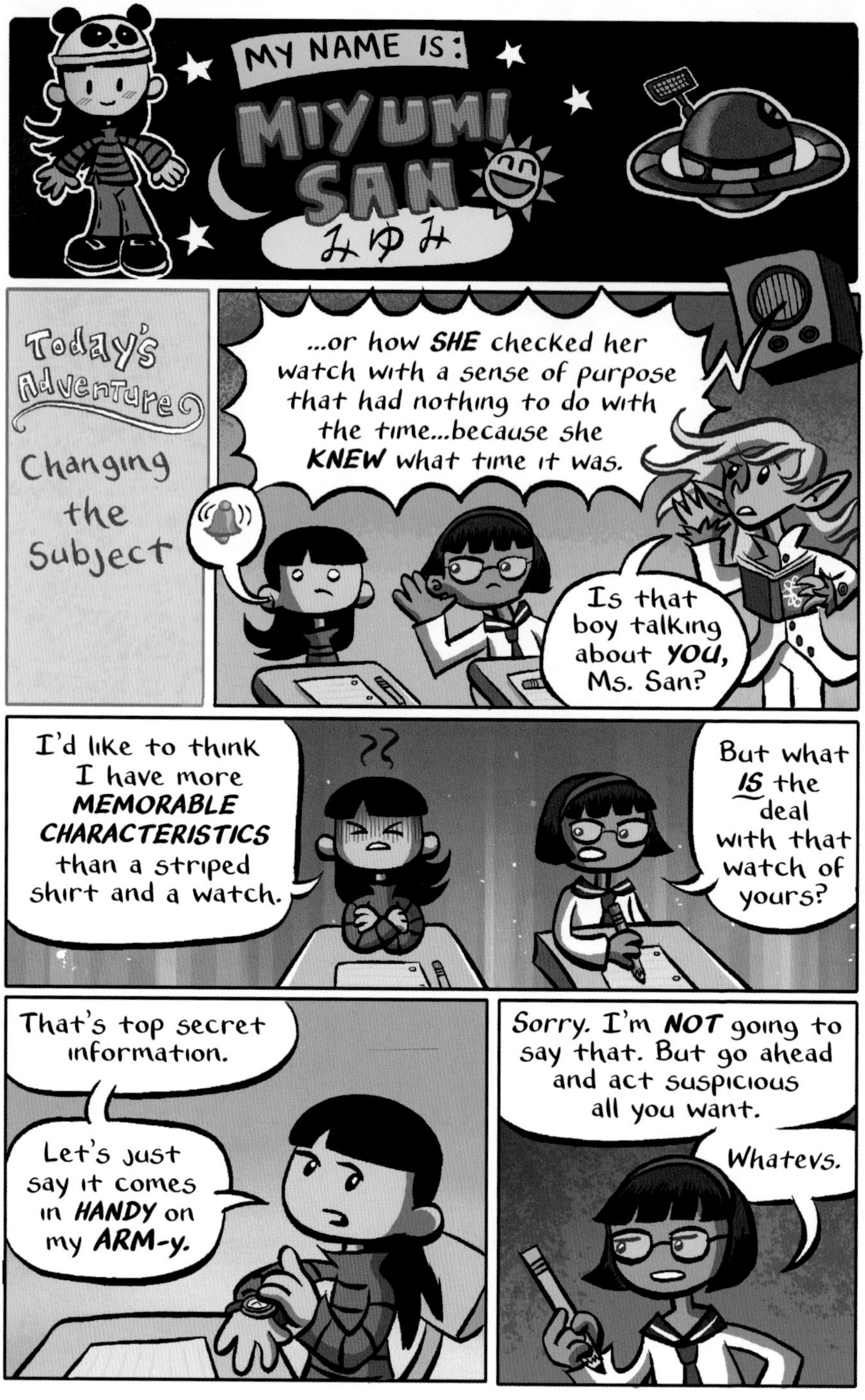
MY NAME IS:
MIYUMI SAN
みゆみ
Today's Adventure
Changing the Subject
...or how SHE checked her watch with a sense of purpose that had nothing to do with the time...because she KNEW what time it was.
Is that boy talking about YOU, Ms. San?
I'd like to think I have more MEMORABLE CHARACTERISTICS than a striped shirt and a watch.
But what IS the deal with that watch of yours?
That's top secret information.
Let's just say it comes in HANDY on my ARM-y.
Sorry. I'm NOT going to say that. But go ahead and act suspicious all you want.
Whatevs.

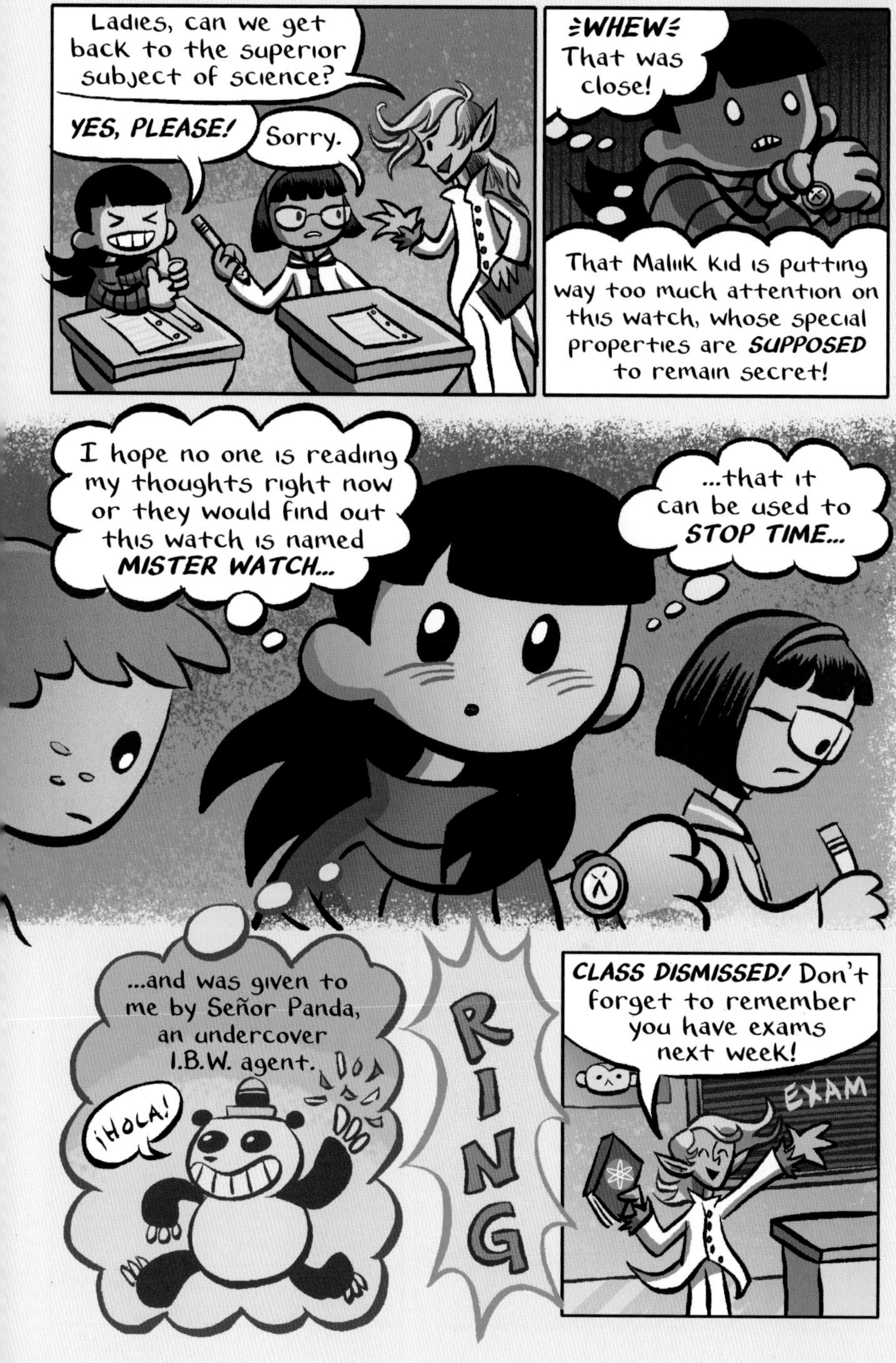

Ladies, can we get back to the superior subject of science?
YES, PLEASE!
Sorry.
WHEW That was close!
That Malik kid is putting way too much attention on this watch, whose special properties are SUPPOSED to remain secret!
I hope no one is reading my thoughts right now or they would find out this watch is named MISTER WATCH...
...that it can be used to STOP TIME...
...and was given to me by Señor Panda, an undercover I.B.W. agent.
¡HOLA!
RING
CLASS DISMISSED! Don't forget to remember you have exams next week!
EXAM

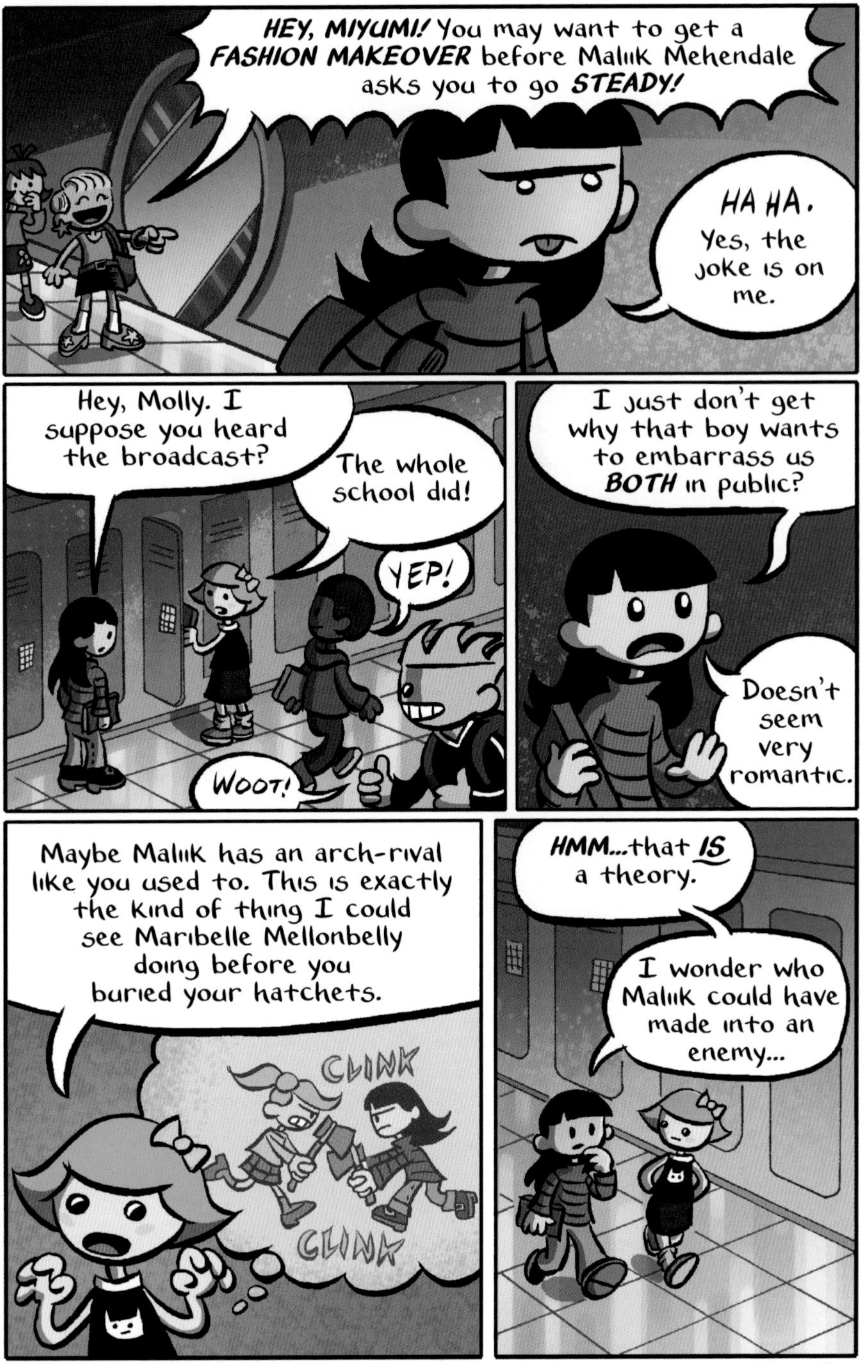
HEY, MIYUMI! You may want to get a FASHION MAKEOVER before Malik Mehendale asks you to go STEADY!
HA HA. Yes, the joke is on me.
Hey, Molly. I suppose you heard the broadcast?
The whole school did!
YEP!
WOOT!
I just don't get why that boy wants to embarrass us BOTH in public?
Doesn't seem very romantic.
Maybe Malik has an arch-rival like you used to. This is exactly the kind of thing I could see Maribelle Mellonbelly doing before you buried your hatchets.
CLINK
CLINK
HMM...that IS a theory.
I wonder who Malik could have made into an enemy...

SEGUE!

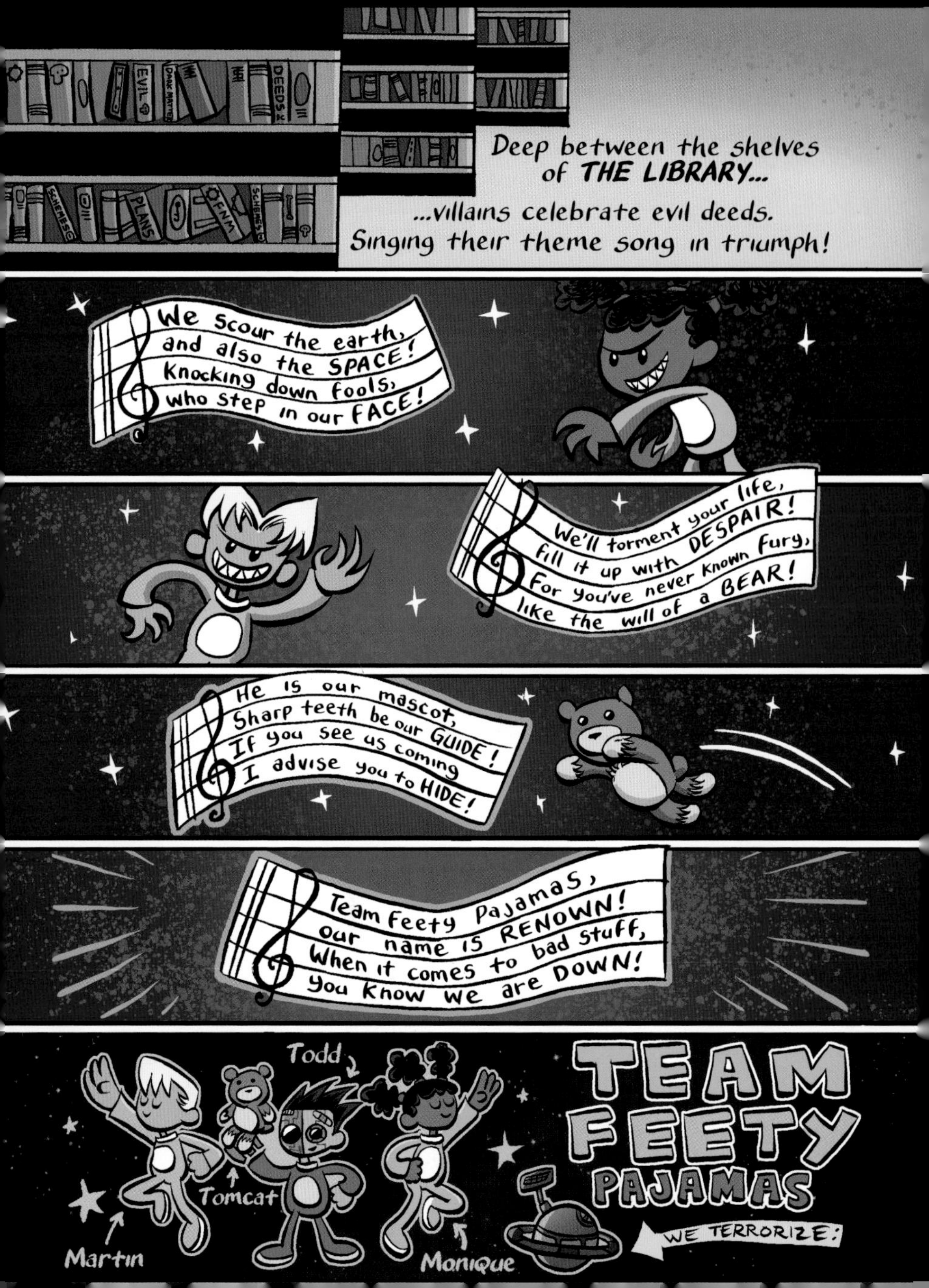
EVIL
DARK MATTER
DEEDS
SCHEMES
PLANS
FNM
SCHEMES
Deep between the shelves of THE LIBRARY...
...villains celebrate evil deeds. Singing their theme song in triumph!
We scour the earth, and also the SPACE! Knocking down fools, who step in our FACE!
We'll torment your life, fill it up with DESPAIR! For you've never known fury, like the will of a BEAR!
He is our mascot, Sharp teeth be our GUIDE! If you see us coming I advise you to HIDE!
Team Feety Pajamas, our name is RENOWN! When it comes to bad stuff, You know we are DOWN!
Todd
Tomcat
Martin
Monique
TEAM FEETY PAJAMAS
WE TERRORIZE!

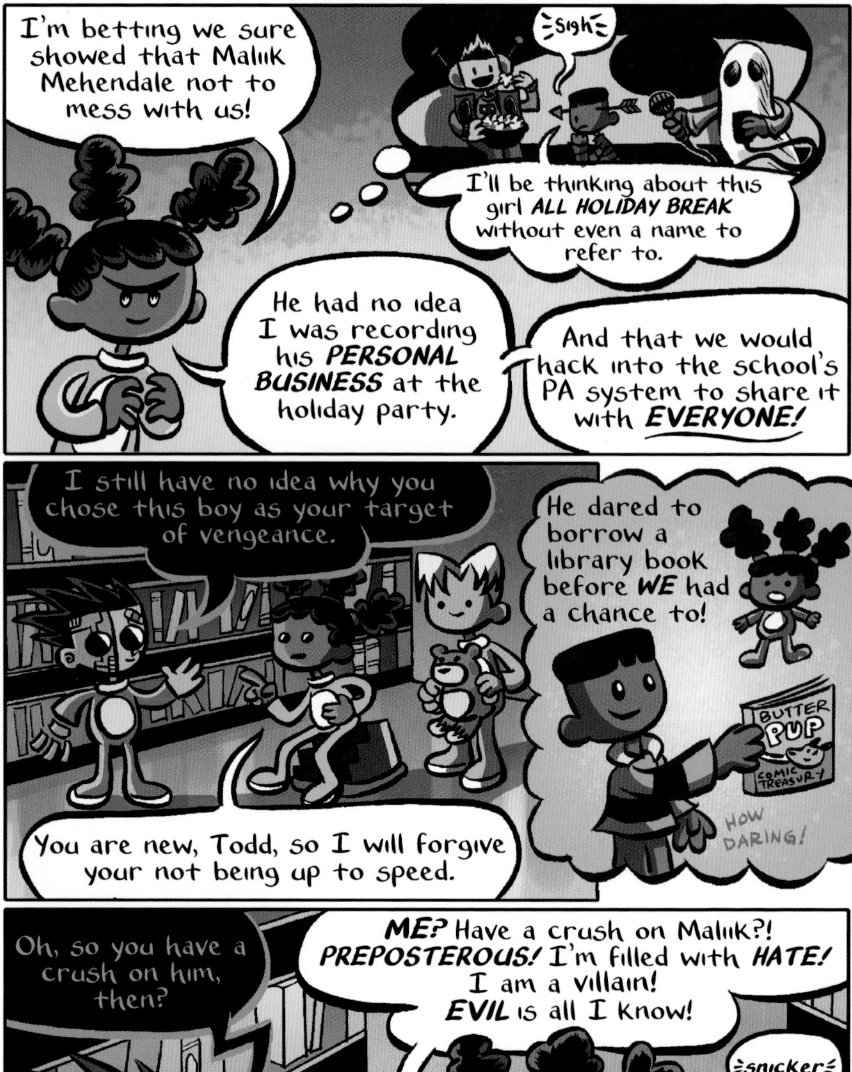

I'm betting we sure showed that Malik Mehendale not to mess with us!
Sigh
I'll be thinking about this girl ALL HOLIDAY BREAK without even a name to refer to.
He had no idea I was recording his PERSONAL BUSINESS at the holiday party.
And that we would hack into the school's PA system to share it with EVERYONE!
I still have no idea why you chose this boy as your target of vengeance.
You are new, Todd, so I will forgive your not being up to speed.
He dared to borrow a library book before WE had a chance to!
BUTTER PUP COMIC TREASURY
HOW DARING!
Oh, so you have a crush on him, then?
ME? Have a crush on Malik?! PREPOSTEROUS! I'm filled with HATE! I am a villain! EVIL is all I know!
snicker
Whatever you say.

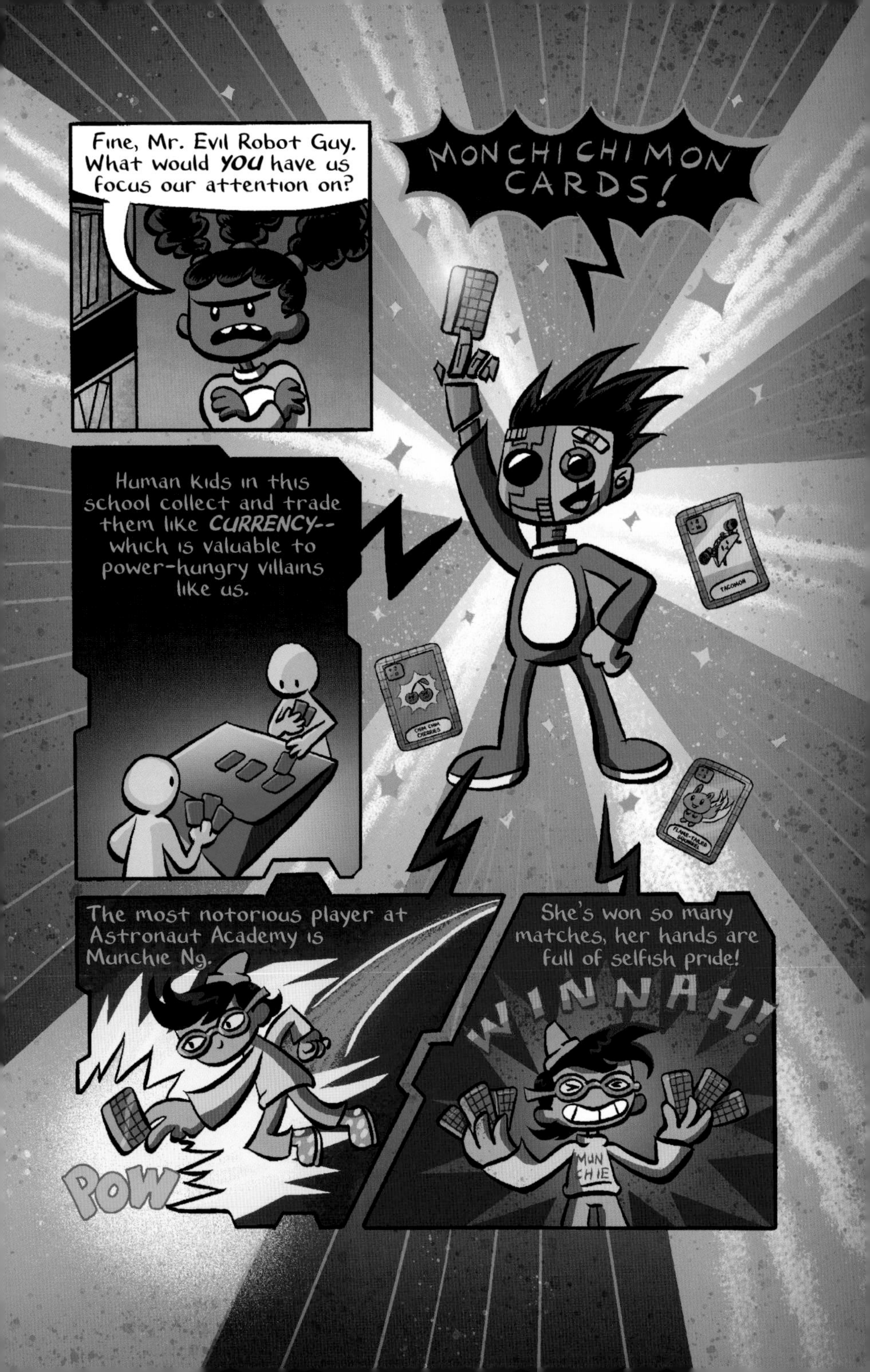

Fine, Mr. Evil Robot Guy. What would YOU have us focus our attention on?
MONCHICHIMON CARDS!
Human kids in this school collect and trade them like CURRENCY--which is valuable to power-hungry villains like us.
TACOMON
CHIM CHIM CHERRIES
FLAME-TAILED SQUIRREL
The most notorious player at Astronaut Academy is Munchie Ng.
POW
She's won so many matches, her hands are full of selfish pride!
WINNAH!
MUNCHIE

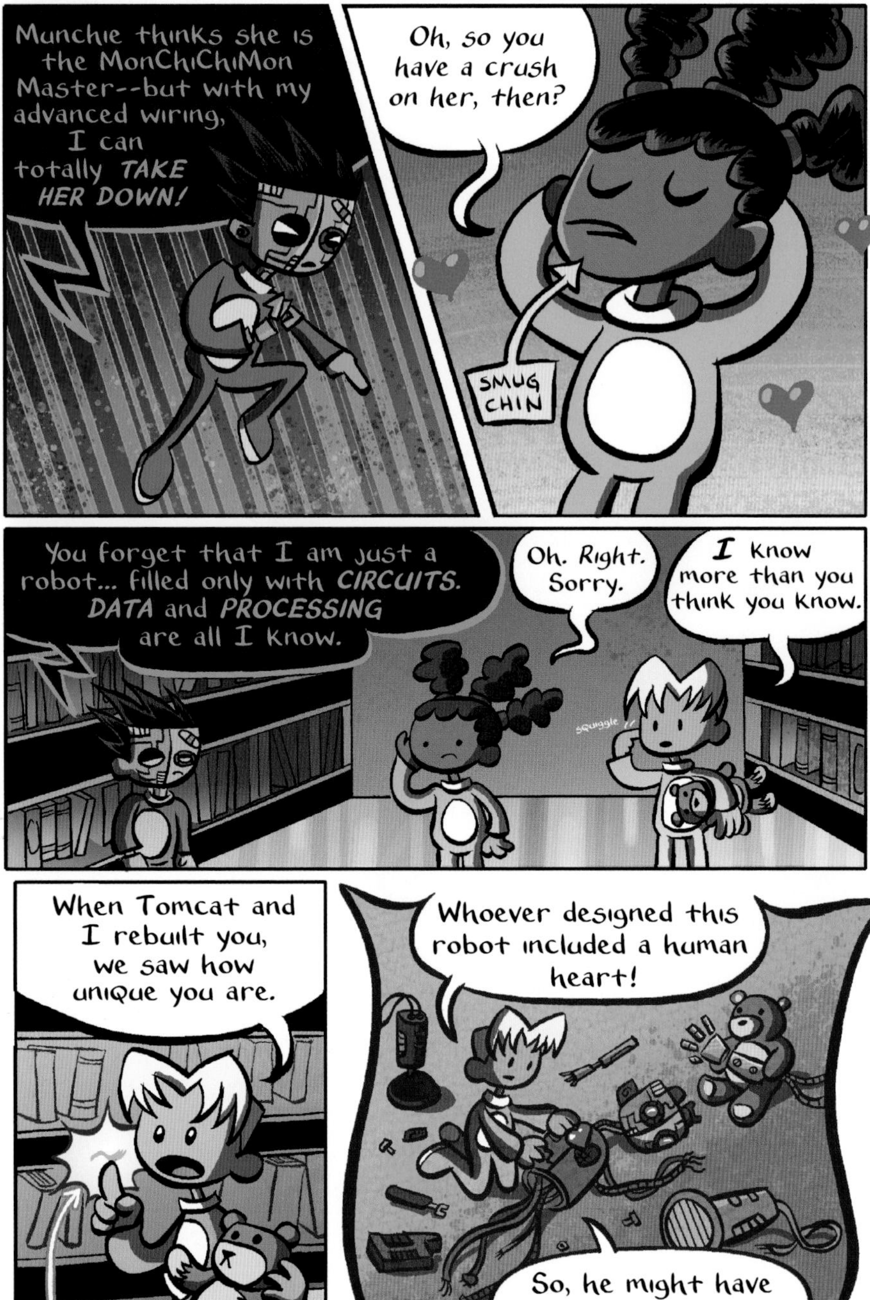
Munchie thinks she is the MonChiChiMon Master--but with my advanced wiring, I can totally TAKE HER DOWN!
Oh, so you have a crush on her, then?
SMUG CHIN
You forget that I am just a robot... filled only with CIRCUITS. DATA and PROCESSING are all I know.
Oh. Right. Sorry.
I know more than you think you know.
squiggle
When Tomcat and I rebuilt you, we saw how unique you are.
FLASHBACK
Whoever designed this robot included a human heart!
So, he might have genuine emotions motivating him!

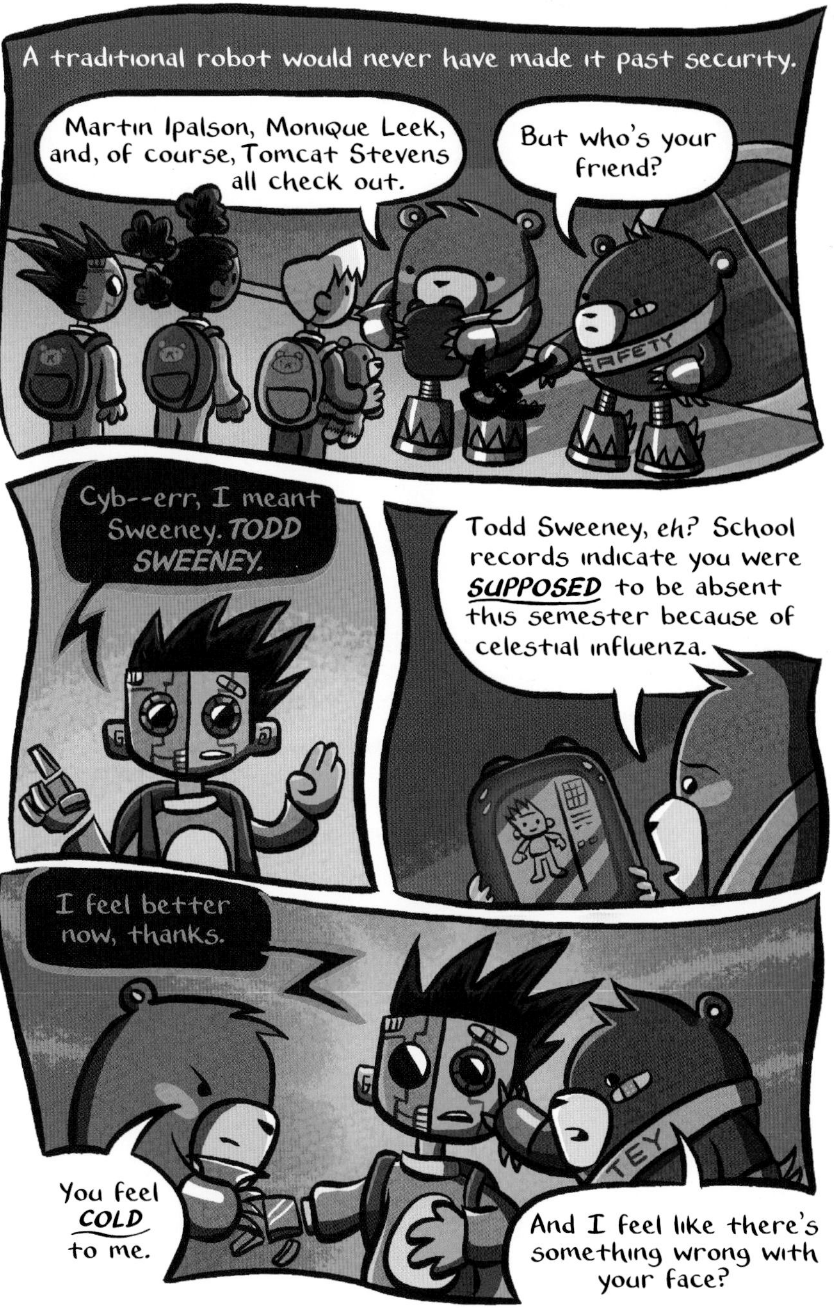
A traditional robot would never have made it past security.
Martin Ipalson, Monique Leek, and, of course, Tomcat Stevens all check out.
But who's your friend?
Cyb--err, I meant Sweeney. *TODD SWEENEY.*
Todd Sweeney, *eh?* School records indicate you were ***SUPPOSED*** to be absent this semester because of celestial influenza.
I feel better now, thanks.
You feel ***COLD*** to me.
And I feel like there's something wrong with your face?

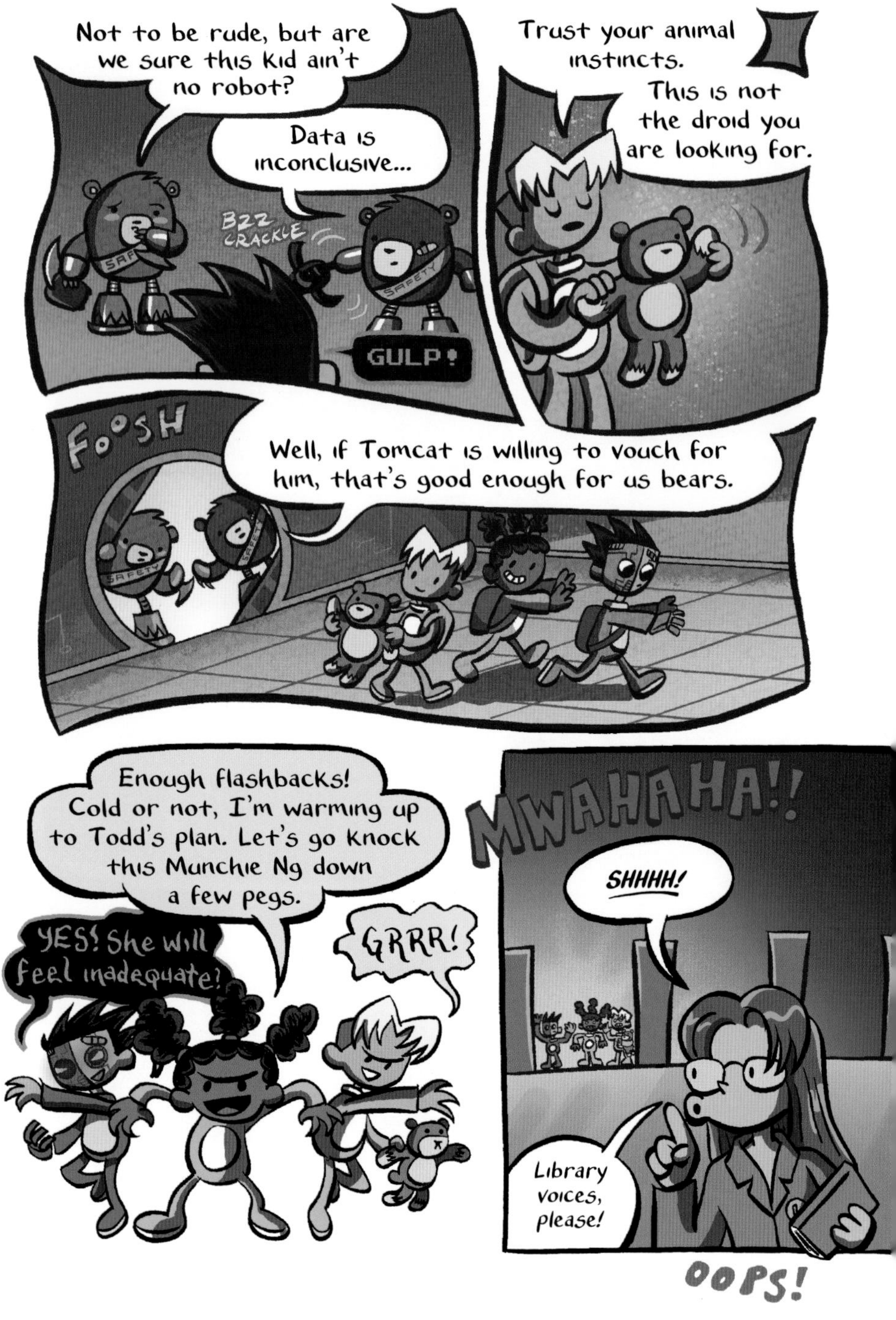

Not to be rude, but are we sure this kid ain't no robot?
Data is inconclusive...
BZZ CRACKLE
GULP!
Trust your animal instincts.
This is not the droid you are looking for.
FOOSH
Well, if Tomcat is willing to vouch for him, that's good enough for us bears.
Enough flashbacks! Cold or not, I'm warming up to Todd's plan. Let's go knock this Munchie Ng down a few pegs.
YES! She will feel inadequate!
GRRR!
MWAHAHA!!
SHHHH!
Library voices, please!
OOPS!

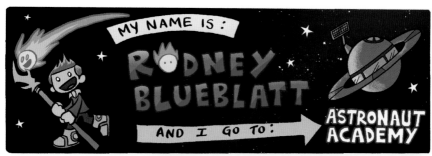

MY NAME IS:
RODNEY BLUEBLATT
AND I GO TO:
ASTRONAUT ACADEMY
What is happening to the Chibi Sesame Seeds that is making me so WORRIED about our potential prospects?
XL FIREBALL
STAR BURGER
ASTRONAUT AC
CURRENT
As team captain, it is my job to make sure everyone is FOCUSED on not being distracted.
Prepared to practice?!
What?
Oops. Yeah. Sorry.
Of course!
02
06
01
12
To make sure they haven't gone crazy.
Malik, please concentrate on the sport at hand!
Do I have to concentrate with my HEARTS...
...as well as brains?

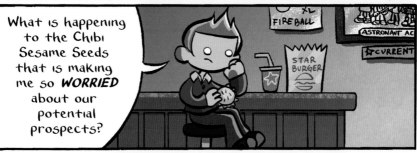

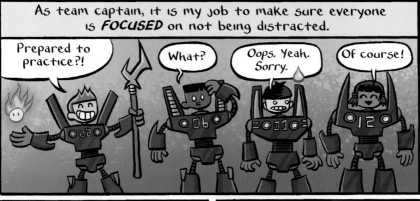

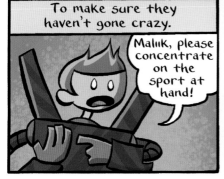

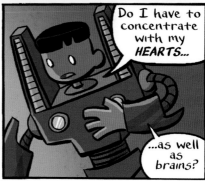

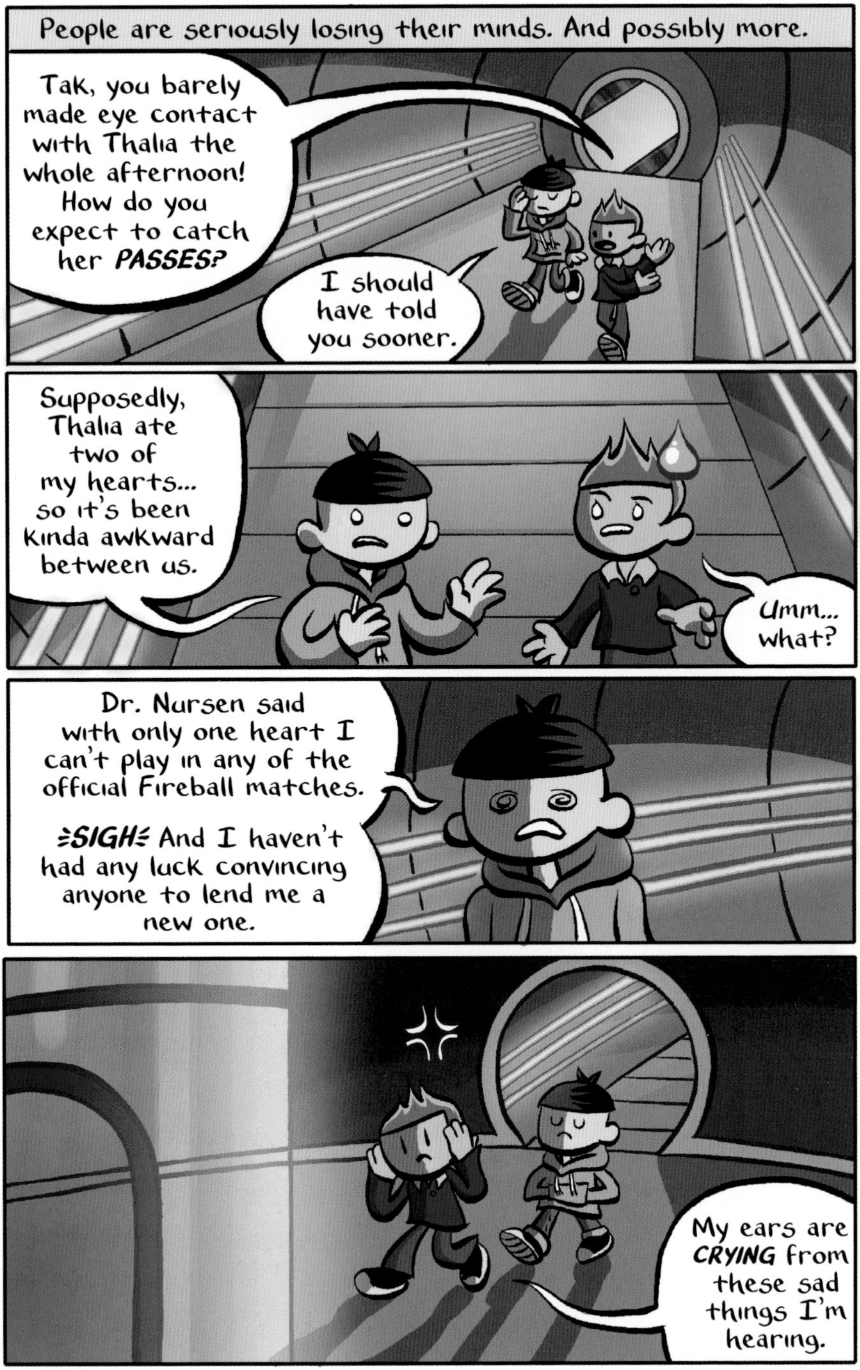
People are seriously losing their minds. And possibly more.
Tak, you barely made eye contact with Thalia the whole afternoon! How do you expect to catch her PASSES?
I should have told you sooner.
Supposedly, Thalia ate two of my hearts... so it's been kinda awkward between us.
Umm... what?
Dr. Nursen said with only one heart I can't play in any of the official Fireball matches.
SIGH And I haven't had any luck convincing anyone to lend me a new one.
My ears are CRYING from these sad things I'm hearing.

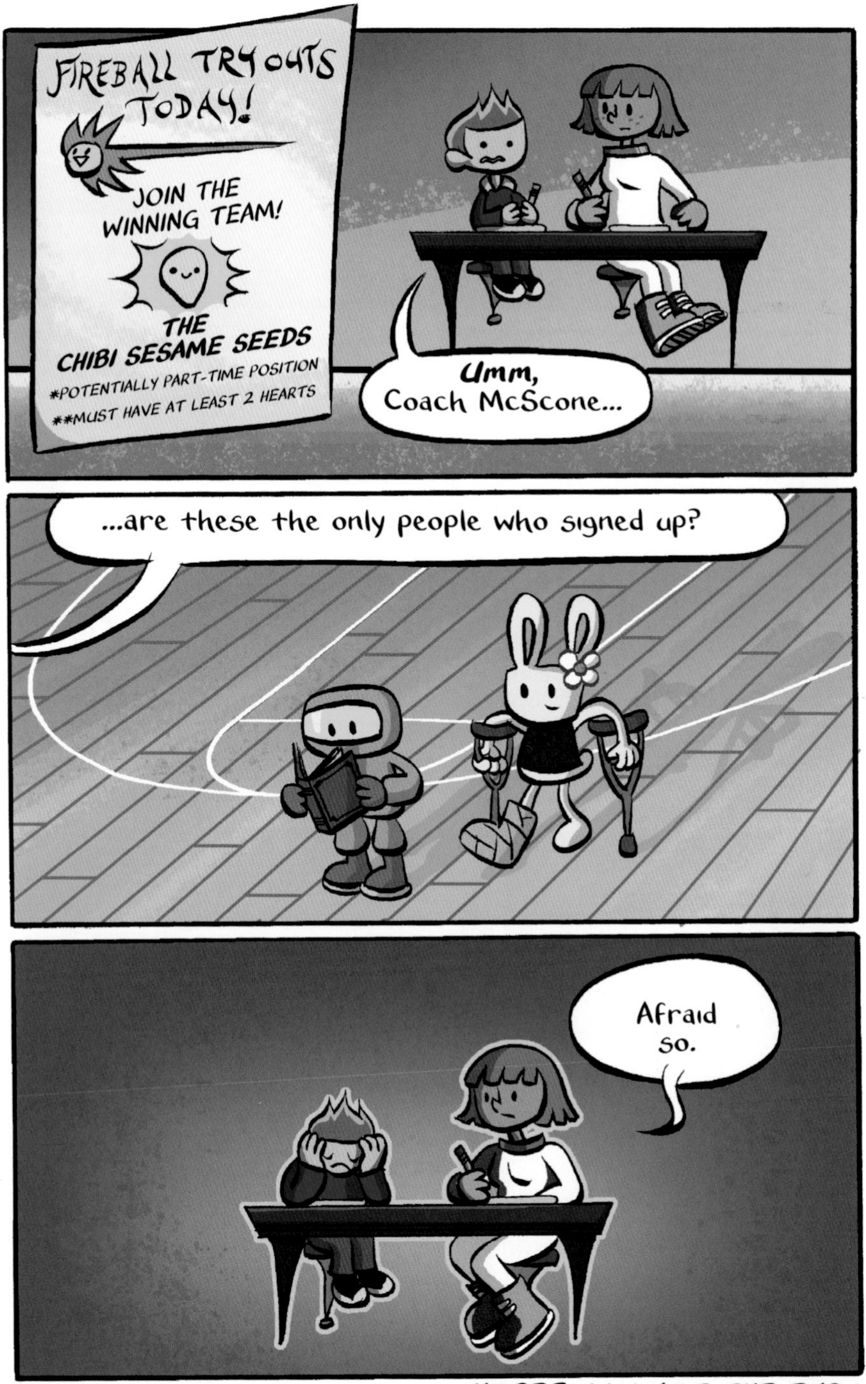
FIREBALL TRYOUTS TODAY!
JOIN THE WINNING TEAM!
THE CHIBI SESAME SEEDS
*POTENTIALLY PART-TIME POSITION
**MUST HAVE AT LEAST 2 HEARTS
Umm, Coach McScone...
...are these the only people who signed up?
Afraid so.

HOPEFULLY NOT THE END!

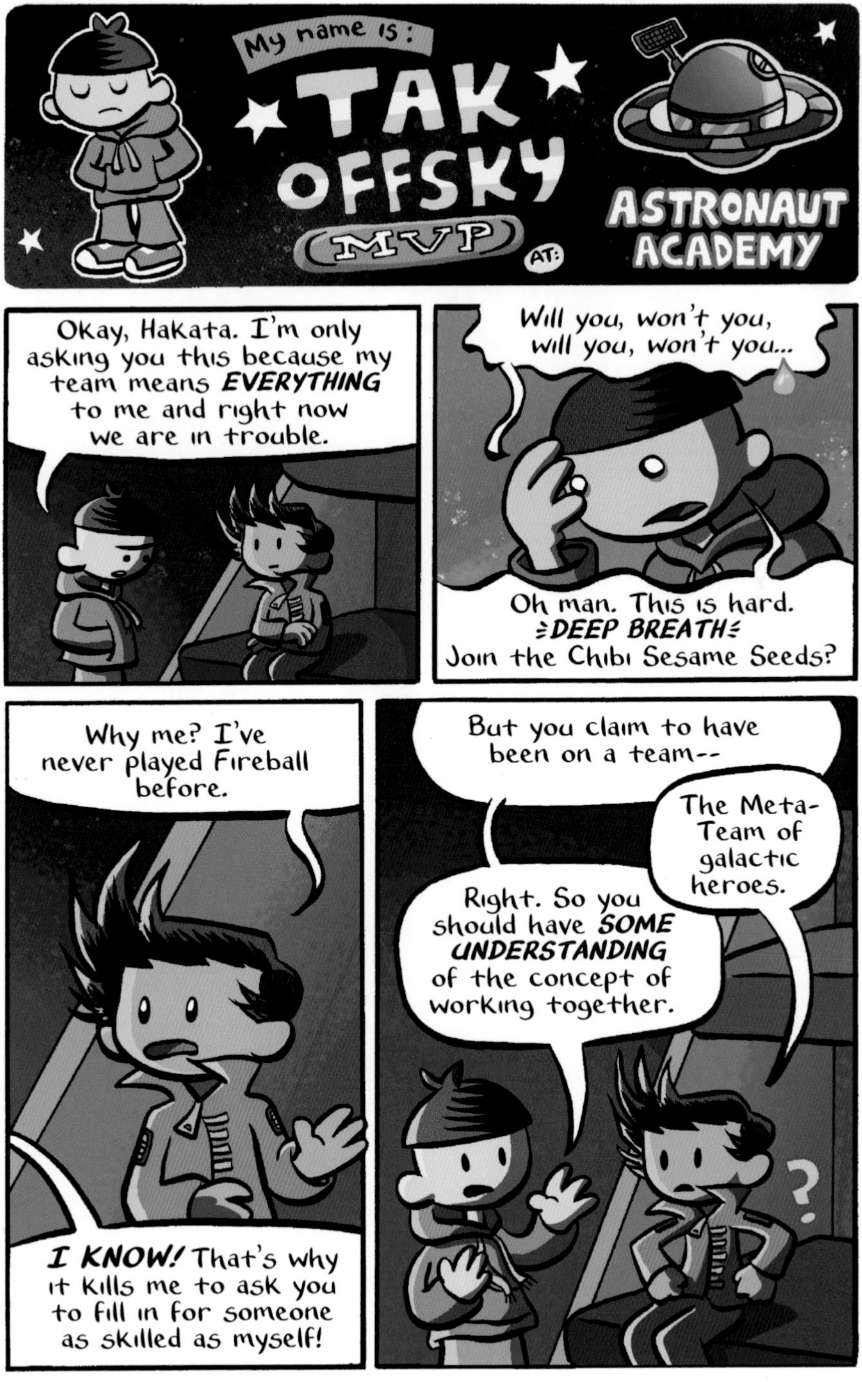
My name is:
TAK OFFSKY
MVP
AT:
ASTRONAUT ACADEMY
Okay, Hakata. I'm only asking you this because my team means *EVERYTHING* to me and right now we are in trouble.
Will you, won't you, will you, won't you...
Oh man. This is hard.
DEEP BREATH
Join the Chibi Sesame Seeds?
Why me? I've never played Fireball before.
I KNOW! That's why it kills me to ask you to fill in for someone as skilled as myself!
But you claim to have been on a team--
The Meta-Team of galactic heroes.
Right. So you should have *SOME UNDERSTANDING* of the concept of working together.
?

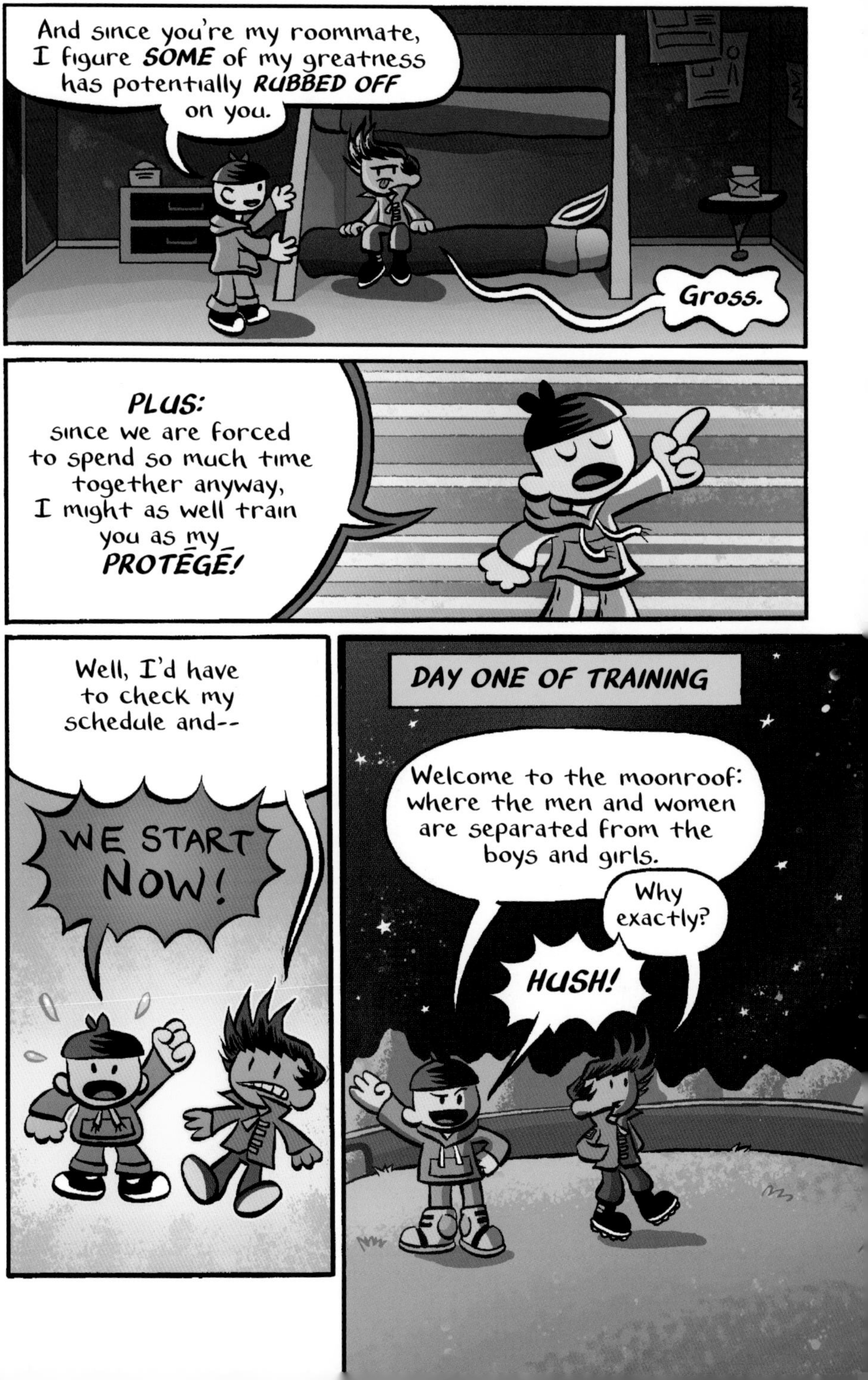

And since you're my roommate, I figure SOME of my greatness has potentially RUBBED OFF on you.
Gross.
PLUS: since we are forced to spend so much time together anyway, I might as well train you as my PROTÉGÉ!
Well, I'd have to check my schedule and--
WE START NOW!
DAY ONE OF TRAINING
Welcome to the moonroof: where the men and women are separated from the boys and girls.
Why exactly?
HUSH!

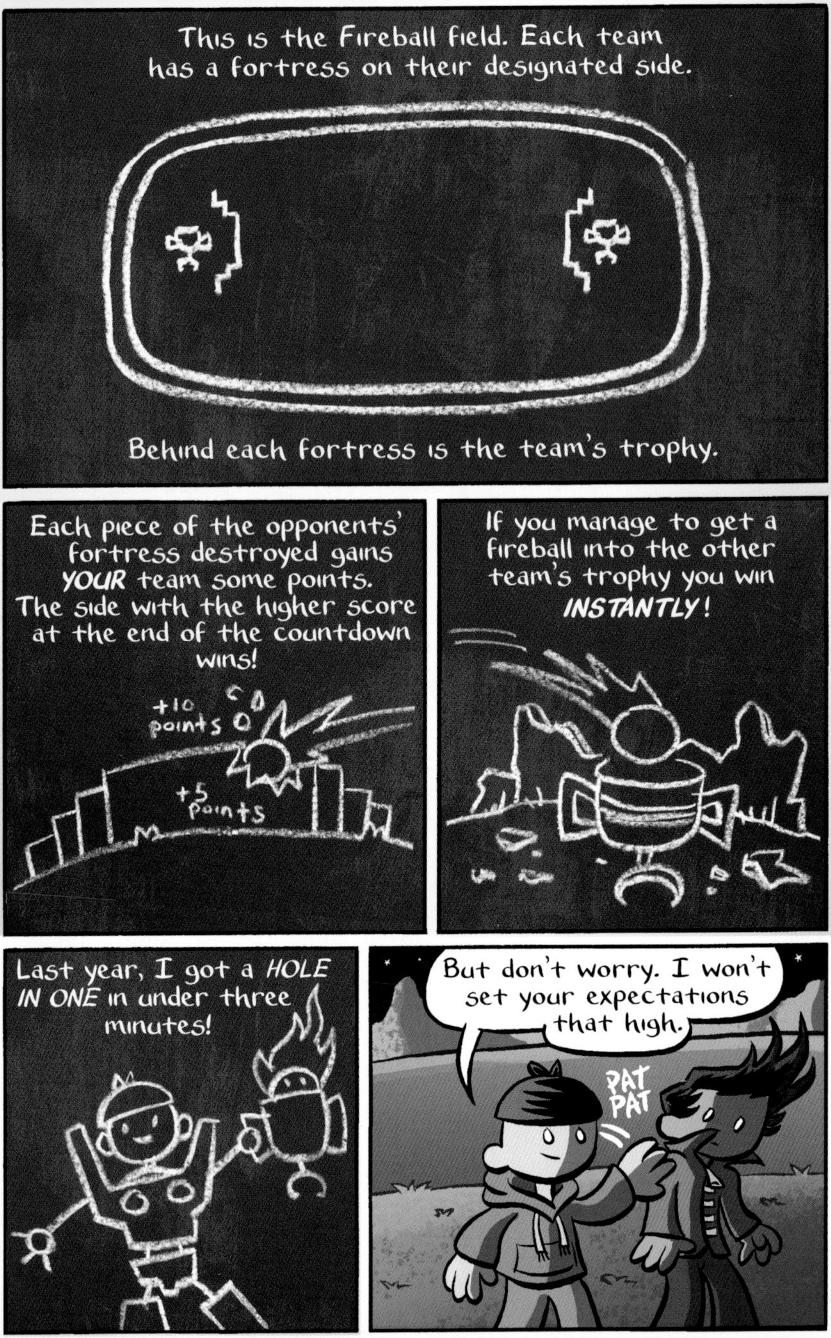
This is the Fireball field. Each team has a fortress on their designated side.
Behind each fortress is the team's trophy.
Each piece of the opponents' fortress destroyed gains *YOUR* team some points. The side with the higher score at the end of the countdown wins!
+10 points
+5 points
If you manage to get a fireball into the other team's trophy you win *INSTANTLY*!
Last year, I got a *HOLE IN ONE* in under three minutes!
But don't worry. I won't set your expectations that high.
PAT PAT

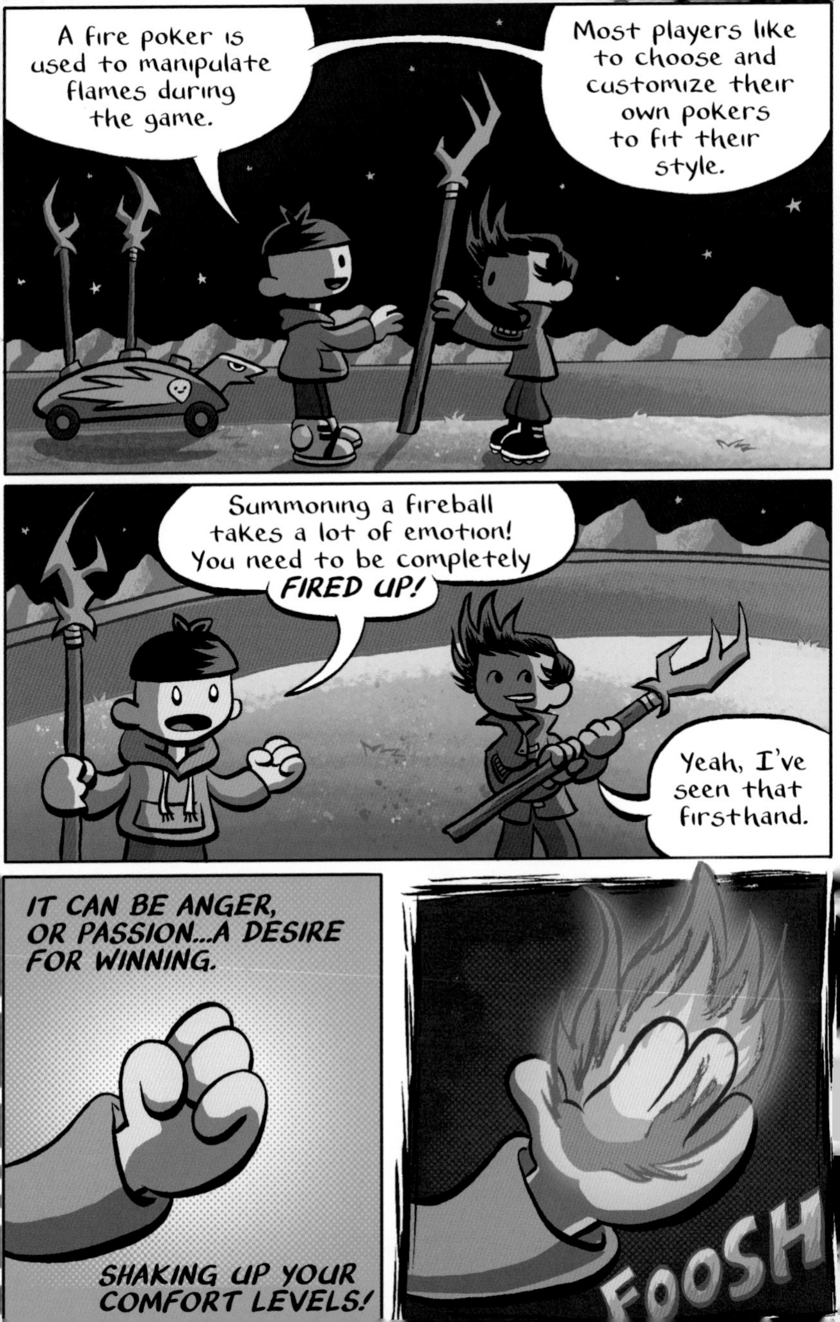
A fire poker is used to manipulate flames during the game.
Most players like to choose and customize their own pokers to fit their style.
Summoning a fireball takes a lot of emotion! You need to be completely FIRED UP!
Yeah, I've seen that firsthand.
IT CAN BE ANGER, OR PASSION...A DESIRE FOR WINNING.
SHAKING UP YOUR COMFORT LEVELS!
FOOSH

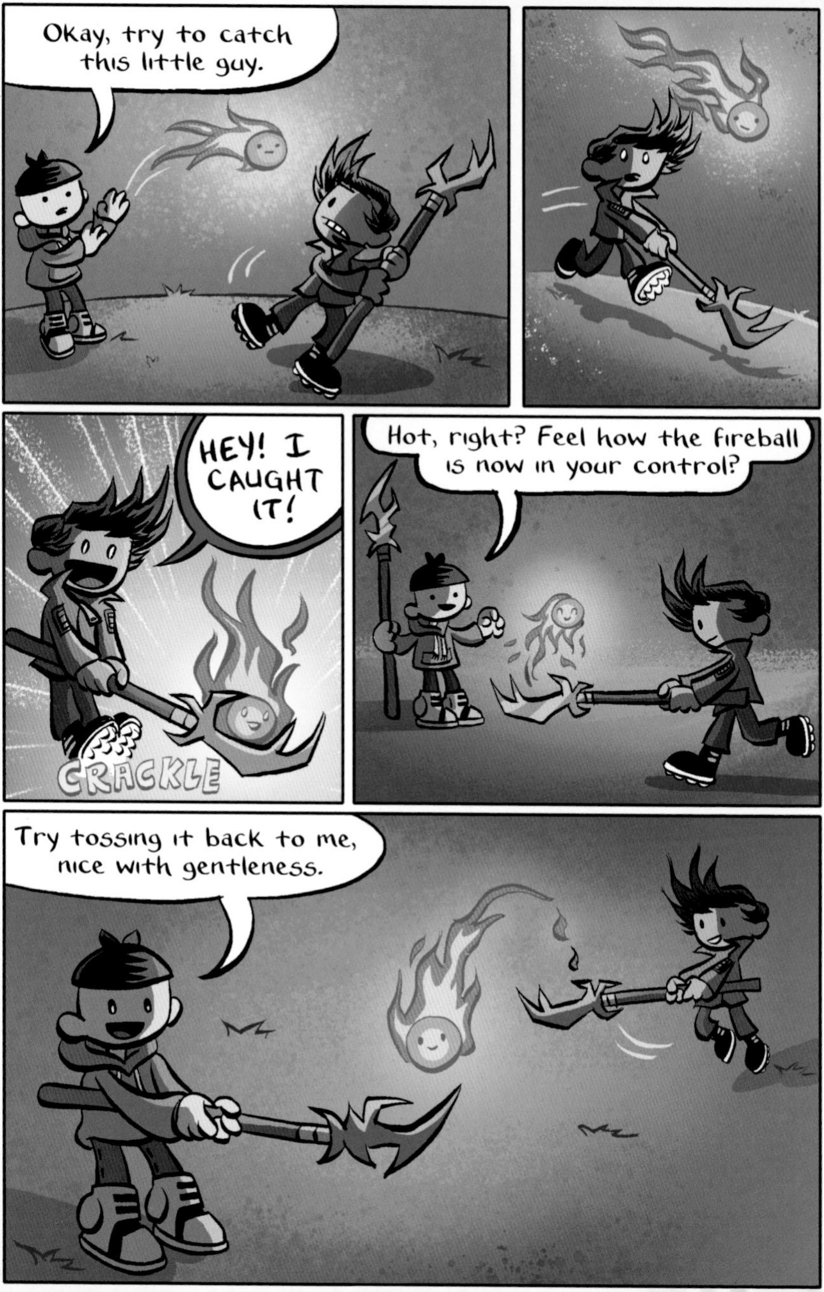
Okay, try to catch this little guy.
HEY! I CAUGHT IT!
CRACKLE
Hot, right? Feel how the fireball is now in your control?
Try tossing it back to me, nice with gentleness.

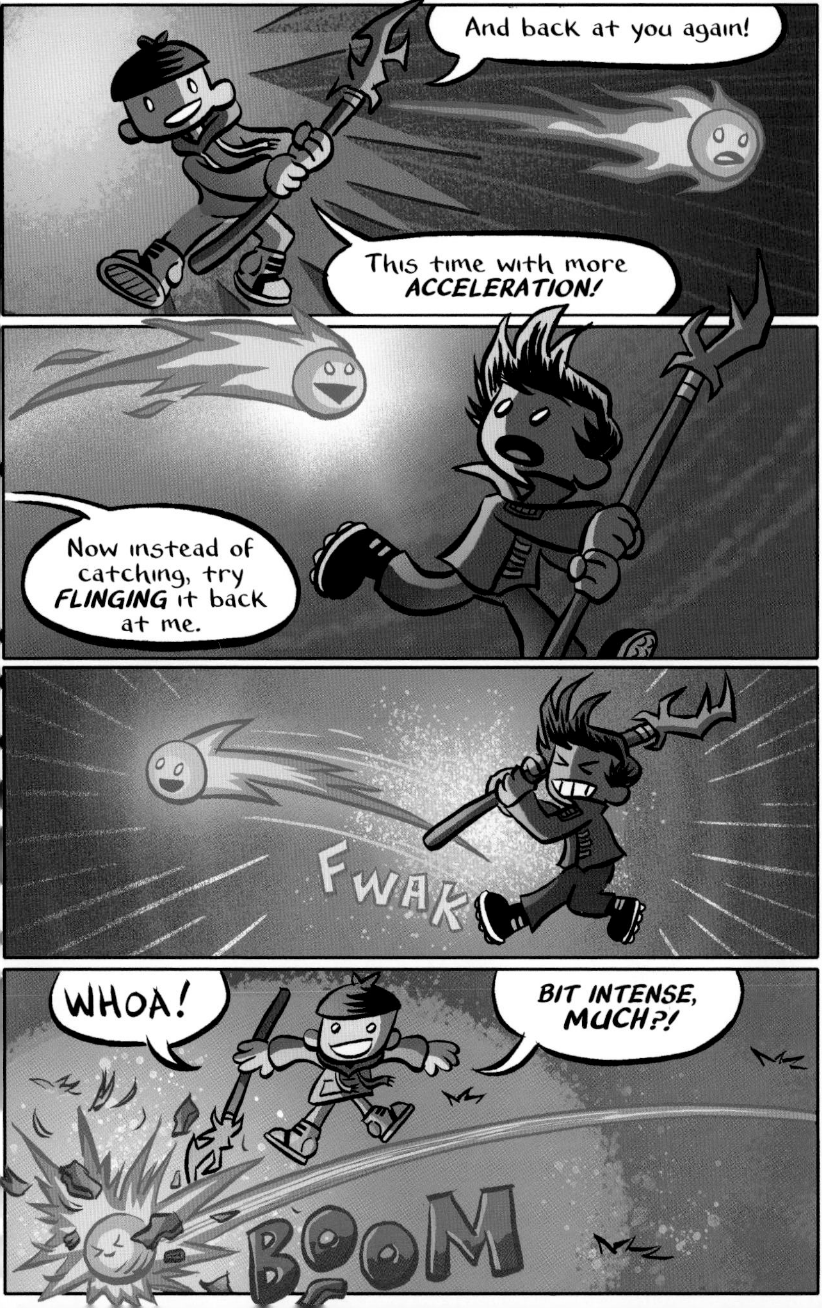
And back at you again!
This time with more ACCELERATION!
Now instead of catching, try FLINGING it back at me.
FWAK
WHOA!
BIT INTENSE, MUCH?!
BOOM

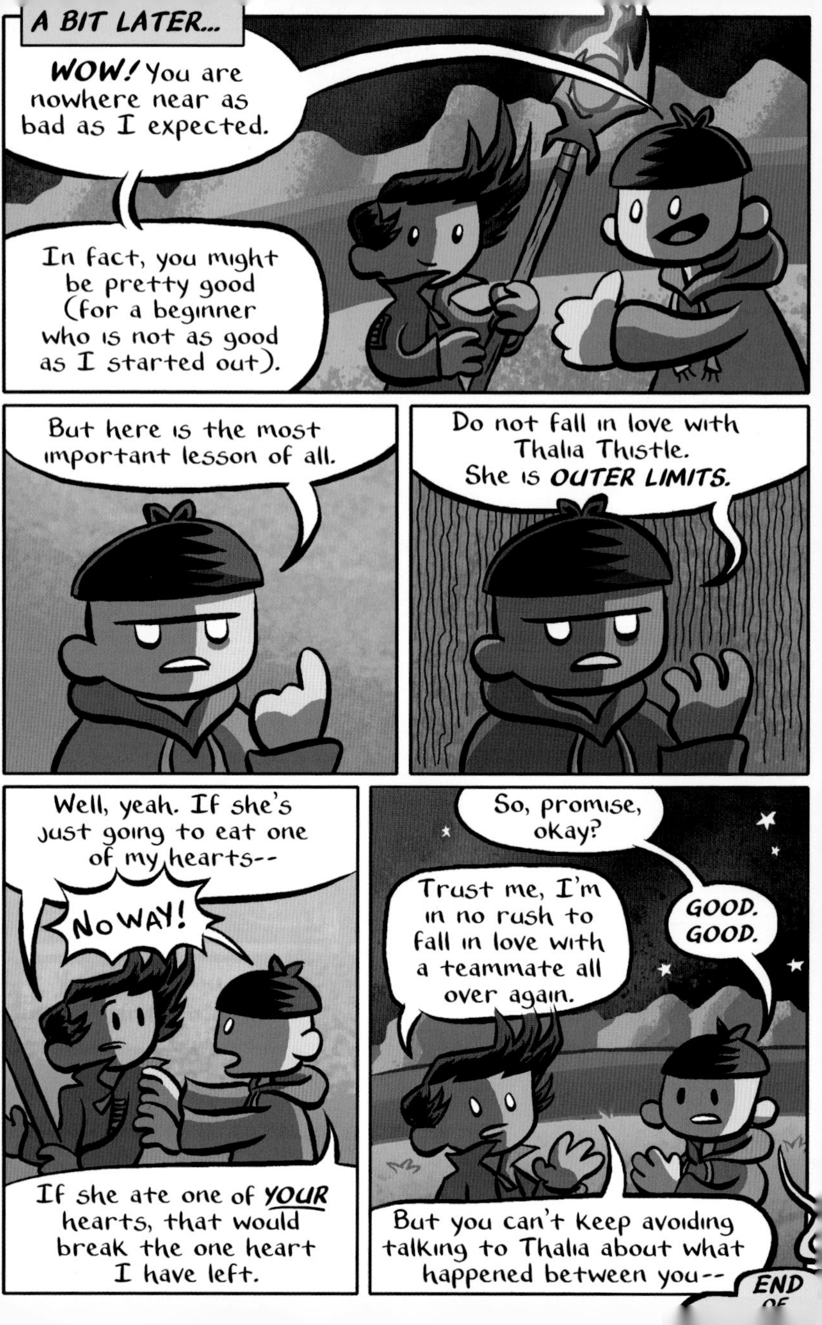
A BIT LATER...
WOW! You are nowhere near as bad as I expected.
In fact, you might be pretty good (for a beginner who is not as good as I started out).
But here is the most important lesson of all.
Do not fall in love with Thalia Thistle. She is OUTER LIMITS.
Well, yeah. If she's just going to eat one of my hearts--
NO WAY!
If she ate one of YOUR hearts, that would break the one heart I have left.
So, promise, okay?
Trust me, I'm in no rush to fall in love with a teammate all over again.
GOOD. GOOD.
But you can't keep avoiding talking to Thalia about what happened between you--
END

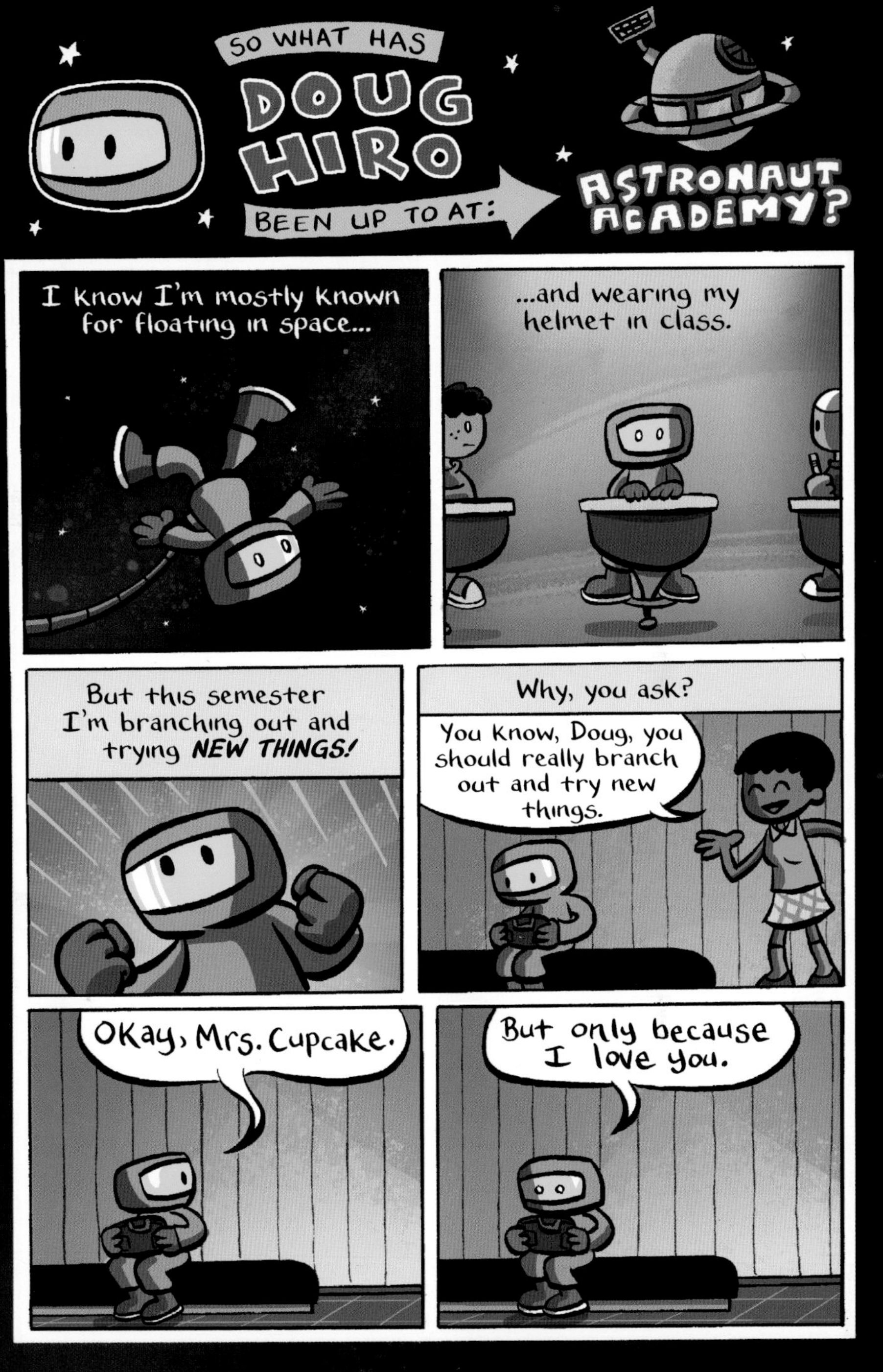

SO WHAT HAS
DOUG HIRO
BEEN UP TO AT:
ASTRONAUT ACADEMY?
I know I'm mostly known for floating in space...
...and wearing my helmet in class.
But this semester I'm branching out and trying NEW THINGS!
Why, you ask?
You know, Doug, you should really branch out and try new things.
Okay, Mrs. Cupcake.
But only because I love you.

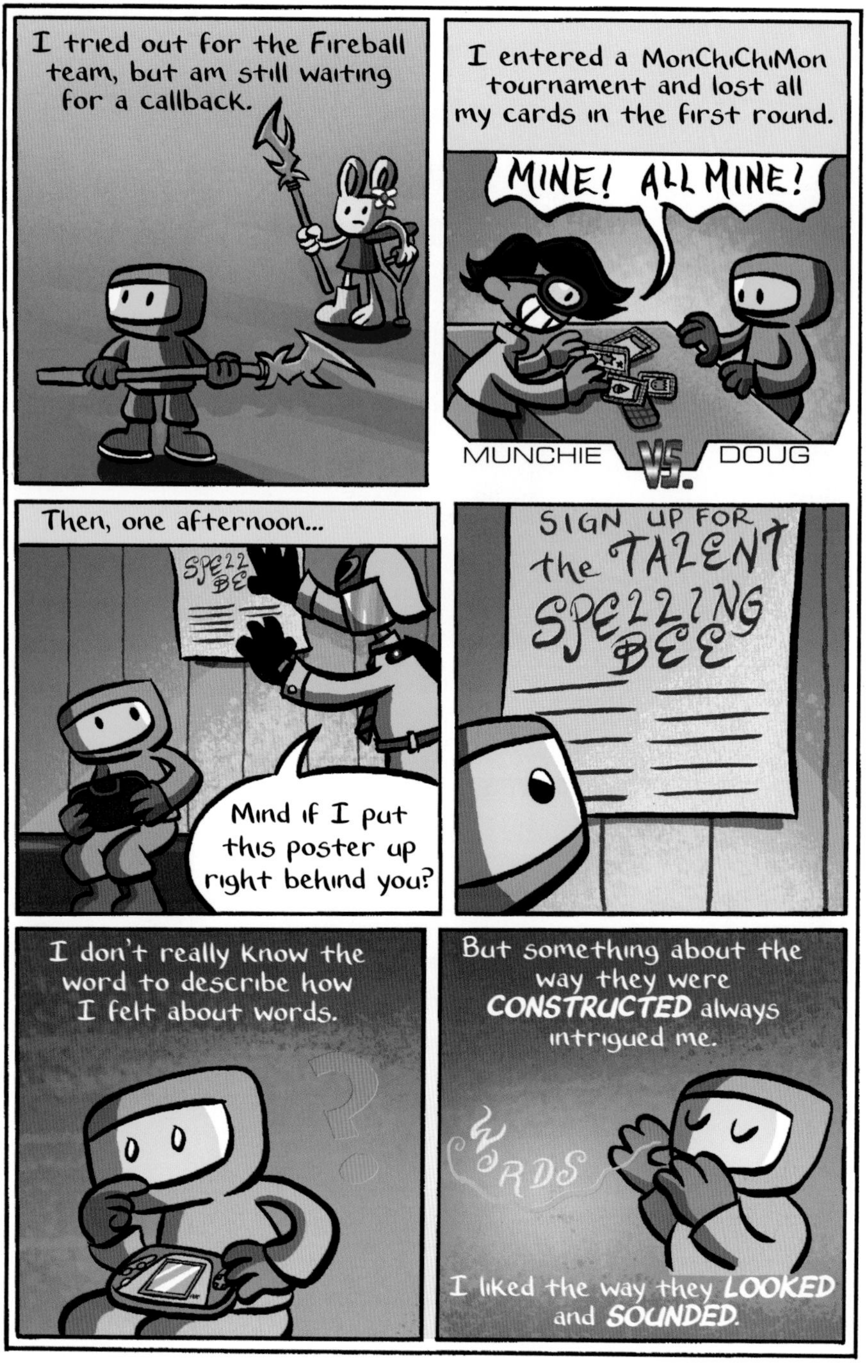
I tried out for the Fireball team, but am still waiting for a callback.
I entered a MonChiChiMon tournament and lost all my cards in the first round.
MINE! ALL MINE!
MUNCHIE
VS.
DOUG
Then, one afternoon...
Mind if I put this poster up right behind you?
SIGN UP FOR the TALENT SPELLING BEE
I don't really know the word to describe how I felt about words.
?
But something about the way they were CONSTRUCTED always intrigued me.
WORDS
I liked the way they LOOKED and SOUNDED.

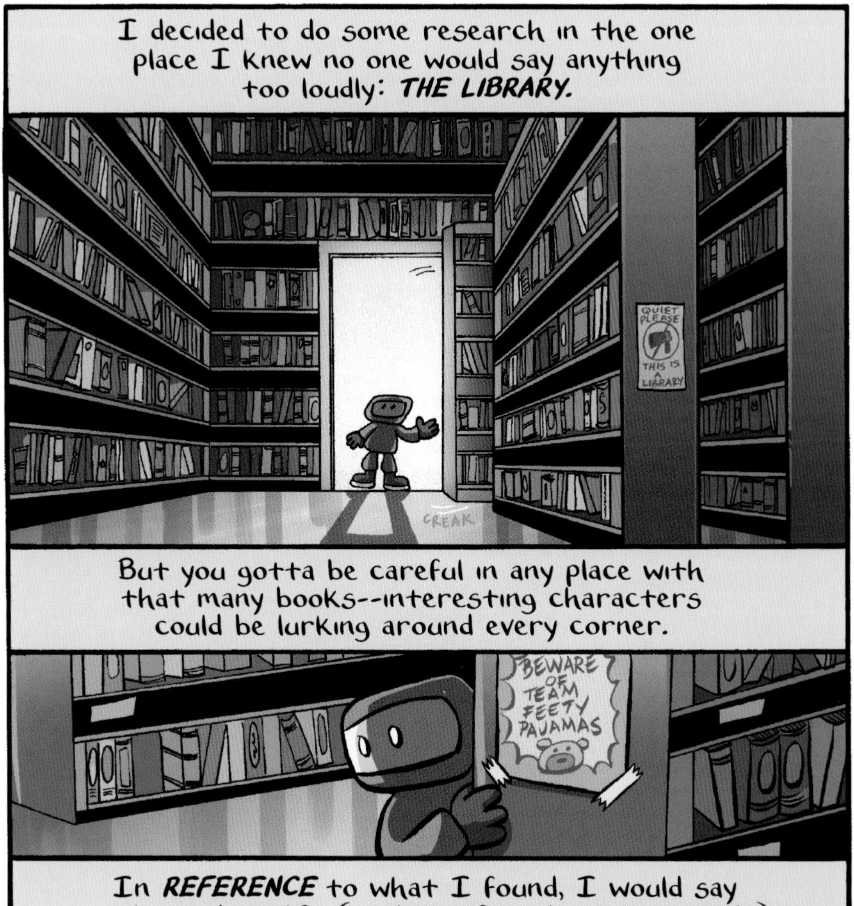
I decided to do some research in the one place I knew no one would say anything too loudly: THE LIBRARY.
QUIET PLEASE
THIS IS A LIBRARY
CREAK
But you gotta be careful in any place with that many books--interesting characters could be lurking around every corner.
BEWARE OF TEAM FEETY PAJAMAS
In REFERENCE to what I found, I would say it changed my life (at least for the next month).
What's this?
THE DICTIONARY

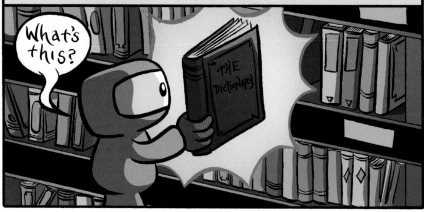

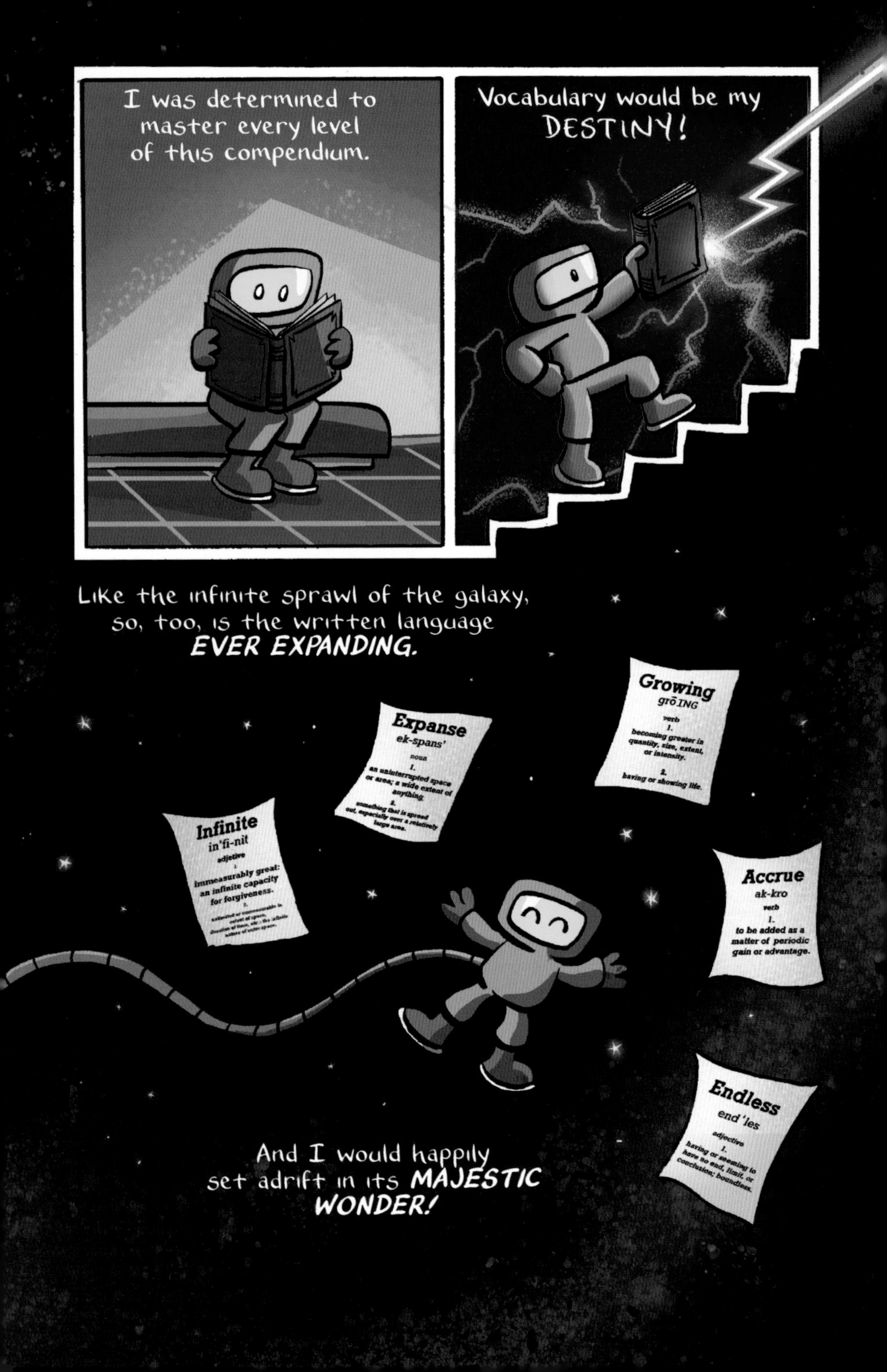

I was determined to master every level of this compendium.
Vocabulary would be my DESTINY!
Like the infinite sprawl of the galaxy, so, too, is the written language EVER EXPANDING.
Expanse
ek-spans'
noun
1.
an uninterrupted space or area; a wide extent of anything.
Growing
grōING
verb
1.
becoming greater in quantity, size, extent, or intensity.
2.
having or showing life.
Infinite
in'fi-nit
adjetive
1.
immeasurably great: an infinite capacity for forgiveness.
2.
Accrue
ak-kro
verb
1.
to be added as a matter of periodic gain or advantage.
Endless
end 'les
adjective
1.
having or seeming to have no end, limit, or conclusion; boundless.
And I would happily set adrift in its MAJESTIC WONDER!

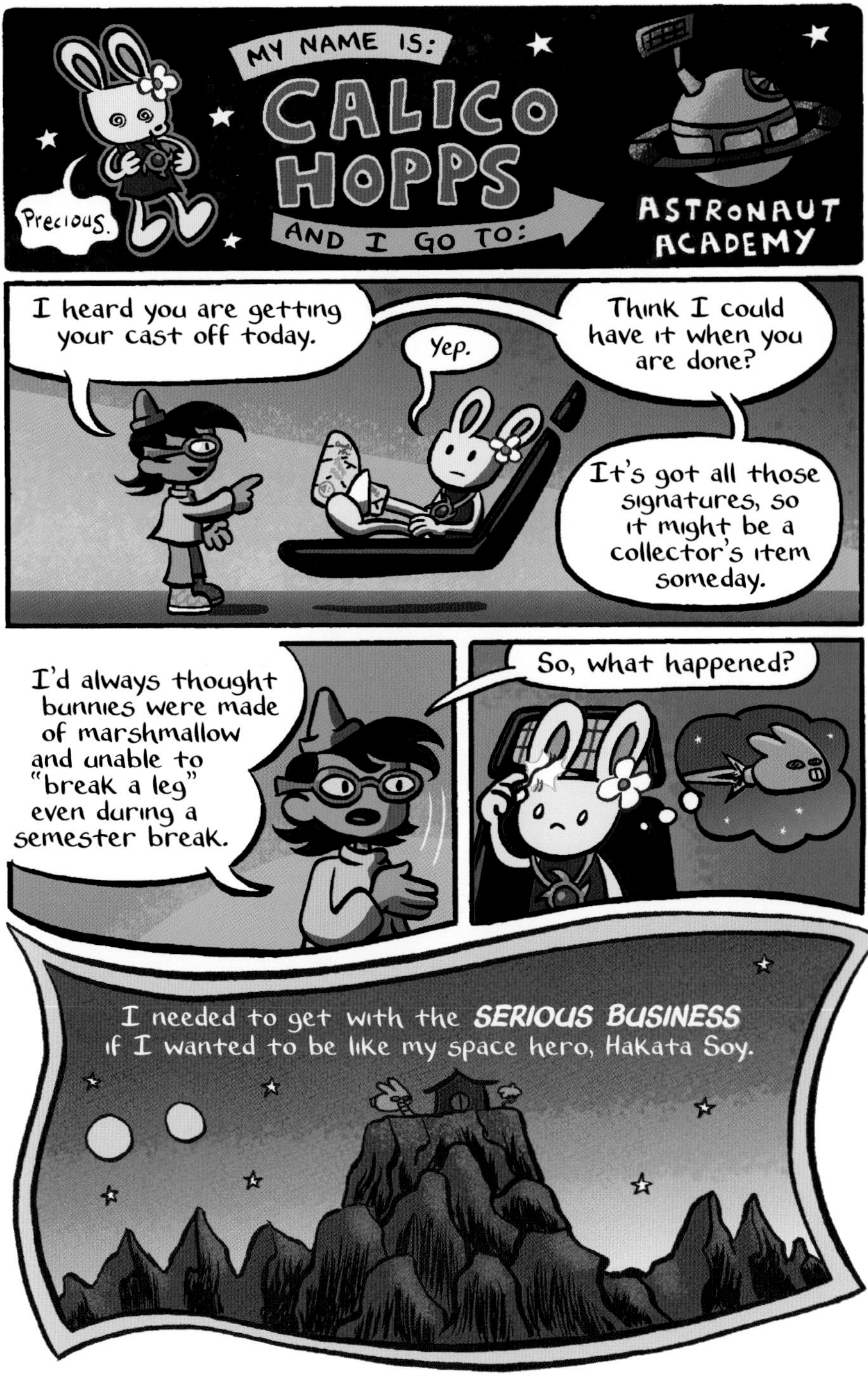

MY NAME IS:
CALICO HOPPS
AND I GO TO:
ASTRONAUT ACADEMY
Precious.
I heard you are getting your cast off today.
Yep.
Think I could have it when you are done?
It's got all those signatures, so it might be a collector's item someday.
I'd always thought bunnies were made of marshmallow and unable to "break a leg" even during a semester break.
So, what happened?
I needed to get with the SERIOUS BUSINESS if I wanted to be like my space hero, Hakata Soy.

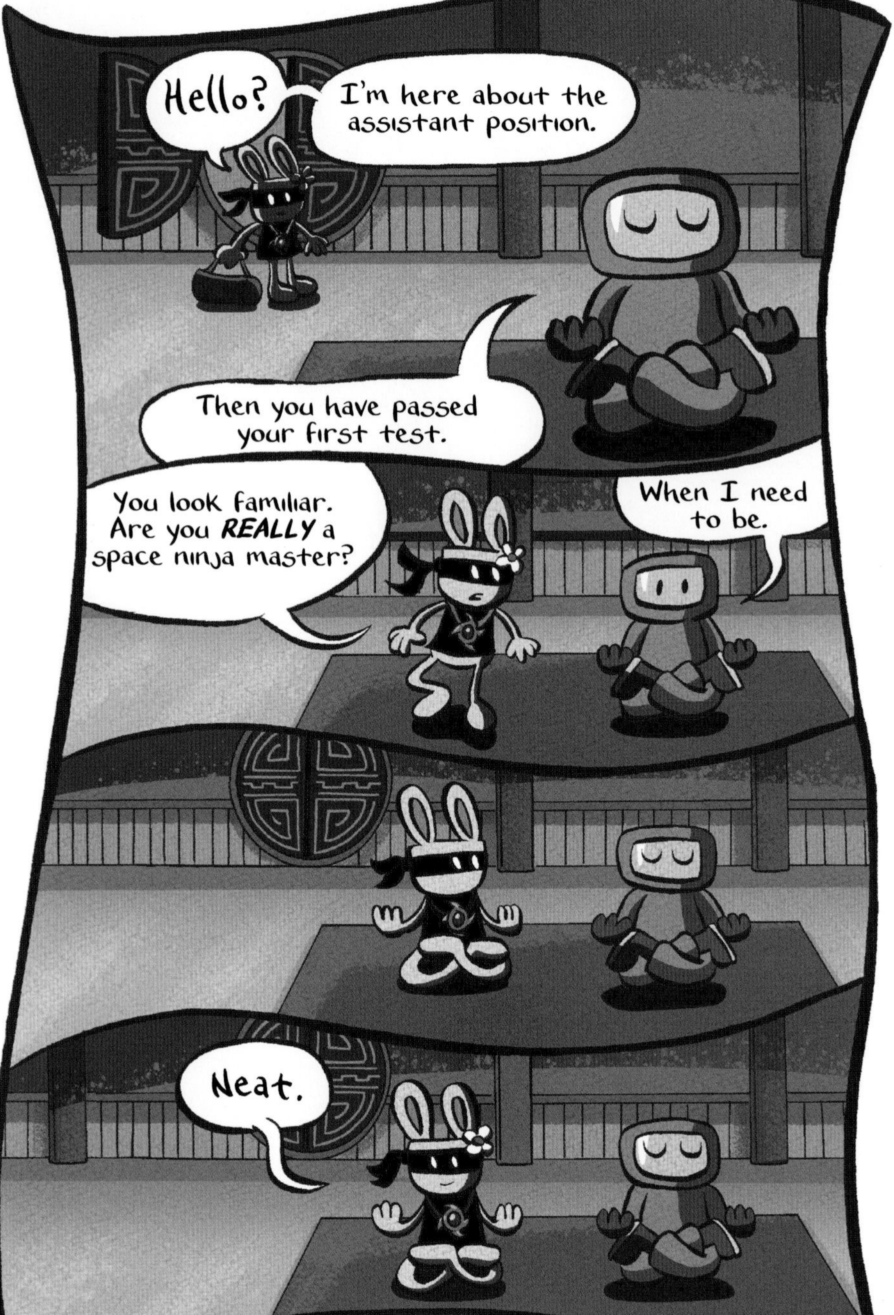
Hello?
I'm here about the assistant position.
Then you have passed your first test.
You look familiar. Are you REALLY a space ninja master?
When I need to be.
Neat.

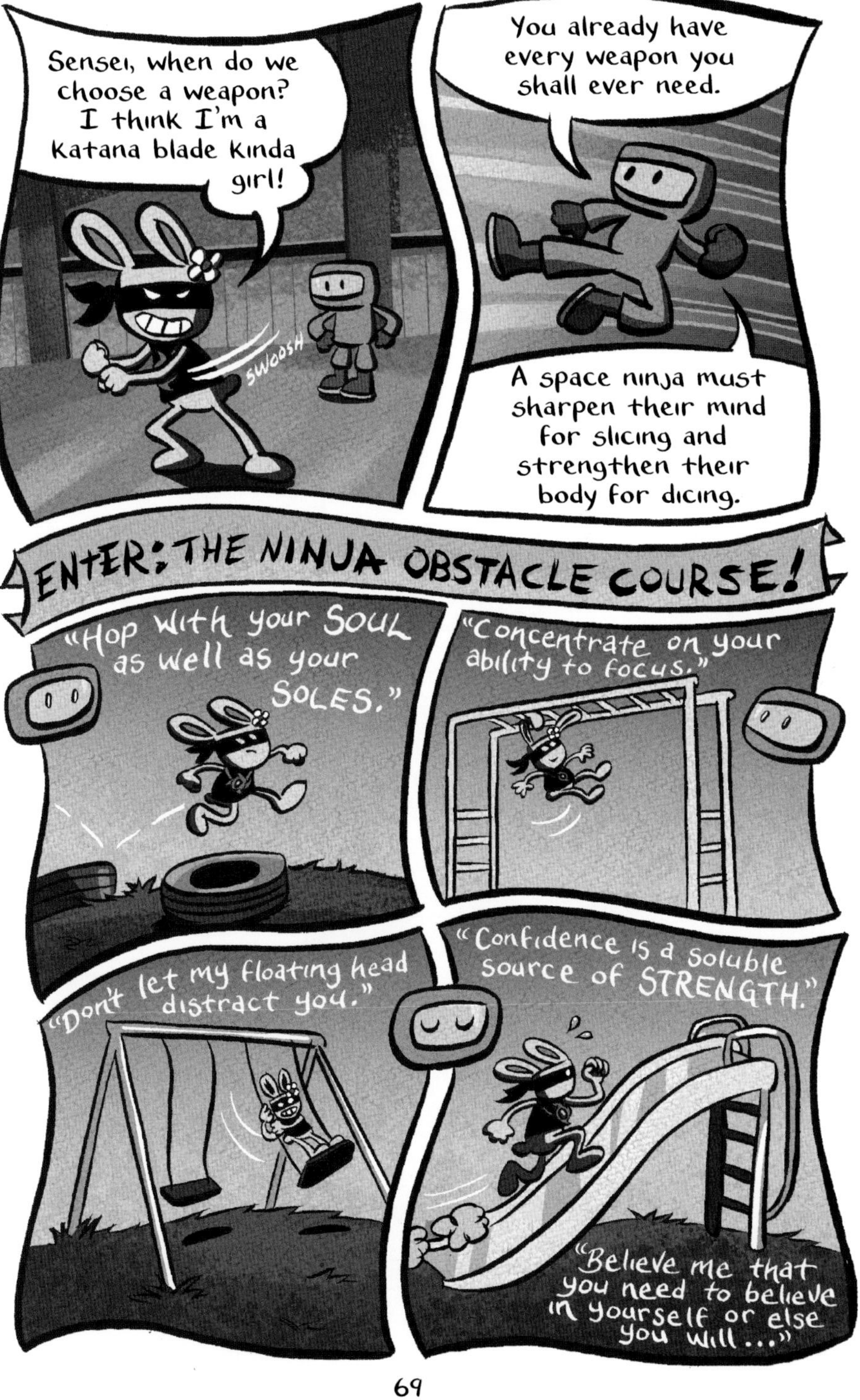

Sensei, when do we choose a weapon? I think I'm a katana blade kinda girl!
SWOOSH
You already have every weapon you shall ever need.
A space ninja must sharpen their mind for slicing and strengthen their body for dicing.
ENTER: THE NINJA OBSTACLE COURSE!
"Hop with your SOUL as well as your SOLES."
"Concentrate on your ability to focus."
"Don't let my floating head distract you."
"Confidence is a soluble source of STRENGTH."
"Believe me that you need to believe in yourself or else you will..."

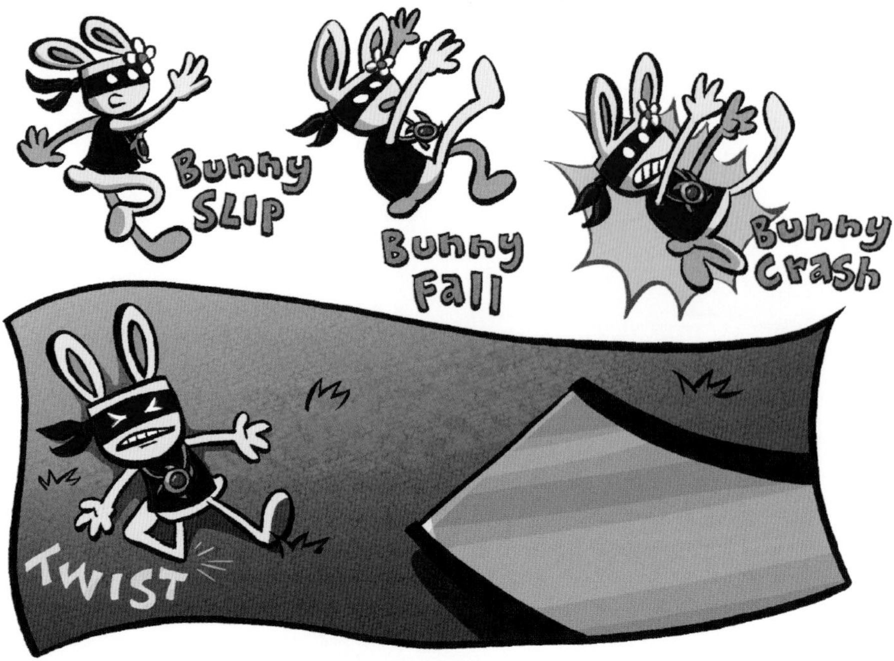
Bunny Slip
Bunny Fall
Bunny Crash
TWIST

I debated using my medallion to call Hakata Soy.

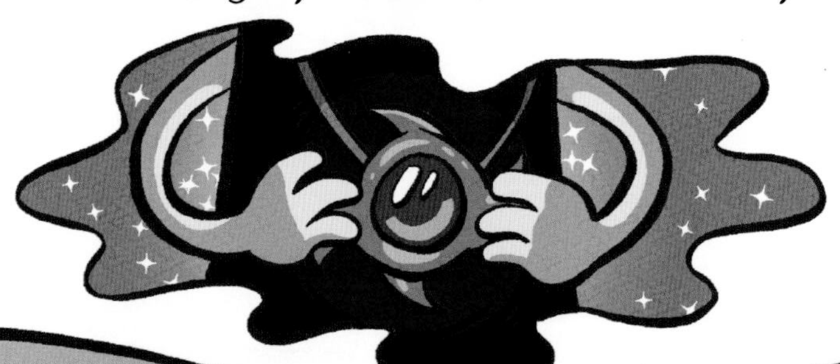

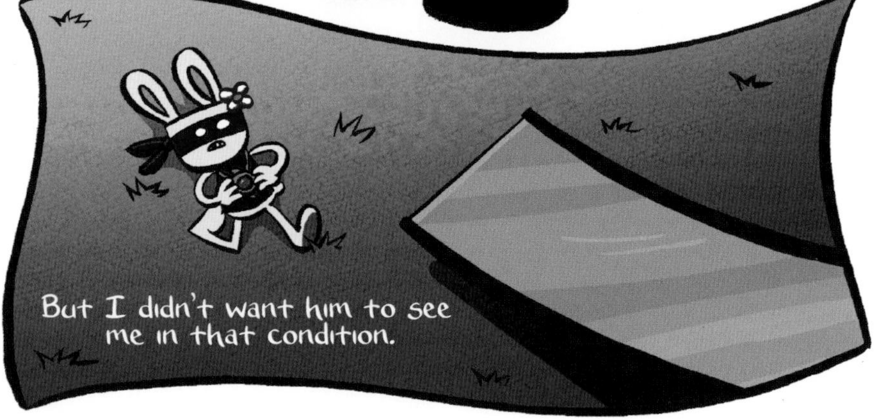
But I didn't want him to see
me in that condition.

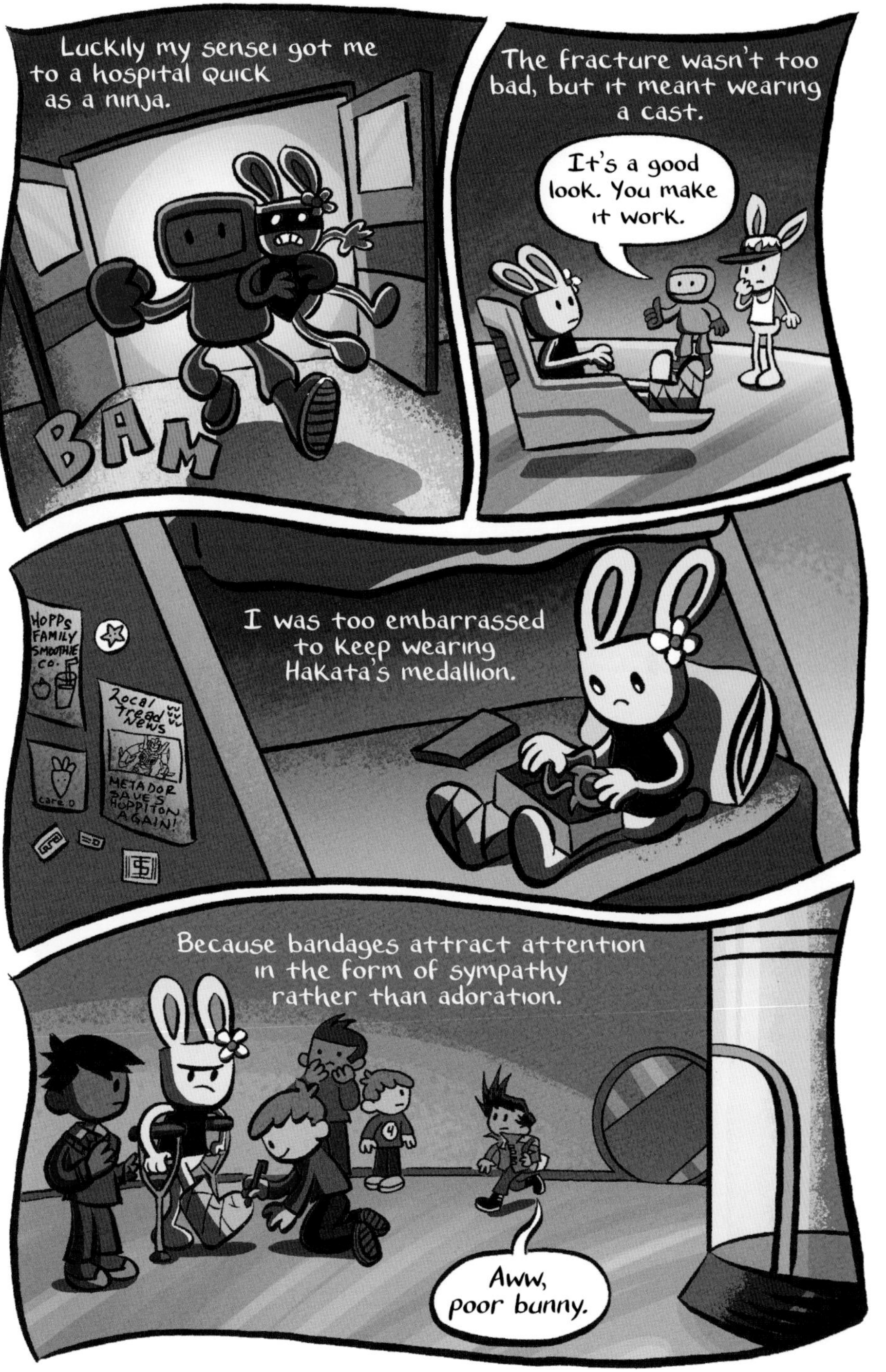
Luckily my sensei got me to a hospital quick as a ninja.
BAM
The fracture wasn't too bad, but it meant wearing a cast.
It's a good look. You make it work.
I was too embarrassed to keep wearing Hakata's medallion.
HOPPS FAMILY SMOOTHIE CO.
Local Tread News
METADOR SAVES HOPPITON AGAIN!
Because bandages attract attention in the form of sympathy rather than adoration.
Aww, poor bunny.

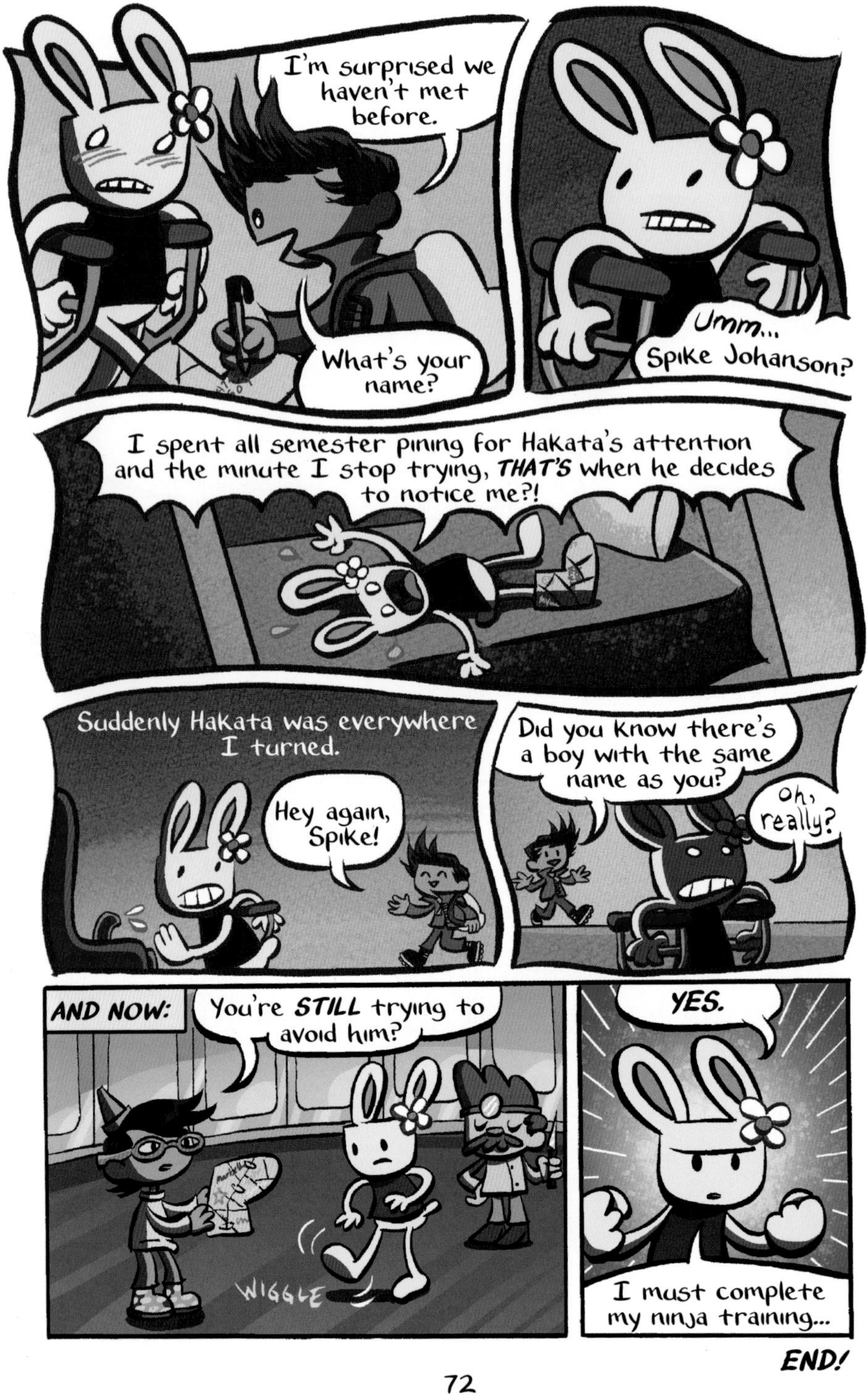
I'm surprised we haven't met before.
What's your name?
Umm... Spike Johanson?
I spent all semester pining for Hakata's attention and the minute I stop trying, THAT'S when he decides to notice me?!
Suddenly Hakata was everywhere I turned.
Hey again, Spike!
Did you know there's a boy with the same name as you?
Oh, really?
AND NOW:
You're STILL trying to avoid him?
WIGGLE
YES.
I must complete my ninja training...
END!

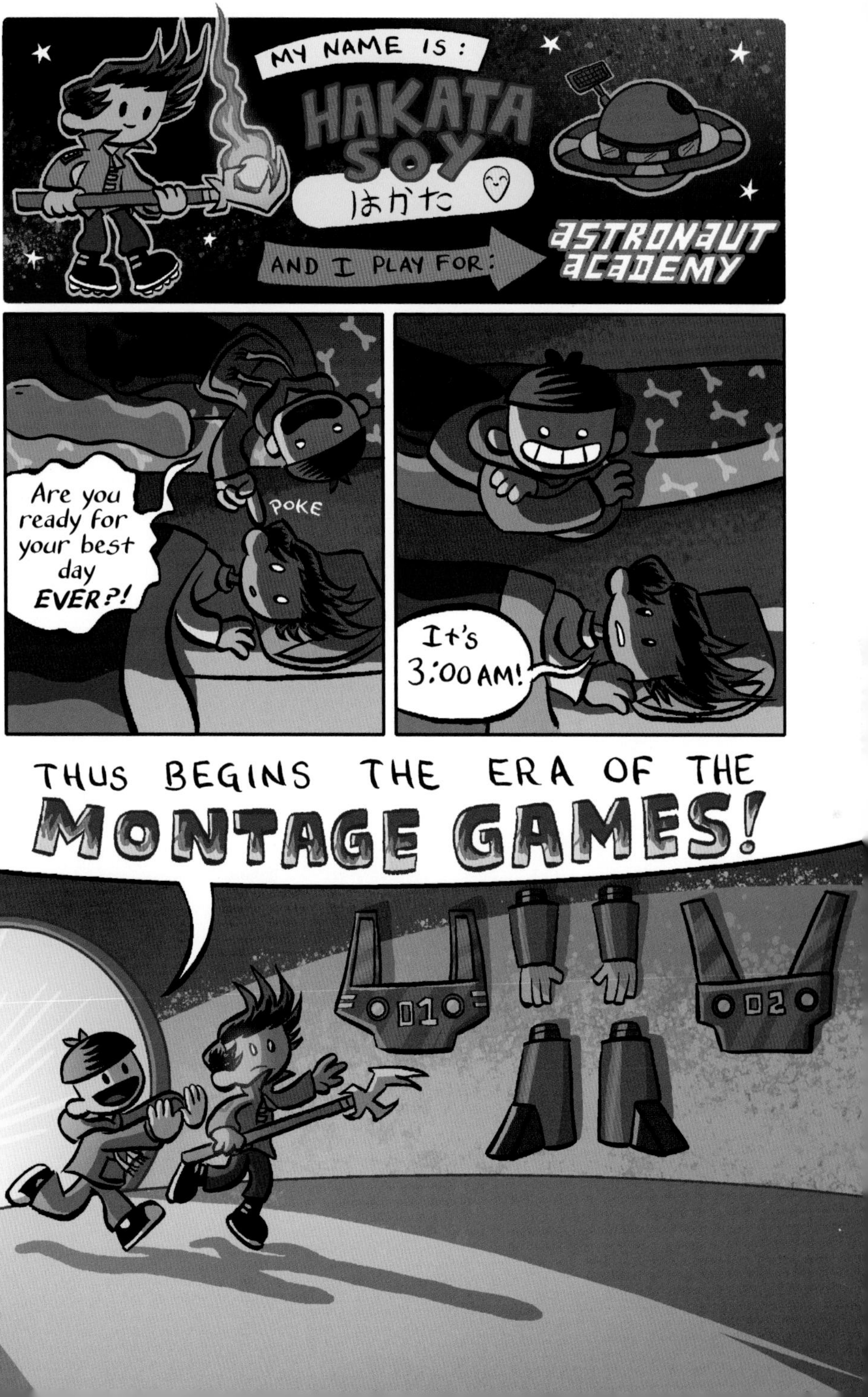
MY NAME IS:
HAKATA SOY
はかた
AND I PLAY FOR:
ASTRONAUT ACADEMY
Are you ready for your best day EVER?!
POKE
It's 3:00 AM!
THUS BEGINS THE ERA OF THE MONTAGE GAMES!
01
02

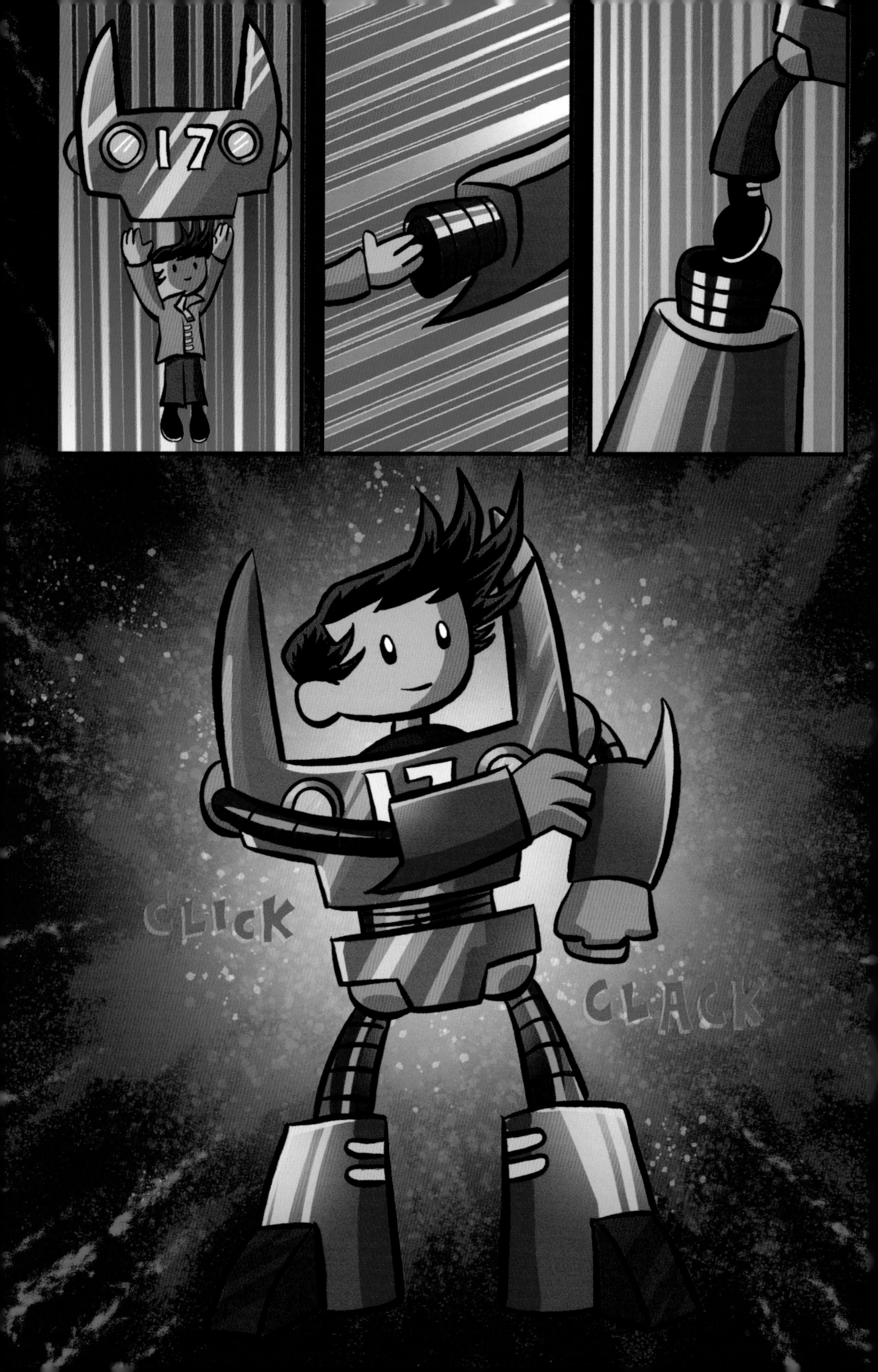
17
CLICK
CLACK

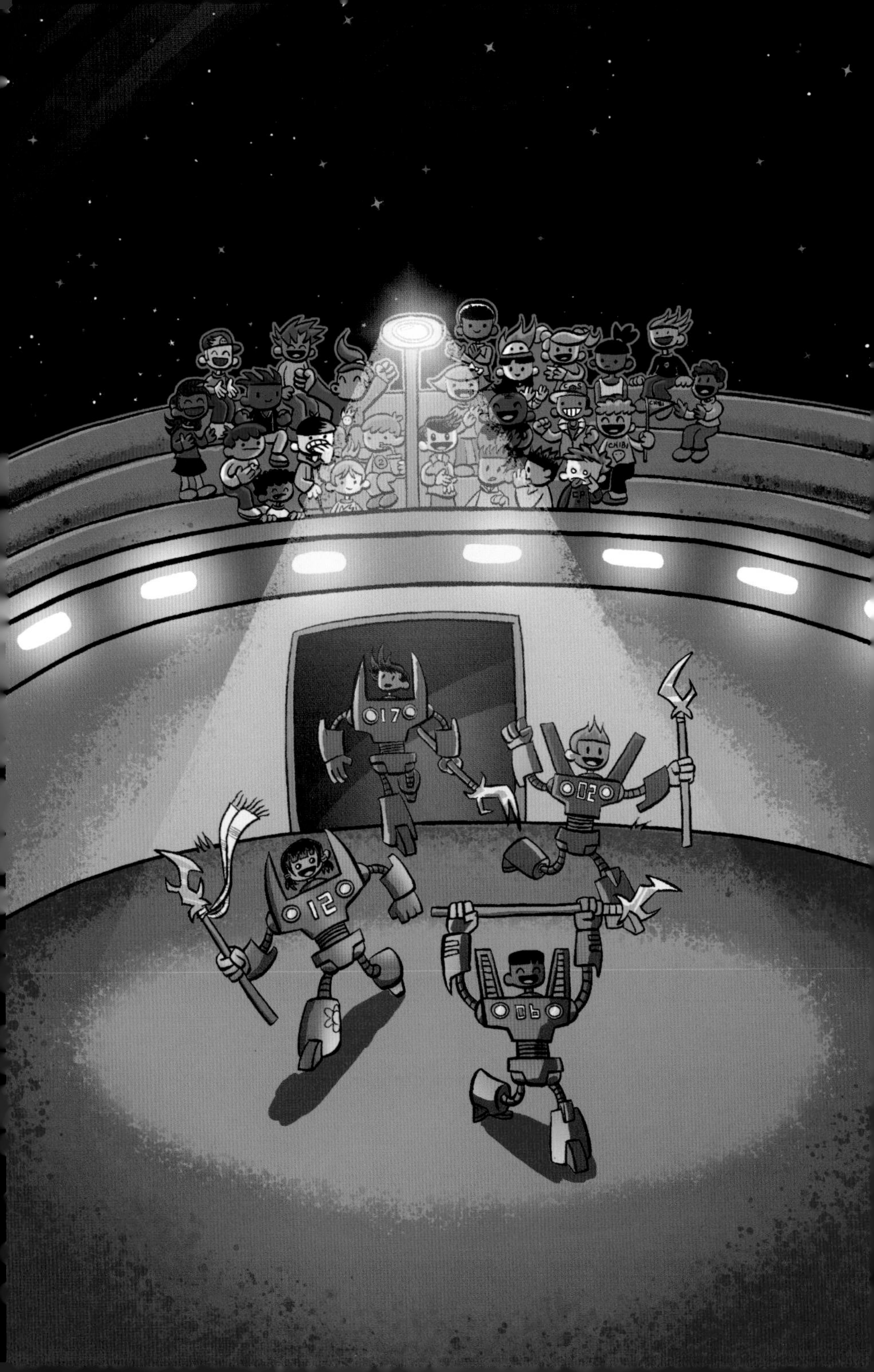
CHIBI
17
02
12
06

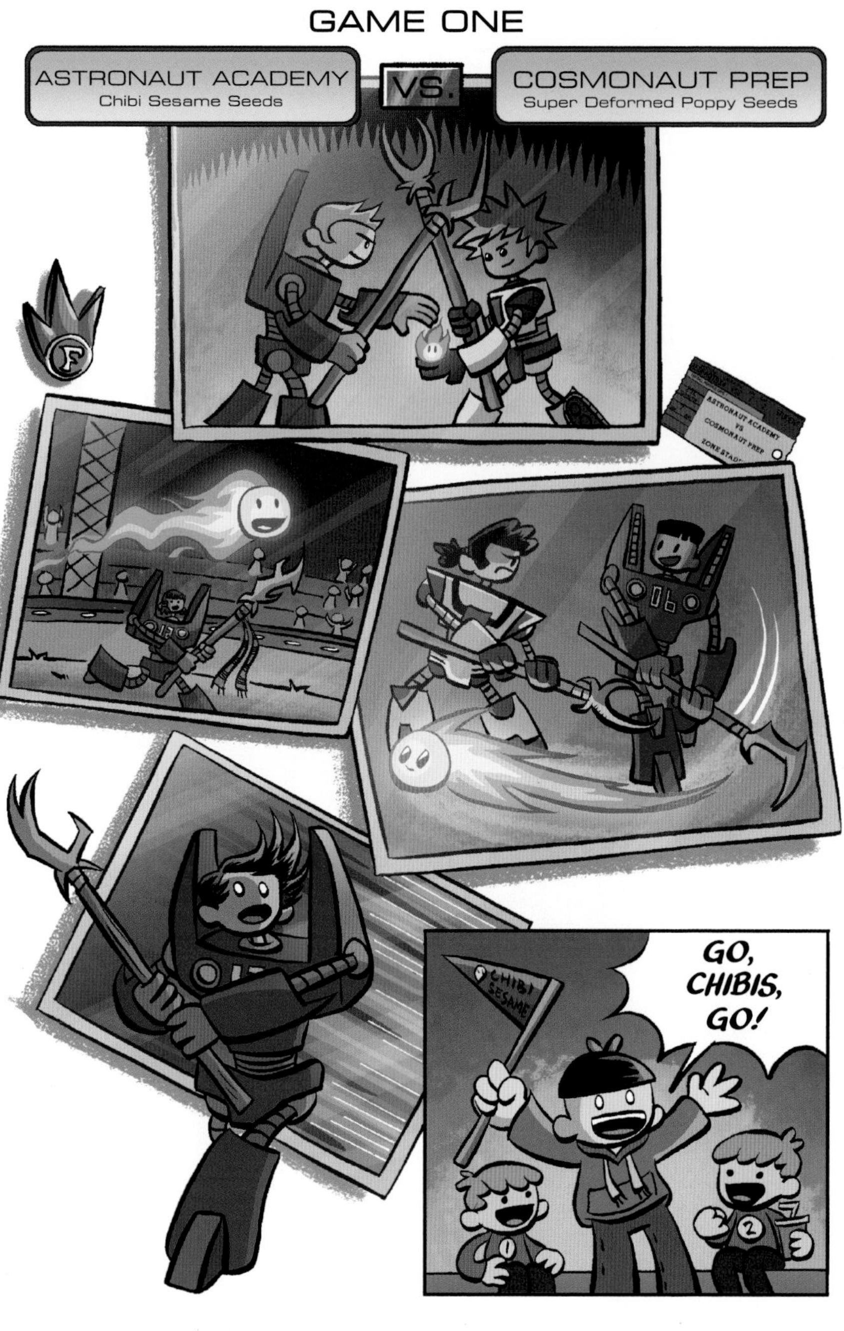
GAME ONE
ASTRONAUT ACADEMY
Chibi Sesame Seeds
VS.
COSMONAUT PREP
Super Deformed Poppy Seeds
CHIBI SESAME
GO, CHIBIS, GO!

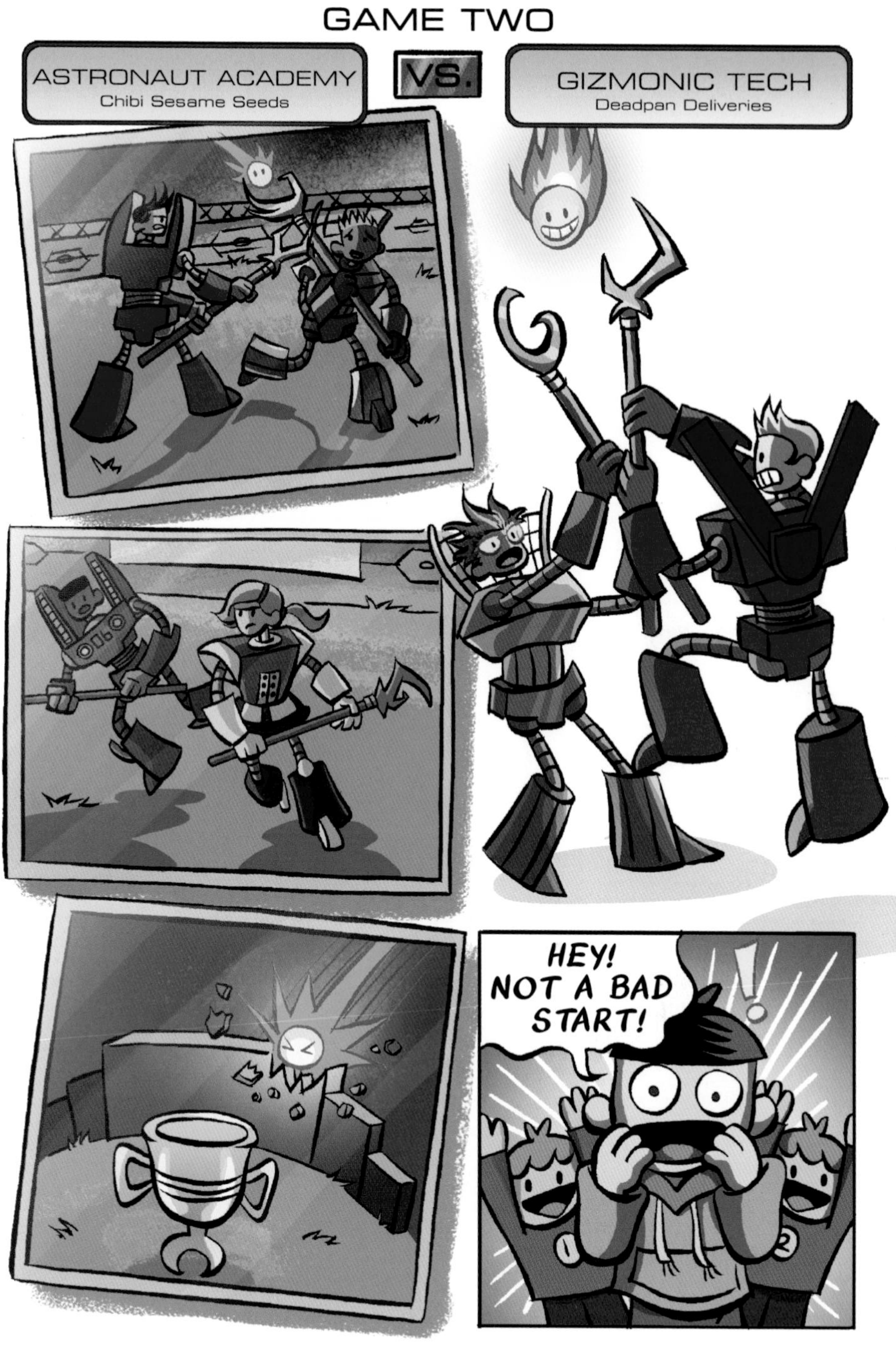
GAME TWO
ASTRONAUT ACADEMY
Chibi Sesame Seeds
VS.
GIZMONIC TECH
Deadpan Deliveries
HEY! NOT A BAD START!

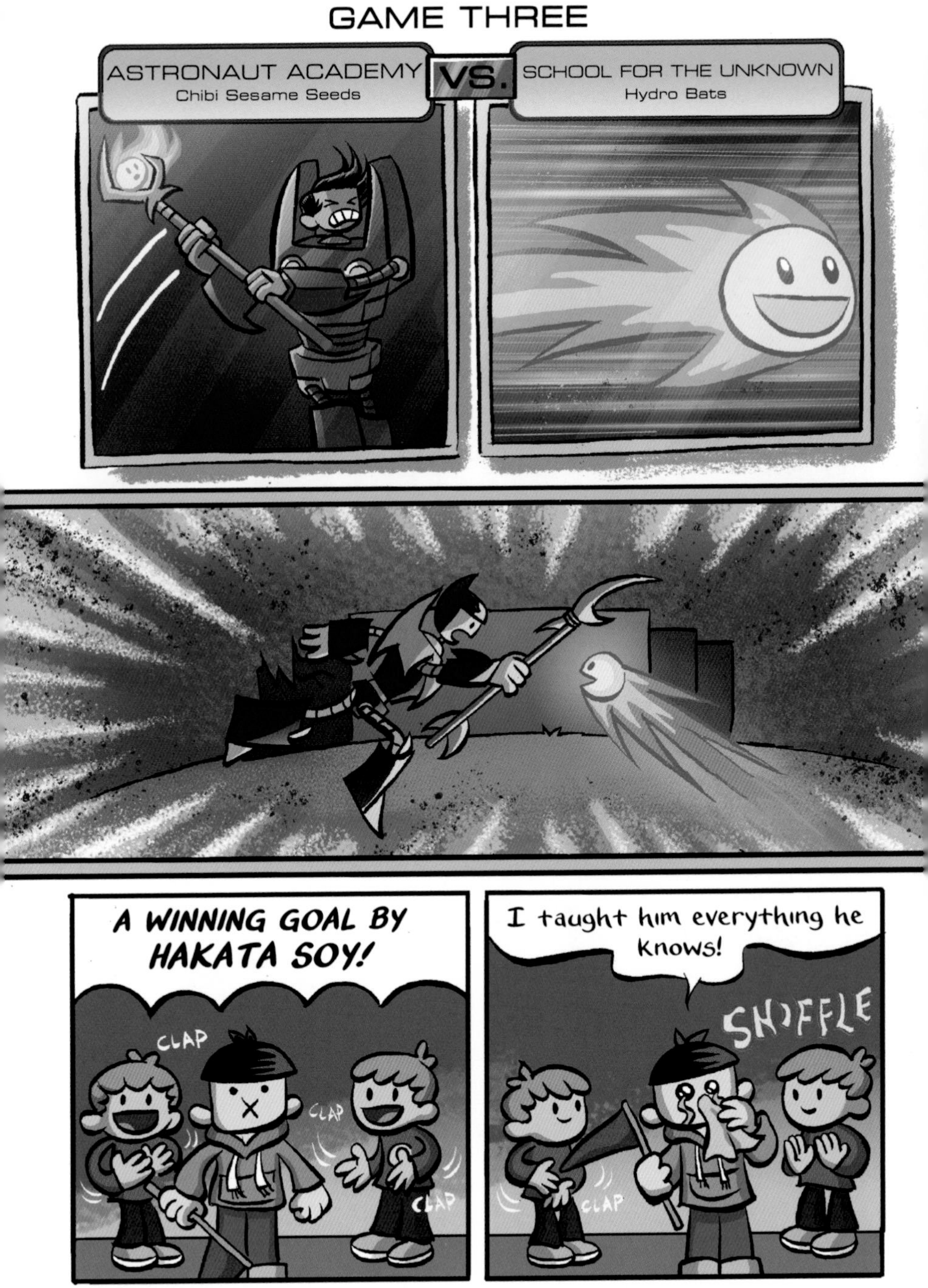
GAME THREE
ASTRONAUT ACADEMY
Chibi Sesame Seeds
VS.
SCHOOL FOR THE UNKNOWN
Hydro Bats
A WINNING GOAL BY HAKATA SOY!
CLAP
CLAP
CLAP
I taught him everything he knows!
SNIFFLE
CLAP

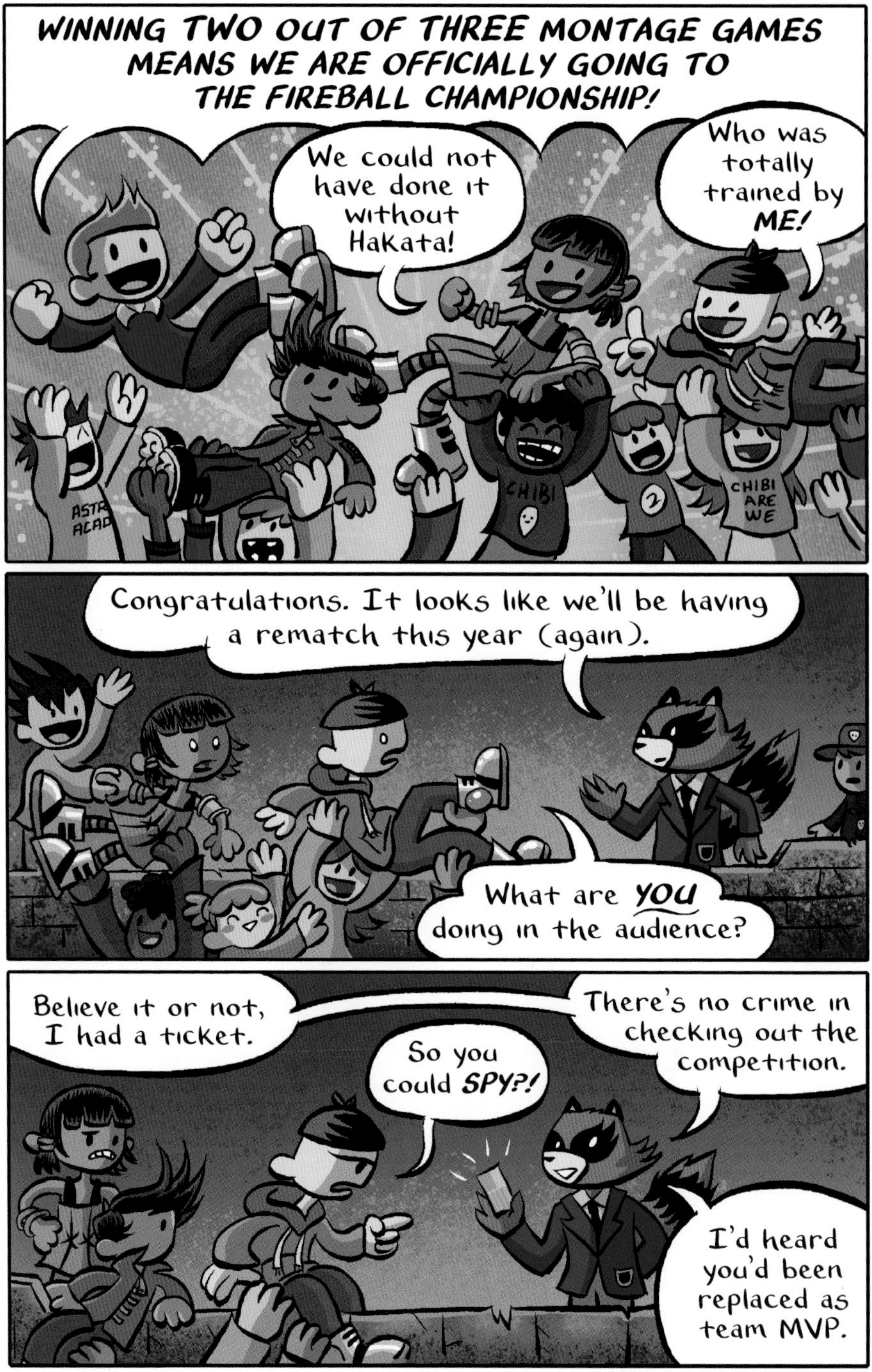
WINNING TWO OUT OF THREE MONTAGE GAMES MEANS WE ARE OFFICIALLY GOING TO THE FIREBALL CHAMPIONSHIP!
We could not have done it without Hakata!
Who was totally trained by ME!
ASTR ACAD
CHIBI
CHIBI ARE WE
Congratulations. It looks like we'll be having a rematch this year (again).
What are YOU doing in the audience?
Believe it or not, I had a ticket.
There's no crime in checking out the competition.
So you could SPY?!
I'd heard you'd been replaced as team MVP.

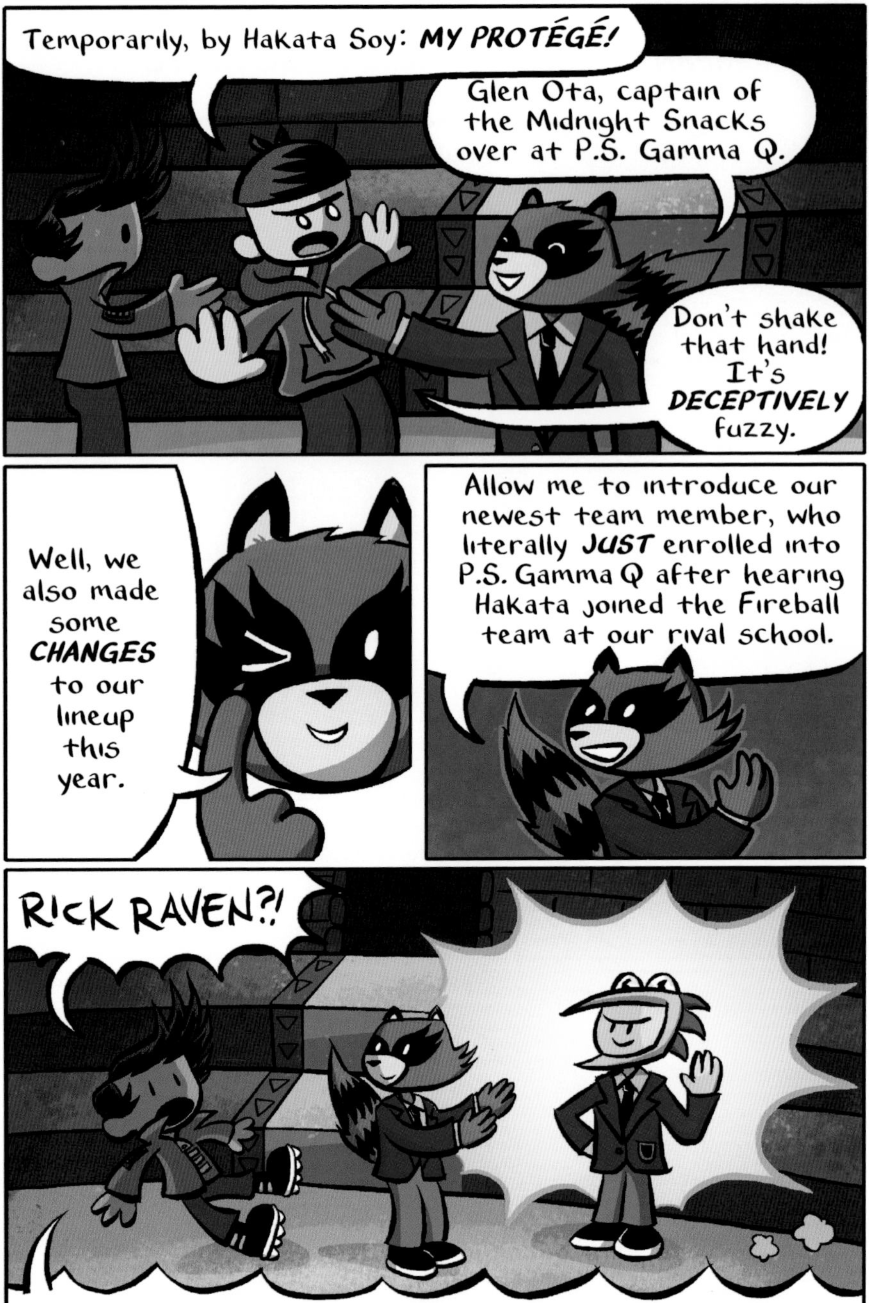
Temporarily, by Hakata Soy: MY PROTÉGÉ!
Glen Ota, captain of the Midnight Snacks over at P.S. Gamma Q.
Don't shake that hand! It's DECEPTIVELY fuzzy.
Well, we also made some CHANGES to our lineup this year.
Allow me to introduce our newest team member, who literally JUST enrolled into P.S. Gamma Q after hearing Hakata joined the Fireball team at our rival school.
RICK RAVEN?!
First you steal my potential girlfriend and now you want to ruin my newfound interest in sports?!

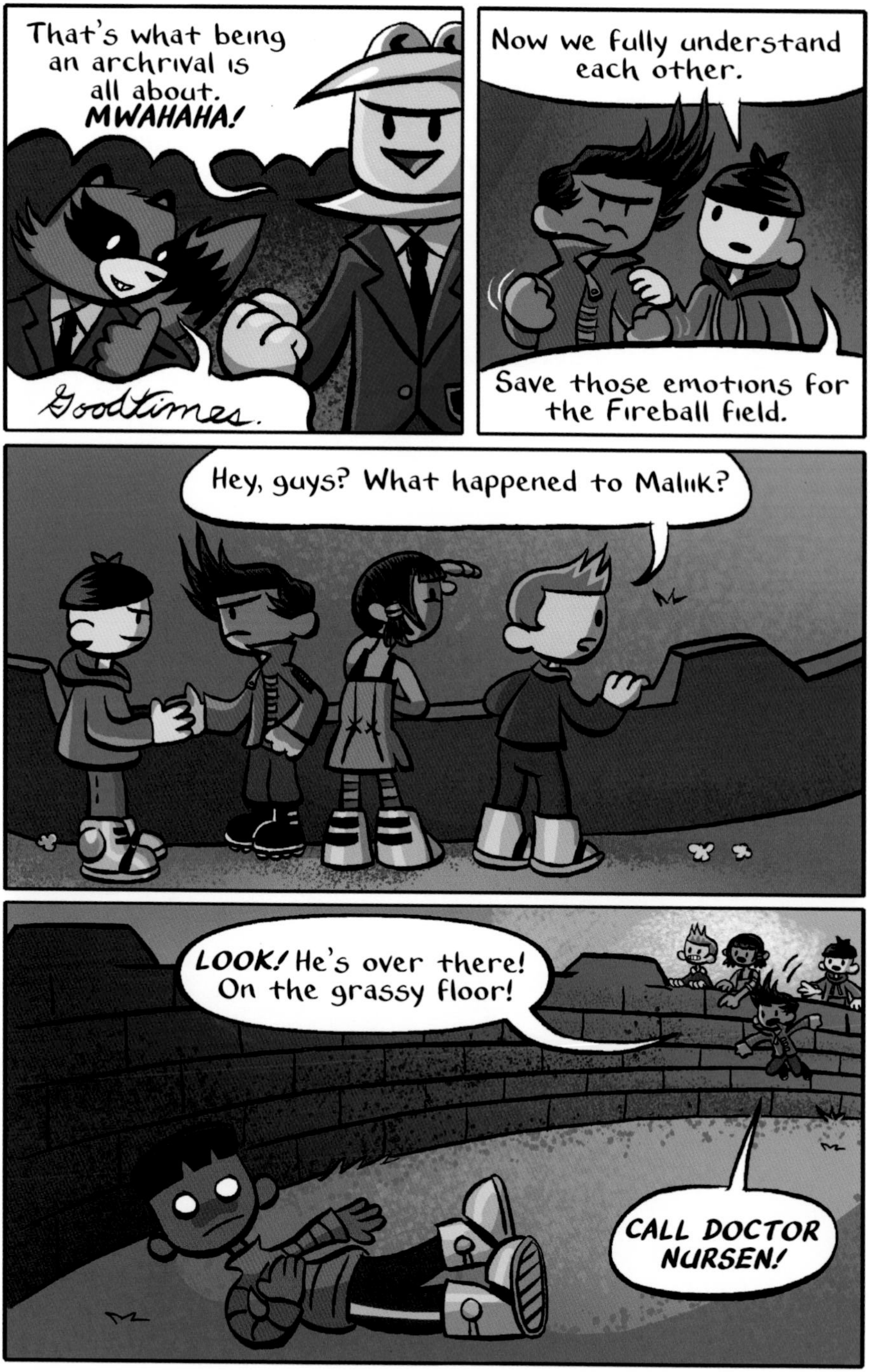
That's what being an archrival is all about. MWAHAHA!
Goodtimes.
Now we fully understand each other.
Save those emotions for the Fireball field.
Hey, guys? What happened to Maliik?
LOOK! He's over there! On the grassy floor!
CALL DOCTOR NURSEN!

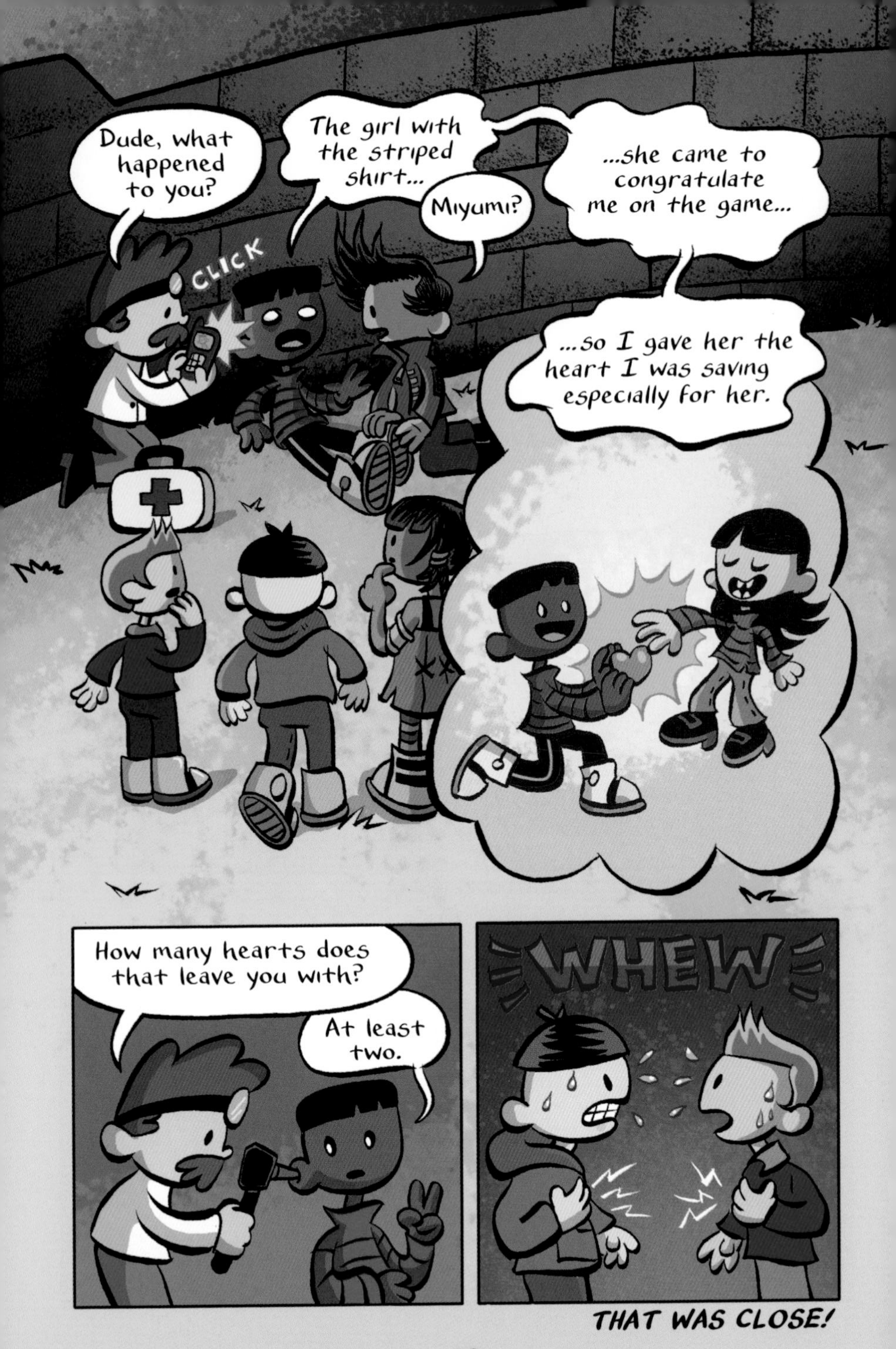
Dude, what happened to you?
CLICK
The girl with the striped shirt...
Miyumi?
...she came to congratulate me on the game...
...so I gave her the heart I was saving especially for her.
How many hearts does that leave you with?
At least two.
WHEW

THAT WAS CLOSE!

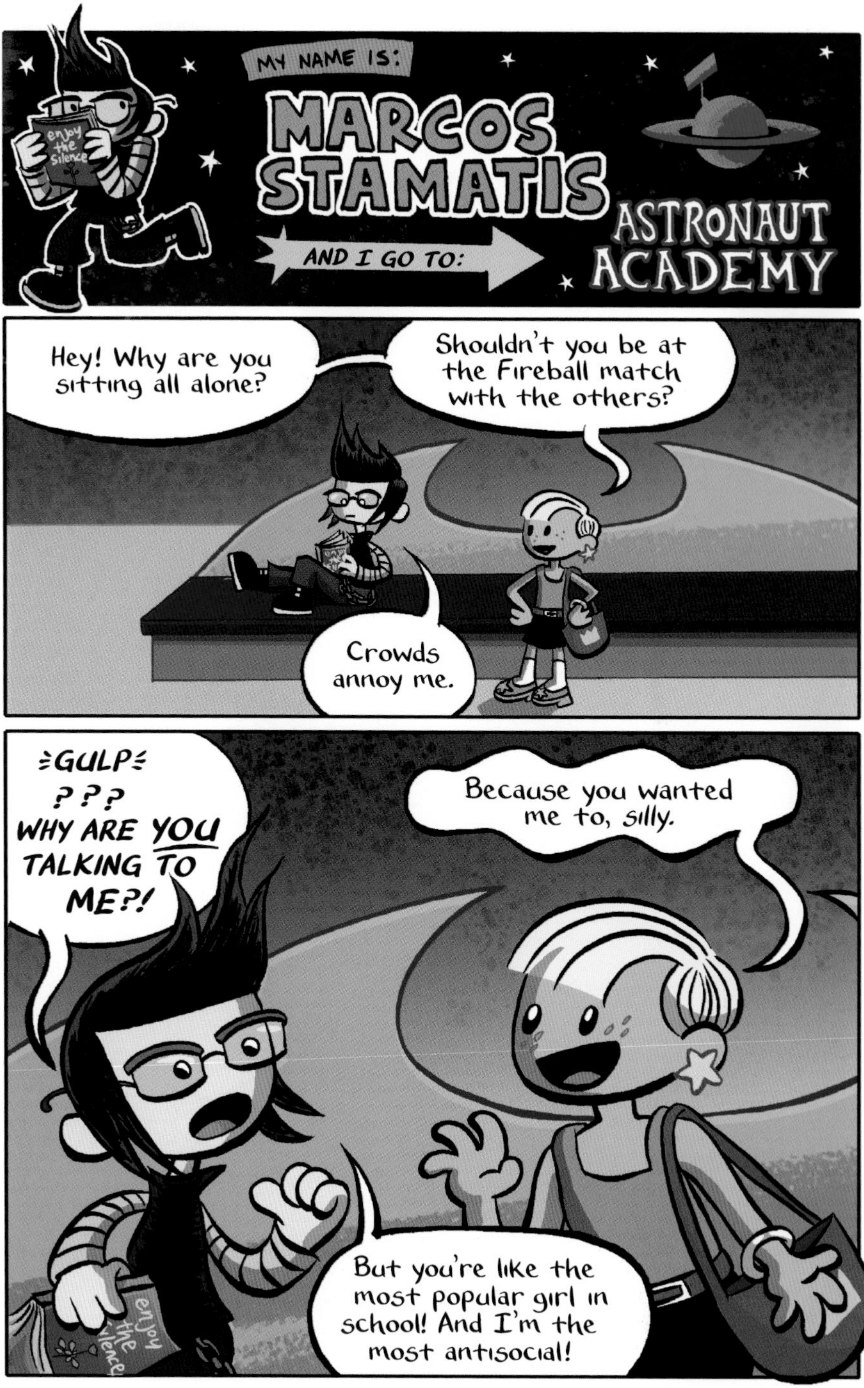
MY NAME IS:
MARCOS STAMATIS
AND I GO TO:
ASTRONAUT ACADEMY
enjoy the silence
Hey! Why are you sitting all alone?
Shouldn't you be at the Fireball match with the others?
Crowds annoy me.
GULP
???
WHY ARE YOU TALKING TO ME?!
Because you wanted me to, silly.
But you're like the most popular girl in school! And I'm the most antisocial!
enjoy the silence

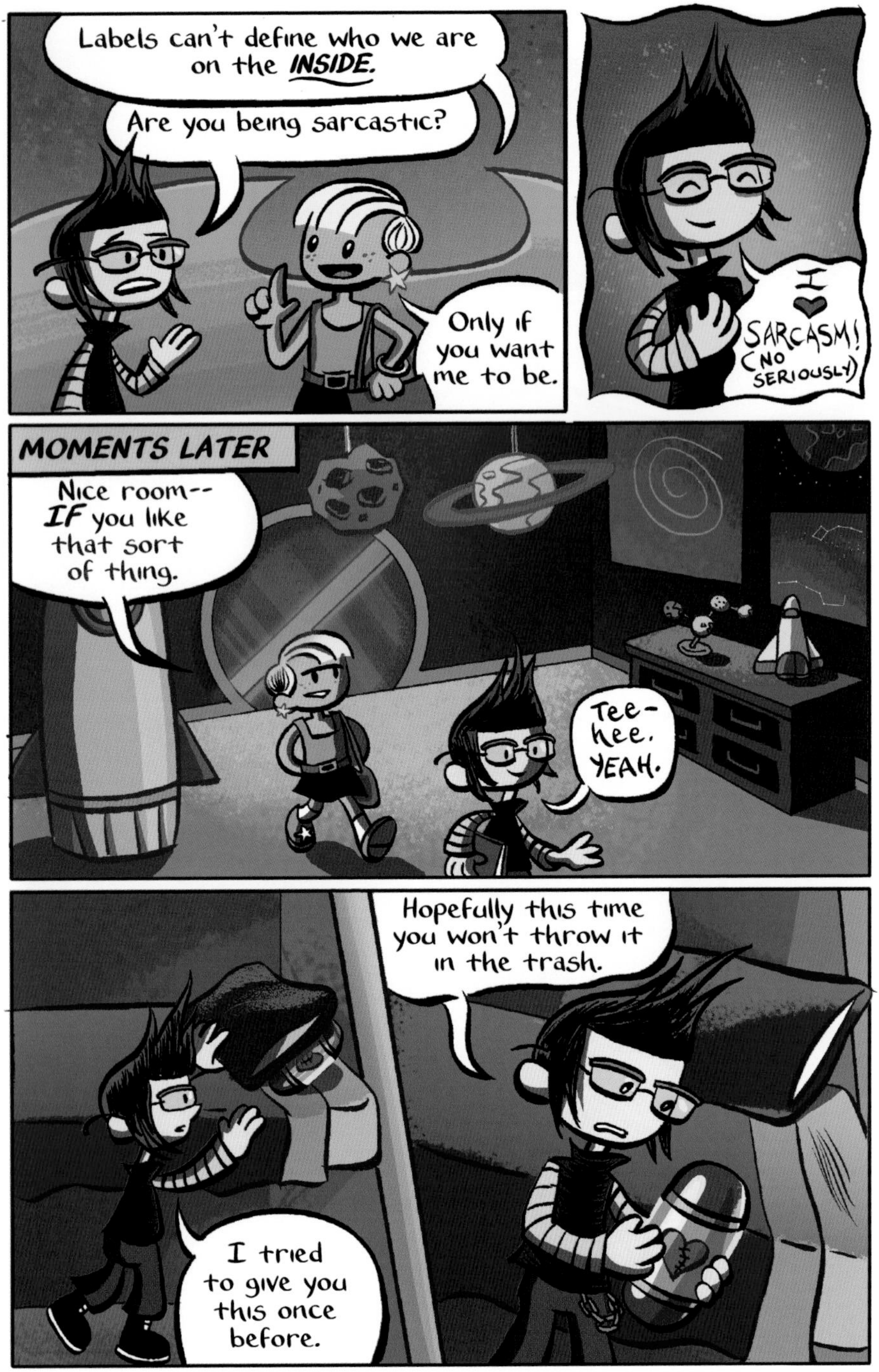
Labels can't define who we are on the INSIDE.
Are you being sarcastic?
Only if you want me to be.
I ♥ SARCASM! (NO SERIOUSLY)
MOMENTS LATER
Nice room-- IF you like that sort of thing.
Tee-hee. YEAH.
Hopefully this time you won't throw it in the trash.
I tried to give you this once before.

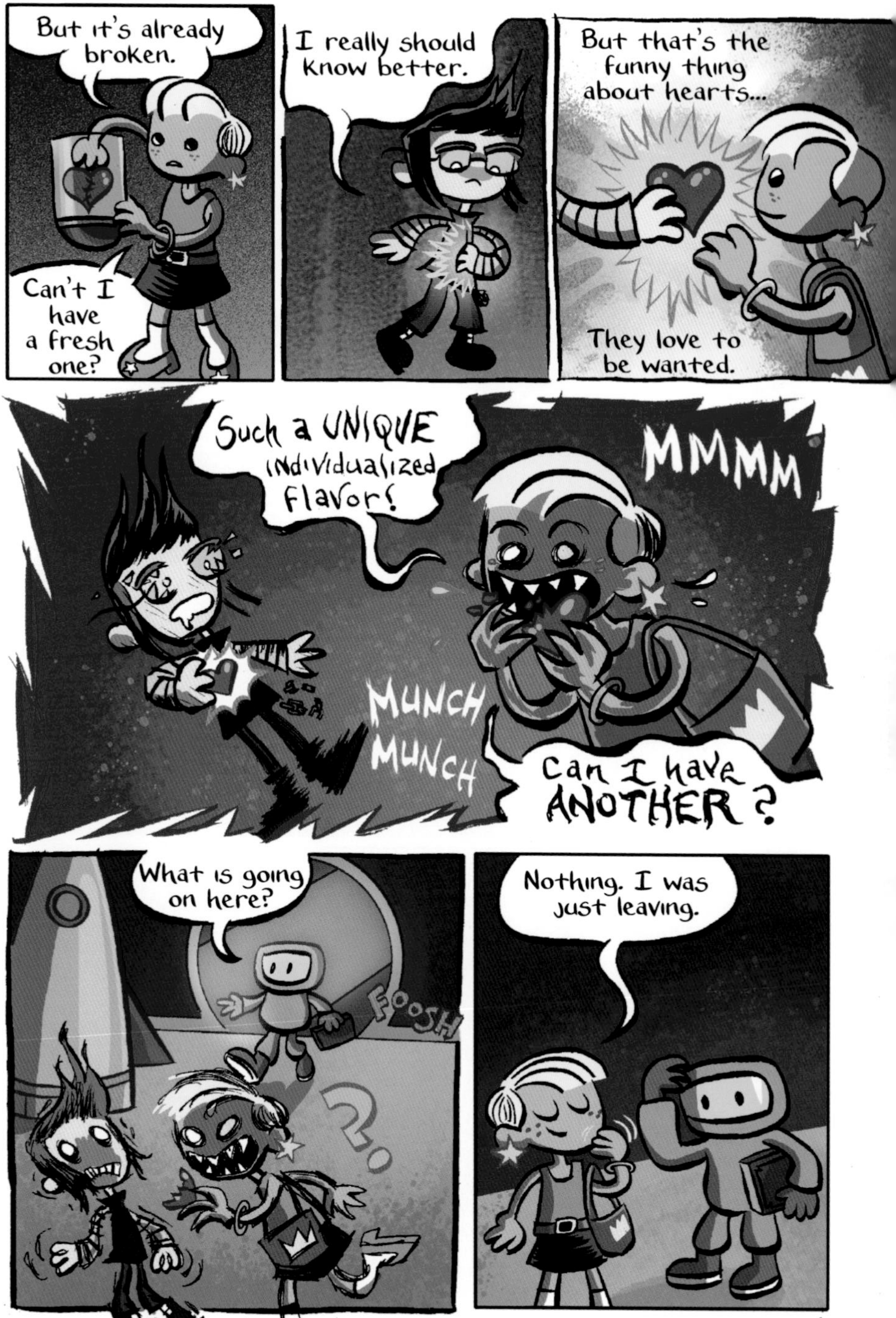
But it's already broken.
Can't I have a fresh one?
I really should know better.
But that's the funny thing about hearts...
They love to be wanted.
Such a UNIQUE individualized flavor!
MMMM
MUNCH MUNCH
Can I have ANOTHER ?
What is going on here?
FOOSH
?
Nothing. I was just leaving.

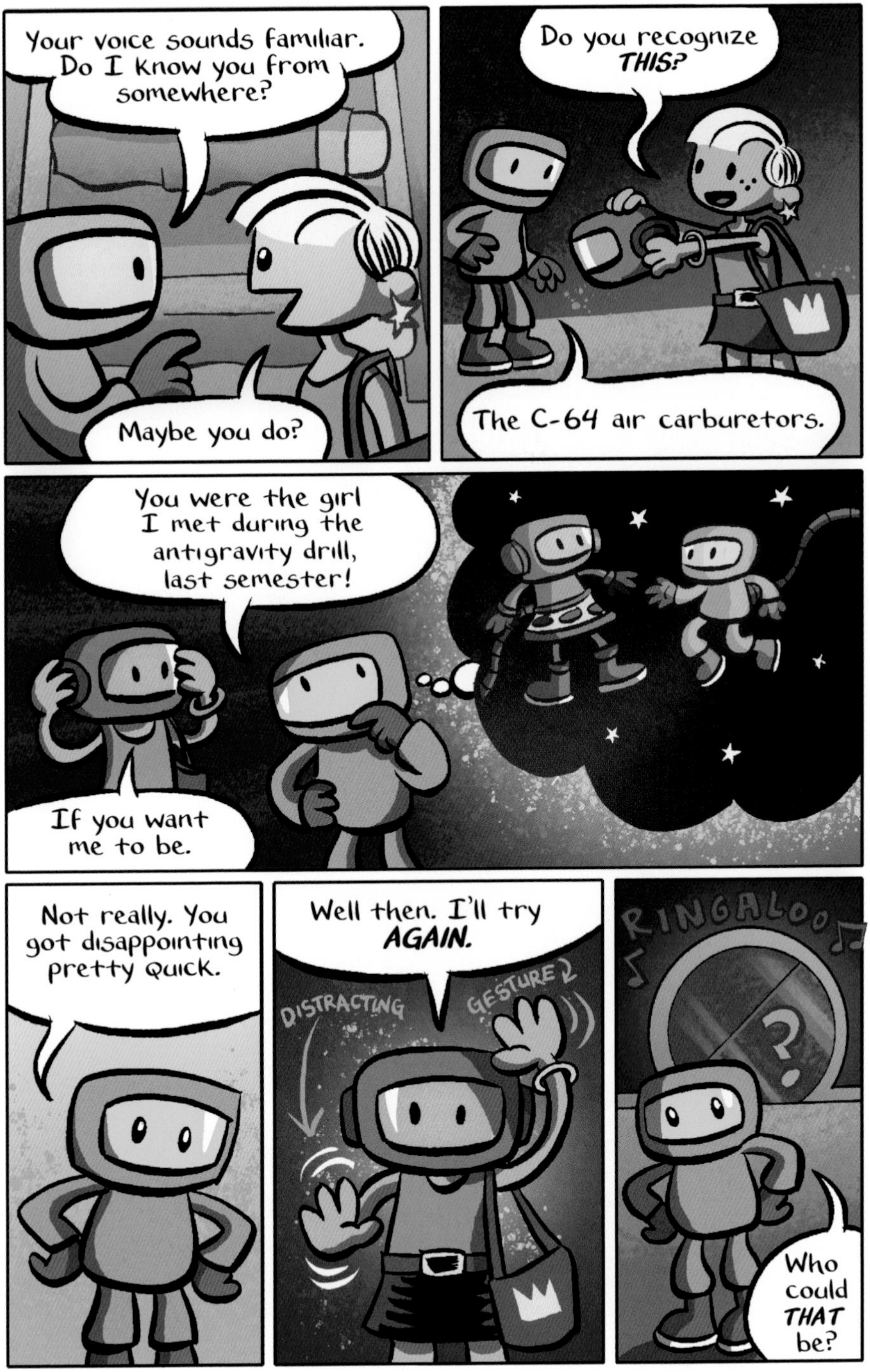
Your voice sounds familiar. Do I know you from somewhere?
Maybe you do?
Do you recognize THIS?
The C-64 air carburetors.
You were the girl I met during the antigravity drill, last semester!
If you want me to be.
Not really. You got disappointing pretty quick.
Well then. I'll try AGAIN.
DISTRACTING
GESTURE
RINGALOO
?
Who could THAT be?

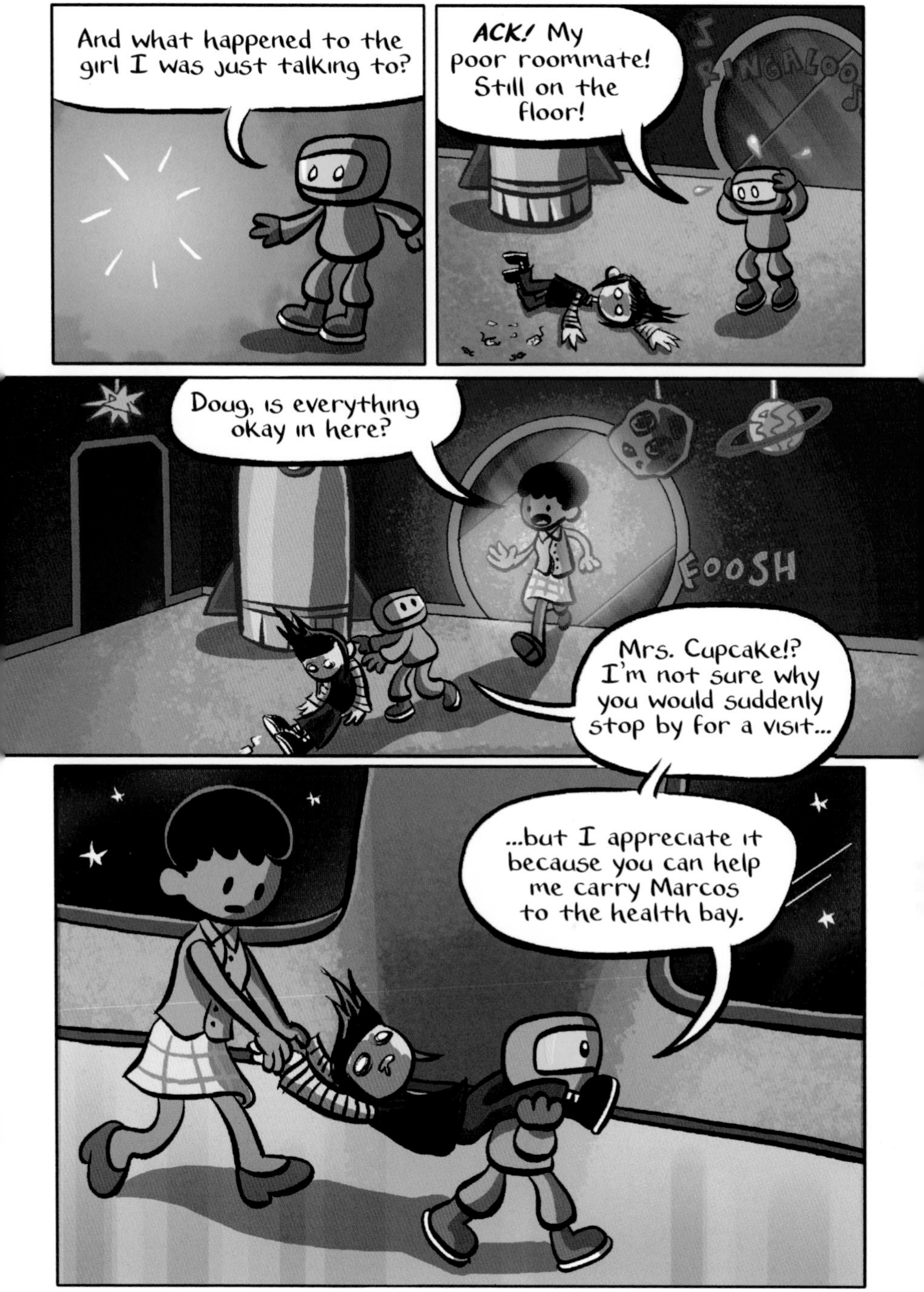
And what happened to the girl I was just talking to?
ACK! My poor roommate! Still on the floor!
RINGALOO
Doug, is everything okay in here?
FOOSH
Mrs. Cupcake!? I'm not sure why you would suddenly stop by for a visit...
...but I appreciate it because you can help me carry Marcos to the health bay.

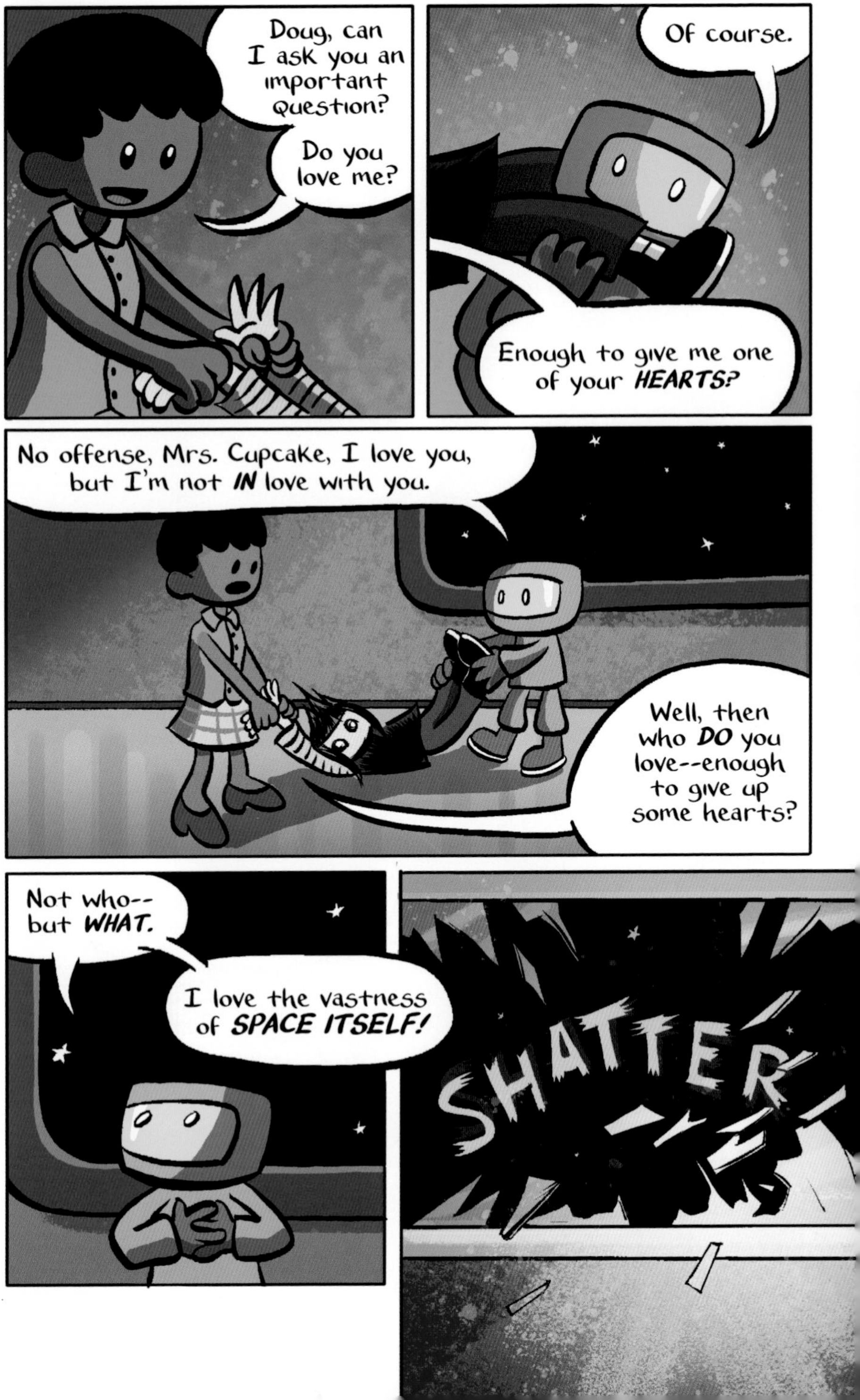
Doug, can I ask you an important question?
Do you love me?
Of course.
Enough to give me one of your **HEARTS?**
No offense, Mrs. Cupcake, I love you, but I'm not **IN** love with you.
Well, then who **DO** you love--enough to give up some hearts?
Not who--but **WHAT.**
I love the vastness of **SPACE ITSELF!**
SHATTER

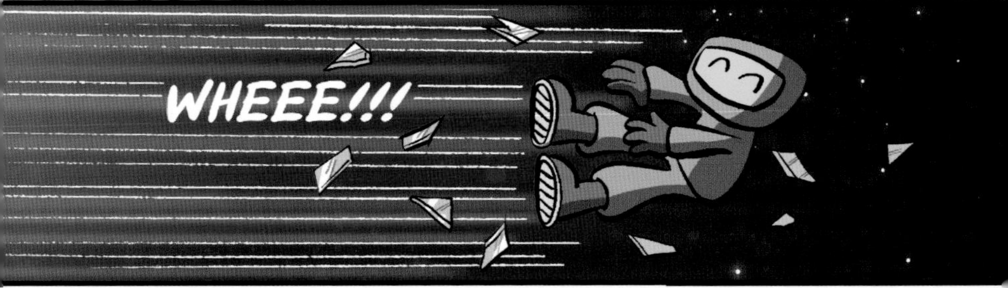
WHEEE!!!

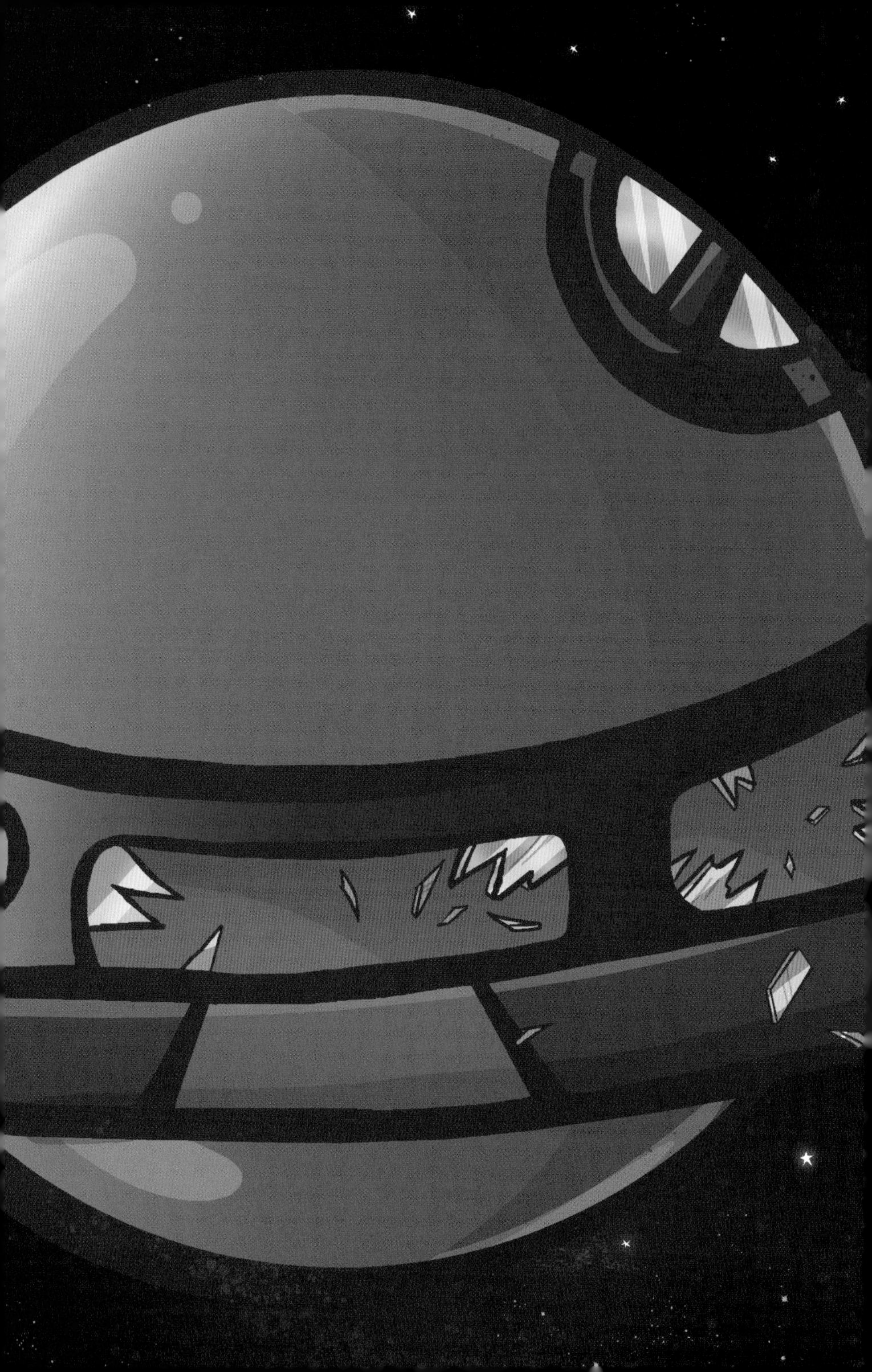

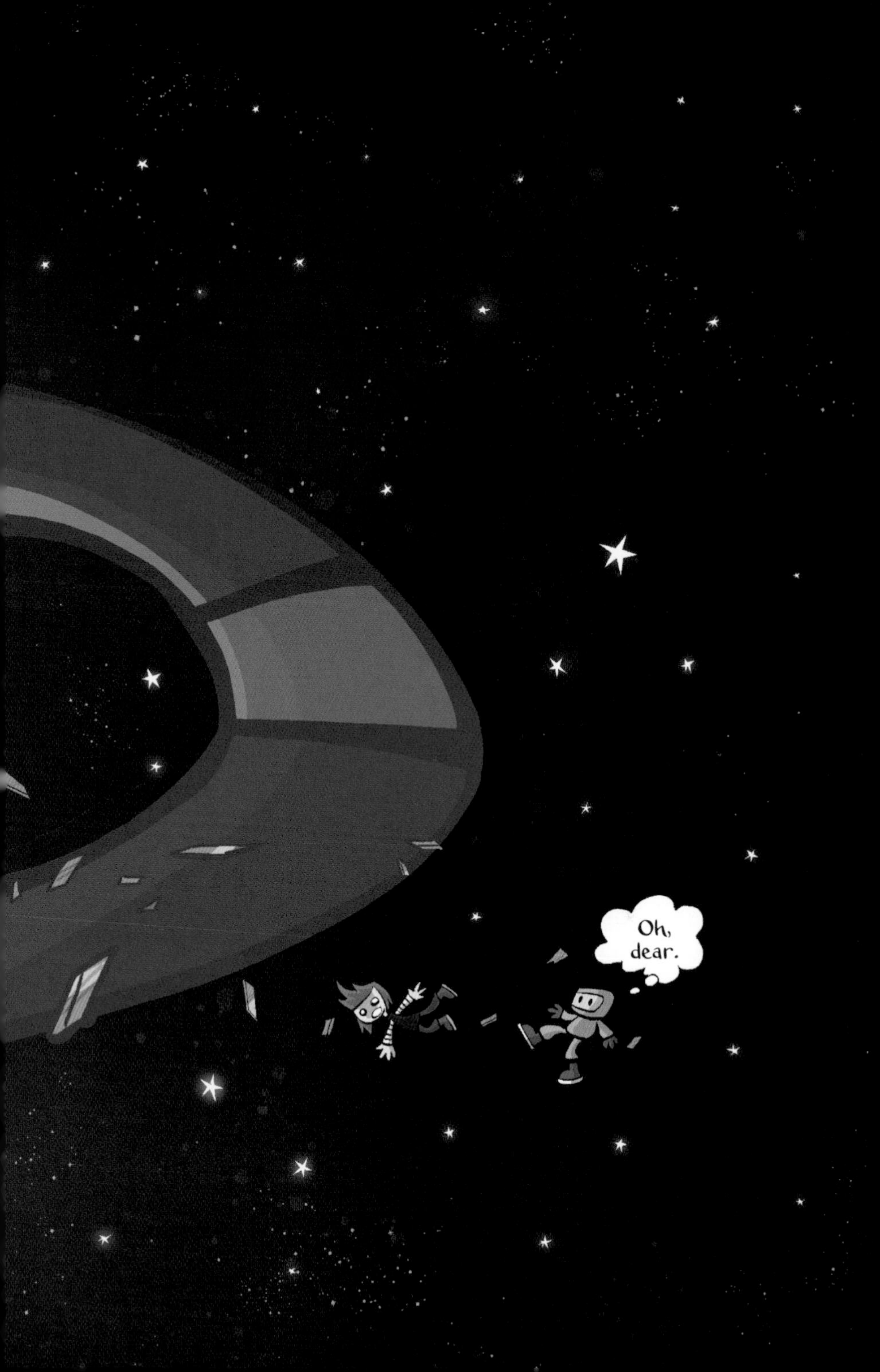
Oh, dear.

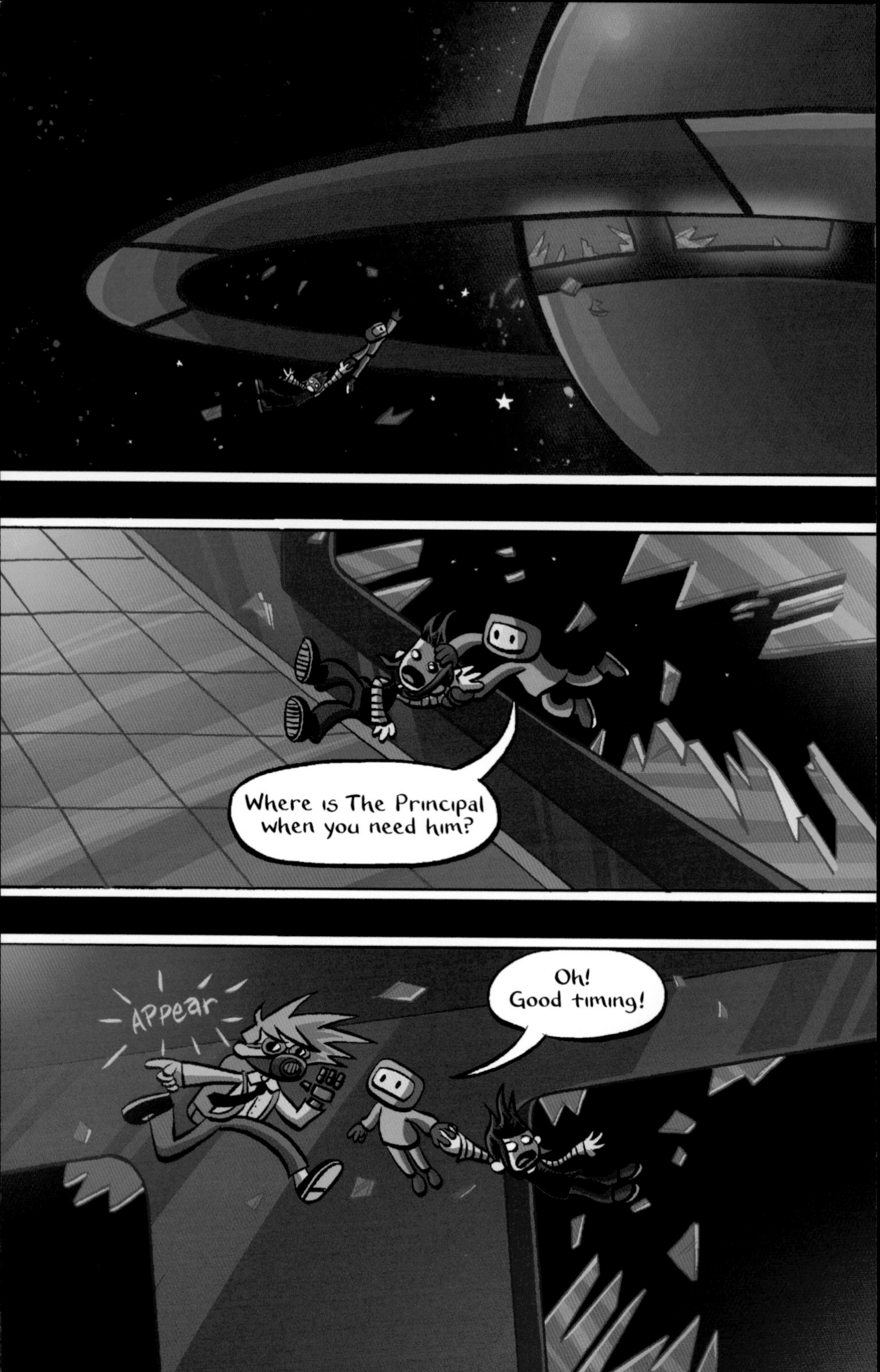
Where is The Principal when you need him?
Appear
Oh! Good timing!

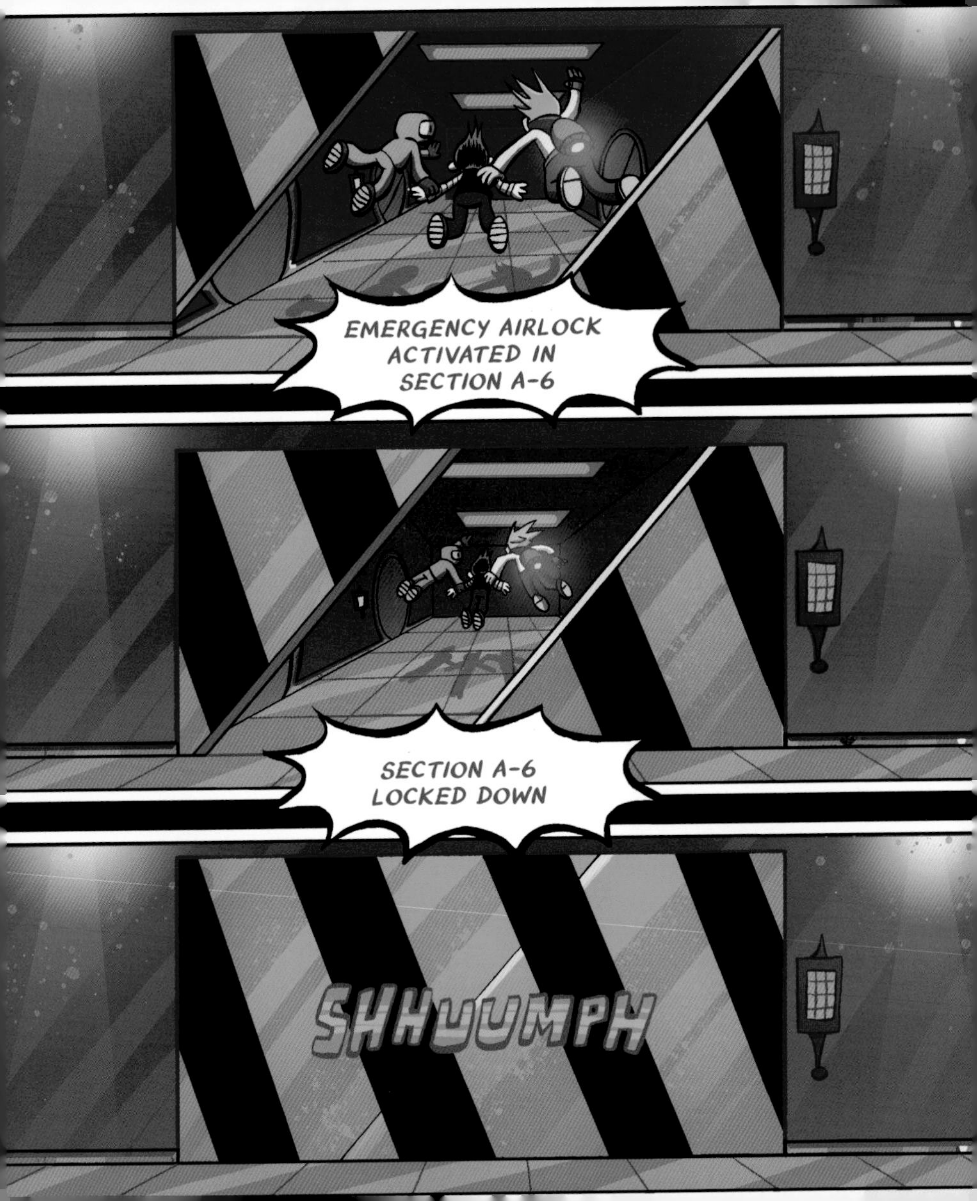
EMERGENCY AIRLOCK ACTIVATED IN SECTION A-6
SECTION A-6 LOCKED DOWN
SHHUUMPH

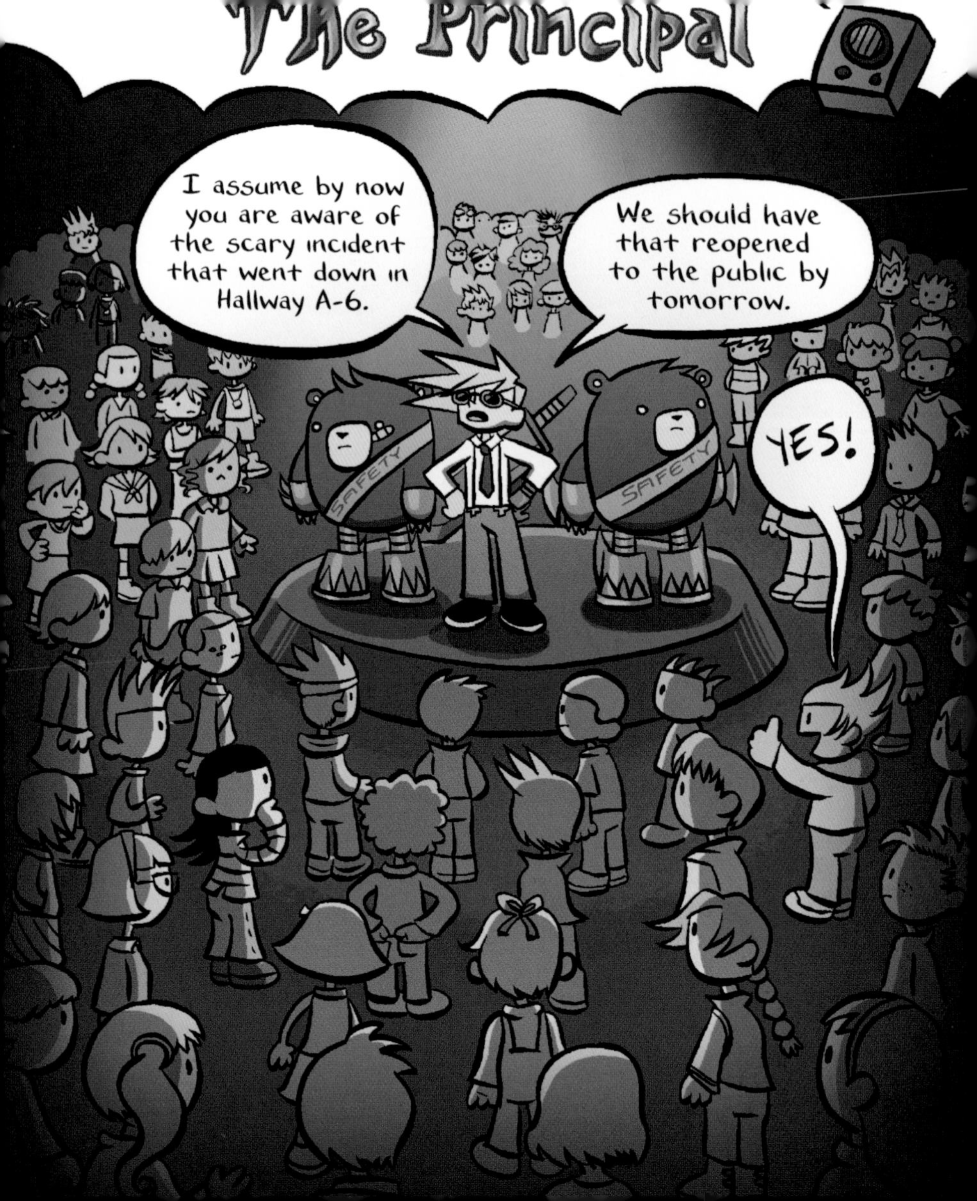
The Principal
I assume by now you are aware of the scary incident that went down in Hallway A-6.
We should have that reopened to the public by tomorrow.
YES!
SAFETY
SAFETY

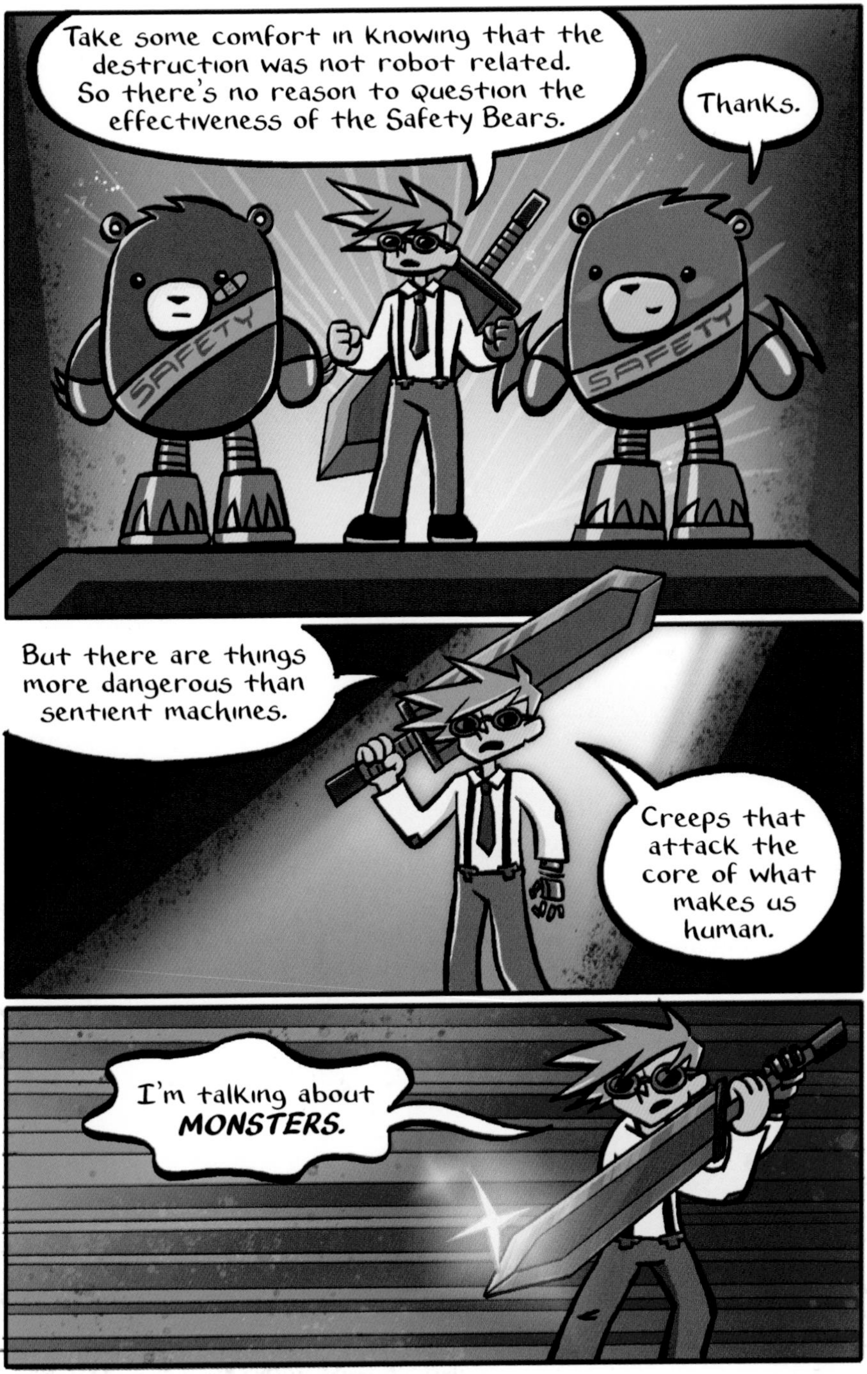
Take some comfort in knowing that the destruction was not robot related. So there's no reason to question the effectiveness of the Safety Bears.
Thanks.
SAFETY
SAFETY
But there are things more dangerous than sentient machines.
Creeps that attack the core of what makes us human.
I'm talking about ***MONSTERS.***

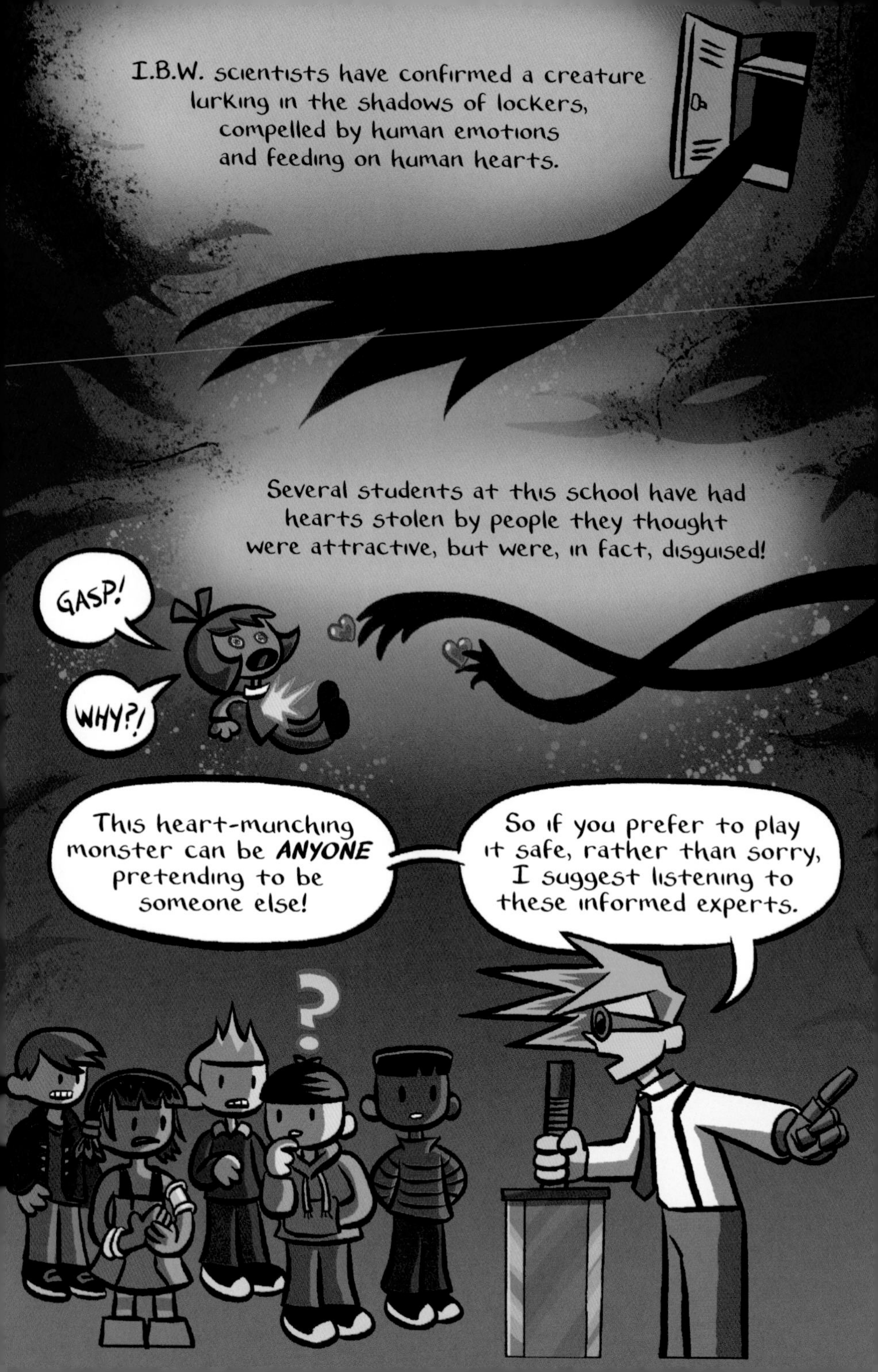
I.B.W. scientists have confirmed a creature lurking in the shadows of lockers, compelled by human emotions and feeding on human hearts.
Several students at this school have had hearts stolen by people they thought were attractive, but were, in fact, disguised!
GASP!
WHY?!
This heart-munching monster can be ANYONE pretending to be someone else!
So if you prefer to play it safe, rather than sorry, I suggest listening to these informed experts.
?

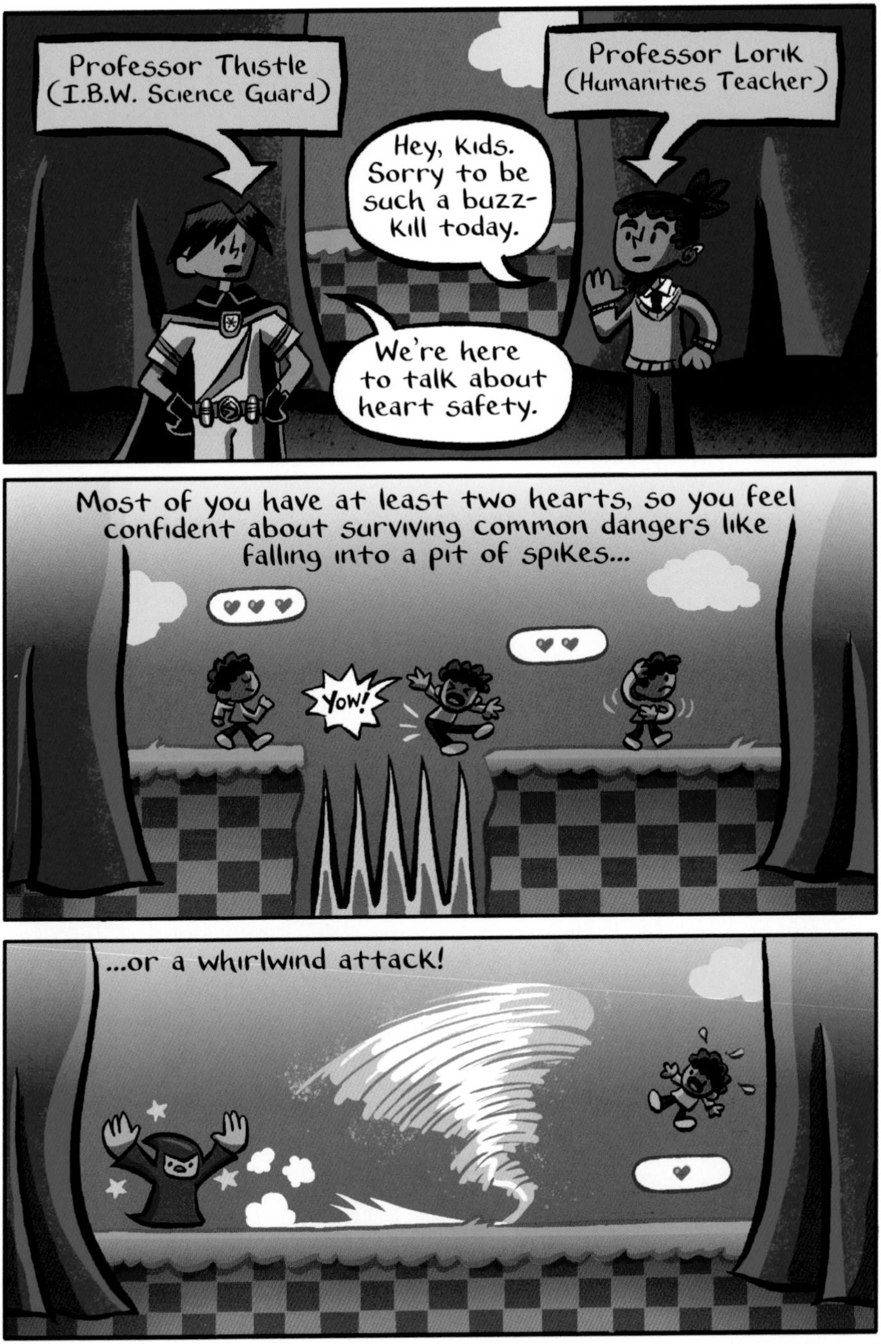
Professor Thistle (I.B.W. Science Guard)
Professor Lorik (Humanities Teacher)
Hey, Kids. Sorry to be such a buzz-kill today.
We're here to talk about heart safety.
Most of you have at least two hearts, so you feel confident about surviving common dangers like falling into a pit of spikes...
YOW!
...or a whirlwind attack!

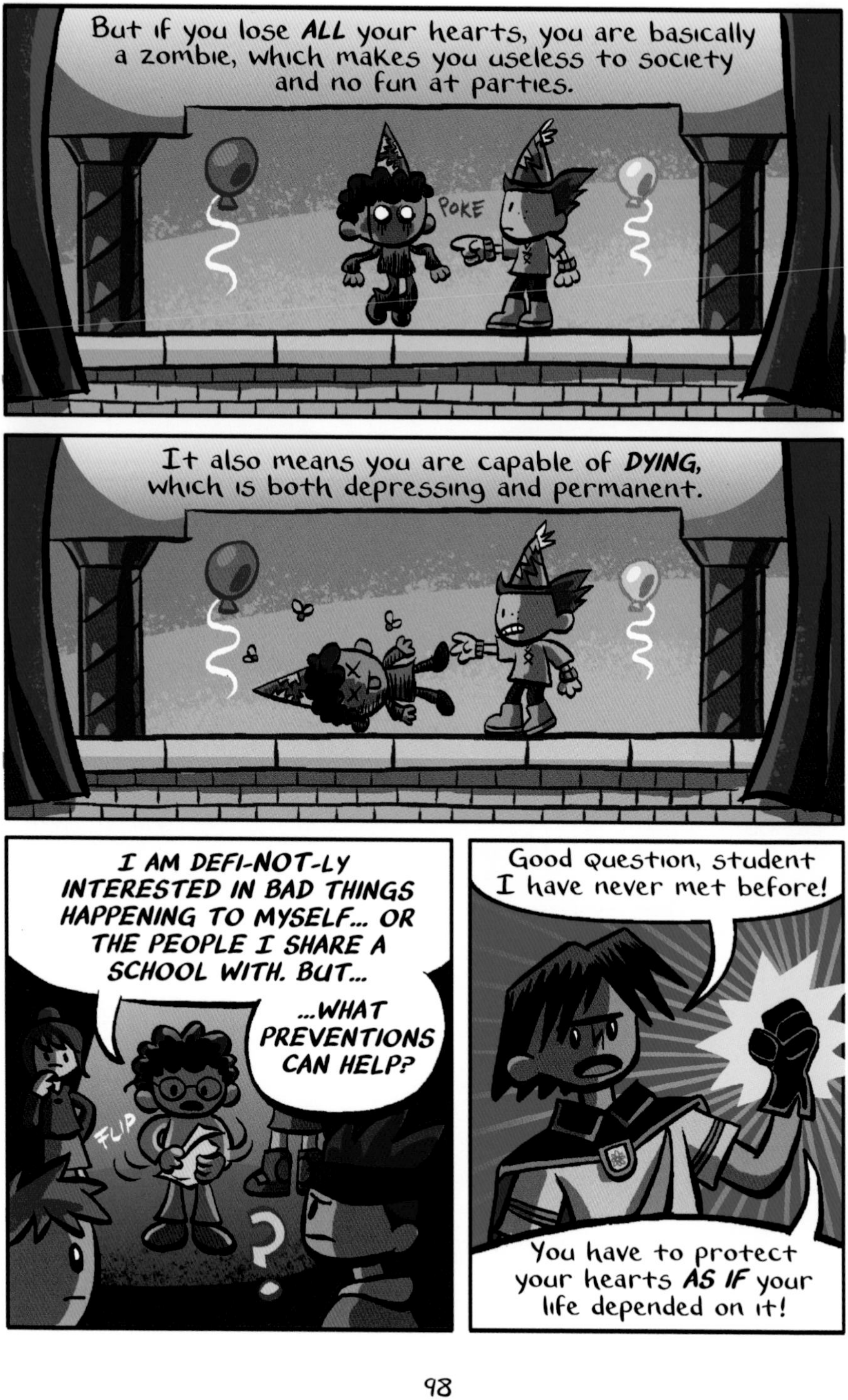

But if you lose ALL your hearts, you are basically a zombie, which makes you useless to society and no fun at parties.
POKE
It also means you are capable of DYING, which is both depressing and permanent.
I AM DEFI-NOT-LY INTERESTED IN BAD THINGS HAPPENING TO MYSELF... OR THE PEOPLE I SHARE A SCHOOL WITH. BUT...
...WHAT PREVENTIONS CAN HELP?
FLIP
Good question, student I have never met before!
You have to protect your hearts AS IF your life depended on it!

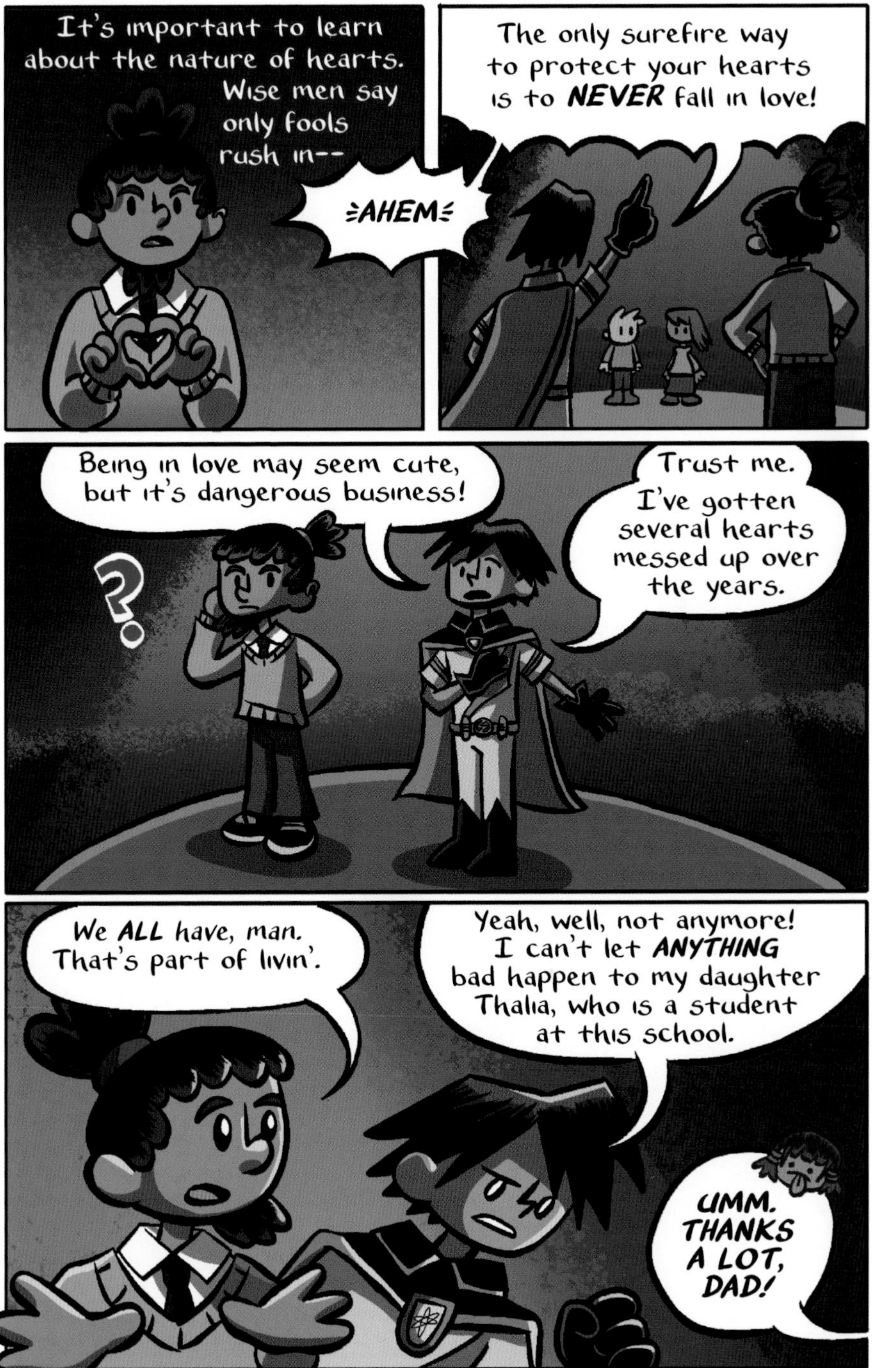
It's important to learn about the nature of hearts.
Wise men say only fools rush in--
AHEM
The only surefire way to protect your hearts is to NEVER fall in love!
Being in love may seem cute, but it's dangerous business!
Trust me.
I've gotten several hearts messed up over the years.
We ALL have, man. That's part of livin'.
Yeah, well, not anymore! I can't let ANYTHING bad happen to my daughter Thalia, who is a student at this school.
UMM. THANKS A LOT, DAD!

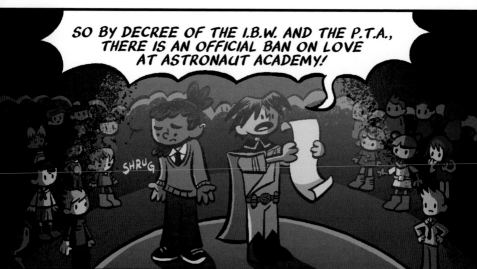

SO BY DECREE OF THE I.B.W. AND THE P.T.A., THERE IS AN OFFICIAL BAN ON LOVE AT ASTRONAUT ACADEMY!

SHRUG

WHAT?! HUH? IS THAT LEGAL?

Stupid acronyms. Think they can tell us what to do. ≤GRUMP≤

We'll be handing out pamphlets with tips and tricks to help you adjust to these physical changes.

I know this seems extreme, but I'm confident in the student body's ability to ADAPT.

So stay safe and trust in our ability as adults to know what's best for you!

OUCH!

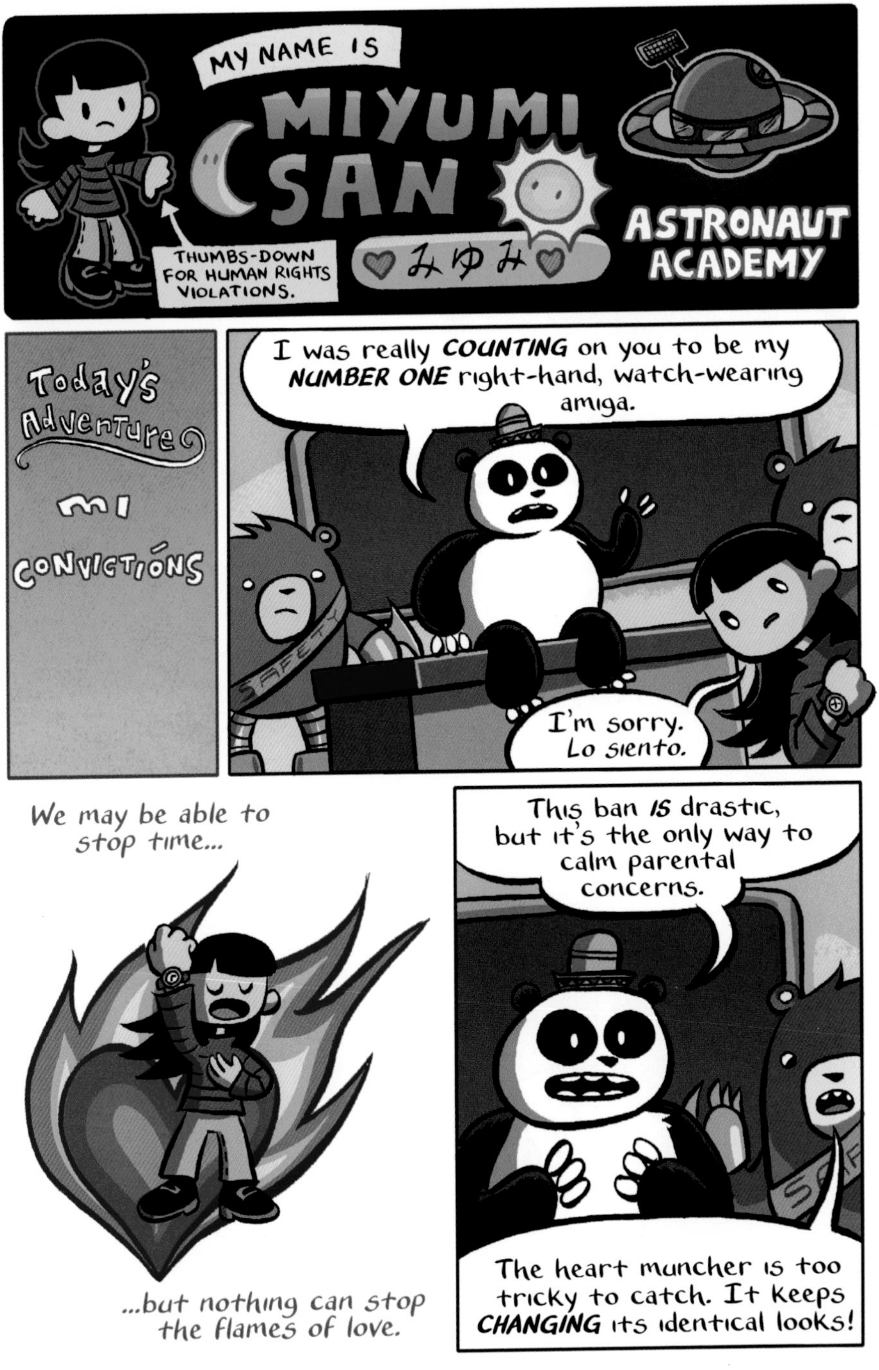
MY NAME IS
MIYUMI SAN
みゆみ
THUMBS-DOWN FOR HUMAN RIGHTS VIOLATIONS.
ASTRONAUT ACADEMY
Today's Adventure
mi CONVICTIÓNS
I was really COUNTING on you to be my NUMBER ONE right-hand, watch-wearing amiga.
SAFETY
I'm sorry. Lo siento.
We may be able to stop time...
...but nothing can stop the flames of love.
This ban IS drastic, but it's the only way to calm parental concerns.
The heart muncher is too tricky to catch. It keeps CHANGING its identical looks!

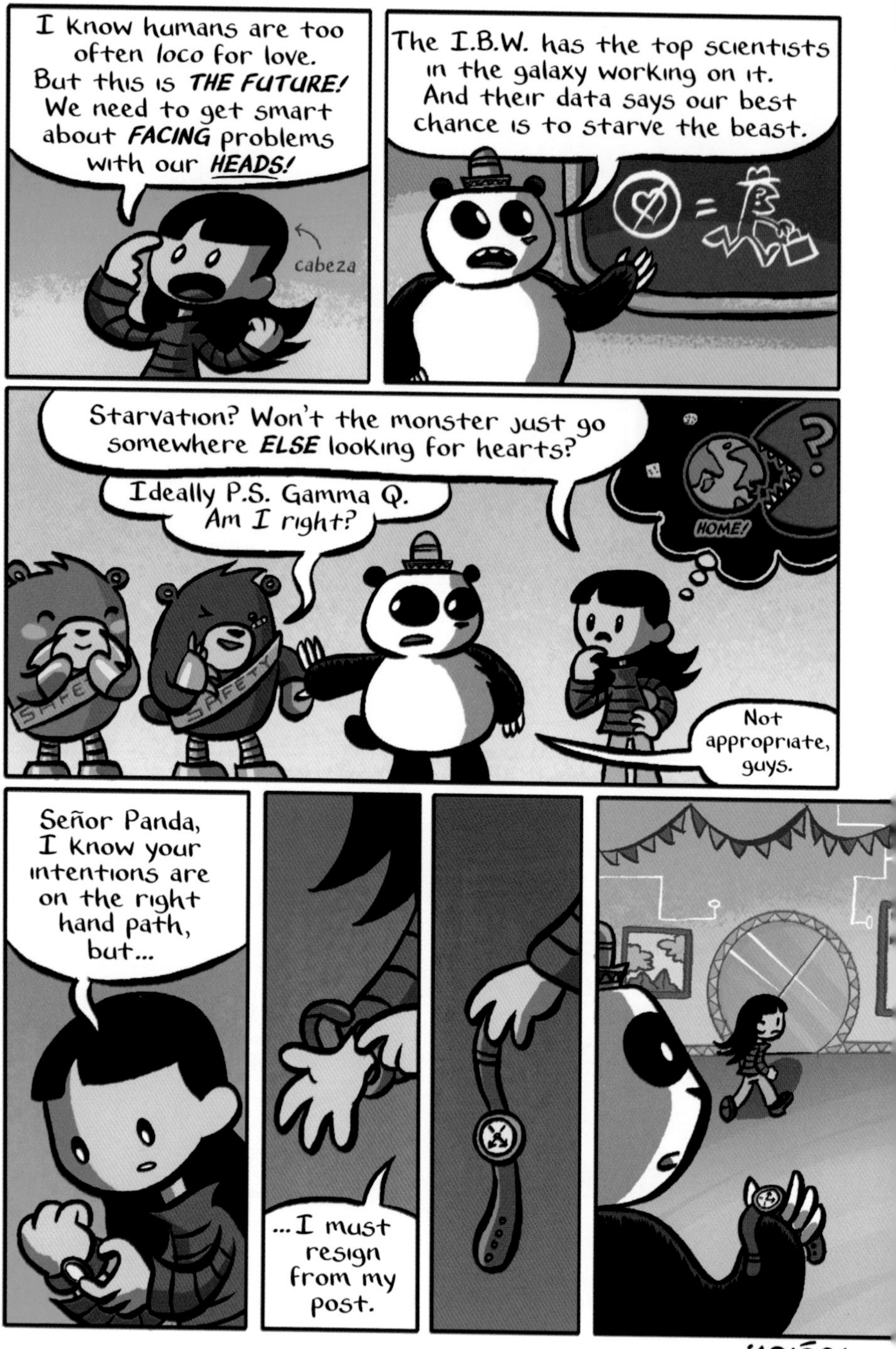
I know humans are too often loco for love. But this is THE FUTURE! We need to get smart about FACING problems with our HEADS!
cabeza
The I.B.W. has the top scientists in the galaxy working on it. And their data says our best chance is to starve the beast.
Starvation? Won't the monster just go somewhere ELSE looking for hearts?
HOME!
Ideally P.S. Gamma Q. Am I right?
SAFETY
SAFETY
Not appropriate, guys.
Señor Panda, I know your intentions are on the right hand path, but...
...I must resign from my post.
¡ADIÓS!

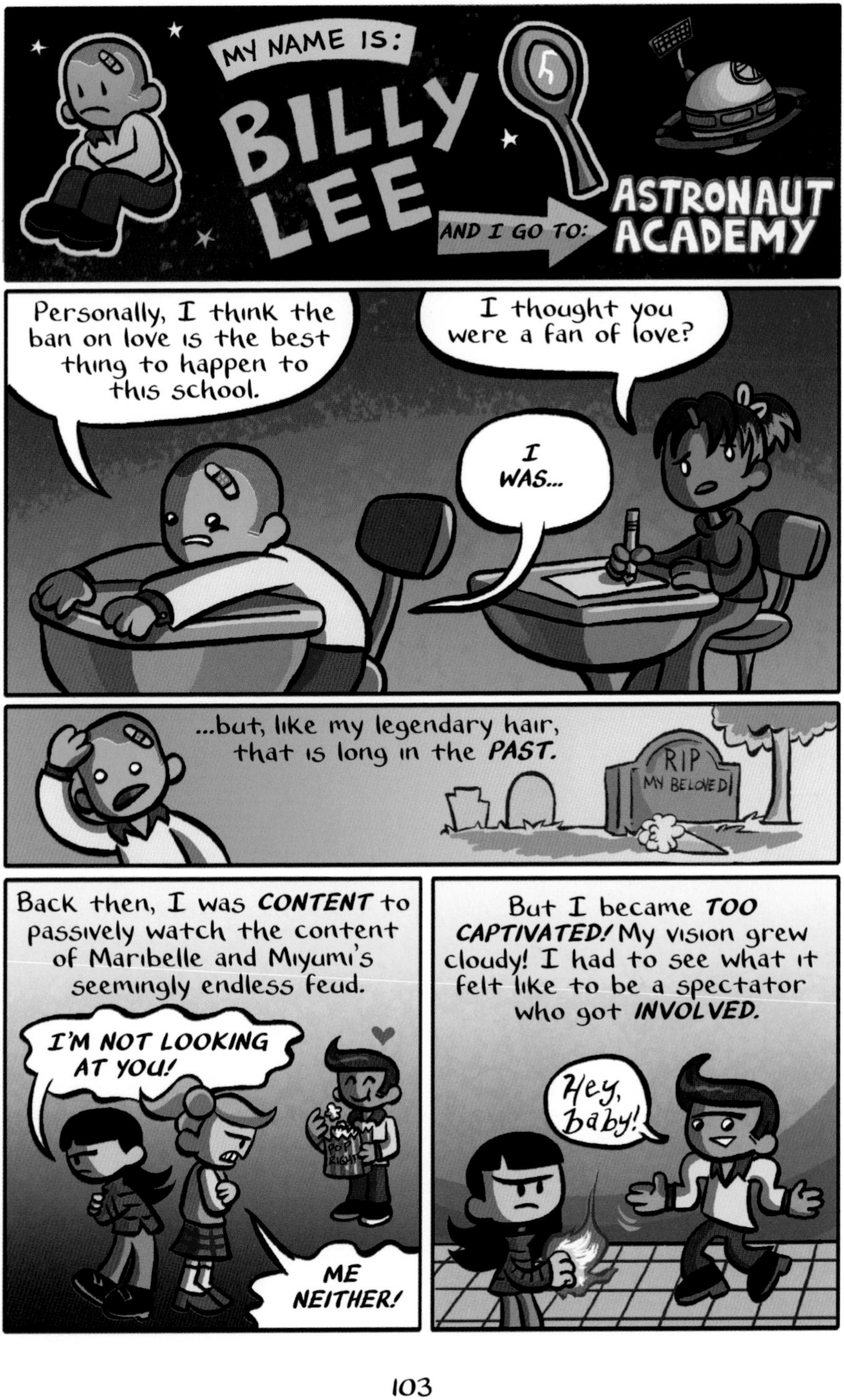
MY NAME IS:
BILLY LEE
AND I GO TO:
ASTRONAUT ACADEMY
Personally, I think the ban on love is the best thing to happen to this school.
I thought you were a fan of love?
I WAS...
...but, like my legendary hair, that is long in the PAST.
RIP
MY BELOVED
Back then, I was CONTENT to passively watch the content of Maribelle and Miyumi's seemingly endless feud.
I'M NOT LOOKING AT YOU!
ME NEITHER!
But I became TOO CAPTIVATED! My vision grew cloudy! I had to see what it felt like to be a spectator who got INVOLVED.
Hey, baby!

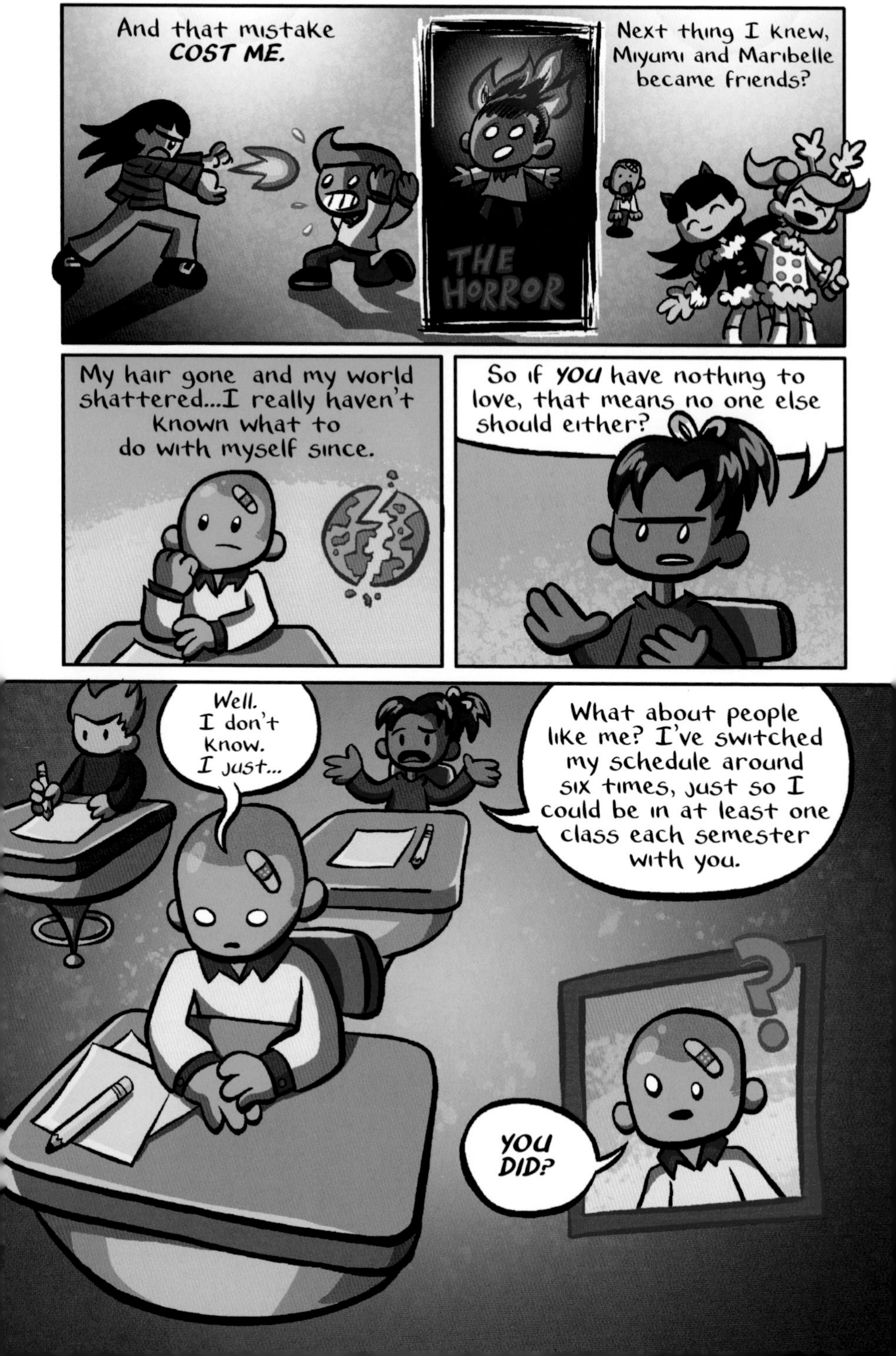
And that mistake **COST ME.**
THE HORROR
Next thing I knew, Miyumi and Maribelle became friends?
My hair gone and my world shattered...I really haven't known what to do with myself since.
So if *YOU* have nothing to love, that means no one else should either?
Well. I don't know. I just...
What about people like me? I've switched my schedule around six times, just so I could be in at least one class each semester with you.
YOU DID?

I must have been crazy, thinking you'd eventually notice.

Wait...are you saying you actually like me?

For some reason I can't explain, yeah.

Even without the pompadour?

YUP.

So, if I asked you on a date...

...you might actually say--

YES.

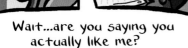

Well, I WOULD have... but there's a BAN ON LOVE, remember?

SORRY.

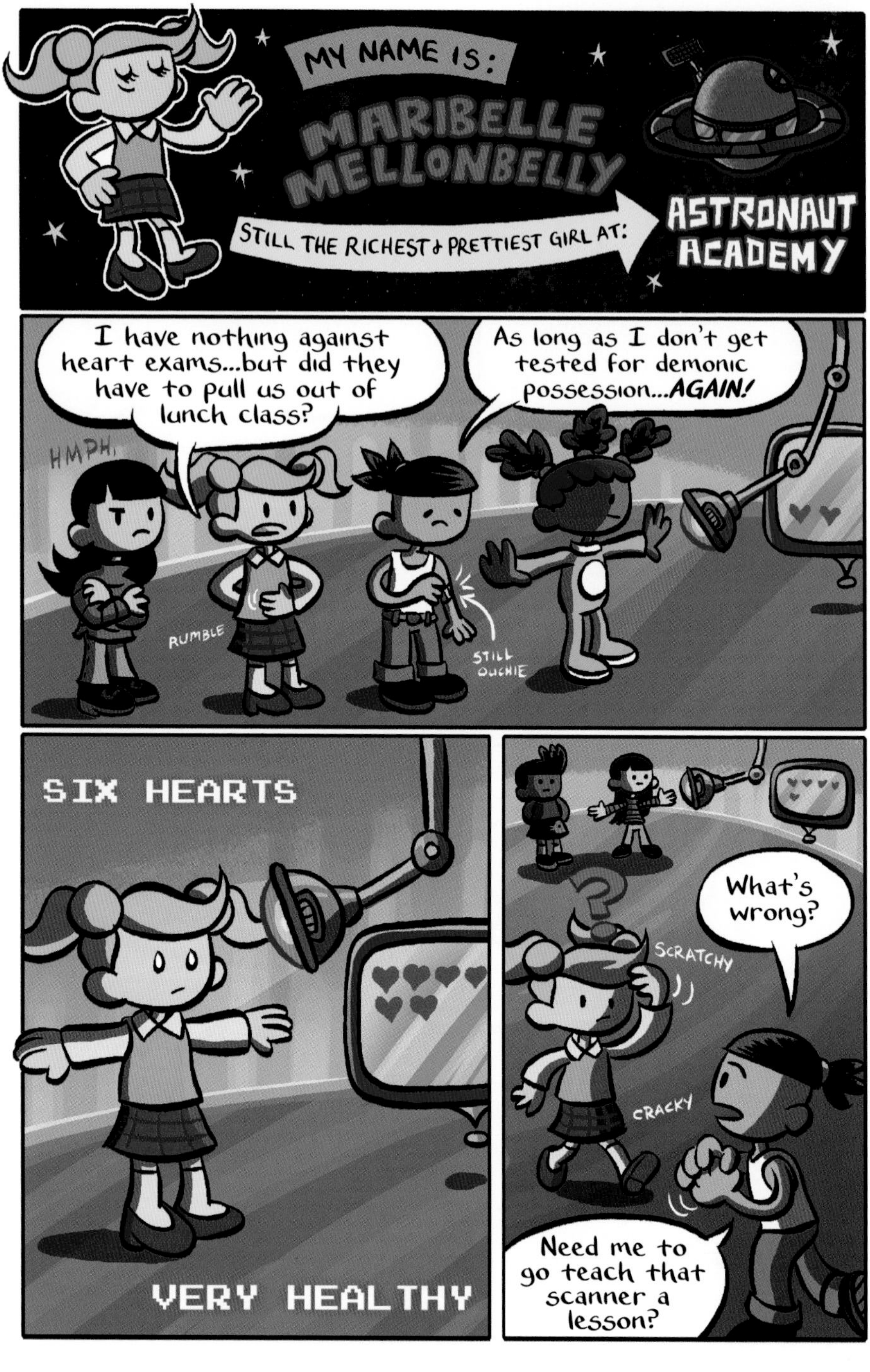
MY NAME IS:
MARIBELLE MELLONBELLY
STILL THE RICHEST & PRETTIEST GIRL AT:
ASTRONAUT ACADEMY
I have nothing against heart exams...but did they have to pull us out of lunch class?
As long as I don't get tested for demonic possession...**AGAIN!**
HMPH.
RUMBLE
STILL OUCHIE
SIX HEARTS
VERY HEALTHY
What's wrong?
SCRATCHY
CRACKY
Need me to go teach that scanner a lesson?

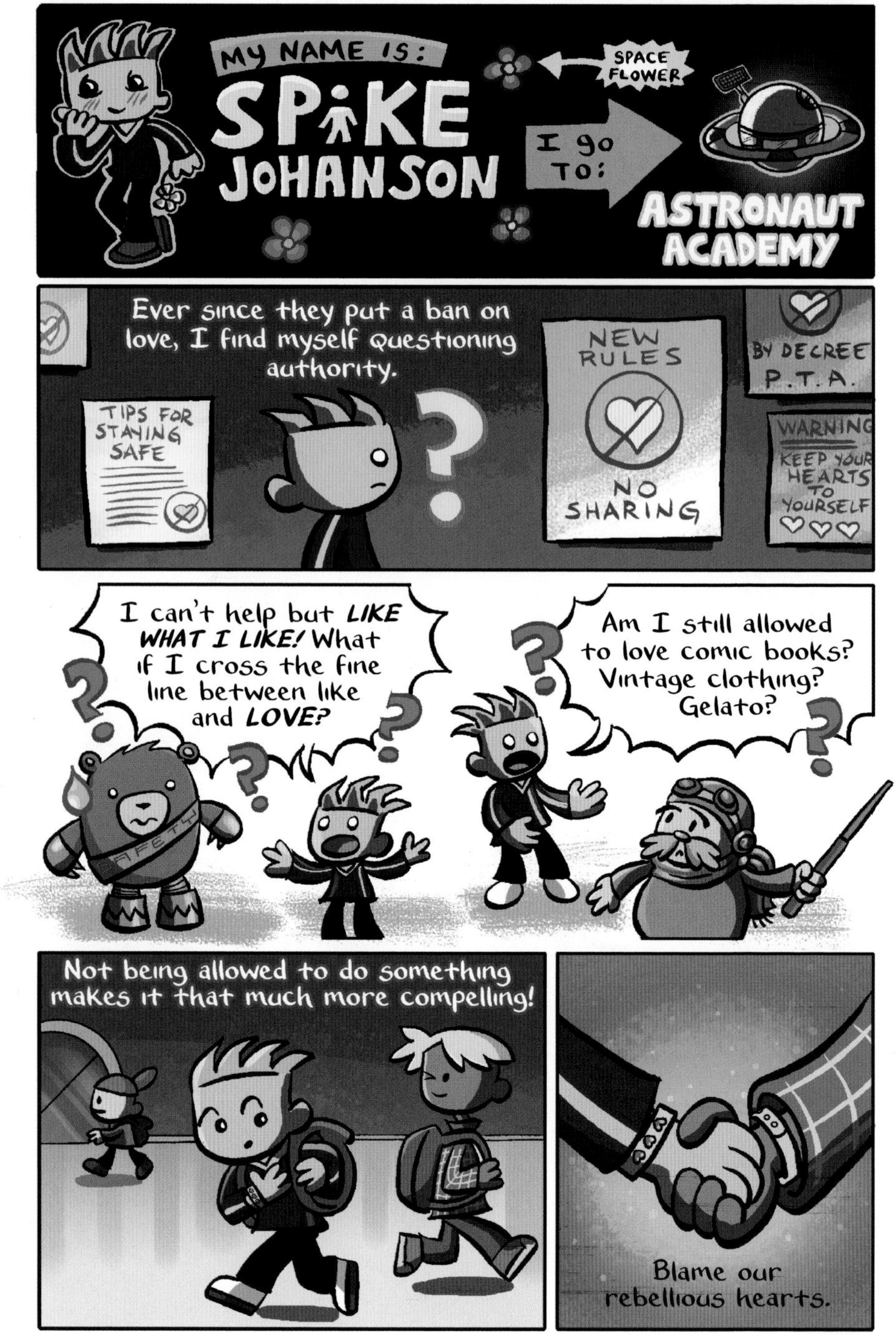
MY NAME IS:
SPIKE JOHANSON
SPACE FLOWER
I go TO:
ASTRONAUT ACADEMY
Ever since they put a ban on love, I find myself questioning authority.
BY DECREE P.T.A.
TIPS FOR STAYING SAFE
NEW RULES
NO SHARING
WARNING
KEEP YOUR HEARTS TO YOURSELF
I can't help but LIKE WHAT I LIKE! What if I cross the fine line between like and LOVE?
Am I still allowed to love comic books? Vintage clothing? Gelato?
SAFETY
Not being allowed to do something makes it that much more compelling!
Blame our rebellious hearts.
END!

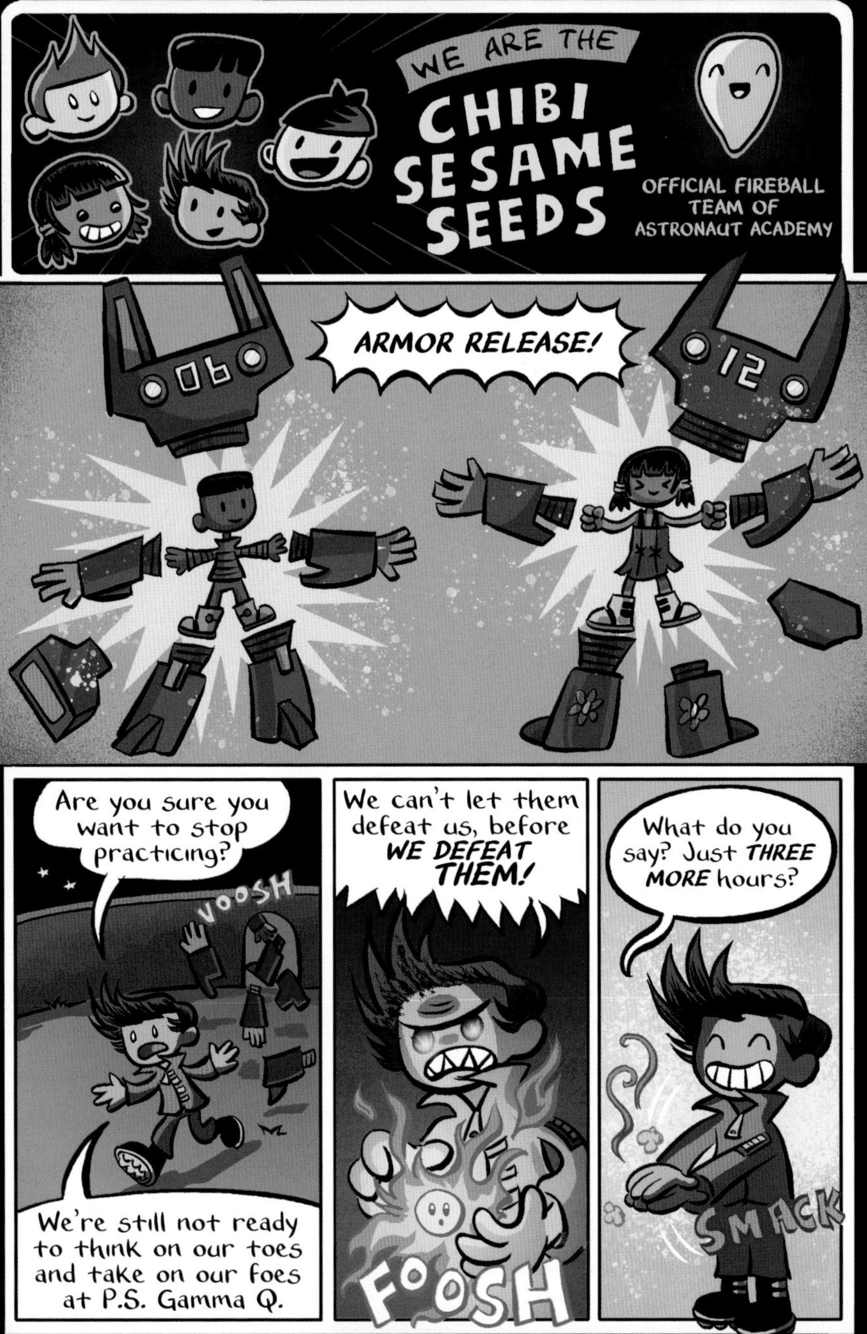
WE ARE THE
CHIBI SESAME SEEDS
OFFICIAL FIREBALL TEAM OF ASTRONAUT ACADEMY
ARMOR RELEASE!
06
12
Are you sure you want to stop practicing?
VOOSH
We're still not ready to think on our toes and take on our foes at P.S. Gamma Q.
We can't let them defeat us, before *WE DEFEAT THEM!*
FOOSH
What do you say? Just *THREE MORE* hours?
SMACK

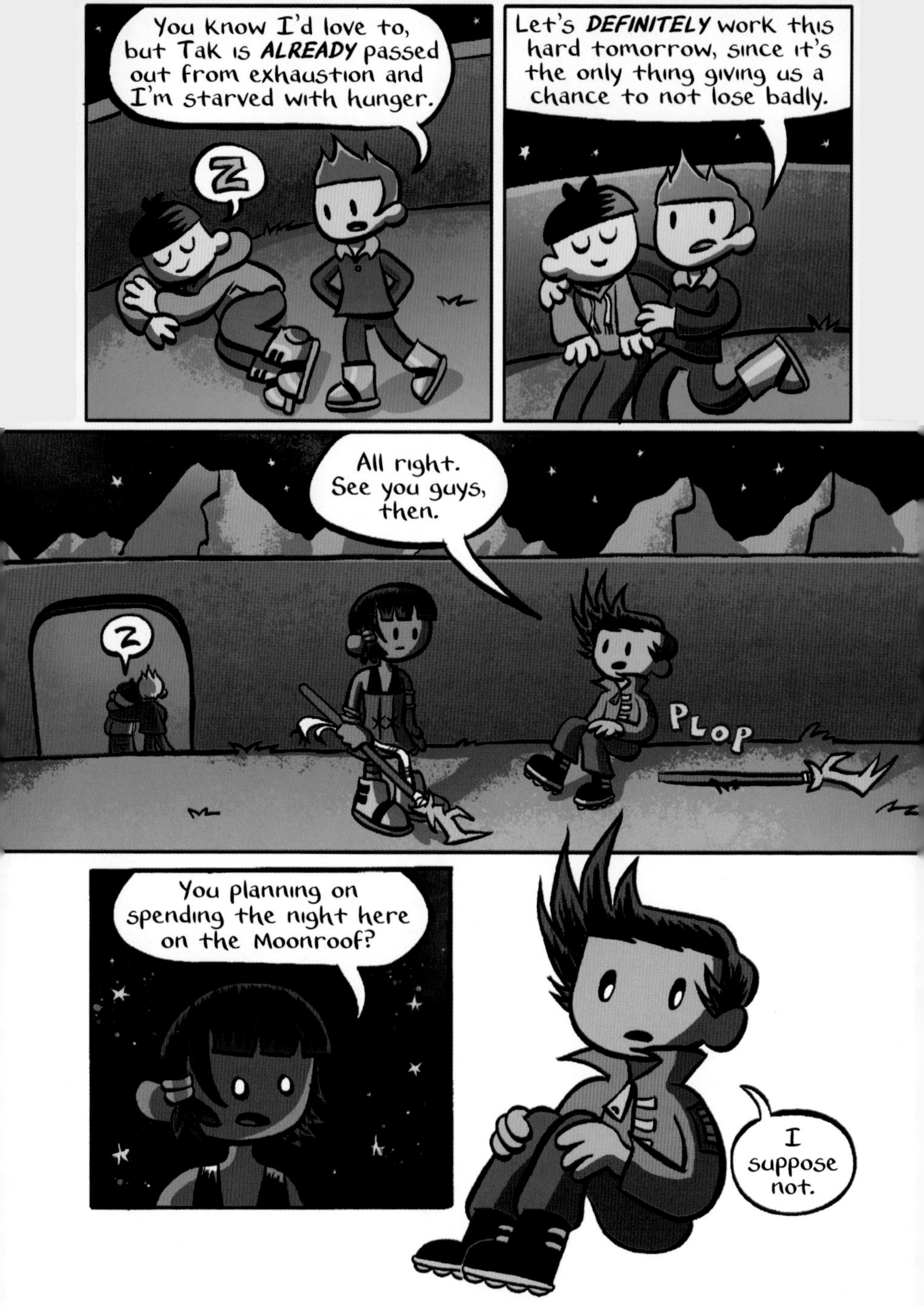
You know I'd love to, but Tak is ALREADY passed out from exhaustion and I'm starved with hunger.
Z
Let's DEFINITELY work this hard tomorrow, since it's the only thing giving us a chance to not lose badly.
All right. See you guys, then.
Z
PLOP
You planning on spending the night here on the Moonroof?
I suppose not.

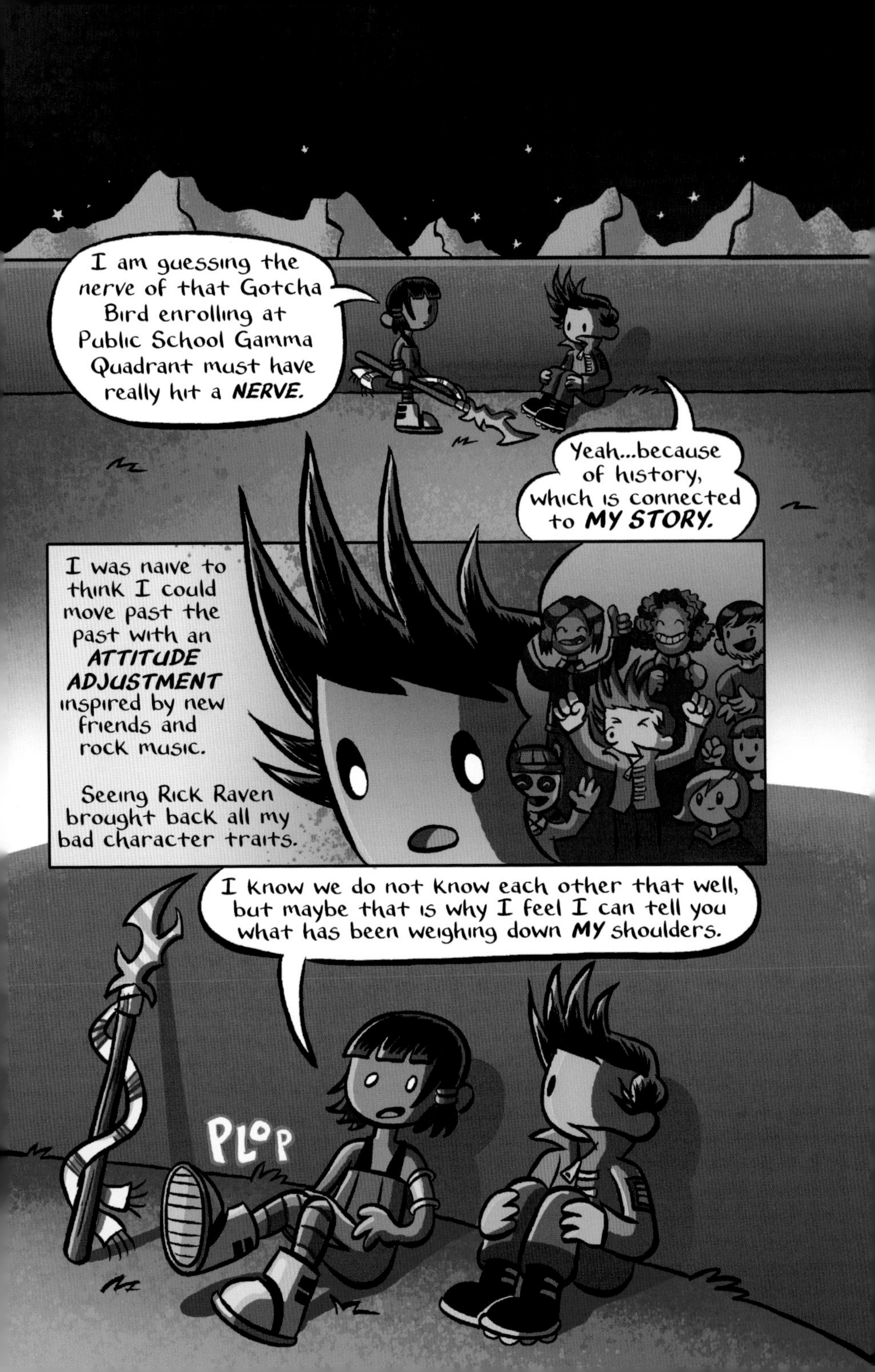
I am guessing the nerve of that Gotcha Bird enrolling at Public School Gamma Quadrant must have really hit a NERVE.
Yeah...because of history, which is connected to MY STORY.
I was naive to think I could move past the past with an ATTITUDE ADJUSTMENT inspired by new friends and rock music.
Seeing Rick Raven brought back all my bad character traits.
I know we do not know each other that well, but maybe that is why I feel I can tell you what has been weighing down MY shoulders.
PLOP

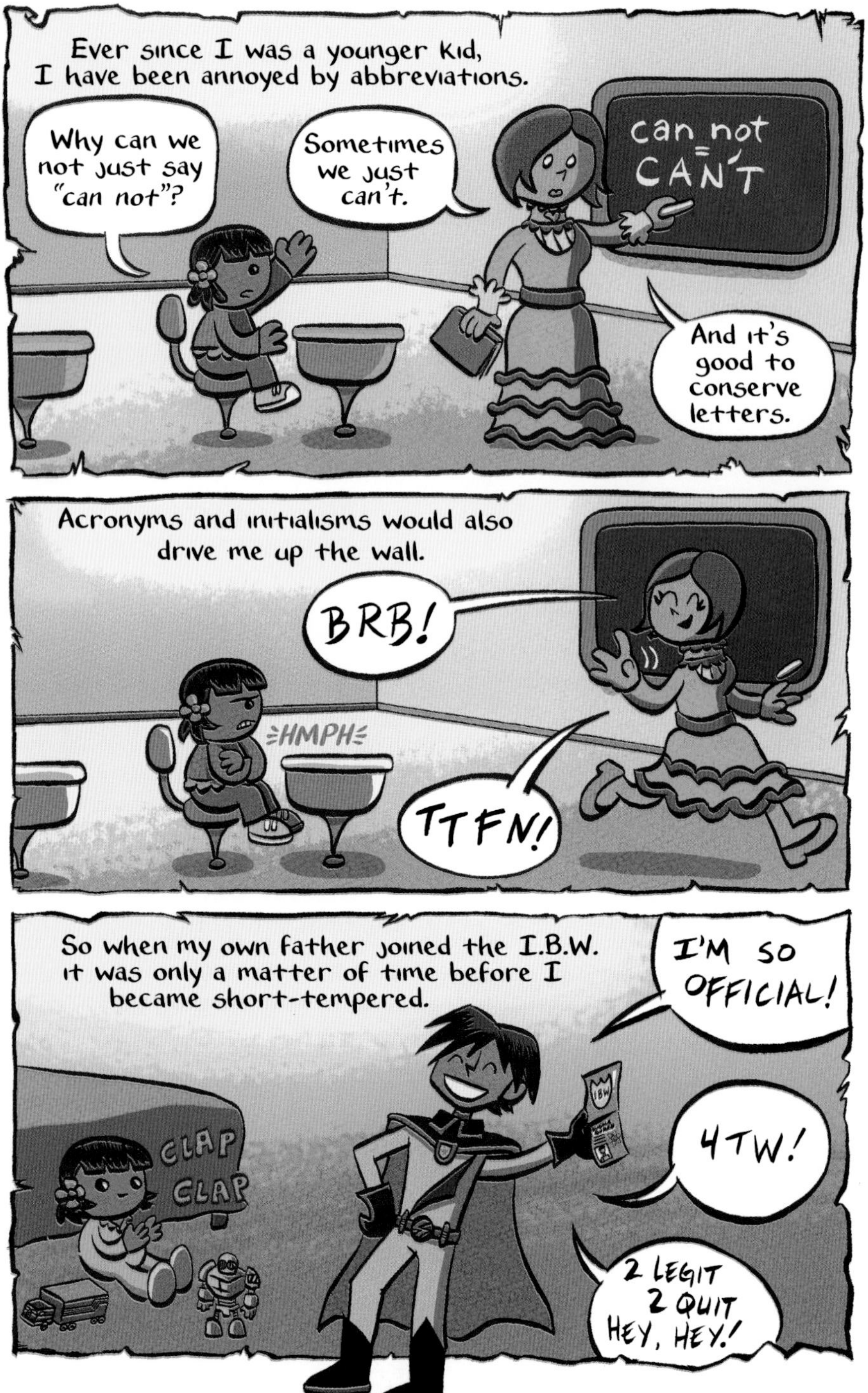
Ever since I was a younger kid, I have been annoyed by abbreviations.
Why can we not just say "can not"?
Sometimes we just can't.
can not = CAN'T
And it's good to conserve letters.
Acronyms and initialisms would also drive me up the wall.
BRB!
HMPH
TTFN!
So when my own father joined the I.B.W. it was only a matter of time before I became short-tempered.
I'M SO OFFICIAL!
CLAP
CLAP
4TW!
2 LEGIT 2 QUIT HEY, HEY!

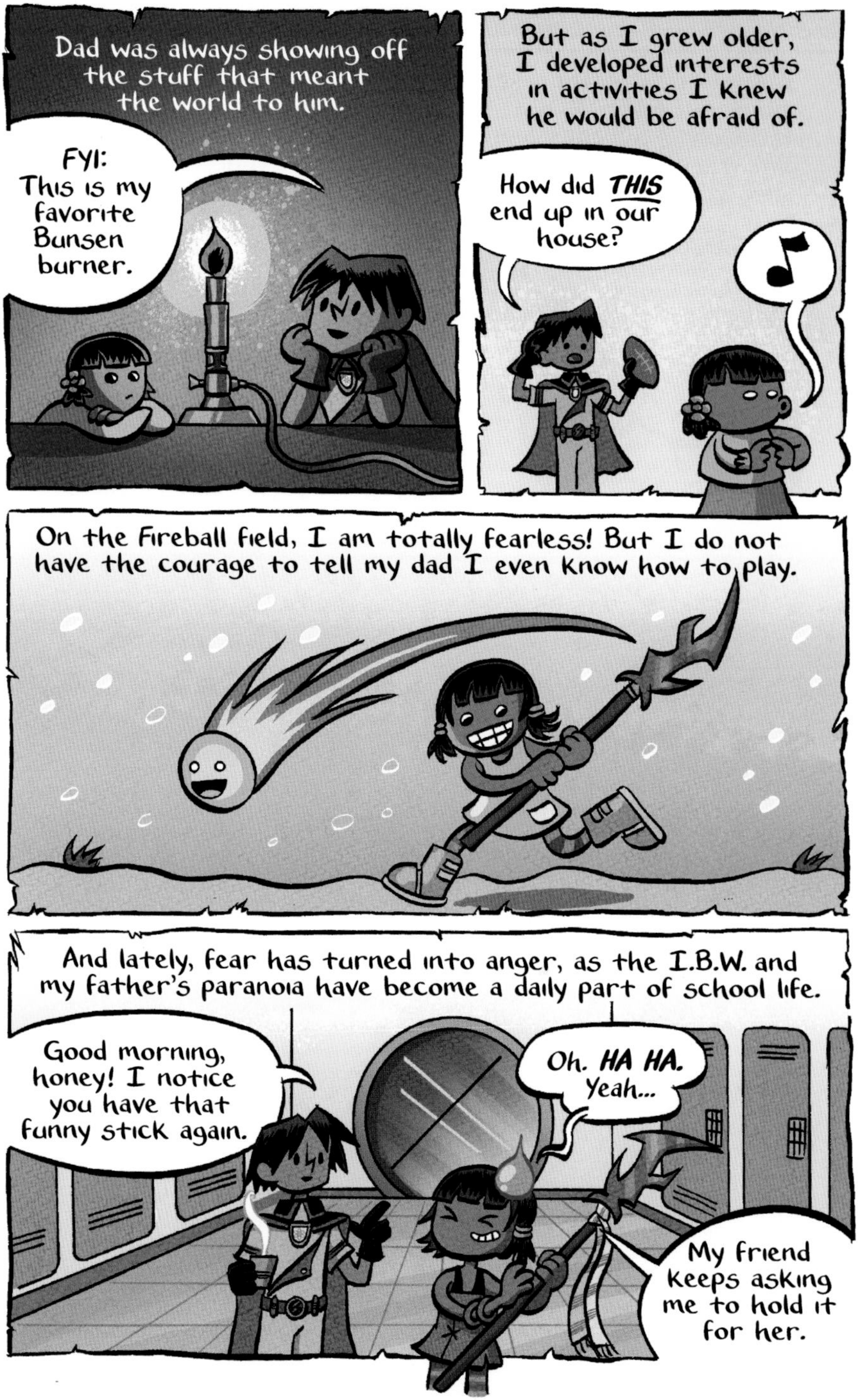

Dad was always showing off the stuff that meant the world to him.
FYI: This is my favorite Bunsen burner.
But as I grew older, I developed interests in activities I knew he would be afraid of.
How did THIS end up in our house?
On the Fireball field, I am totally fearless! But I do not have the courage to tell my dad I even know how to play.
And lately, fear has turned into anger, as the I.B.W. and my father's paranoia have become a daily part of school life.
Good morning, honey! I notice you have that funny stick again.
Oh. HA HA. Yeah...
My friend keeps asking me to hold it for her.

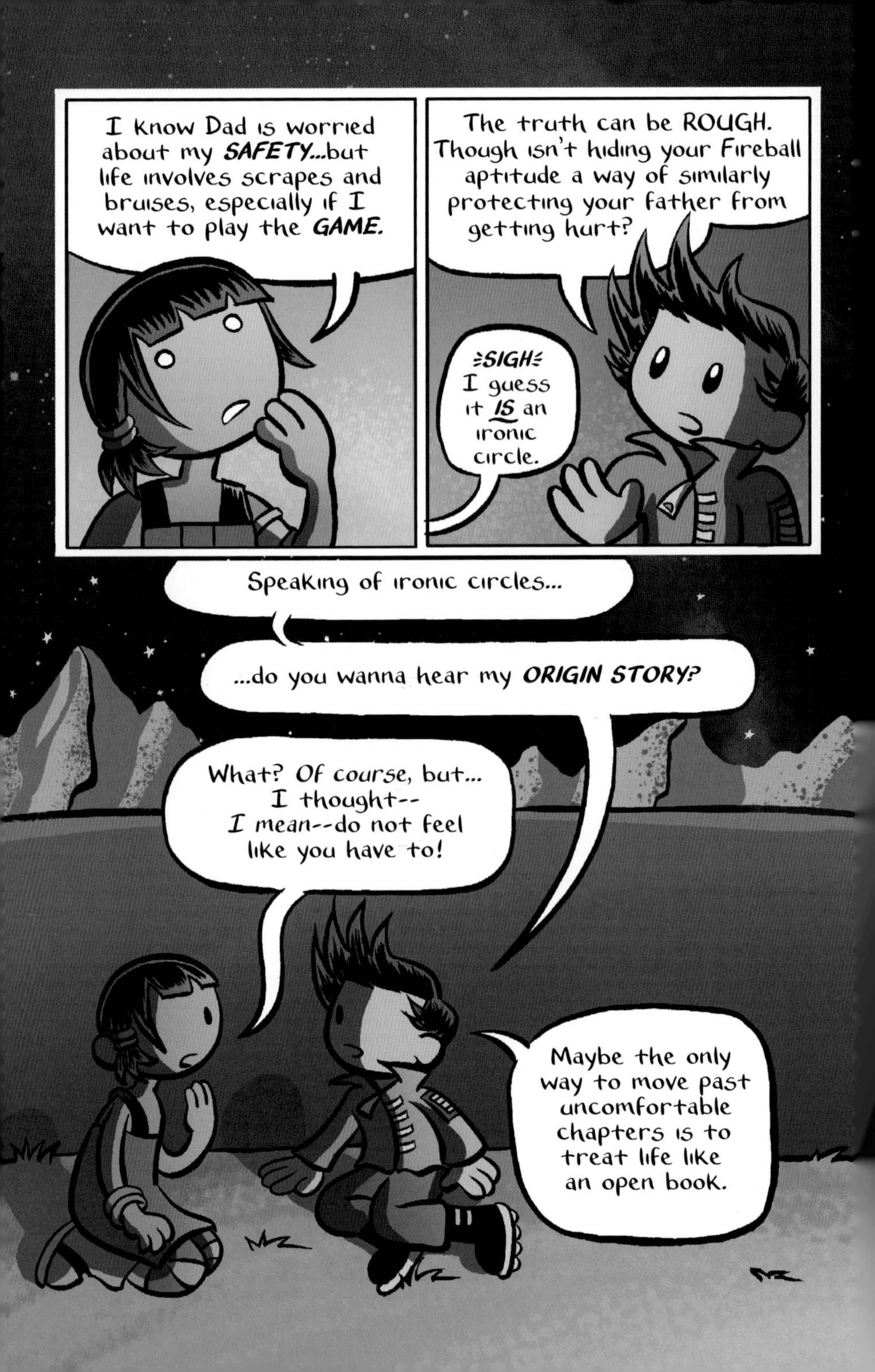
I know Dad is worried about my SAFETY...but life involves scrapes and bruises, especially if I want to play the GAME.
The truth can be ROUGH. Though isn't hiding your Fireball aptitude a way of similarly protecting your father from getting hurt?
SIGH I guess it IS an ironic circle.
Speaking of ironic circles...
...do you wanna hear my ORIGIN STORY?
What? Of course, but... I thought-- I mean--do not feel like you have to!
Maybe the only way to move past uncomfortable chapters is to treat life like an open book.

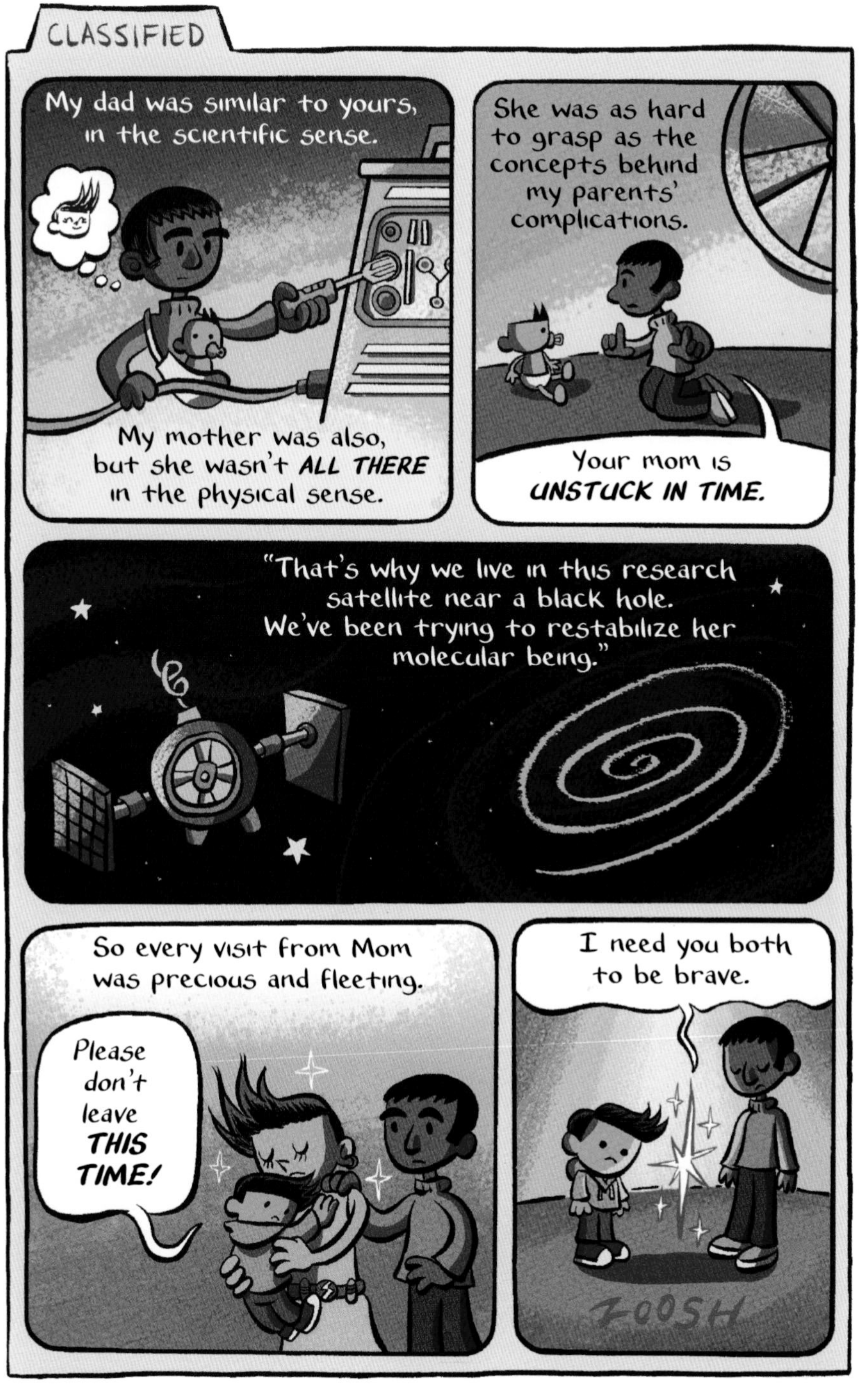
CLASSIFIED
My dad was similar to yours, in the scientific sense.
My mother was also, but she wasn't ALL THERE in the physical sense.
She was as hard to grasp as the concepts behind my parents' complications.
Your mom is UNSTUCK IN TIME.
"That's why we live in this research satellite near a black hole. We've been trying to restabilize her molecular being."
So every visit from Mom was precious and fleeting.
Please don't leave THIS TIME!
I need you both to be brave.
ZOOSH

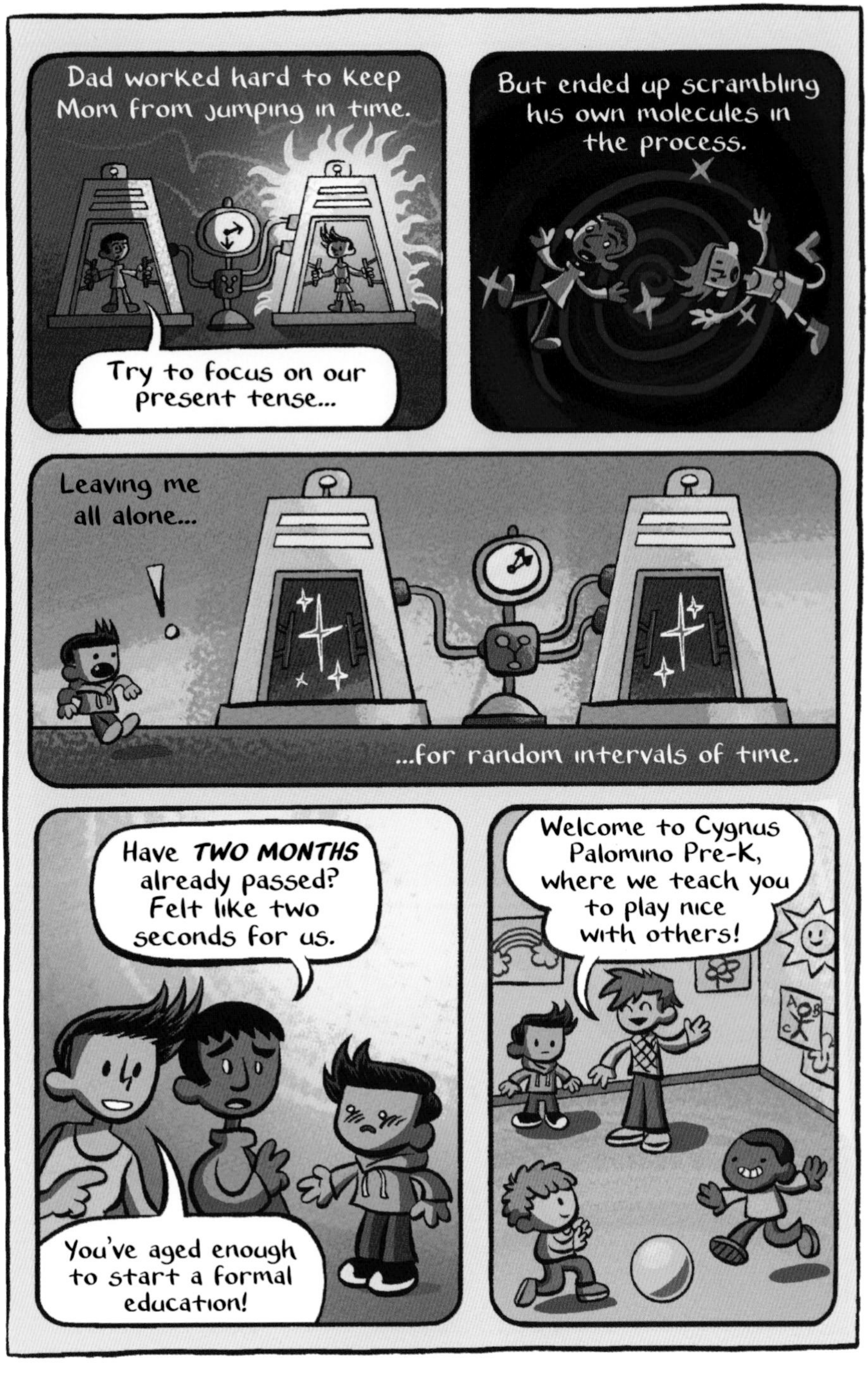

Dad worked hard to keep Mom from jumping in time.
Try to focus on our present tense...
But ended up scrambling his own molecules in the process.
Leaving me all alone...
!
...for random intervals of time.
Have TWO MONTHS already passed? Felt like two seconds for us.
You've aged enough to start a formal education!
Welcome to Cygnus Palomino Pre-K, where we teach you to play nice with others!

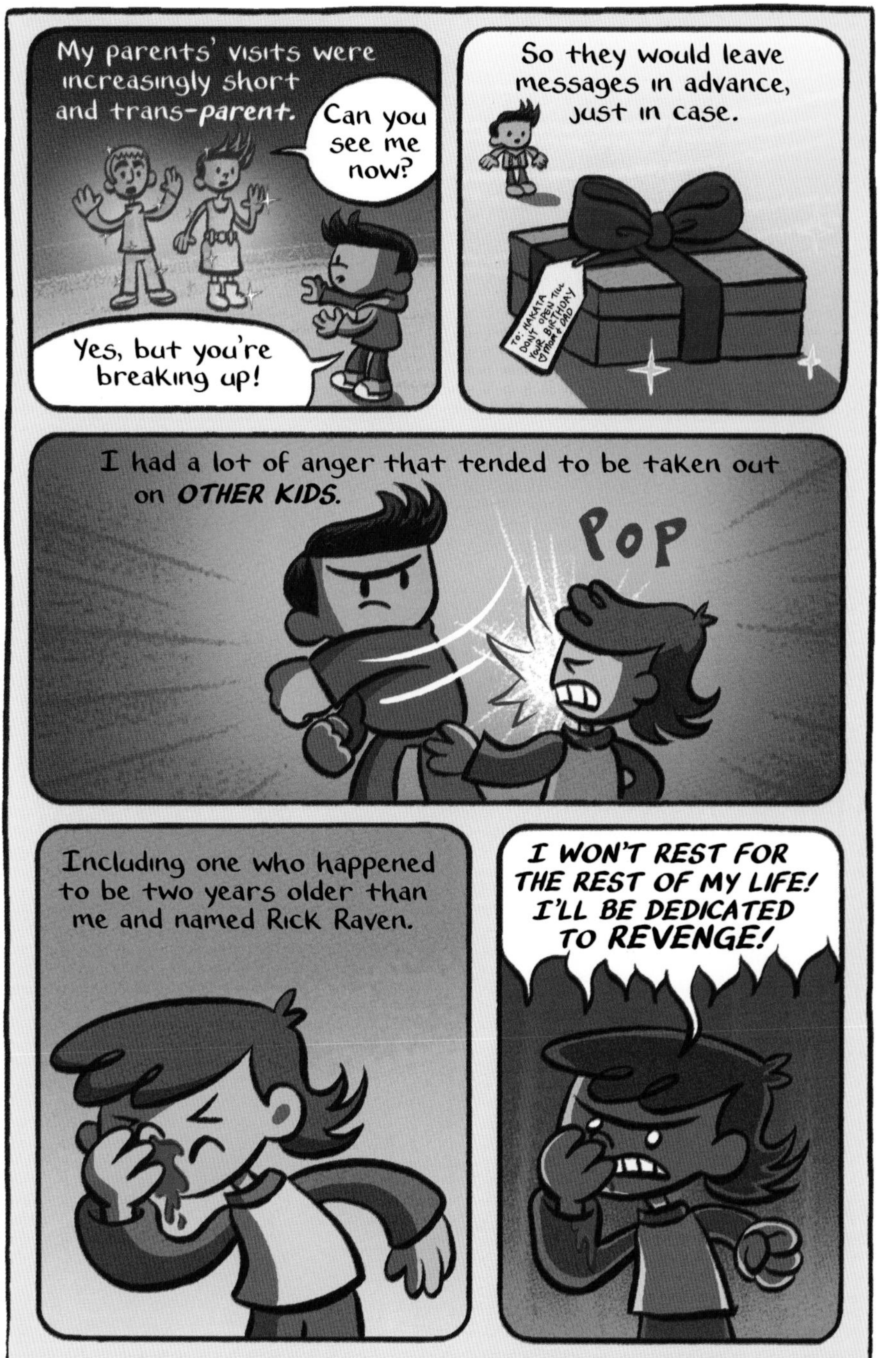
My parents' visits were increasingly short and trans-*parent.*
Can you see me now?
Yes, but you're breaking up!
So they would leave messages in advance, just in case.
TO: HAKATA DON'T OPEN TILL YOUR BIRTHDAY ♡MOM & DAD
I had a lot of anger that tended to be taken out on *OTHER KIDS.*
POP
Including one who happened to be two years older than me and named Rick Raven.
I WON'T REST FOR THE REST OF MY LIFE! I'LL BE DEDICATED TO **REVENGE!**

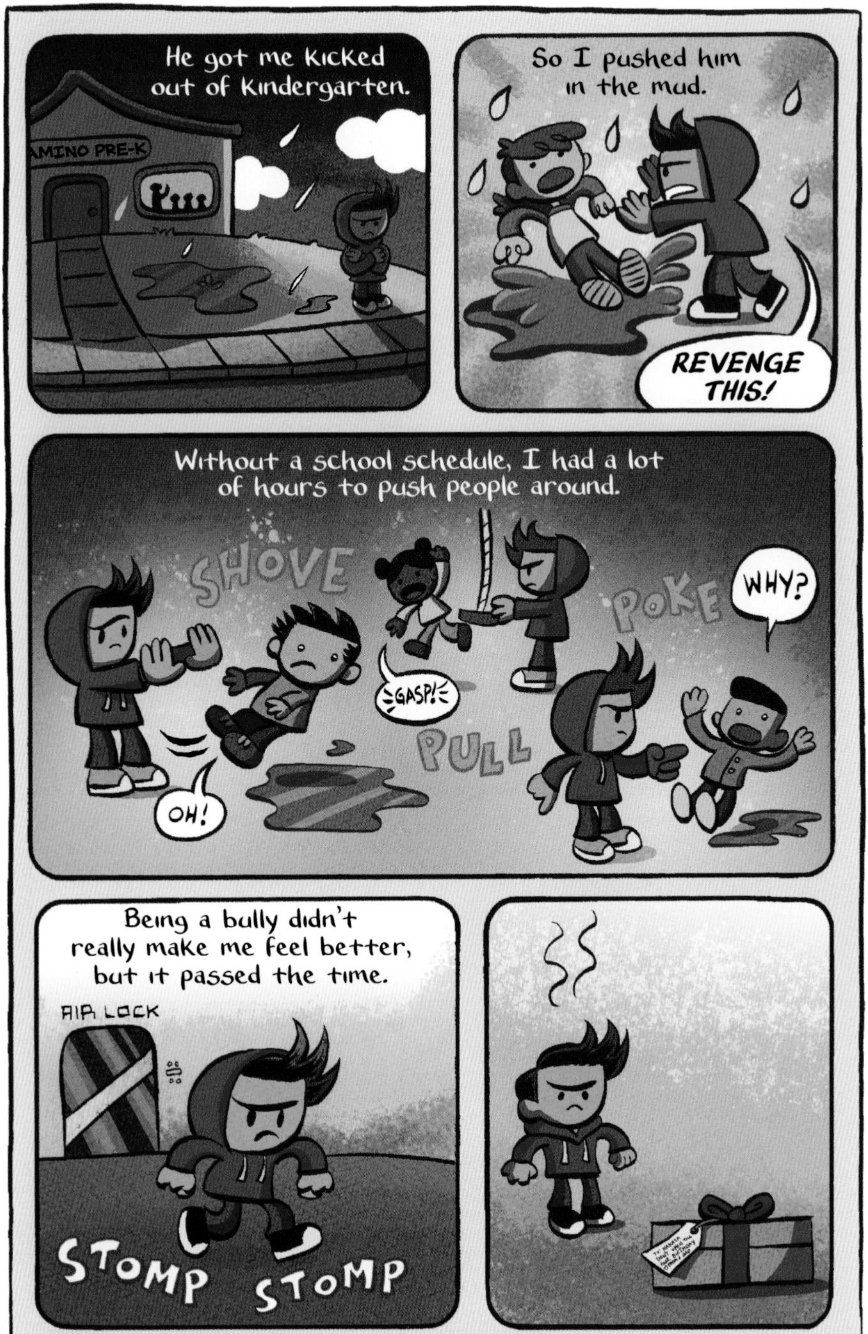
He got me kicked out of kindergarten.
AMINO PRE-K
So I pushed him in the mud.
REVENGE THIS!
Without a school schedule, I had a lot of hours to push people around.
SHOVE
GASP!
POKE
WHY?
OH!
PULL
Being a bully didn't really make me feel better, but it passed the time.
AIR LOCK
STOMP STOMP

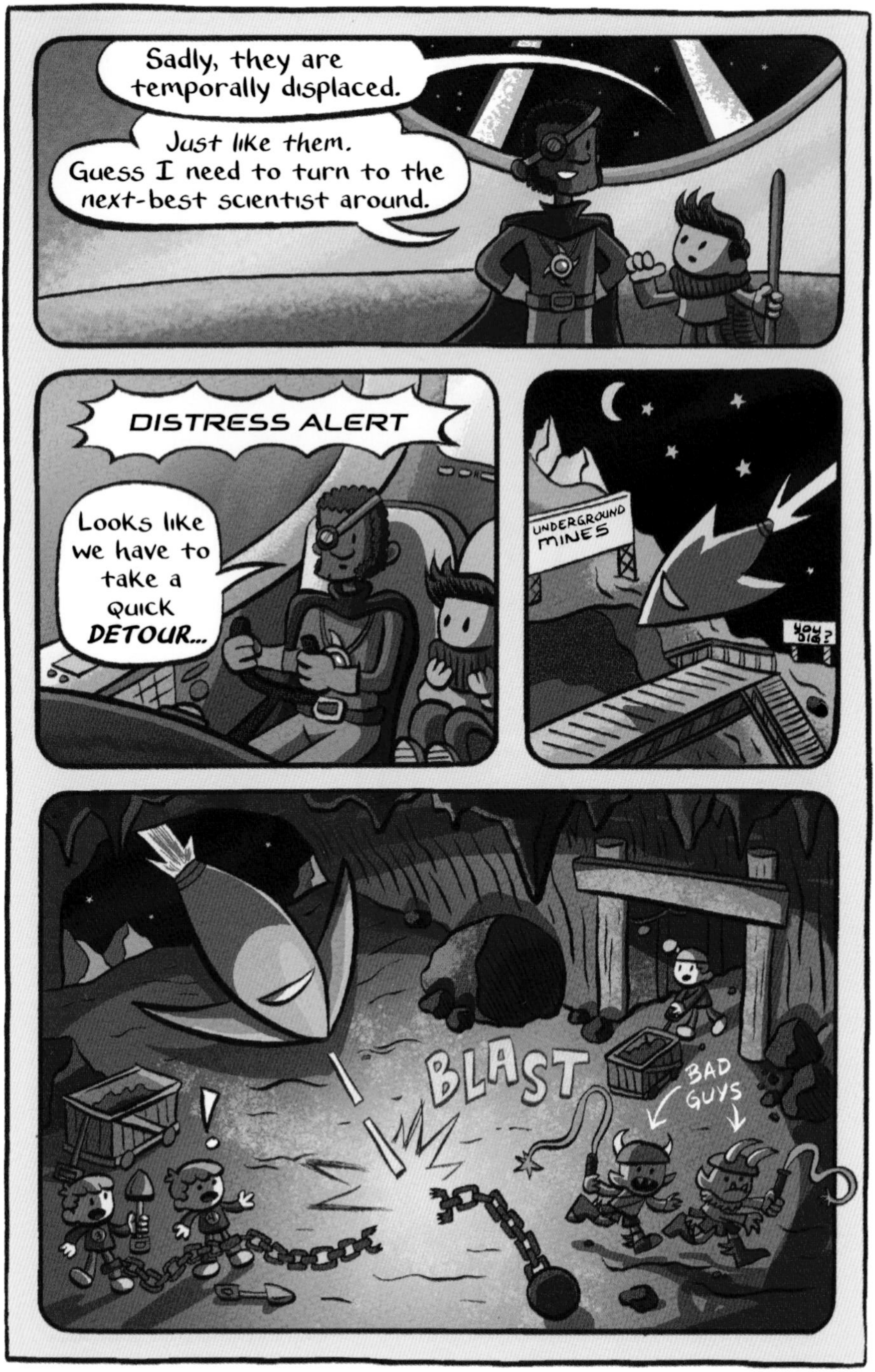
Sadly, they are temporally displaced.
Just like them. Guess I need to turn to the next-best scientist around.
DISTRESS ALERT
Looks like we have to take a quick DETOUR...
UNDERGROUND MINES
YOU DIG?
BLAST
BAD GUYS

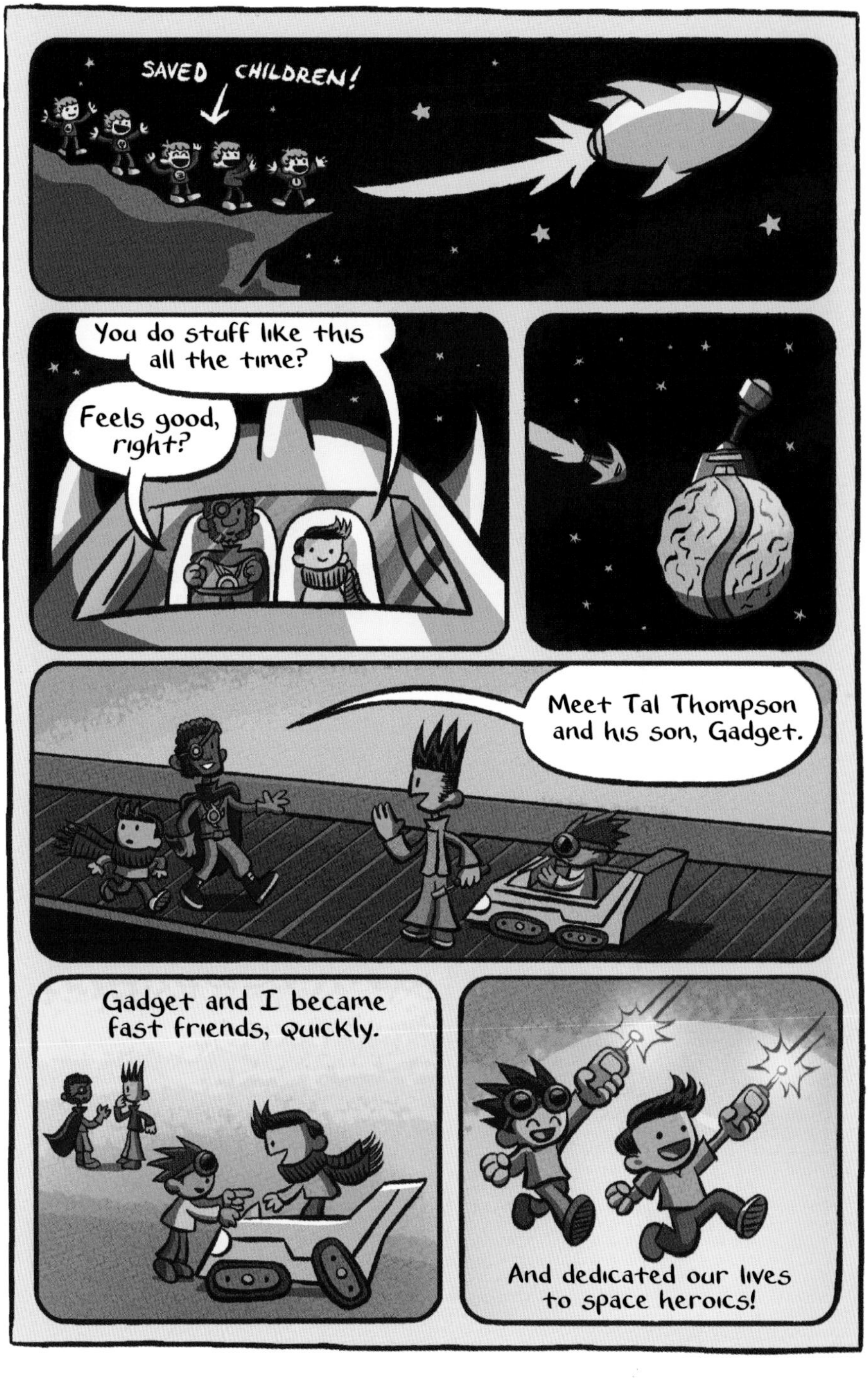

SAVED CHILDREN!
You do stuff like this all the time?
Feels good, right?
Meet Tal Thompson and his son, Gadget.
Gadget and I became fast friends, quickly.
And dedicated our lives to space heroics!

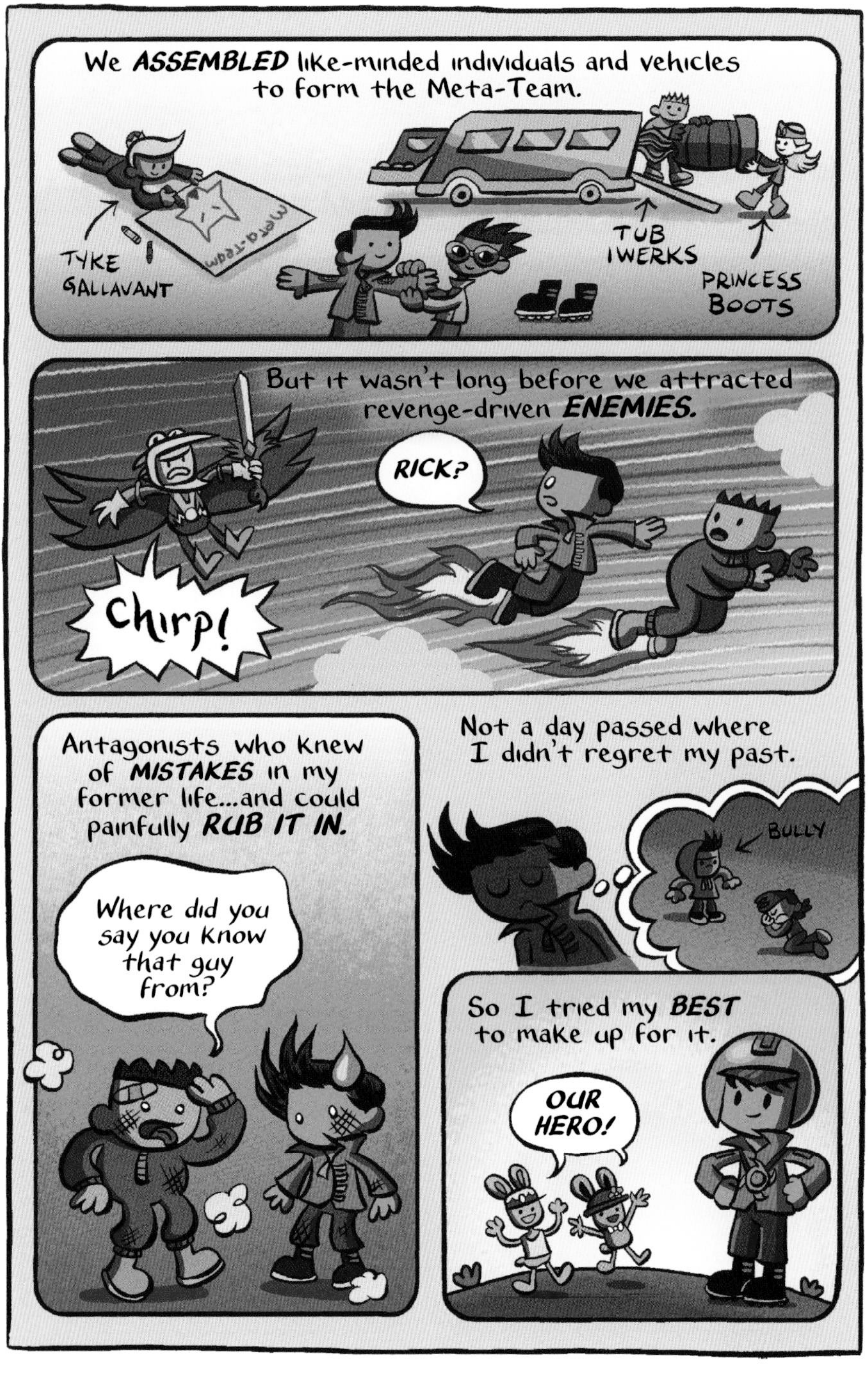
We ASSEMBLED like-minded individuals and vehicles to form the Meta-Team.
META-TEAM
TYKE GALLAVANT
TUB IWERKS
PRINCESS BOOTS
But it wasn't long before we attracted revenge-driven ENEMIES.
RICK?
Chirp!
Antagonists who knew of MISTAKES in my former life...and could painfully RUB IT IN.
Where did you say you know that guy from?
Not a day passed where I didn't regret my past.
BULLY
So I tried my BEST to make up for it.
OUR HERO!

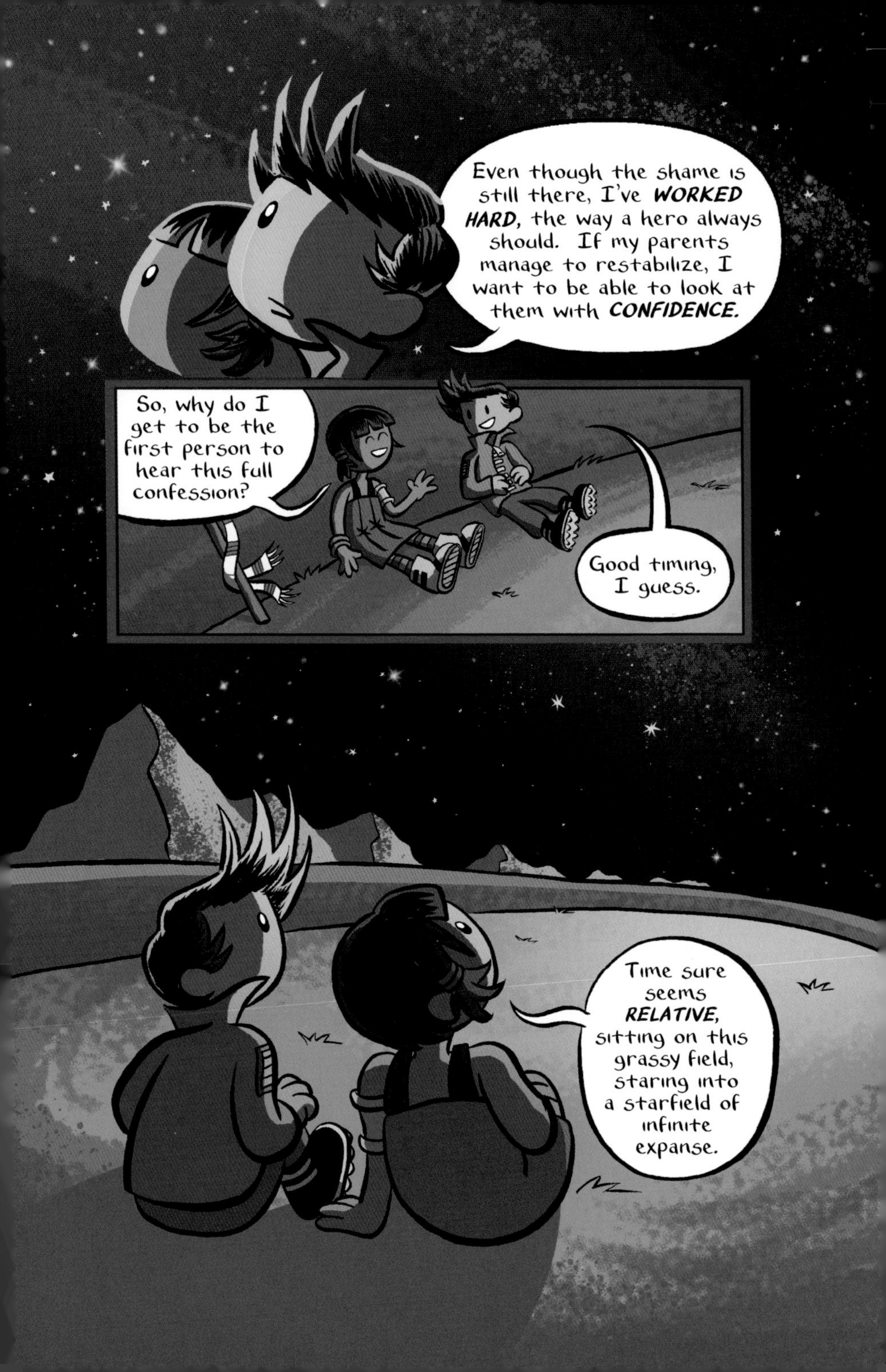
Even though the shame is still there, I've WORKED HARD, the way a hero always should. If my parents manage to restabilize, I want to be able to look at them with CONFIDENCE.
So, why do I get to be the first person to hear this full confession?
Good timing, I guess.
Time sure seems RELATIVE, sitting on this grassy field, staring into a starfield of infinite expanse.

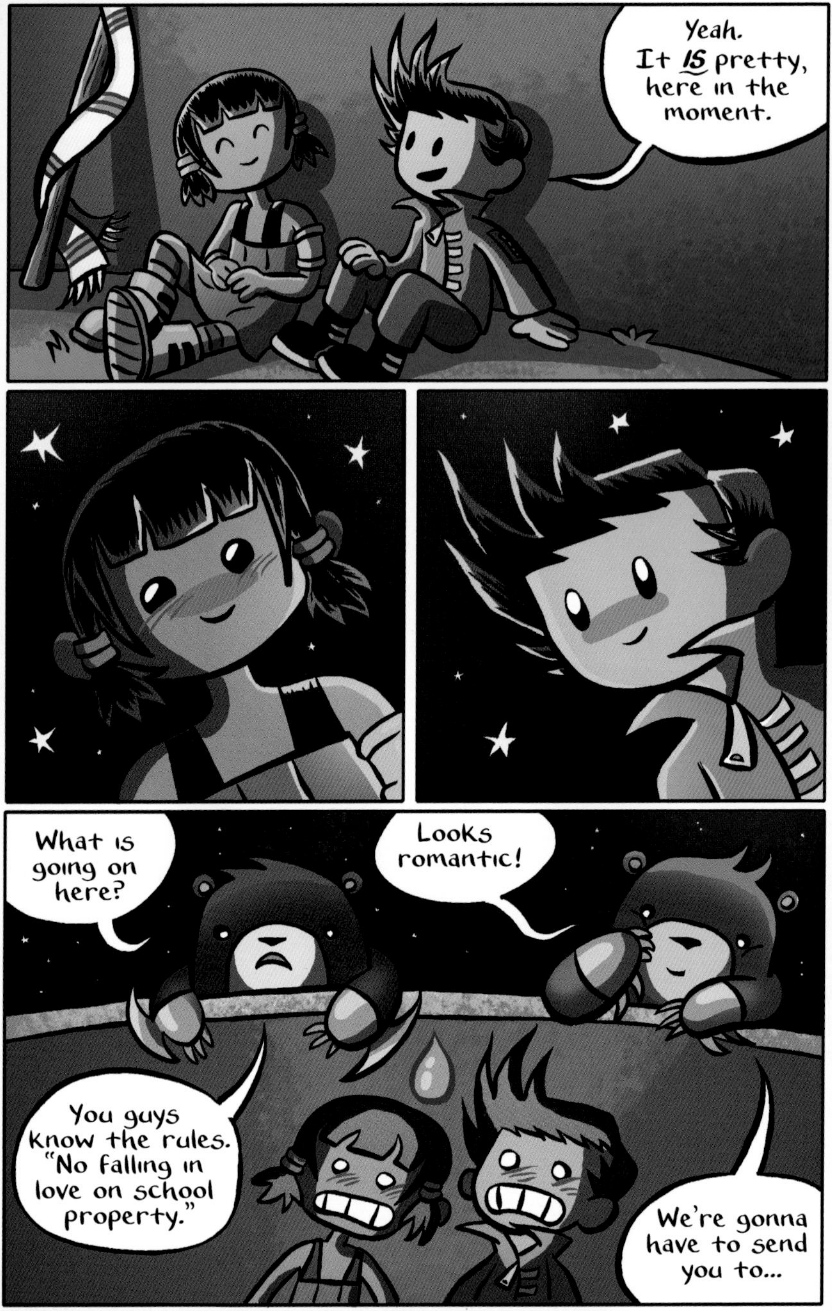

Yeah. It IS pretty, here in the moment.
What is going on here?
Looks romantic!
You guys know the rules. "No falling in love on school property."
We're gonna have to send you to...

DETENTION

Make sure they don't serve in the same cell!

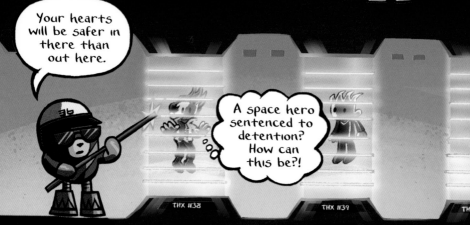

Your hearts will be safer in there than out here.

A space hero sentenced to detention? How can this be?!

THX 1138   THX 1139   THX

PSST--Hey, Soy! Whatcha in fer? I's caught holdin' hands wit a **KID IN THE HALL!** How is d<u>a</u>t a crime?

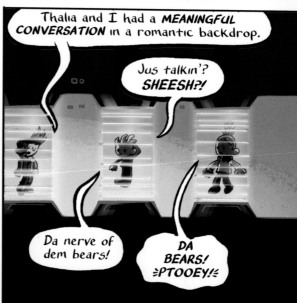

Thalia and I had a **MEANINGFUL CONVERSATION** in a romantic backdrop.

Jus talkin'? **SHEESH?!**

Da nerve of dem bears!

DA BEARS! ≥PTOOEY!≤

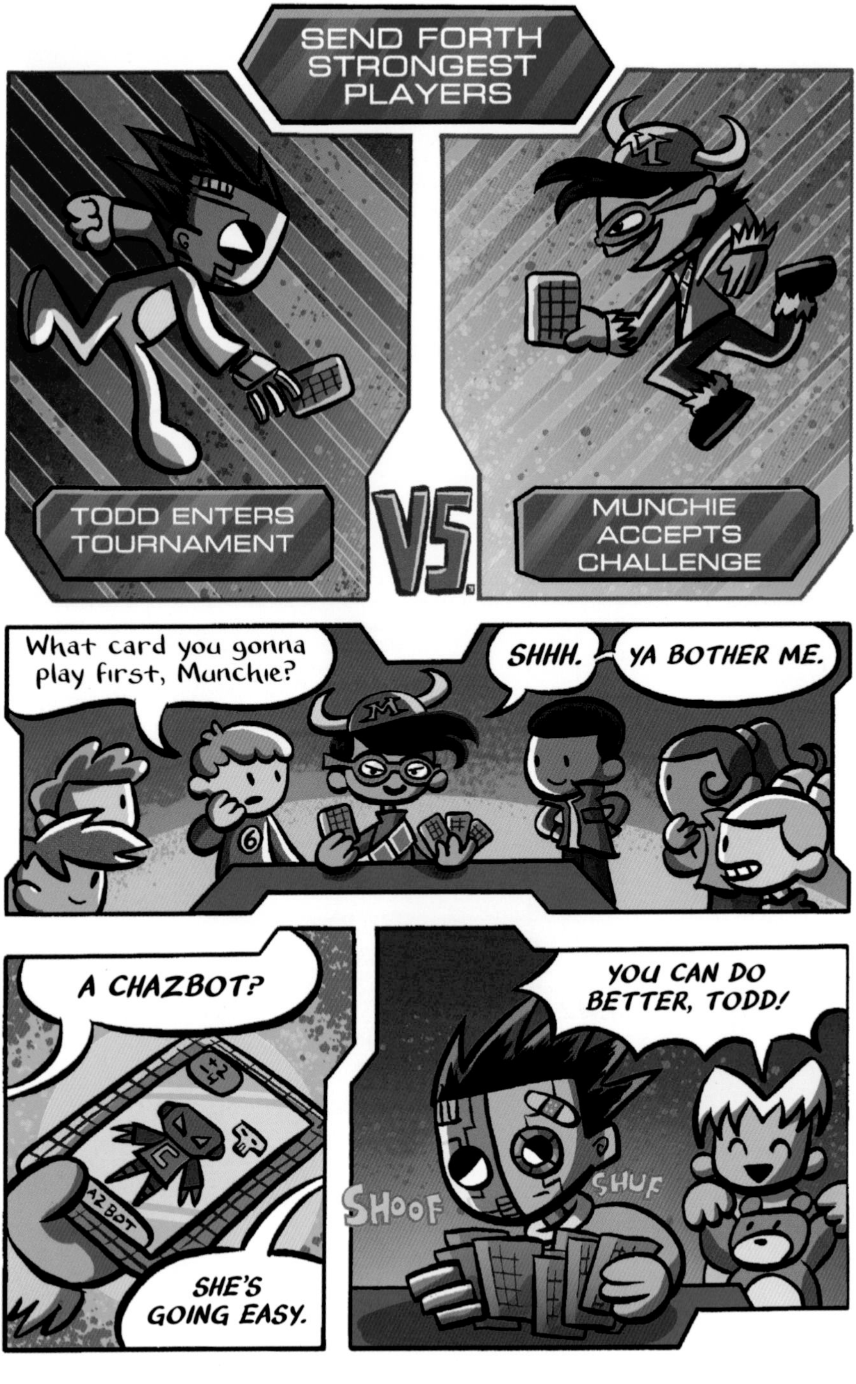
SEND FORTH STRONGEST PLAYERS
TODD ENTERS TOURNAMENT
VS.
MUNCHIE ACCEPTS CHALLENGE
What card you gonna play first, Munchie?
SHHH.
YA BOTHER ME.
A CHAZBOT?
SHE'S GOING EASY.
YOU CAN DO BETTER, TODD!
SHOOF
SHUF

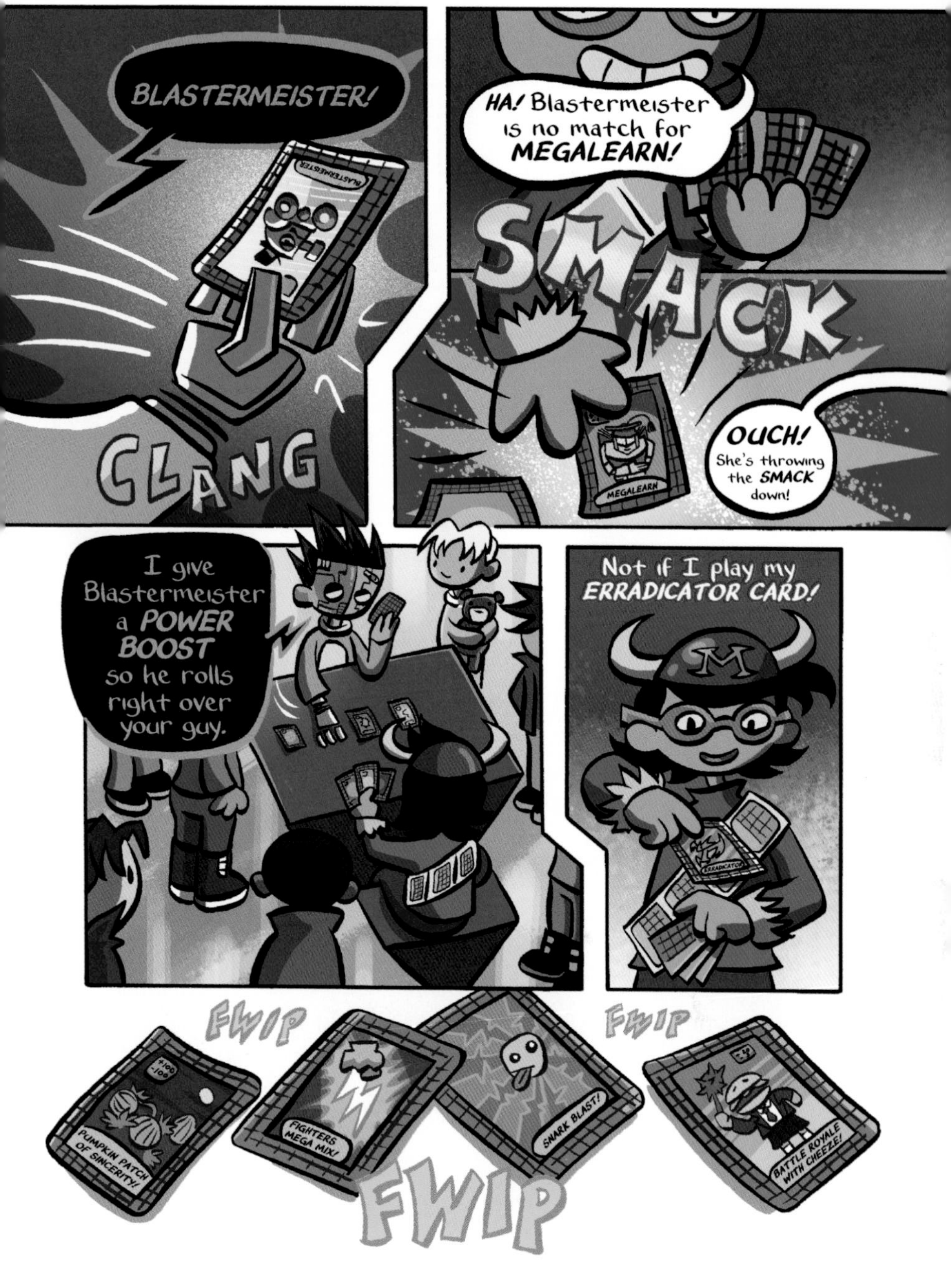
BLASTERMEISTER!
BLASTERMEISTER
CLANG
HA! Blastermeister is no match for MEGALEARN!
SMACK
MEGALEARN
OUCH! She's throwing the SMACK down!
I give Blastermeister a POWER BOOST so he rolls right over your guy.
Not if I play my ERRADICATOR CARD!
FWIP
FWIP
+100
-100
PUMPKIN PATCH OF SINCERITY!
FIGHTERS MEGA MIX!
SNARK BLAST!
BATTLE ROYALE WITH CHEEZE!
FWIP

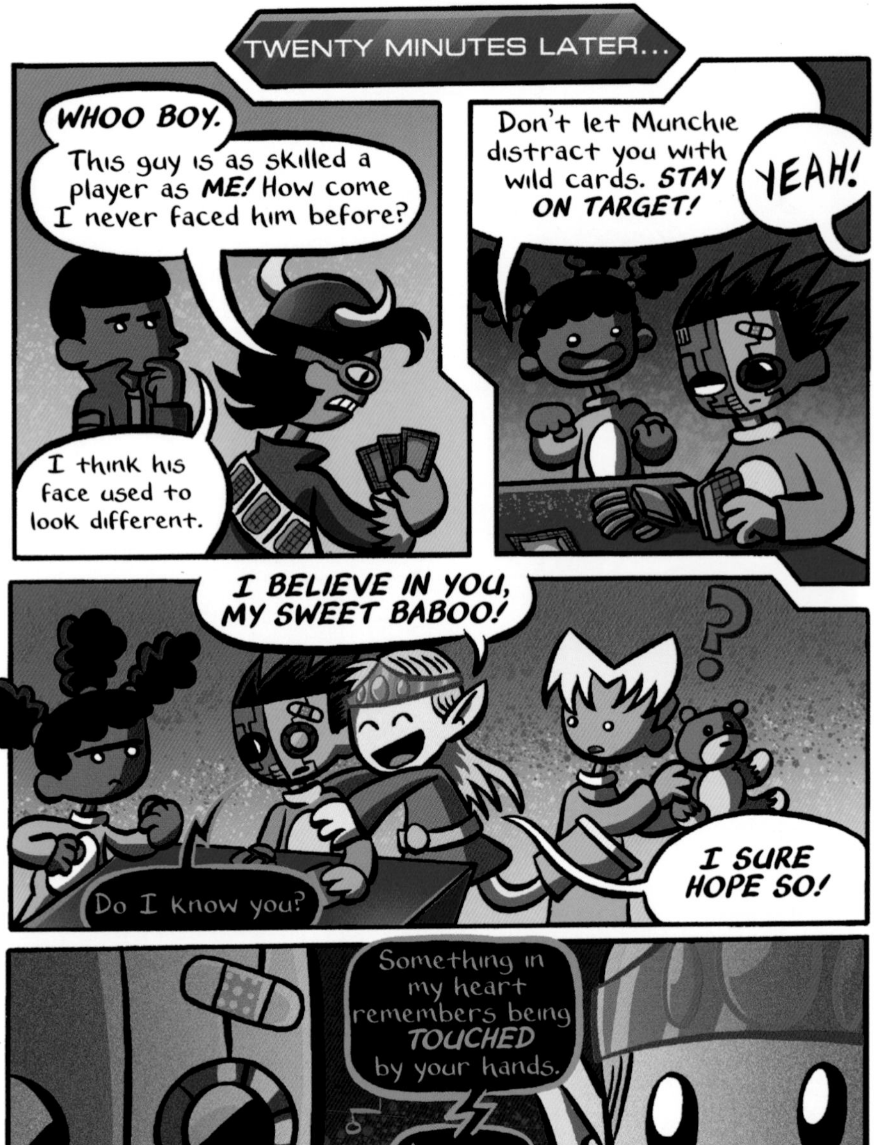
TWENTY MINUTES LATER...
WHOO BOY.
This guy is as skilled a player as ME! How come I never faced him before?
I think his face used to look different.
Don't let Munchie distract you with wild cards. STAY ON TARGET!
YEAH!
I BELIEVE IN YOU, MY SWEET BABOO!
?
Do I know you?
I SURE HOPE SO!
Something in my heart remembers being TOUCHED by your hands.
Are you... Princess Boots?
Why not?

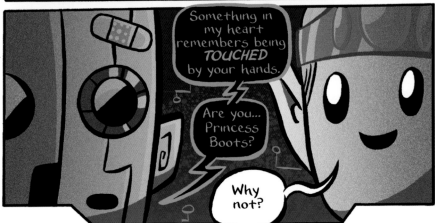

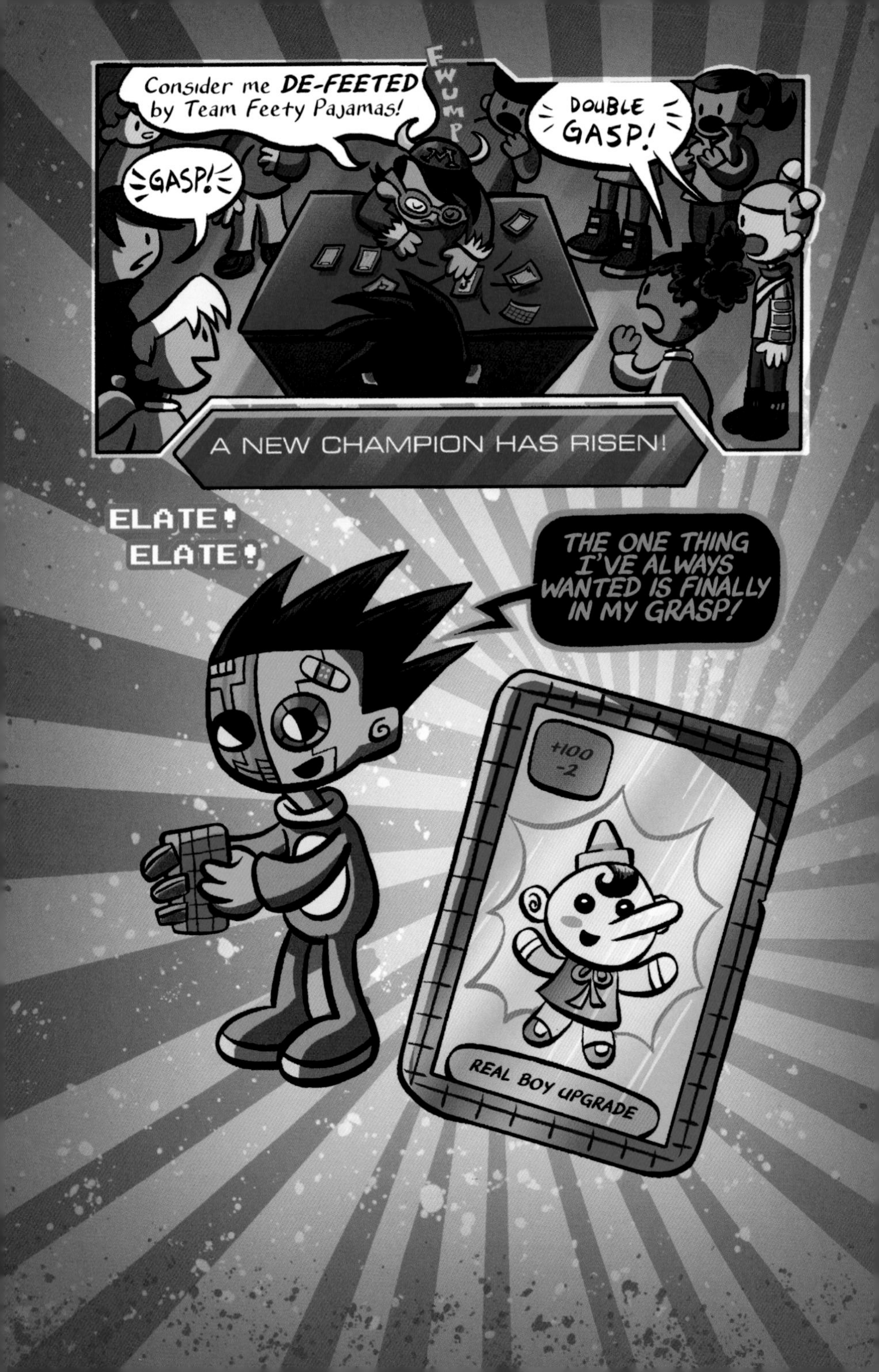

Consider me DE-FEETED by Team Feety Pajamas!
FWUMP
GASP!
DOUBLE GASP!
A NEW CHAMPION HAS RISEN!
ELATE!
ELATE!
THE ONE THING I'VE ALWAYS WANTED IS FINALLY IN MY GRASP!
+100
-2
REAL BOY UPGRADE

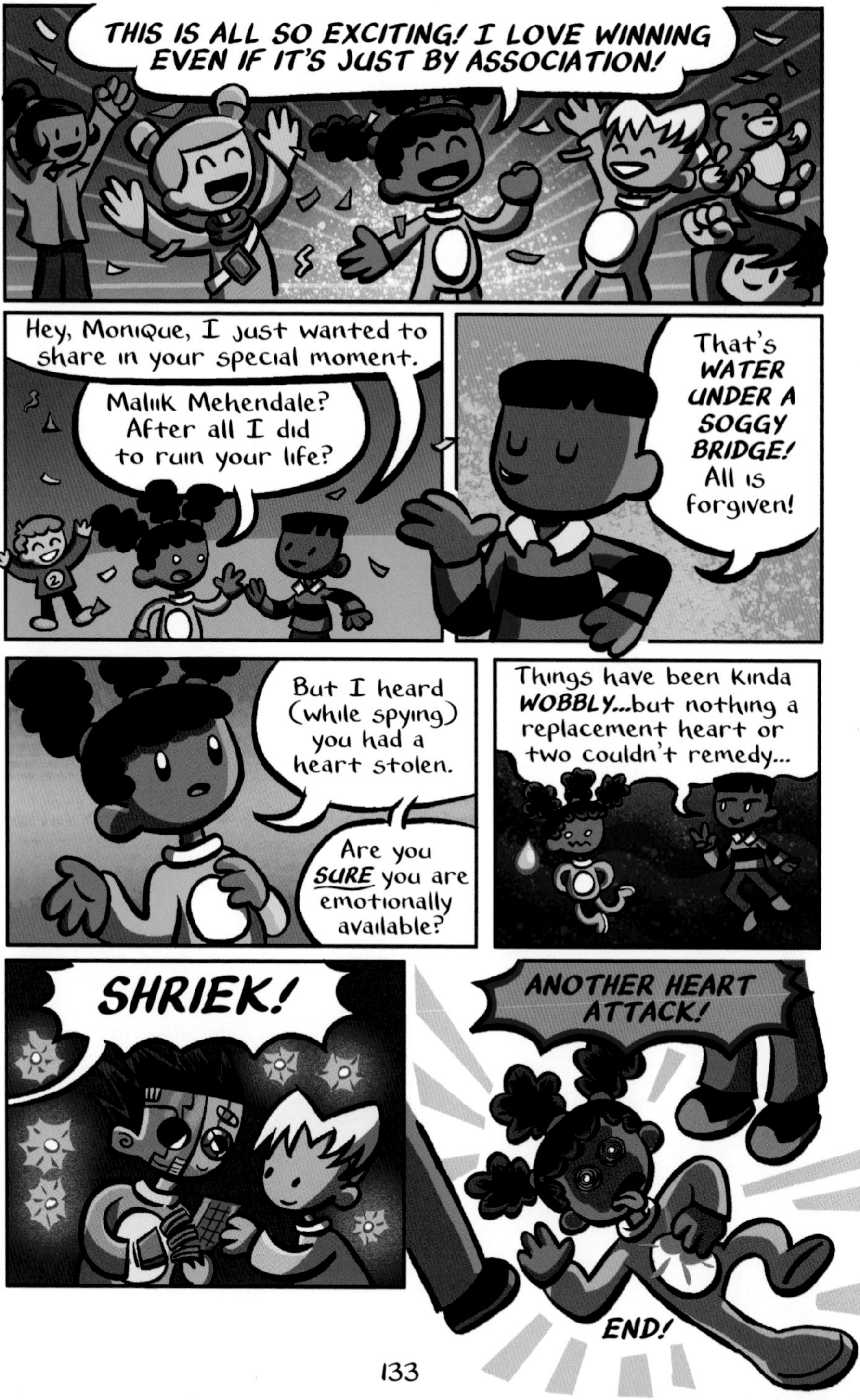
THIS IS ALL SO EXCITING! I LOVE WINNING EVEN IF IT'S JUST BY ASSOCIATION!
Hey, Monique, I just wanted to share in your special moment.
Malik Mehendale? After all I did to ruin your life?
That's WATER UNDER A SOGGY BRIDGE! All is forgiven!
But I heard (while spying) you had a heart stolen.
Are you SURE you are emotionally available?
Things have been kinda WOBBLY...but nothing a replacement heart or two couldn't remedy...
SHRIEK!
ANOTHER HEART ATTACK!
END!

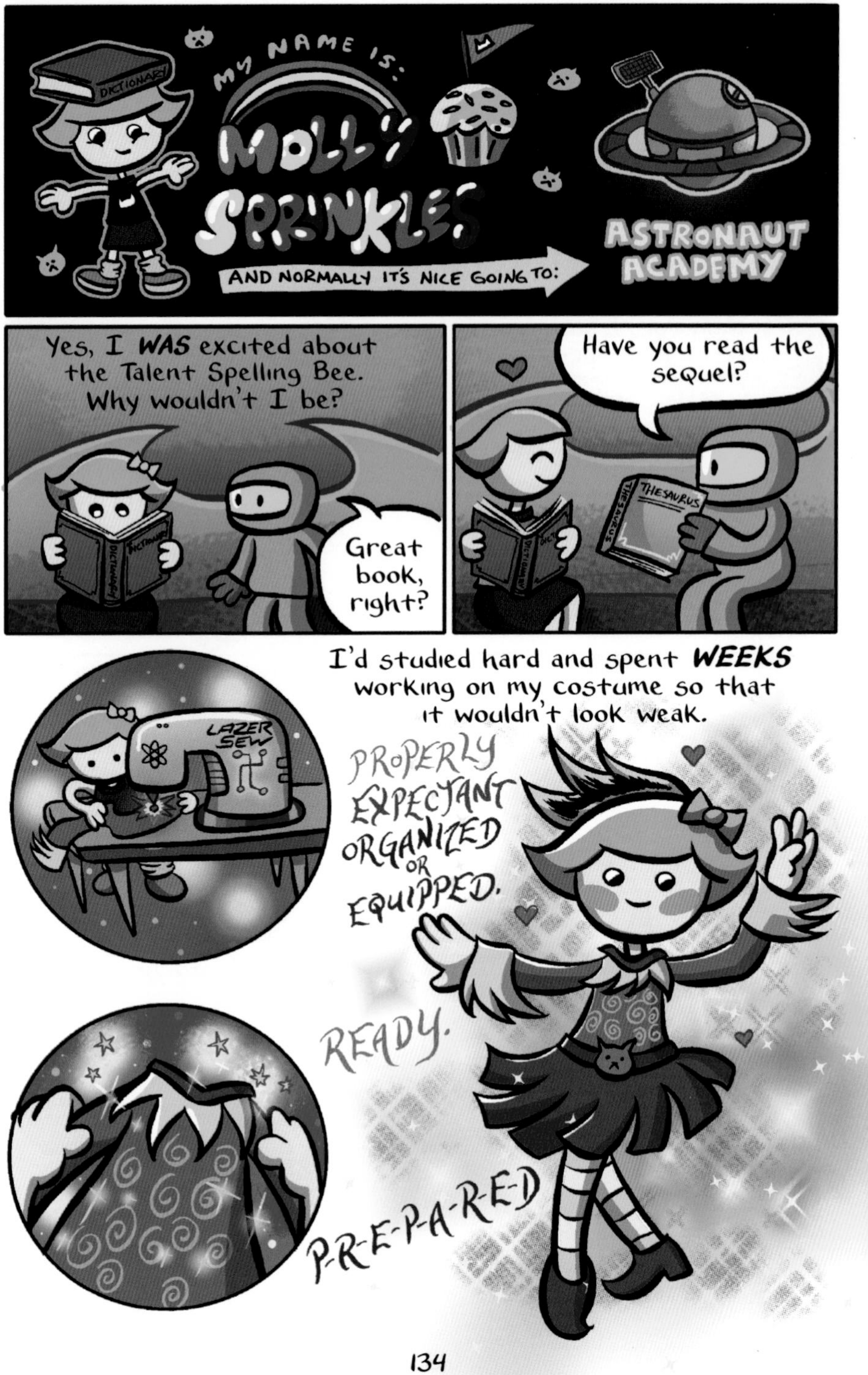

MY NAME IS:
MOLLY SPRINKLES
AND NORMALLY IT'S NICE GOING TO:
ASTRONAUT ACADEMY
DICTIONARY
Yes, I WAS excited about the Talent Spelling Bee. Why wouldn't I be?
Great book, right?
Have you read the sequel?
THESAURUS
I'd studied hard and spent WEEKS working on my costume so that it wouldn't look weak.
LAZER SEW
PROPERLY
EXPECTANT
ORGANIZED
OR
EQUIPPED.
READY.
P-R-E-P-A-R-E-D

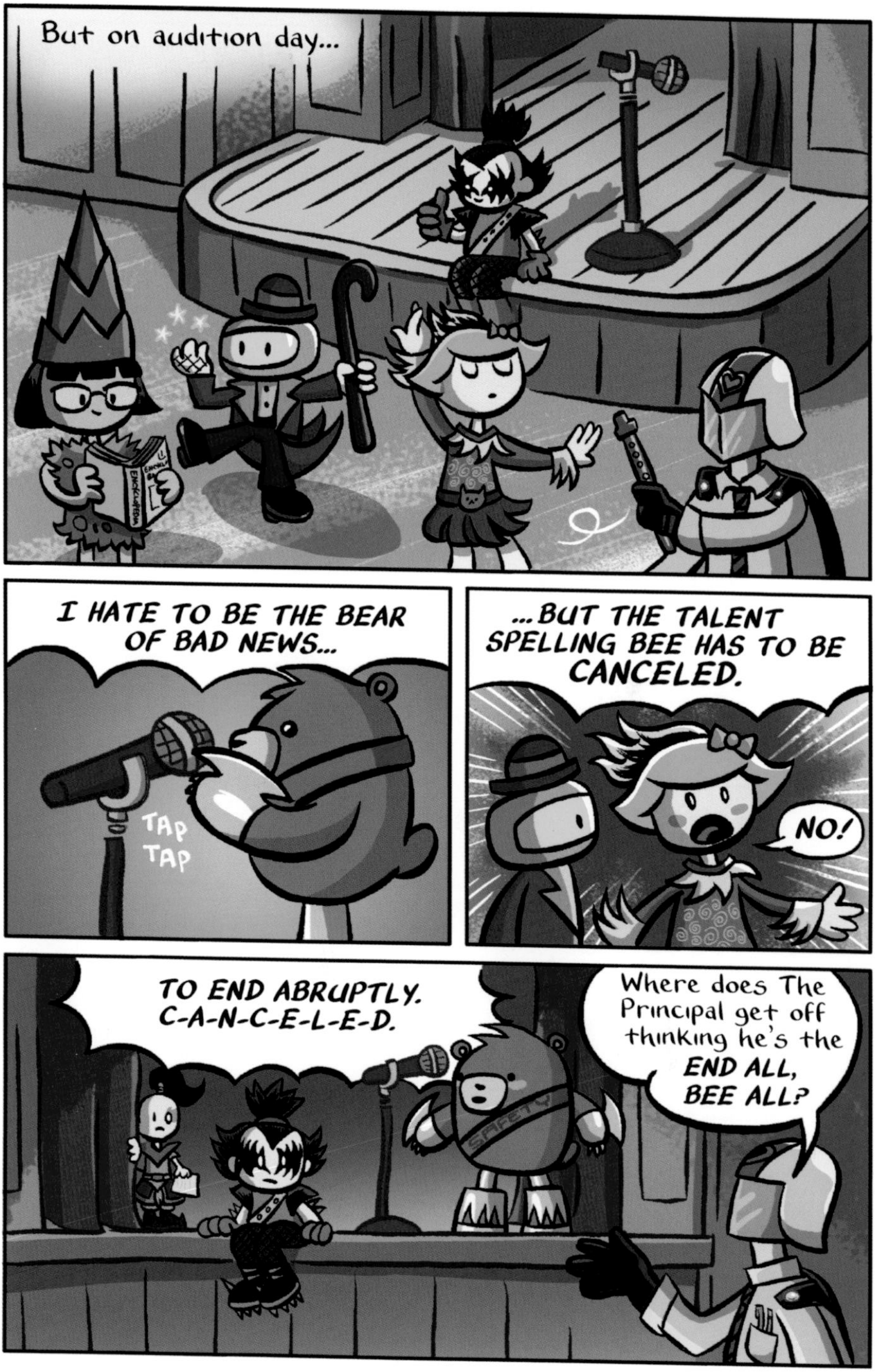

But on audition day...
ENCYCLOPEDIA
I HATE TO BE THE BEAR OF BAD NEWS...
TAP TAP
...BUT THE TALENT SPELLING BEE HAS TO BE CANCELED.
NO!
TO END ABRUPTLY. C-A-N-C-E-L-E-D.
Where does The Principal get off thinking he's the END ALL, BEE ALL?
SAFETY

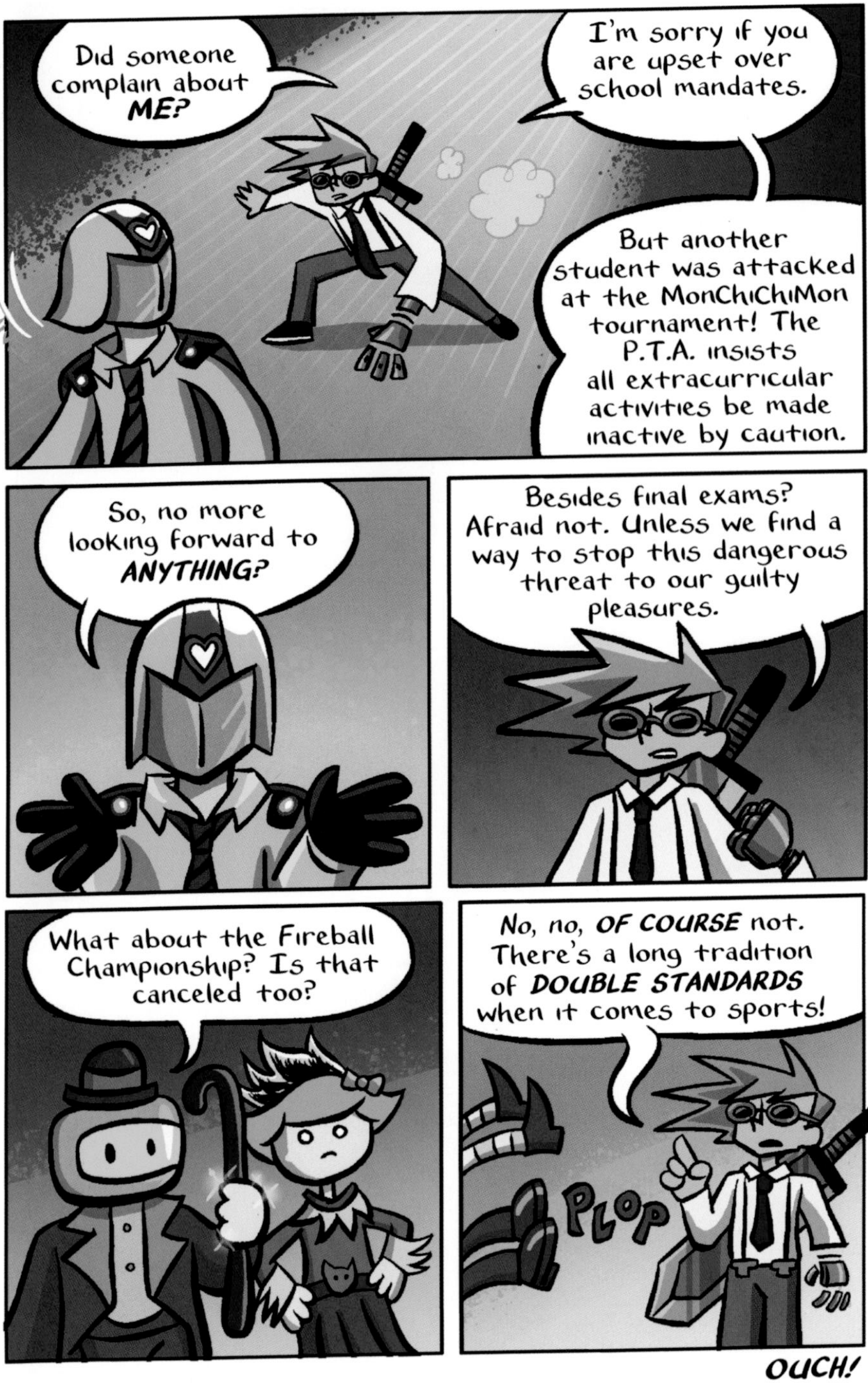
Did someone complain about ME?
I'm sorry if you are upset over school mandates.
But another student was attacked at the MonChiChiMon tournament! The P.T.A. insists all extracurricular activities be made inactive by caution.
So, no more looking forward to ANYTHING?
Besides final exams? Afraid not. Unless we find a way to stop this dangerous threat to our guilty pleasures.
What about the Fireball Championship? Is that canceled too?
No, no, OF COURSE not. There's a long tradition of DOUBLE STANDARDS when it comes to sports!
PLOP
OUCH!

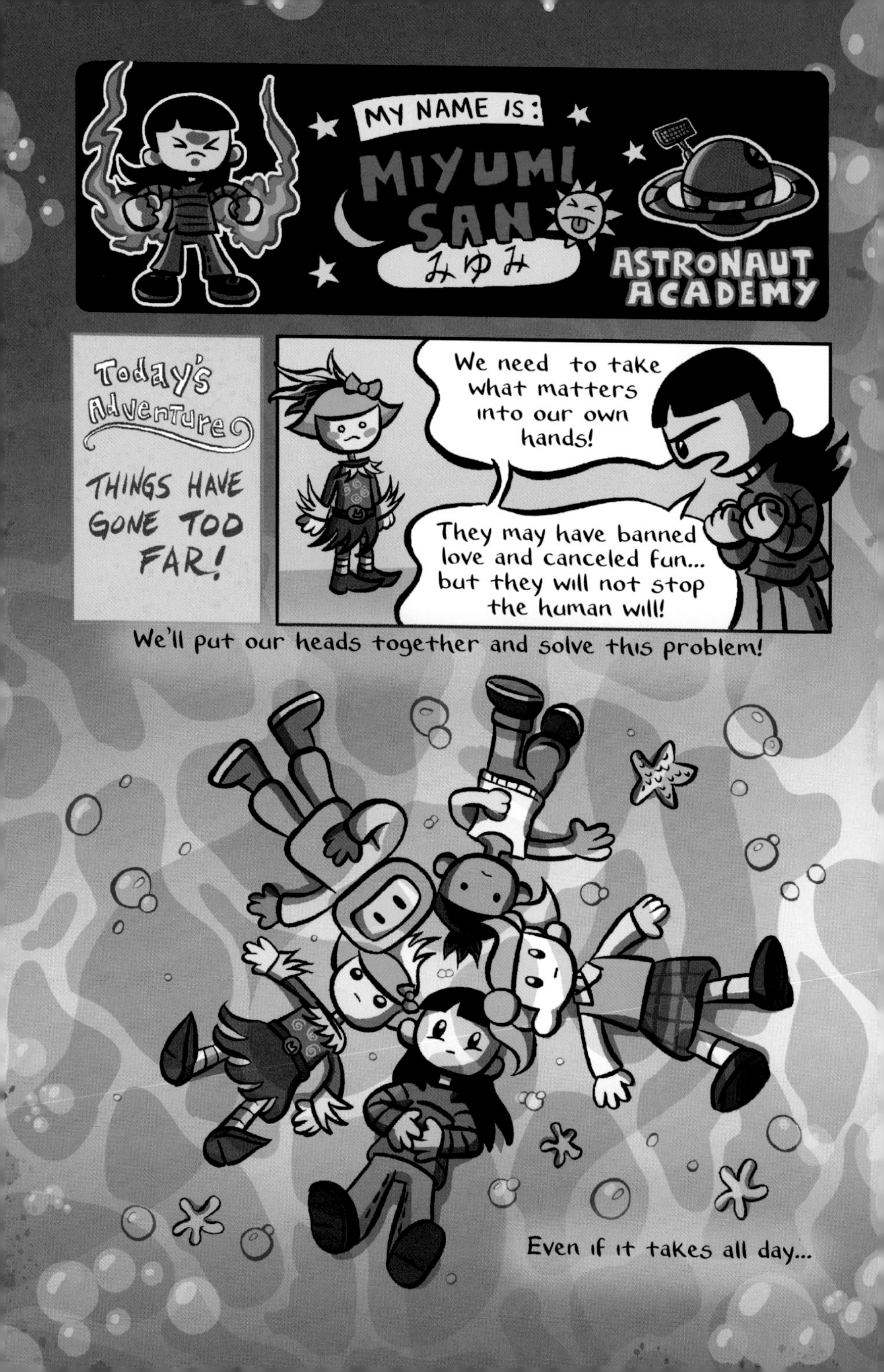

MY NAME IS:
MIYUMI SAN
みゆみ
ASTRONAUT ACADEMY
Today's Adventure
THINGS HAVE GONE TOO FAR!
We need to take what matters into our own hands!
They may have banned love and canceled fun... but they will not stop the human will!
We'll put our heads together and solve this problem!
Even if it takes all day...

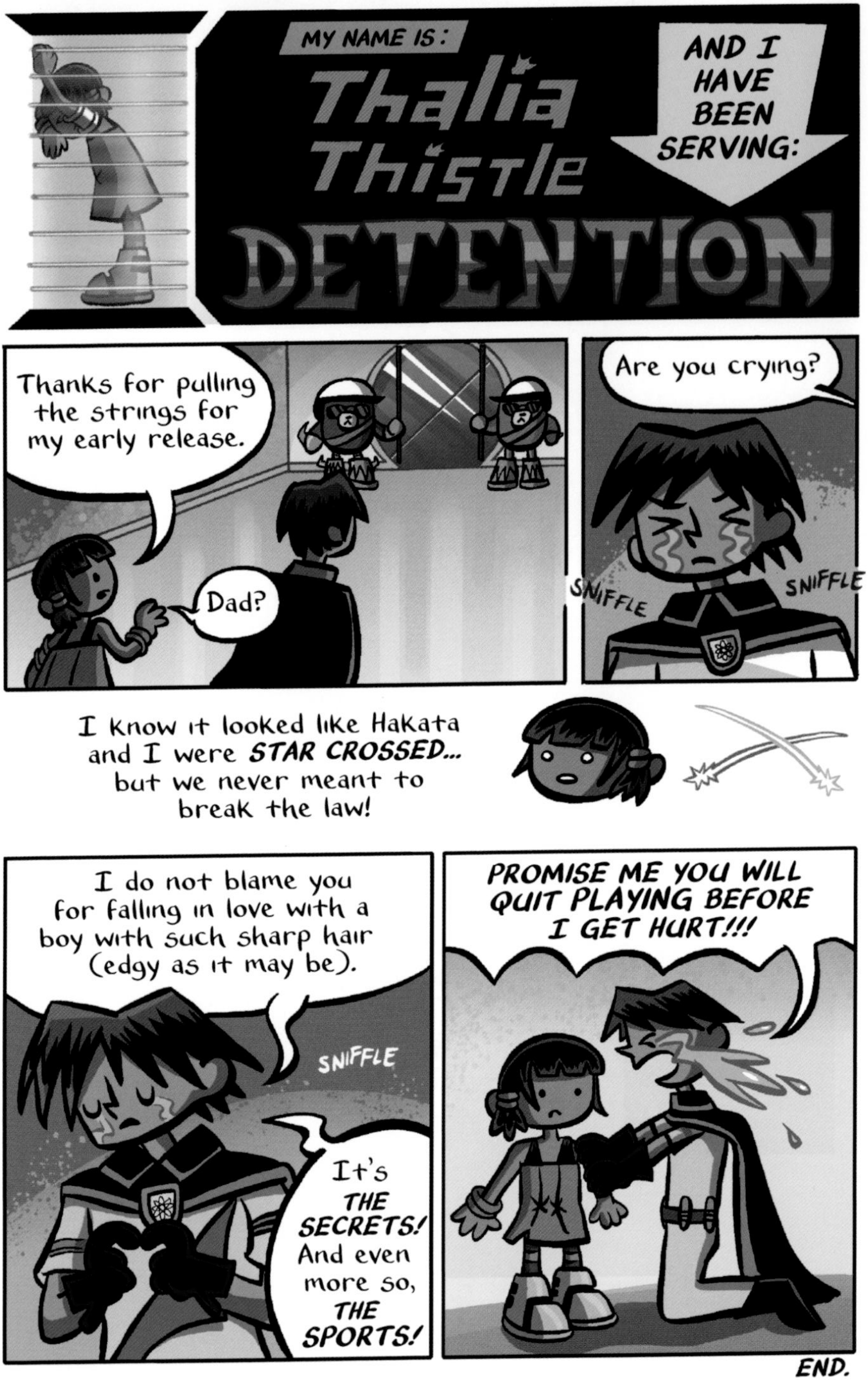
MY NAME IS:
Thalia Thistle
AND I HAVE BEEN SERVING:
DETENTION
Thanks for pulling the strings for my early release.
Dad?
Are you crying?
SNIFFLE
SNIFFLE
I know it looked like Hakata and I were STAR CROSSED... but we never meant to break the law!
I do not blame you for falling in love with a boy with such sharp hair (edgy as it may be).
SNIFFLE
It's THE SECRETS! And even more so, THE SPORTS!
PROMISE ME YOU WILL QUIT PLAYING BEFORE I GET HURT!!!
END.

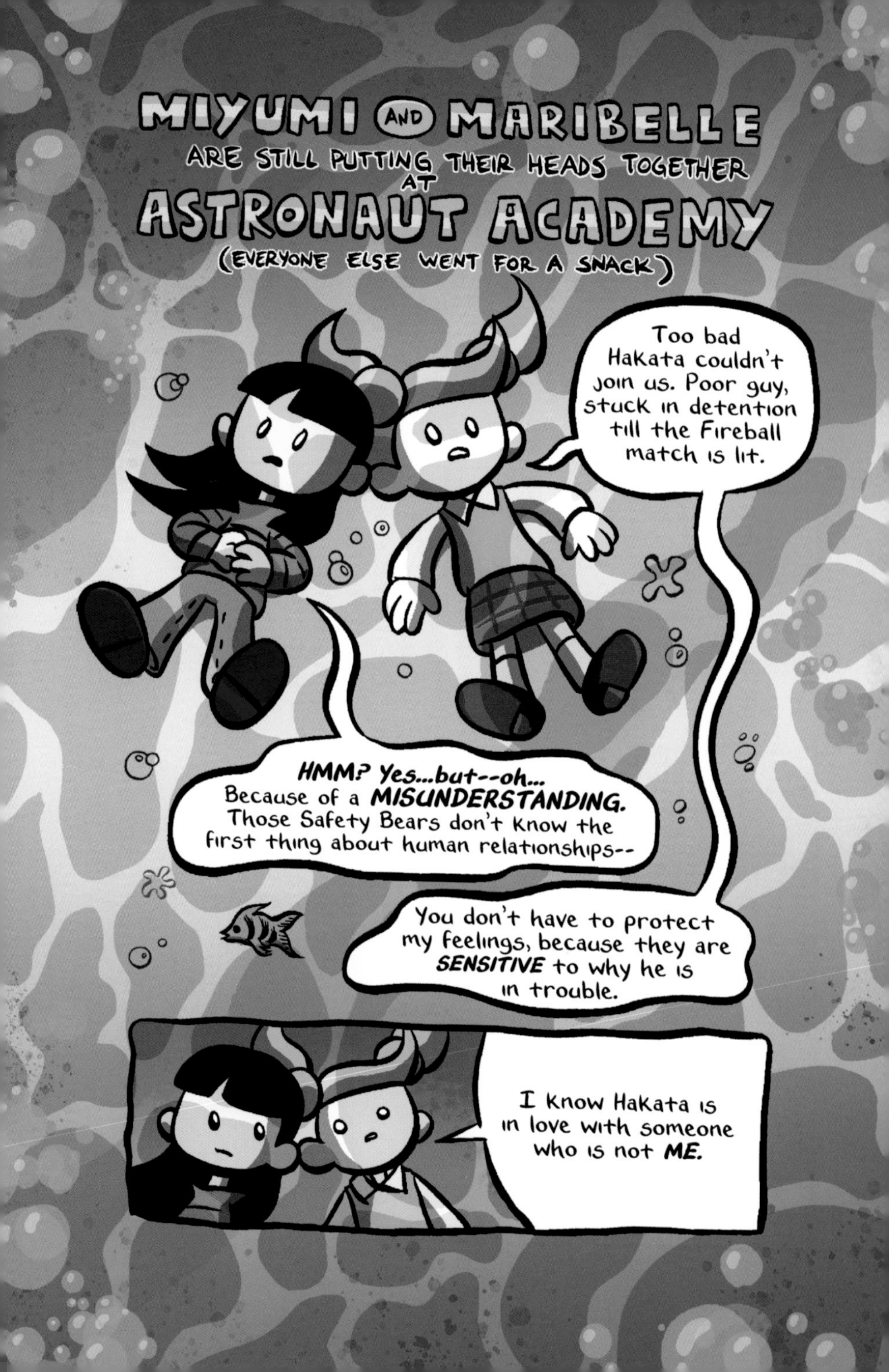
MIYUMI AND MARIBELLE
ARE STILL PUTTING THEIR HEADS TOGETHER AT
ASTRONAUT ACADEMY
(EVERYONE ELSE WENT FOR A SNACK)
Too bad Hakata couldn't join us. Poor guy, stuck in detention till the Fireball match is lit.
HMM? Yes...but--oh... Because of a MISUNDERSTANDING. Those Safety Bears don't know the first thing about human relationships--
You don't have to protect my feelings, because they are SENSITIVE to why he is in trouble.
I know Hakata is in love with someone who is not ME.

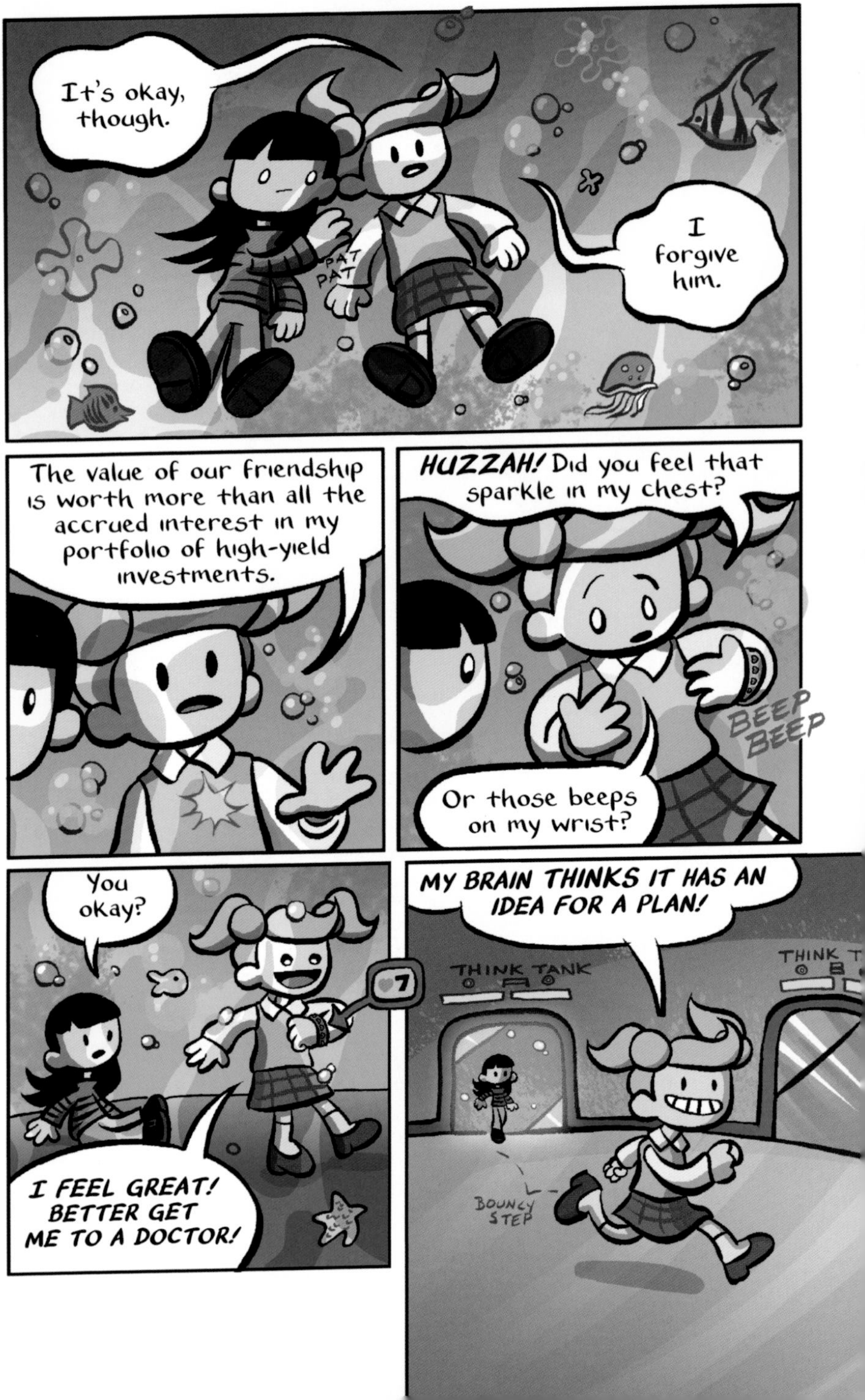
It's okay, though.
PAT PAT
I forgive him.
The value of our friendship is worth more than all the accrued interest in my portfolio of high-yield investments.
HUZZAH! Did you feel that sparkle in my chest?
BEEP BEEP
Or those beeps on my wrist?
You okay?
7
I FEEL GREAT! BETTER GET ME TO A DOCTOR!
MY BRAIN THINKS IT HAS AN IDEA FOR A PLAN!
THINK TANK
BOUNCY STEP

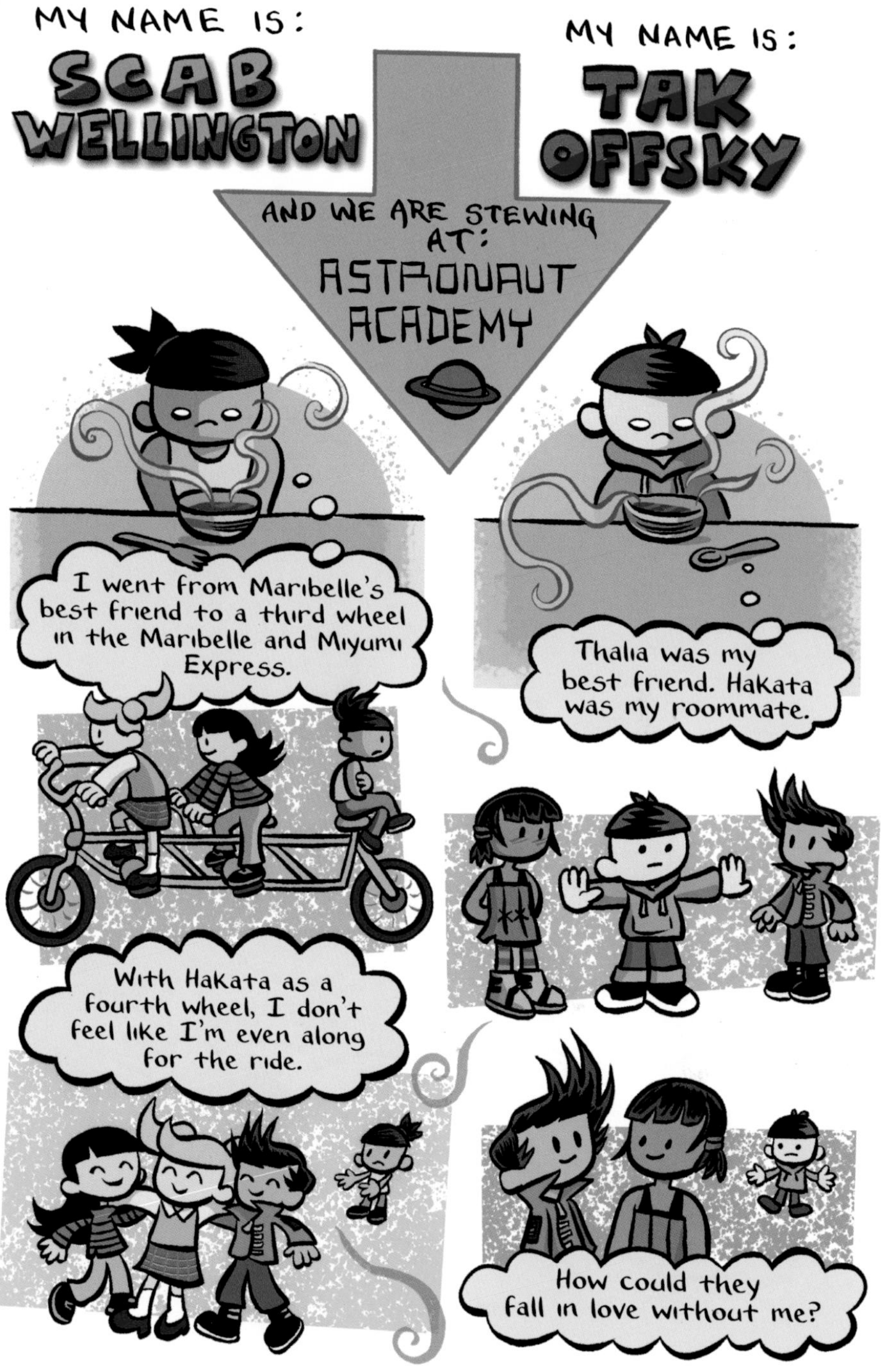
MY NAME IS:
SCAB WELLINGTON
MY NAME IS:
TAK OFFSKY
AND WE ARE STEWING AT:
ASTRONAUT ACADEMY
I went from Maribelle's best friend to a third wheel in the Maribelle and Miyumi Express.
Thalia was my best friend. Hakata was my roommate.
With Hakata as a fourth wheel, I don't feel like I'm even along for the ride.
How could they fall in love without me?

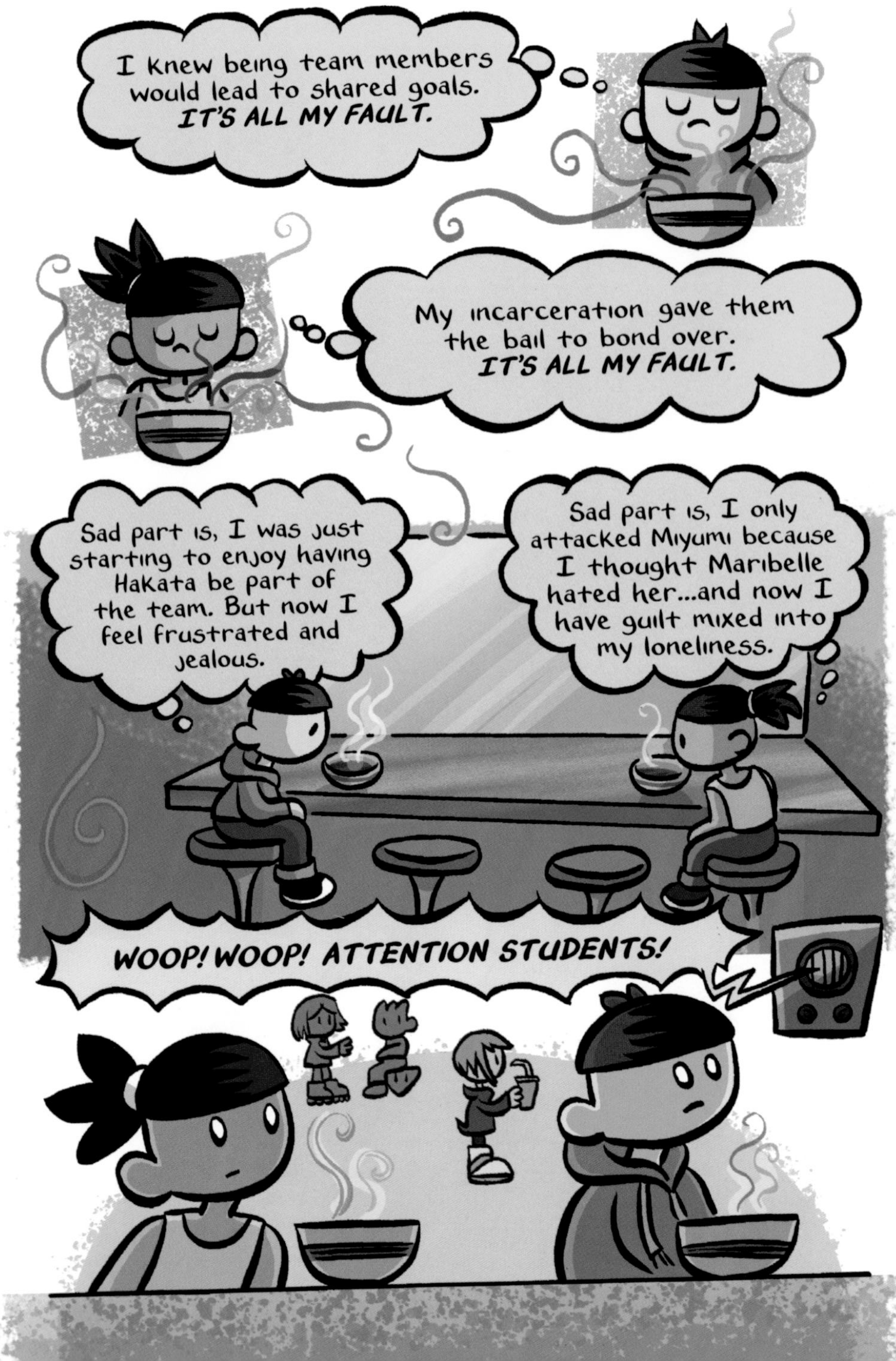
I knew being team members would lead to shared goals. IT'S ALL MY FAULT.
My incarceration gave them the bail to bond over. IT'S ALL MY FAULT.
Sad part is, I was just starting to enjoy having Hakata be part of the team. But now I feel frustrated and jealous.
Sad part is, I only attacked Miyumi because I thought Maribelle hated her...and now I have guilt mixed into my loneliness.
WOOP! WOOP! ATTENTION STUDENTS!

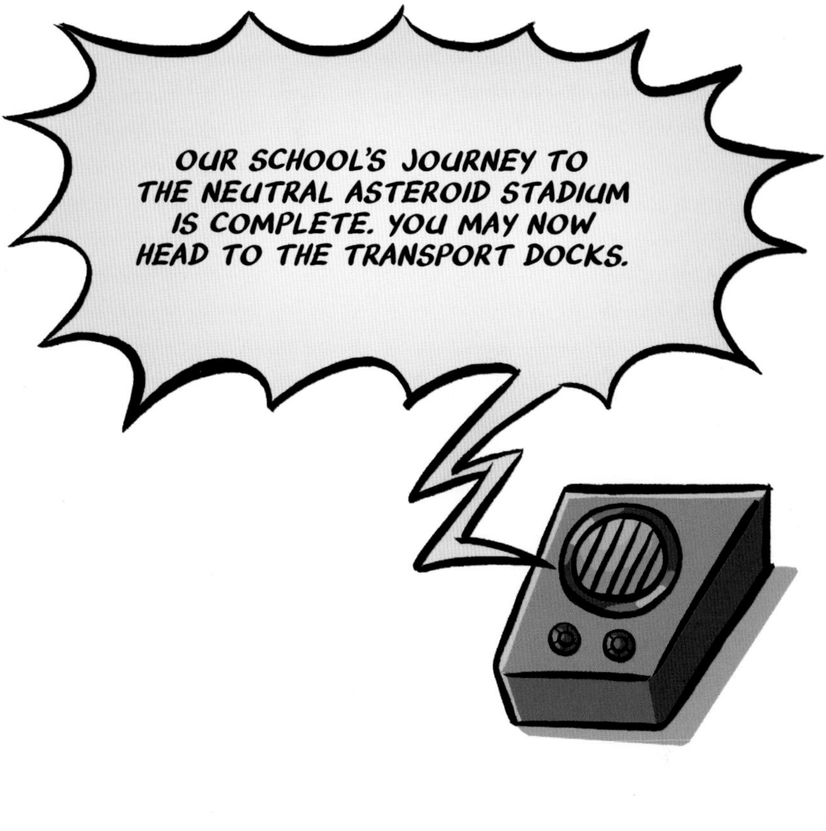
OUR SCHOOL'S JOURNEY TO THE NEUTRAL ASTEROID STADIUM IS COMPLETE. YOU MAY NOW HEAD TO THE TRANSPORT DOCKS.

FIREBALL

Welcome to Neutral Asteroid Stadium!
Location of the annual event in which
this year will be no exception
to the exceptional
excitement we've come to expect,
again and AGAIN!

P.S. GAMMA Q

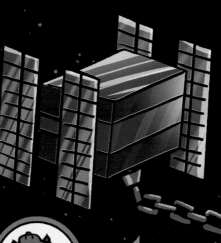

Coach
PomPoko

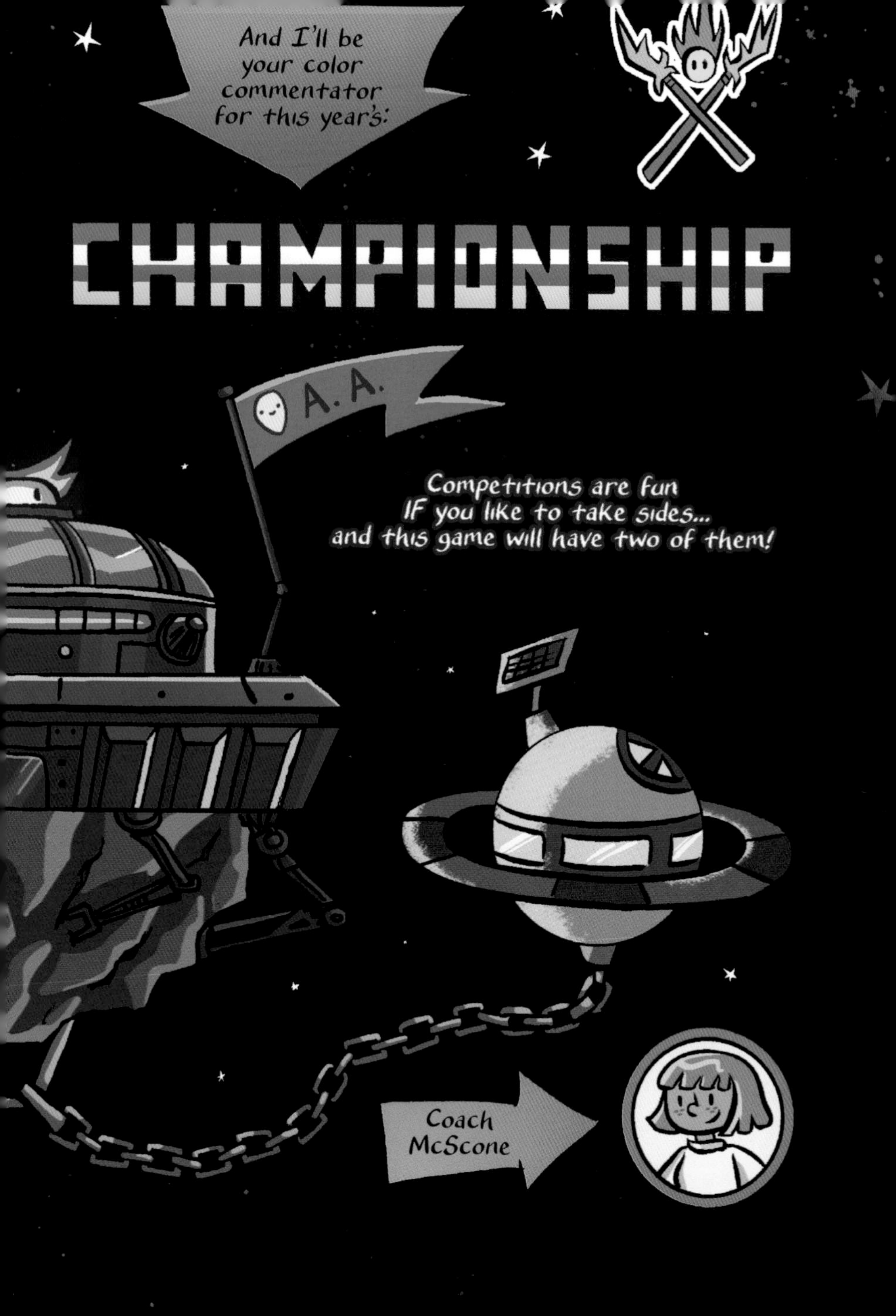
And I'll be your color commentator for this year's:
CHAMPIONSHIP
A. A.
Competitions are fun IF you like to take sides... and this game will have two of them!
Coach McScone

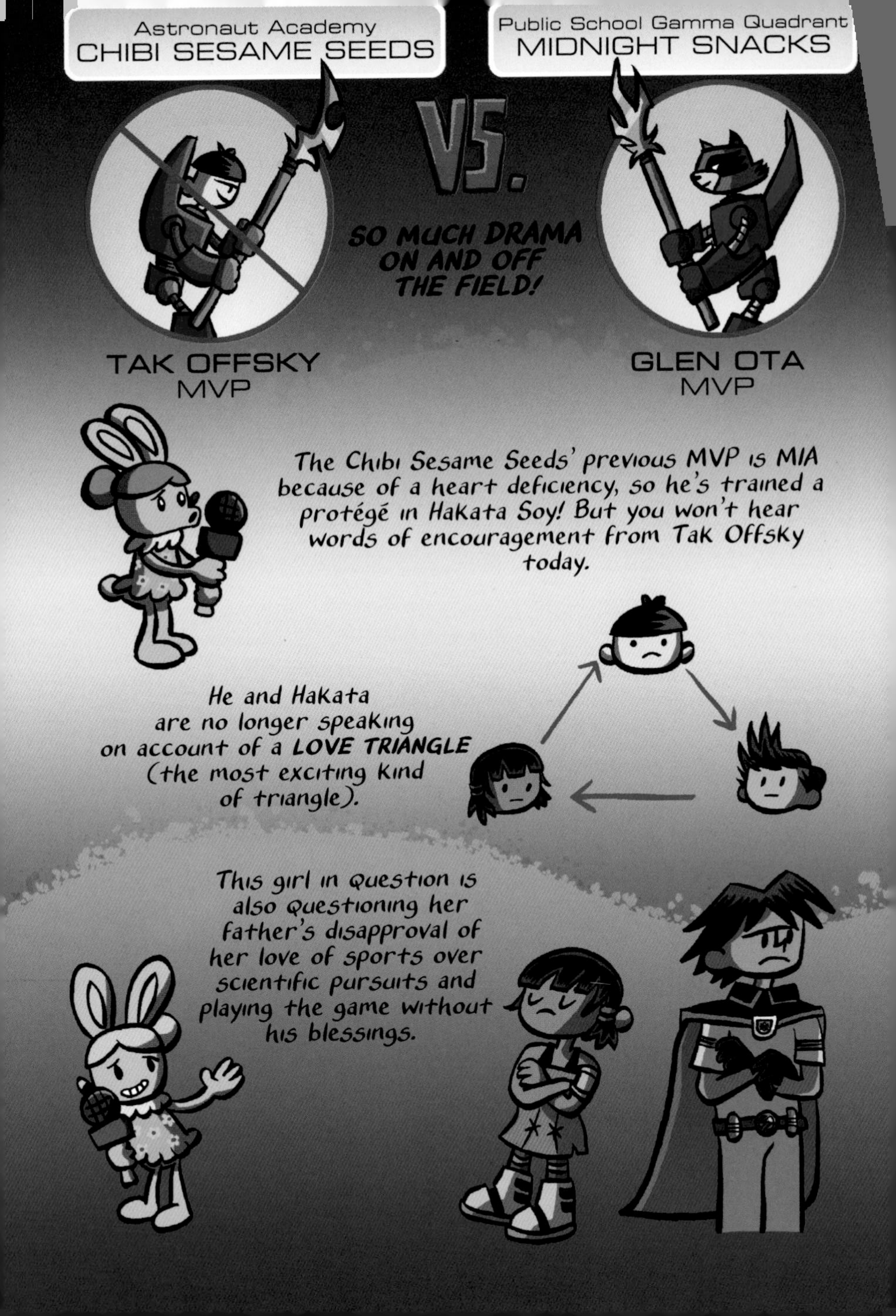

Astronaut Academy
CHIBI SESAME SEEDS
Public School Gamma Quadrant
MIDNIGHT SNACKS
VS.
SO MUCH DRAMA ON AND OFF THE FIELD!
TAK OFFSKY
MVP
GLEN OTA
MVP
The Chibi Sesame Seeds' previous MVP is MIA because of a heart deficiency, so he's trained a protégé in Hakata Soy! But you won't hear words of encouragement from Tak Offsky today.
He and Hakata are no longer speaking on account of a LOVE TRIANGLE (the most exciting kind of triangle).
This girl in question is also questioning her father's disapproval of her love of sports over scientific pursuits and playing the game without his blessings.

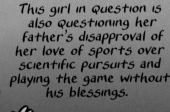

Speaking of old people, the Council of Elders have canceled the Grand Fire Ball (the usual dance party held after the game) in accordance with the P.T.A.'s ban on love.

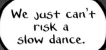

We just can't risk a slow dance.

And a stool pigeon has revealed that Hakata Soy is also conflicted about his ongoing conflict with Rick Raven, leader of the Gotcha Birds and latest addition to the Midnight Snacks!

ZAP

If you are a conflict enthusiast like myself, this is the **GOOD STUFF.** And things are just getting started!

Each of the school principals are entering the field...

...Let's watch!

THE CEREMONIAL CLASHING OF THE SWORDS!

SHING

SHING

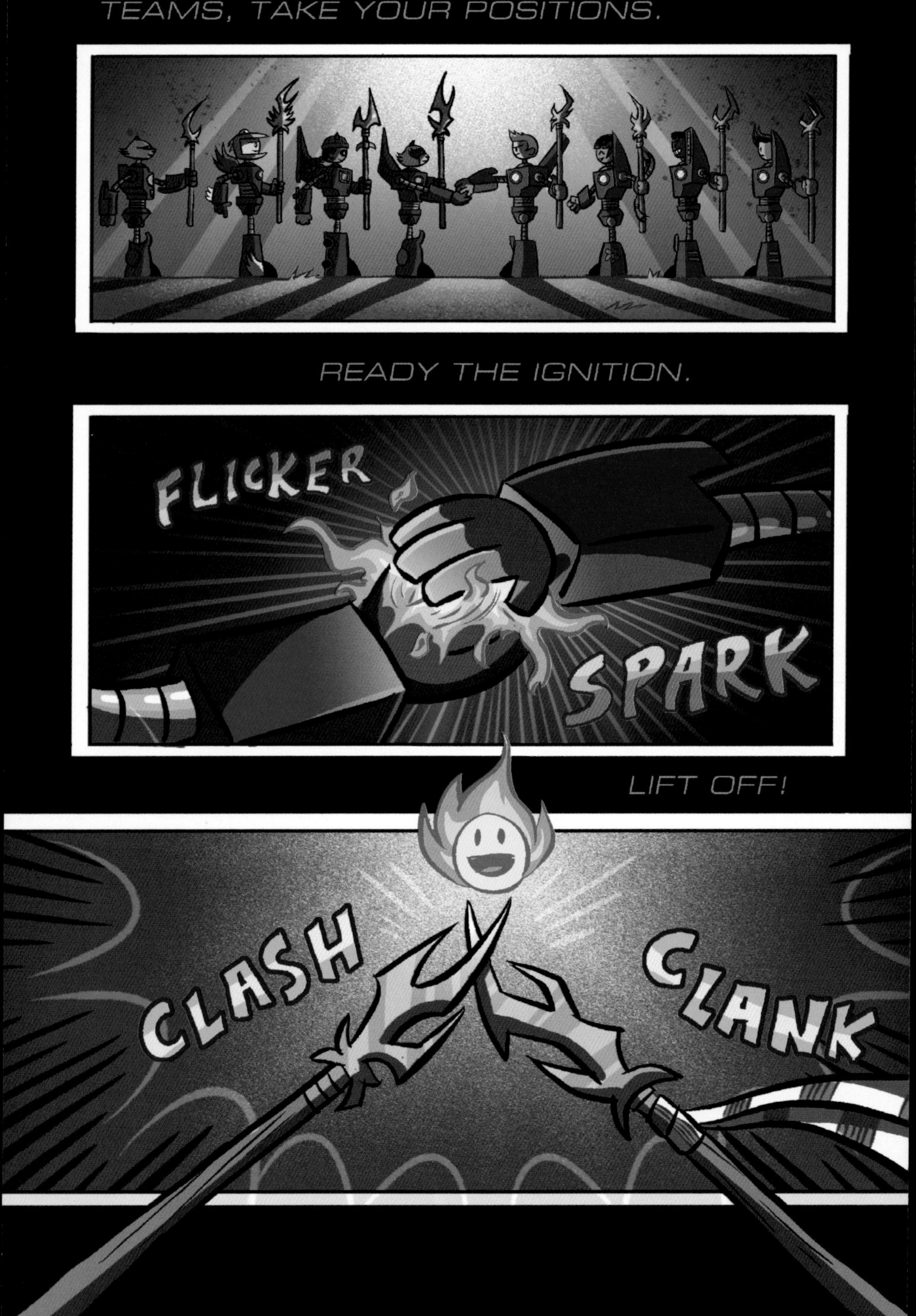
TEAMS, TAKE YOUR POSITIONS.
READY THE IGNITION.
FLICKER
SPARK
LIFT OFF!
CLASH
CLANK

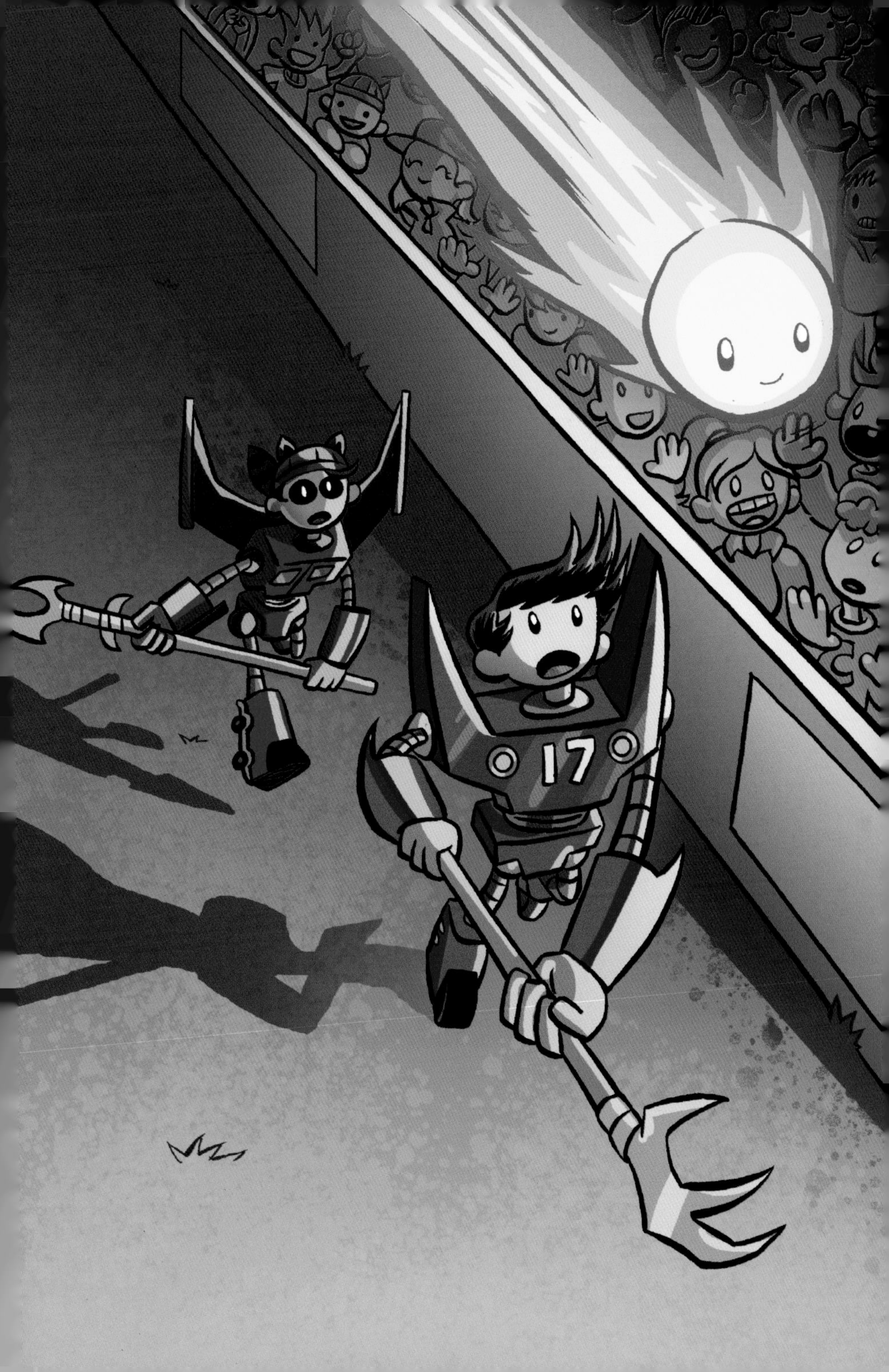
17

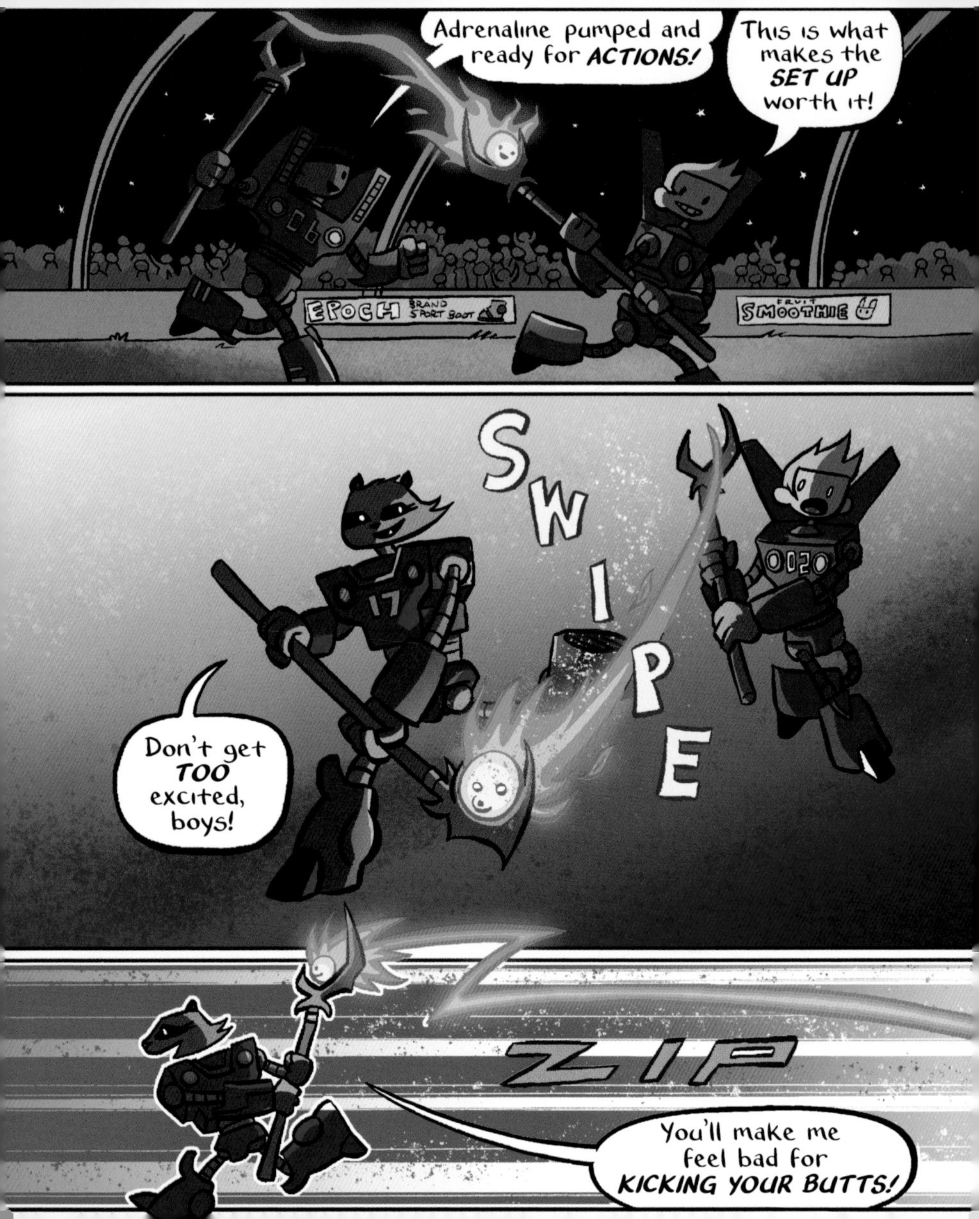
Adrenaline pumped and ready for ACTIONS!
This is what makes the SET UP worth it!
EPOCH BRAND SPORT BOOT
FRUIT SMOOTHIE
SWIPE
17
0020
Don't get TOO excited, boys!
ZIP
You'll make me feel bad for KICKING YOUR BUTTS!

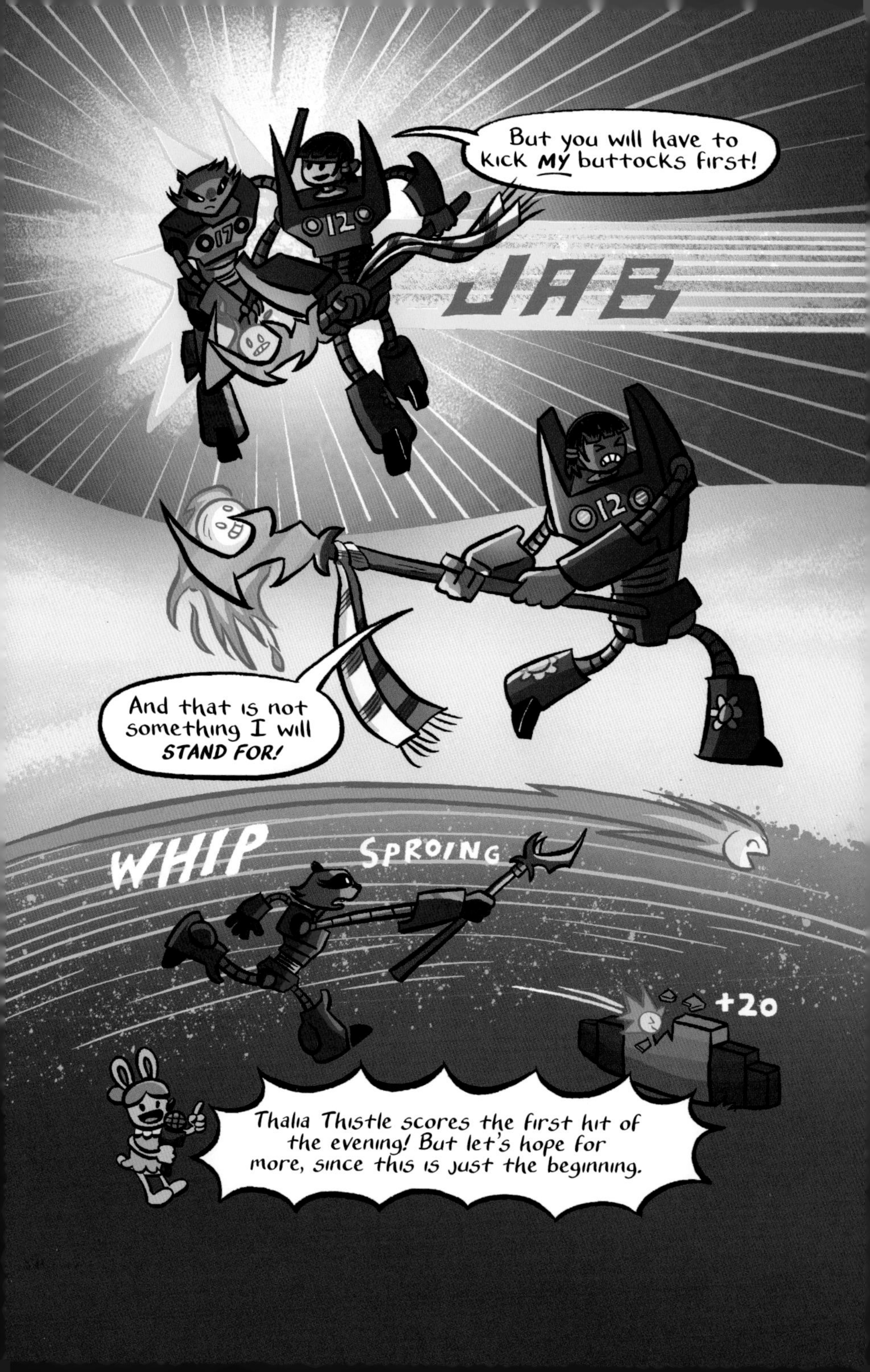

But you will have to kick MY buttocks first!
JAB
And that is not something I will STAND FOR!
WHIP
SPROING
+20
Thalia Thistle scores the first hit of the evening! But let's hope for more, since this is just the beginning.

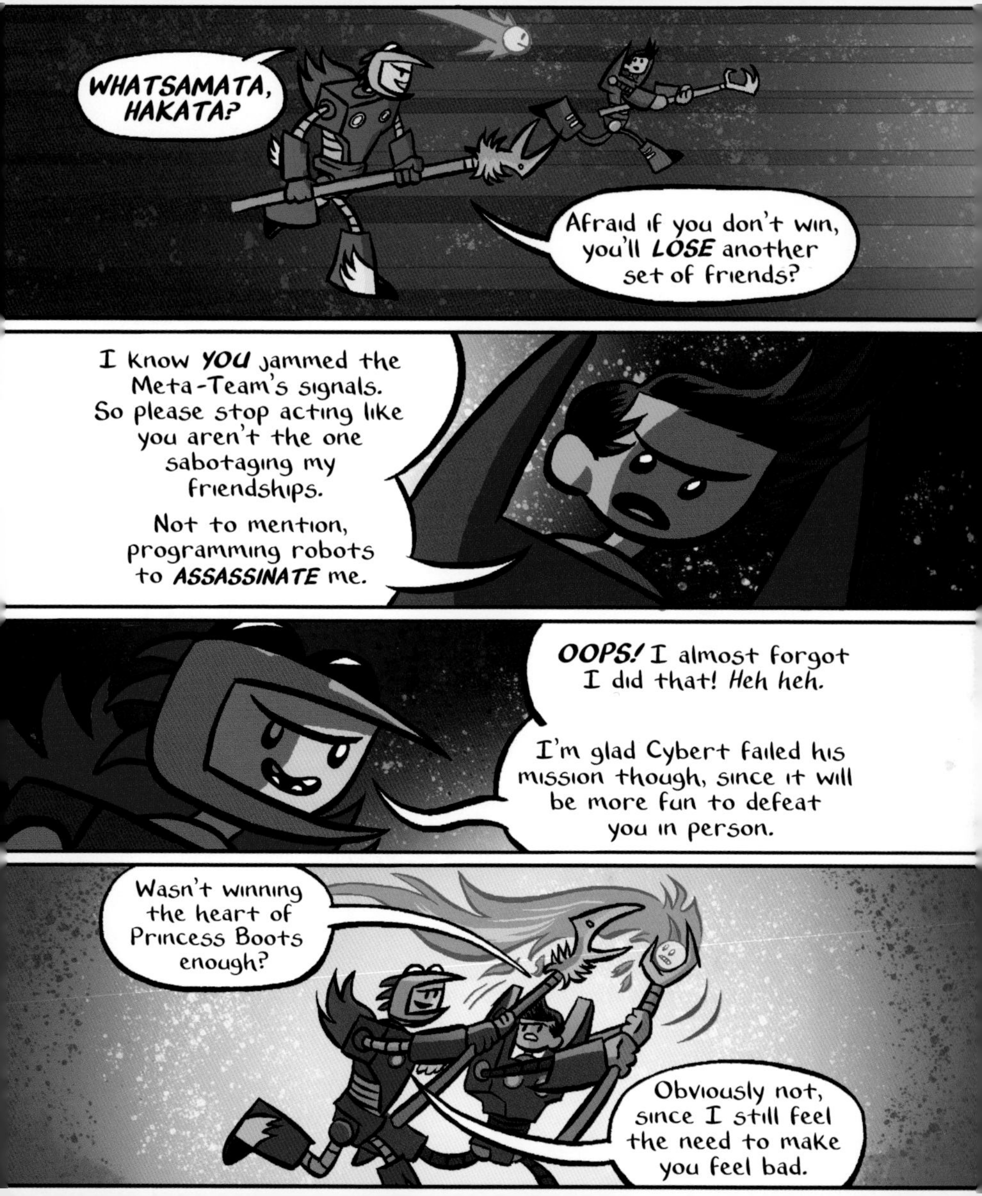

WHATSAMATA, HAKATA?
Afraid if you don't win, you'll LOSE another set of friends?
I know YOU jammed the Meta-Team's signals. So please stop acting like you aren't the one sabotaging my friendships.
Not to mention, programming robots to ASSASSINATE me.
OOPS! I almost forgot I did that! Heh heh.
I'm glad Cybert failed his mission though, since it will be more fun to defeat you in person.
Wasn't winning the heart of Princess Boots enough?
Obviously not, since I still feel the need to make you feel bad.

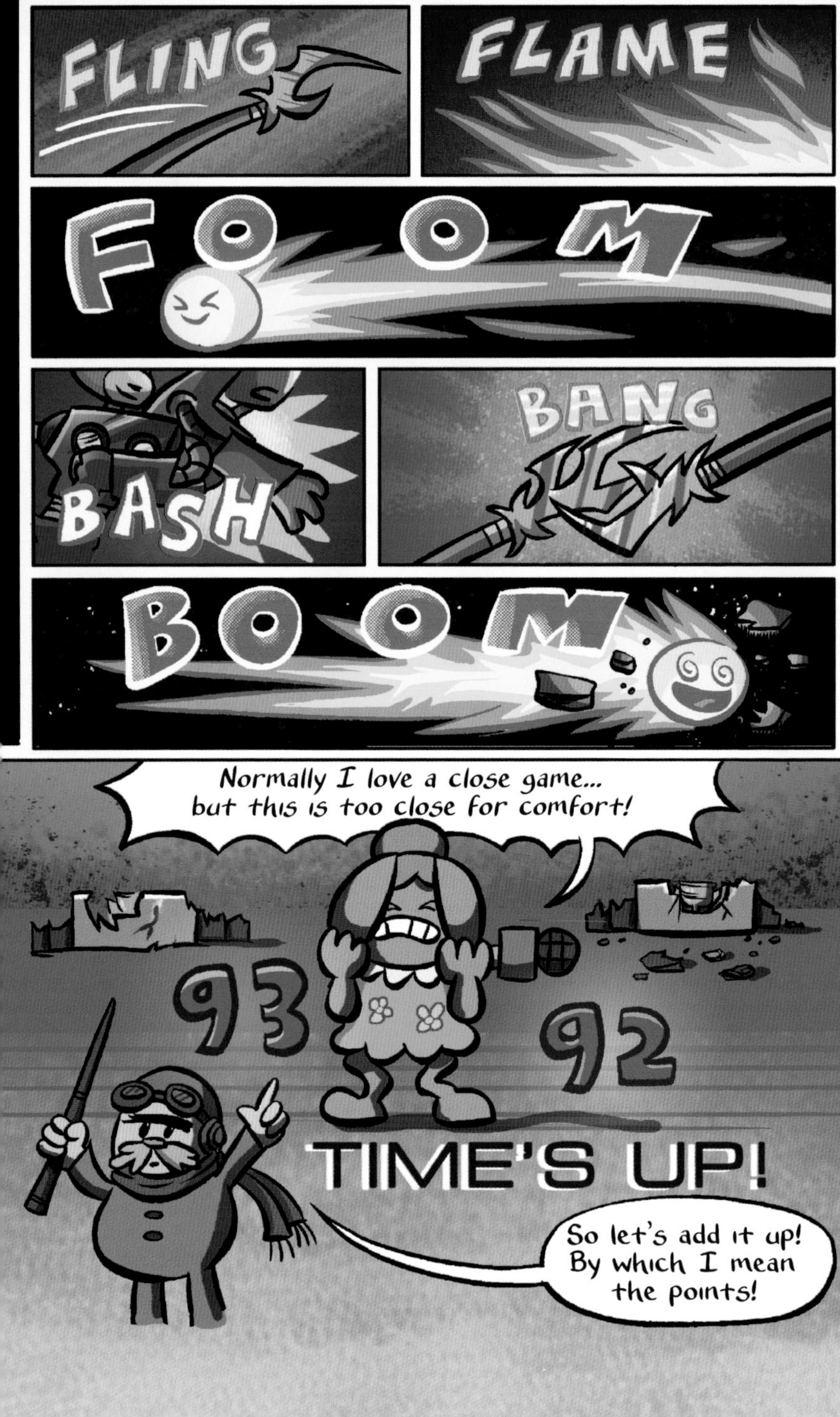
FLING
FLAME
FOOM
BASH
BANG
BOOM
Normally I love a close game... but this is too close for comfort!
93
92
TIME'S UP!
So let's add it up! By which I mean the points!

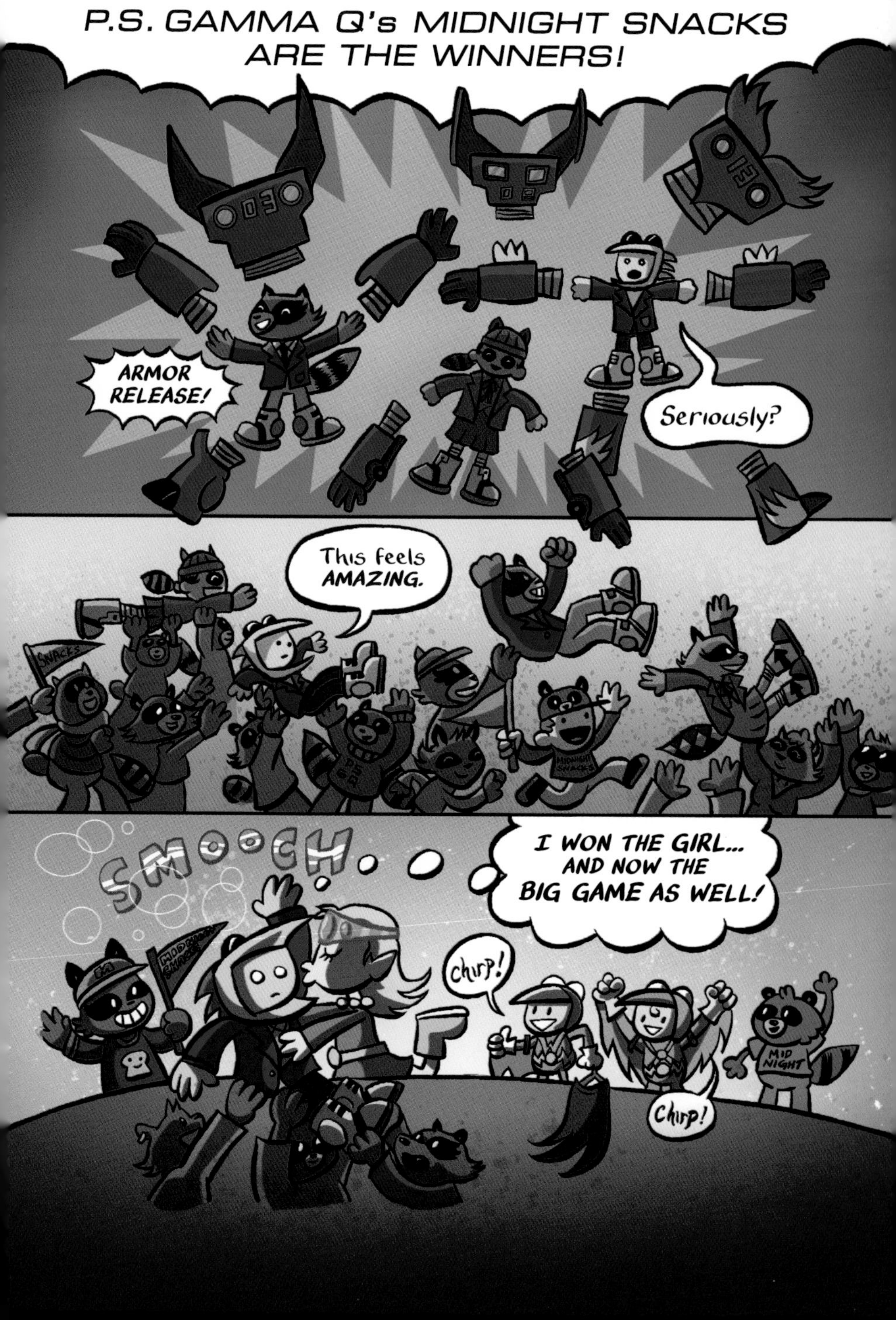
P.S. GAMMA Q's MIDNIGHT SNACKS ARE THE WINNERS!
ARMOR RELEASE!
Seriously?
This feels AMAZING.
SNACKS
MIDNIGHT SNACKS
SMOOCH
I WON THE GIRL... AND NOW THE BIG GAME AS WELL!
Chirp!
MID NIGHT
Chirp!

158

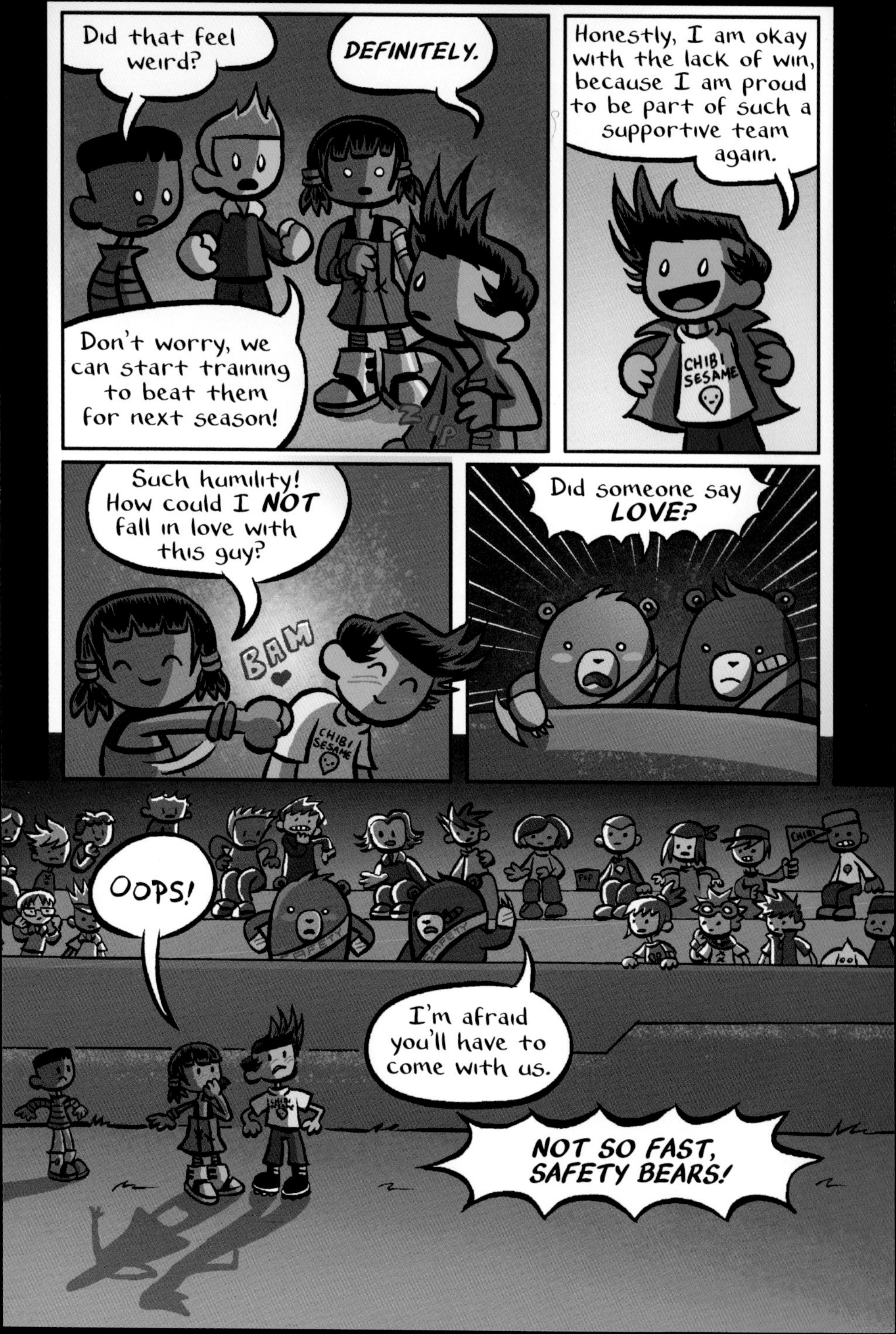
Did that feel weird?
DEFINITELY.
Don't worry, we can start training to beat them for next season!
ZIP
Honestly, I am okay with the lack of win, because I am proud to be part of such a supportive team again.
CHIBI SESAME
Such humility! How could I NOT fall in love with this guy?
BAM
CHIBI SESAME
Did someone say LOVE?
OOPS!
I'm afraid you'll have to come with us.
NOT SO FAST, SAFETY BEARS!

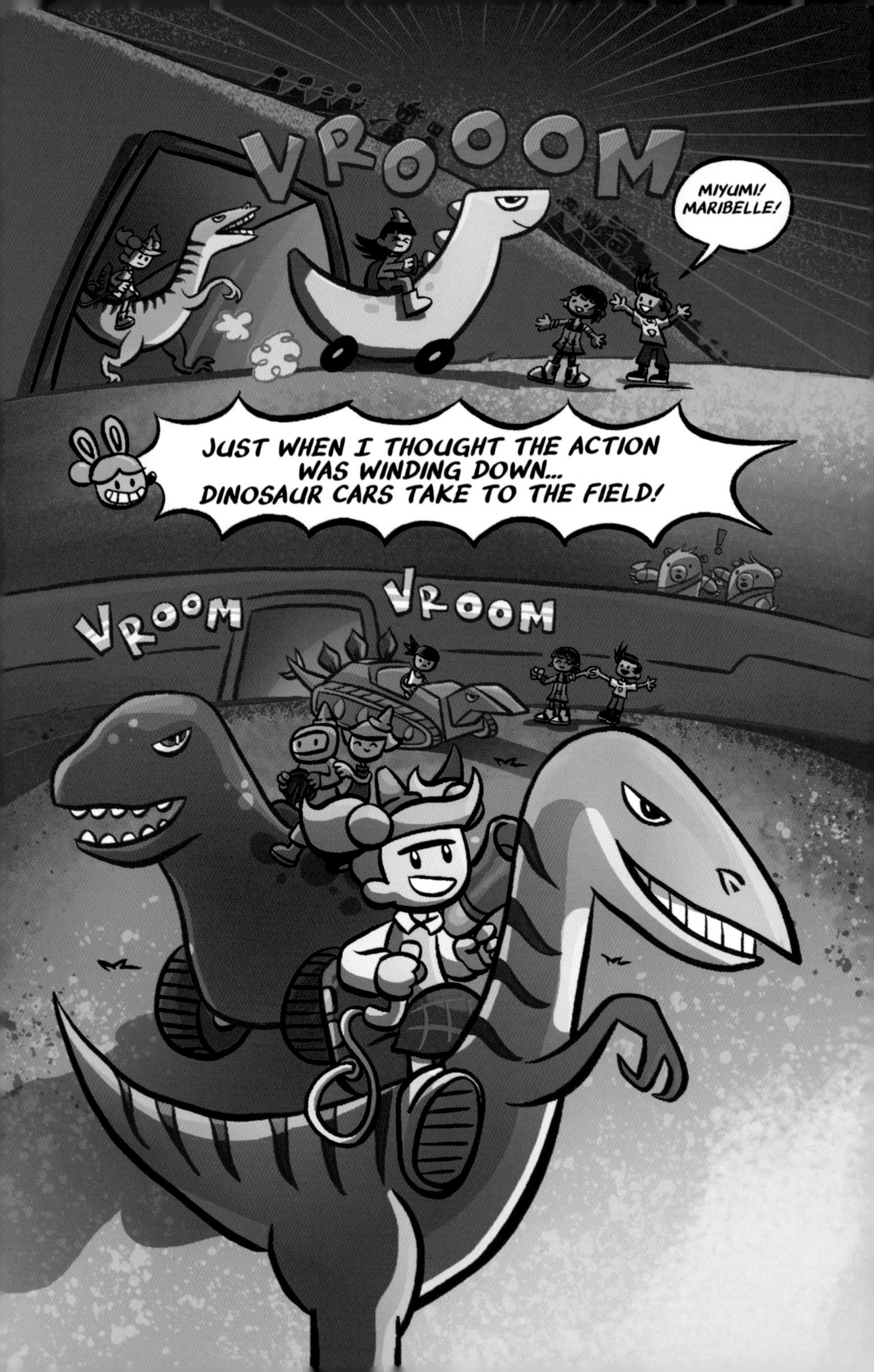
VROOOM
MIYUMI! MARIBELLE!
JUST WHEN I THOUGHT THE ACTION WAS WINDING DOWN... DINOSAUR CARS TAKE TO THE FIELD!
!
VROOM
VROOM

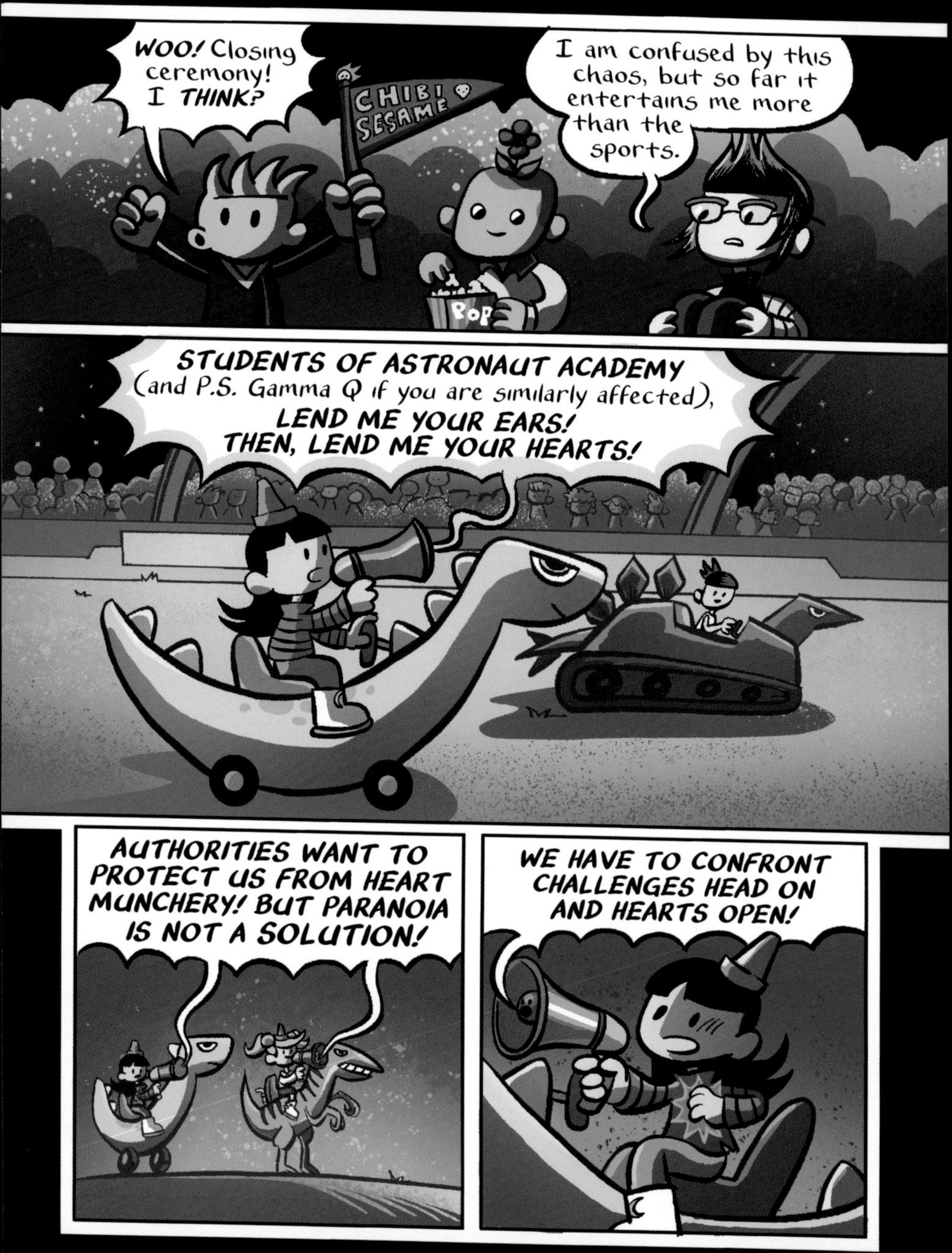
WOO! Closing ceremony! I THINK?
CHIBI SESAME
POP
I am confused by this chaos, but so far it entertains me more than the sports.
STUDENTS OF ASTRONAUT ACADEMY (and P.S. Gamma Q if you are similarly affected), LEND ME YOUR EARS! THEN, LEND ME YOUR HEARTS!
AUTHORITIES WANT TO PROTECT US FROM HEART MUNCHERY! BUT PARANOIA IS NOT A SOLUTION!
WE HAVE TO CONFRONT CHALLENGES HEAD ON AND HEARTS OPEN!

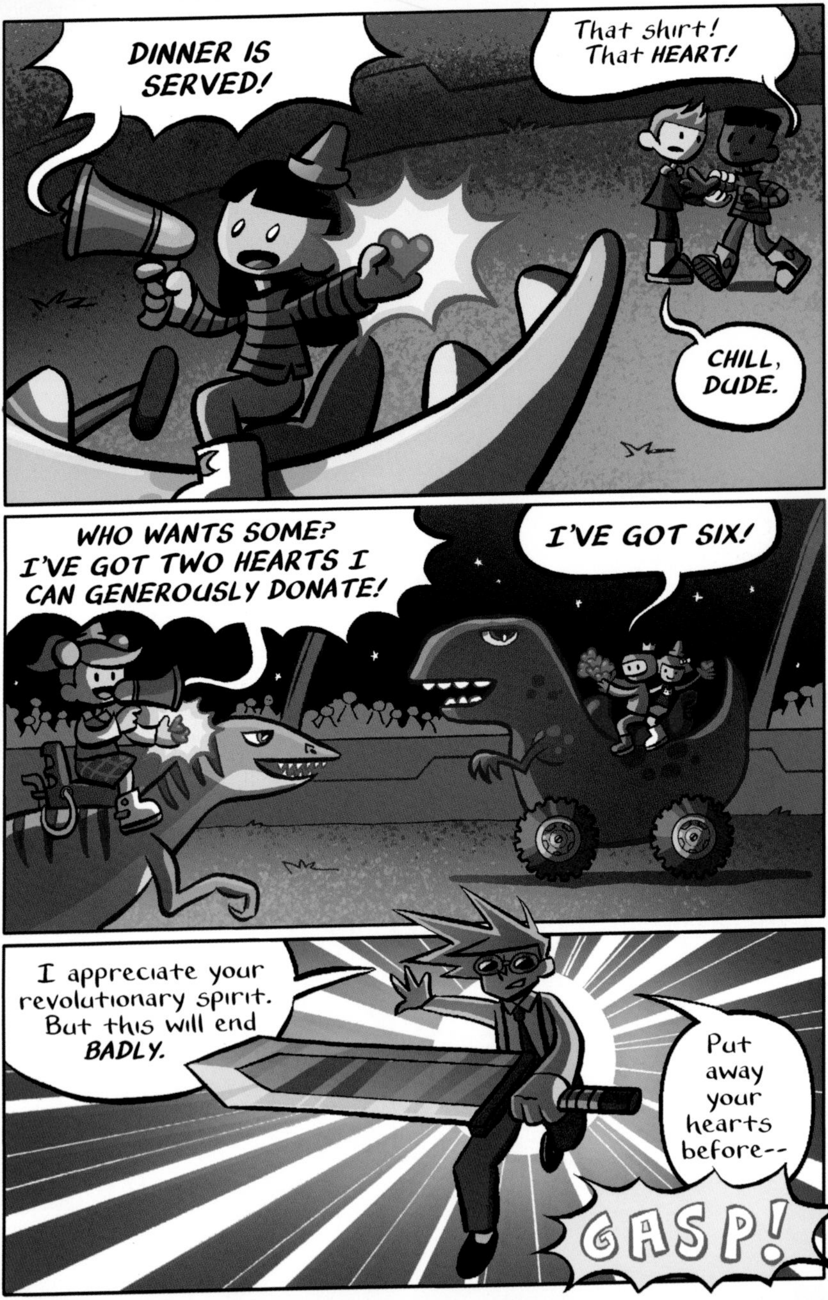
DINNER IS SERVED!
That shirt! That HEART!
CHILL, DUDE.
WHO WANTS SOME? I'VE GOT TWO HEARTS I CAN GENEROUSLY DONATE!
I'VE GOT SIX!
I appreciate your revolutionary spirit. But this will end BADLY.
Put away your hearts before--
GASP!

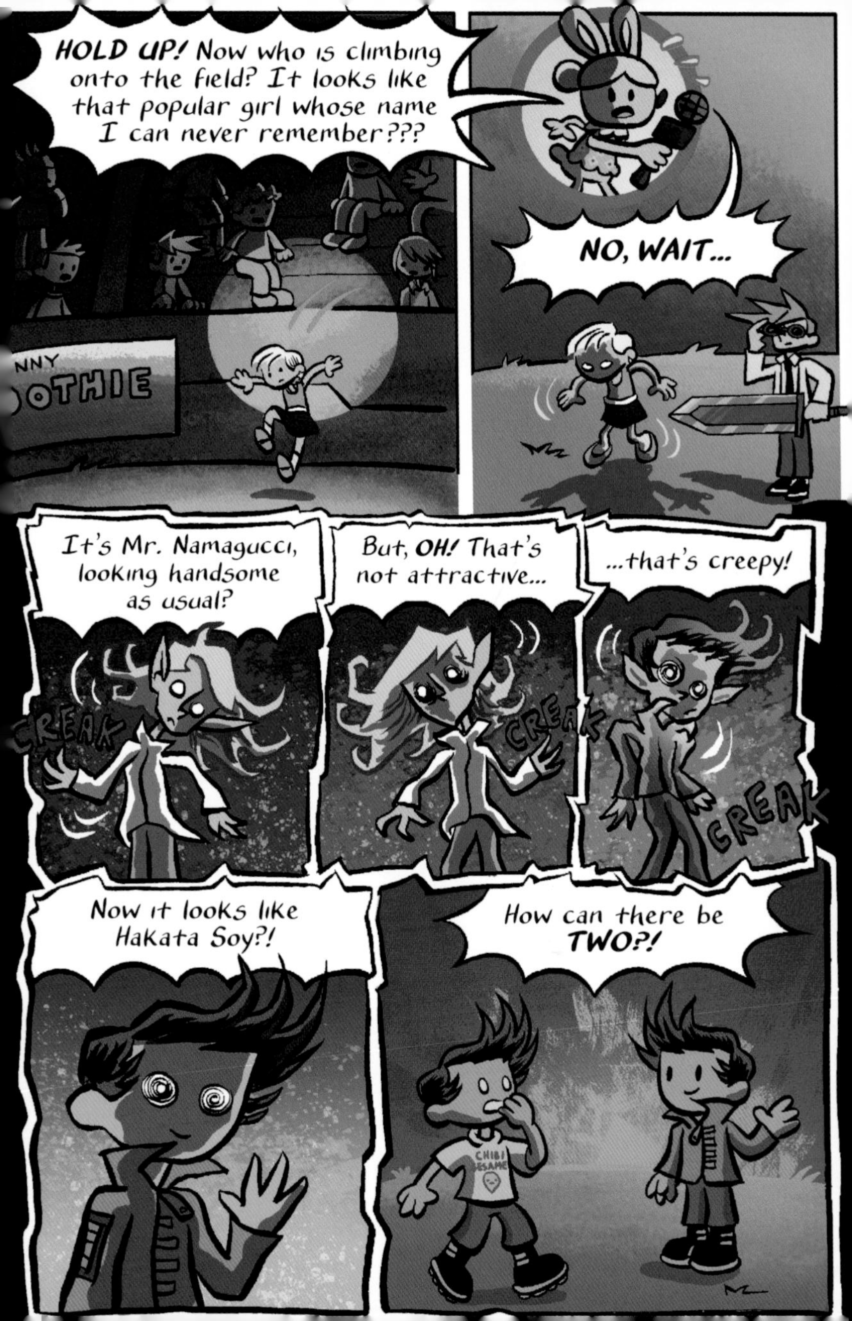
HOLD UP! Now who is climbing onto the field? It looks like that popular girl whose name I can never remember???
NNY
OTHIE
NO, WAIT...
It's Mr. Namagucci, looking handsome as usual?
CREAK
But, OH! That's not attractive...
CREAK
...that's creepy!
CREAK
Now it looks like Hakata Soy?!
How can there be TWO?!
CHIBI SESAME

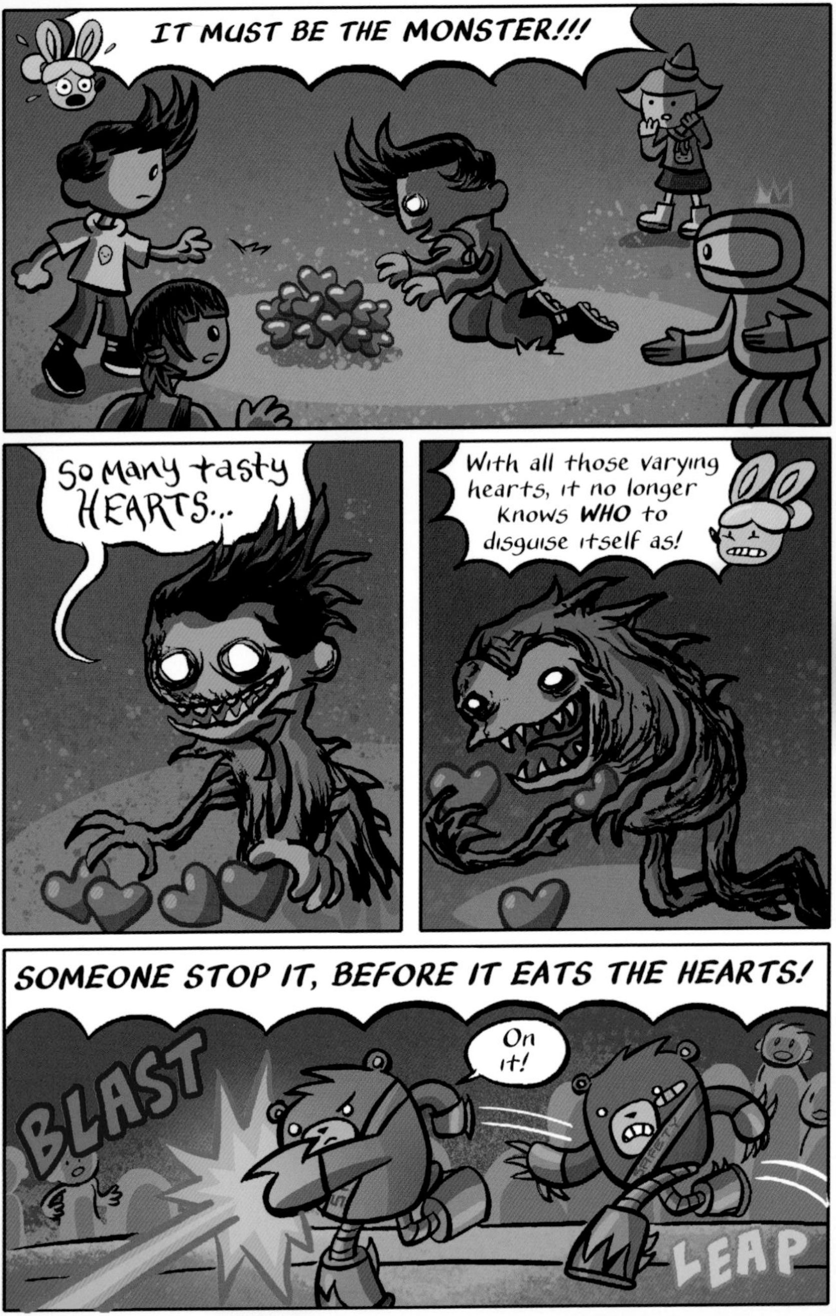
IT MUST BE THE MONSTER!!!
So Many tasty HEARTS...
With all those varying hearts, it no longer knows WHO to disguise itself as!
SOMEONE STOP IT, BEFORE IT EATS THE HEARTS!
BLAST
On it!
LEAP

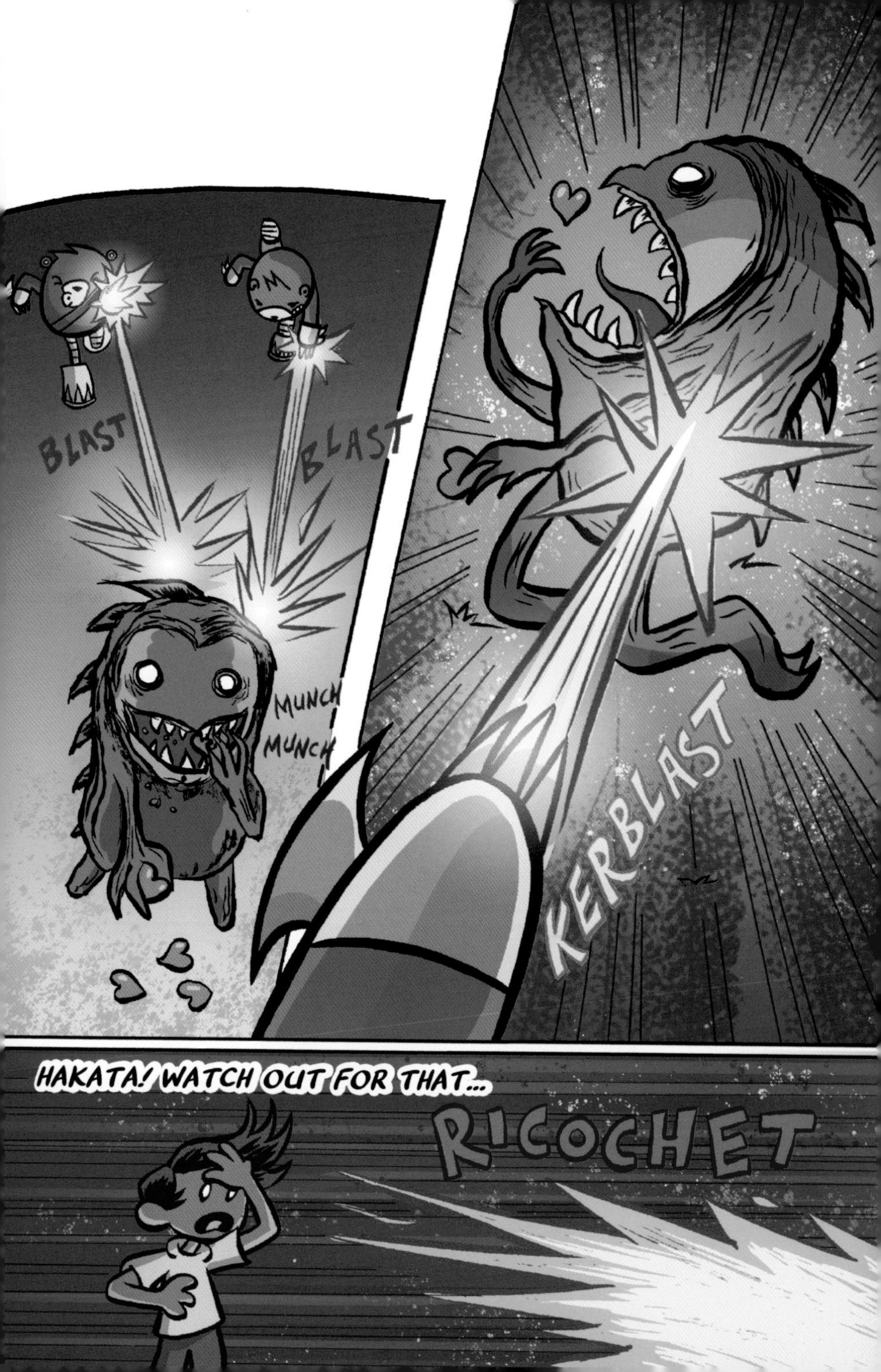
BLAST
BLAST
MUNCH
MUNCH
KERBLAST
HAKATA! WATCH OUT FOR THAT...
RICOCHET

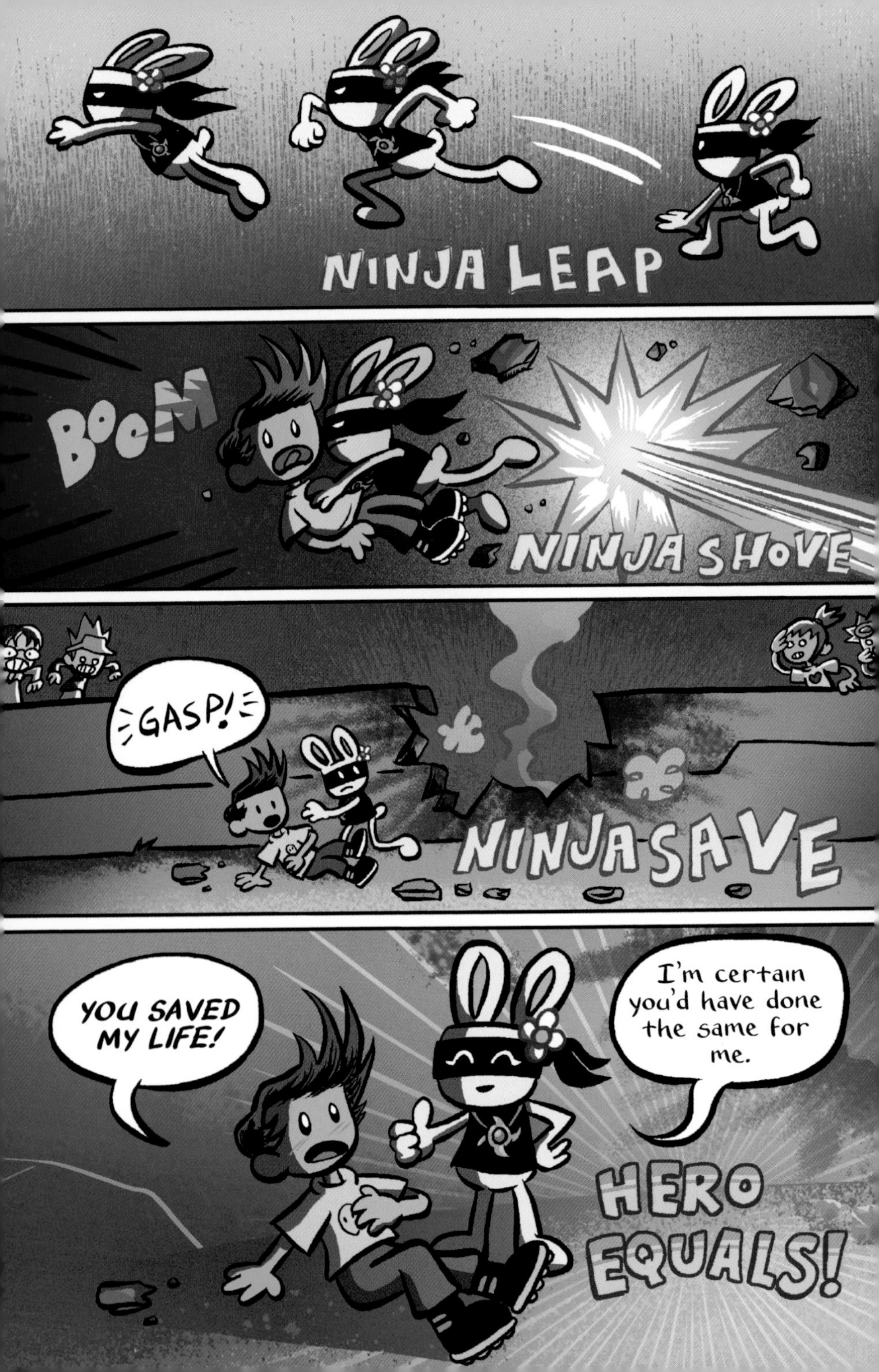
NINJA LEAP
BOOM
NINJA SHOVE
GASP!
NINJA SAVE
YOU SAVED MY LIFE!
I'm certain you'd have done the same for me.
HERO EQUALS!

Eating all those hearts has made the monster **SO CHUNKY!**

SWOOSH

RICOCHET

POP

Even **MY SWORD** has no effect!

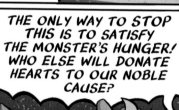

THE ONLY WAY TO STOP THIS IS TO SATISFY THE MONSTER'S HUNGER! WHO ELSE WILL DONATE HEARTS TO OUR NOBLE CAUSE?

No offense, but that's kind of asking a lot.

Can't I just donate my naturally curly hair?

At least that tends to **GROW BACK!**

THAT'S OUR POINT! MARIBELLE HERE DISCOVERED YOUR HEARTS CAN--

Um, Maribelle?

HEY! Who turned off the time?

POKE POKE

← TOTALLY FROZEN

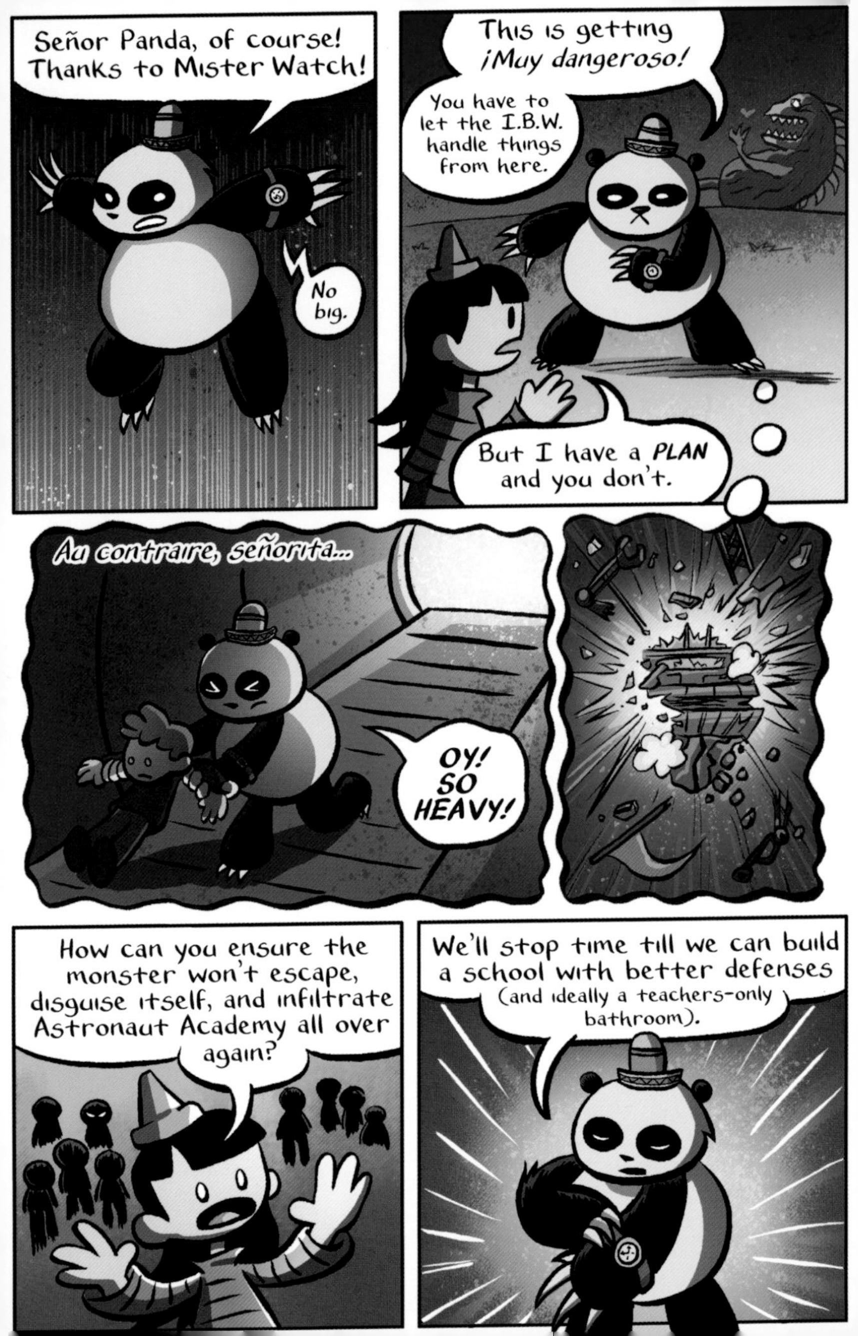
Señor Panda, of course! Thanks to Mister Watch!
No big.
This is getting ¡Muy dangeroso!
You have to let the I.B.W. handle things from here.
But I have a PLAN and you don't.
Au contraire, señorita...
OY! SO HEAVY!
How can you ensure the monster won't escape, disguise itself, and infiltrate Astronaut Academy all over again?
We'll stop time till we can build a school with better defenses
(and ideally a teachers-only bathroom).

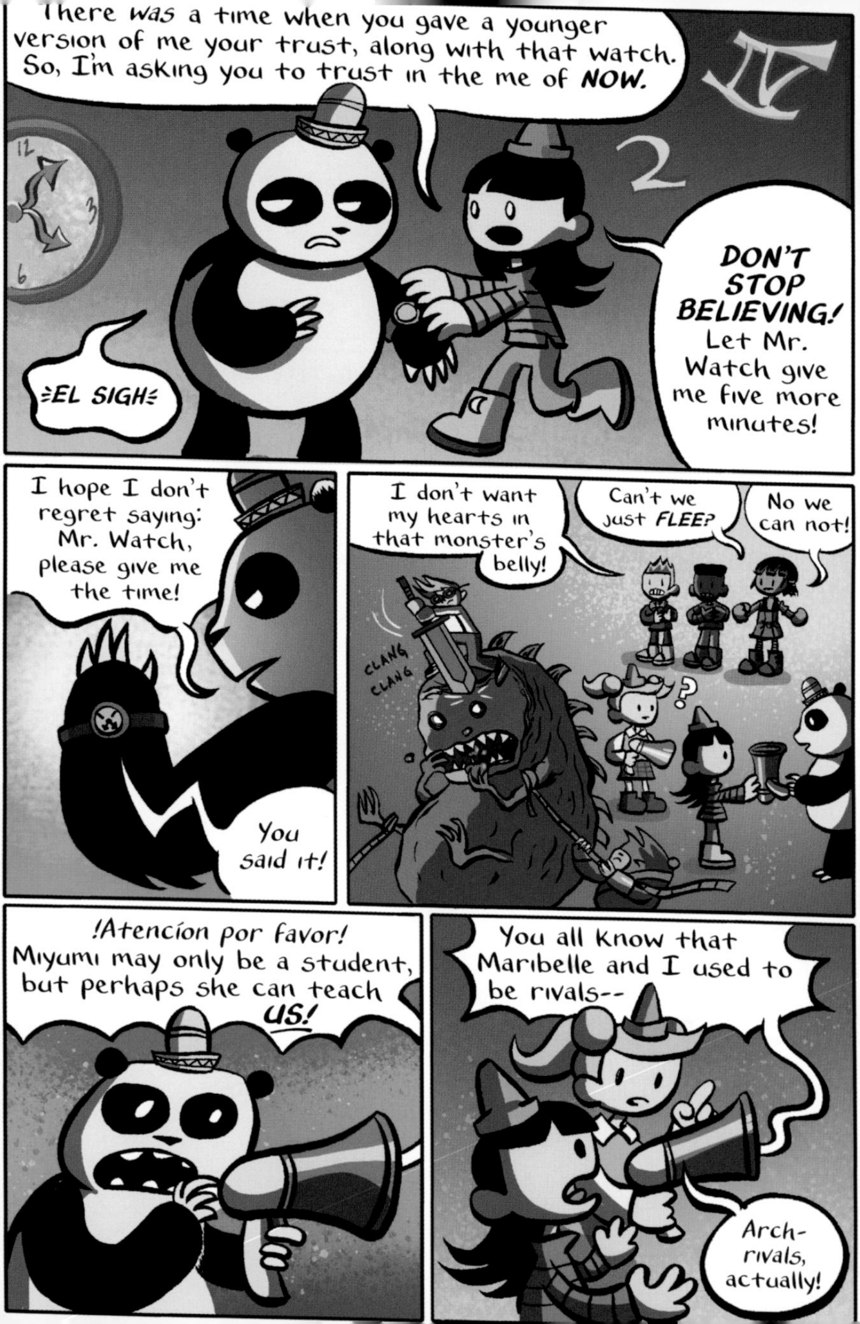
There was a time when you gave a younger version of me your trust, along with that watch. So, I'm asking you to trust in the me of NOW.
≶EL SIGH≶
DON'T STOP BELIEVING! Let Mr. Watch give me five more minutes!
I hope I don't regret saying: Mr. Watch, please give me the time!
You said it!
I don't want my hearts in that monster's belly!
Can't we just FLEE?
No we can not!
CLANG CLANG
?
!Atencíon por favor! Miyumi may only be a student, but perhaps she can teach US!
You all know that Maribelle and I used to be rivals--
Arch-rivals, actually!

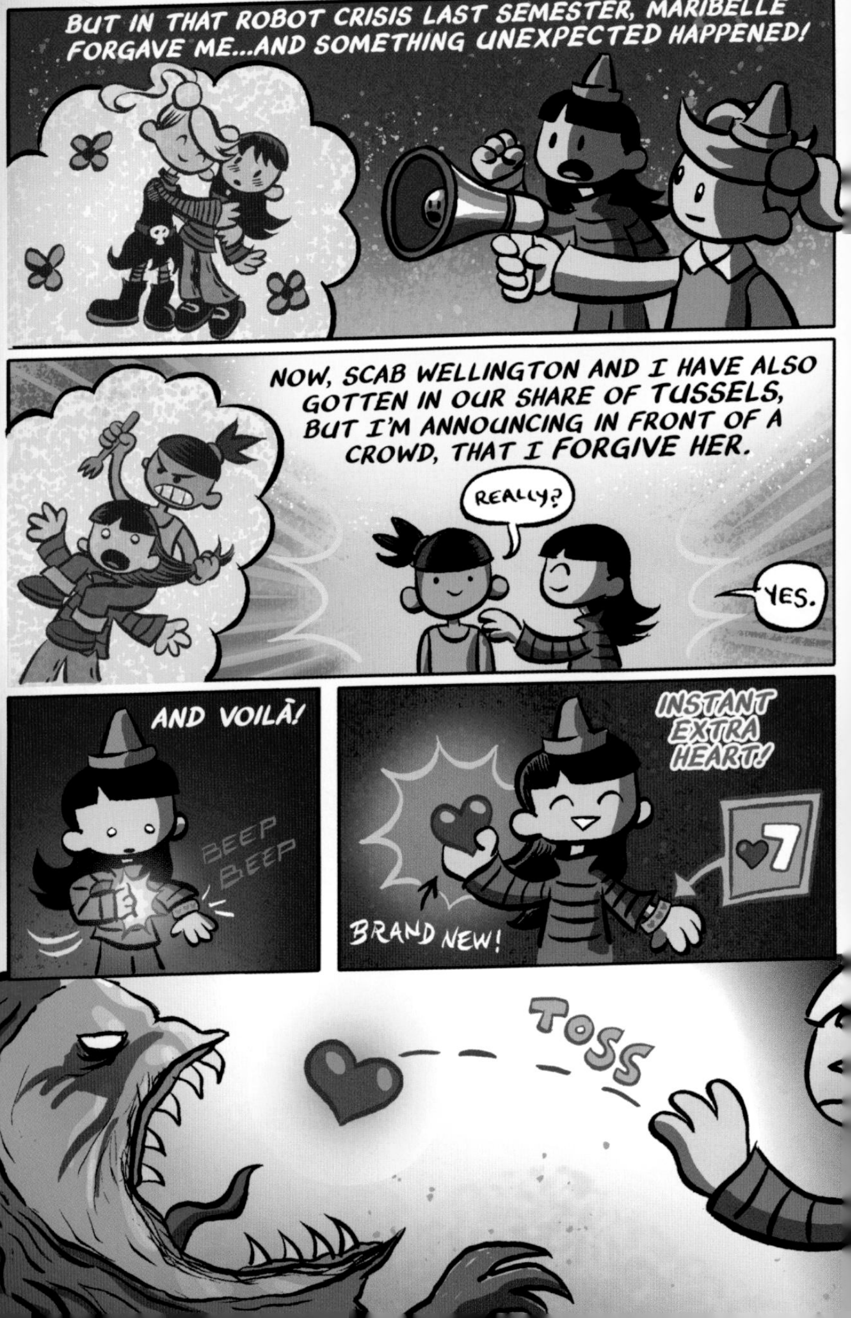
BUT IN THAT ROBOT CRISIS LAST SEMESTER, MARIBELLE FORGAVE ME...AND SOMETHING UNEXPECTED HAPPENED!
NOW, SCAB WELLINGTON AND I HAVE ALSO GOTTEN IN OUR SHARE OF TUSSELS, BUT I'M ANNOUNCING IN FRONT OF A CROWD, THAT I FORGIVE HER.
REALLY?
YES.
AND VOILÀ!
BEEP BEEP
INSTANT EXTRA HEART!
BRAND NEW!
7
TOSS

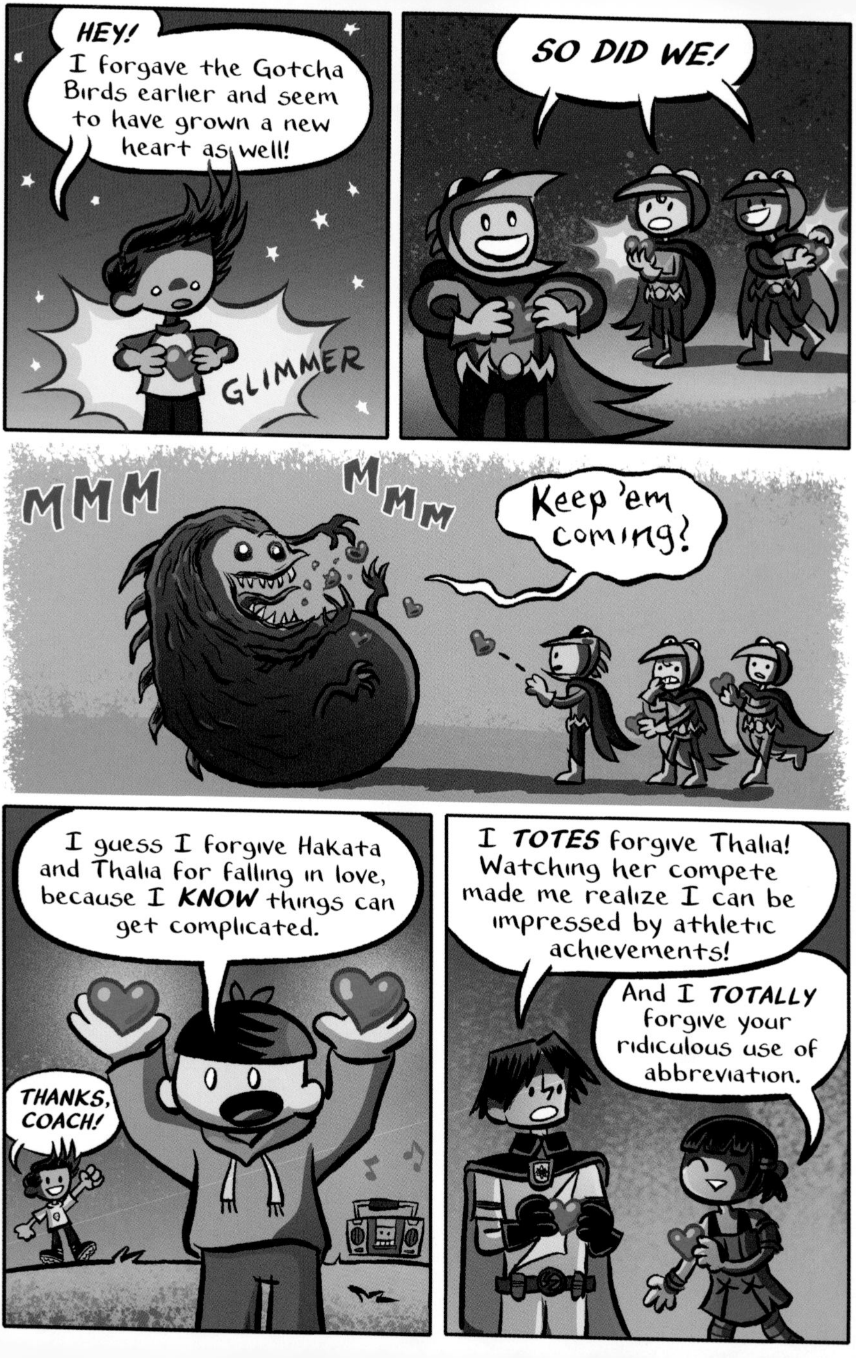
HEY!
I forgave the Gotcha Birds earlier and seem to have grown a new heart as well!
GLIMMER
SO DID WE!
MMM
MMM
Keep 'em coming?
I guess I forgive Hakata and Thalia for falling in love, because I KNOW things can get complicated.
THANKS, COACH!
I TOTES forgive Thalia! Watching her compete made me realize I can be impressed by athletic achievements!
And I TOTALLY forgive your ridiculous use of abbreviation.

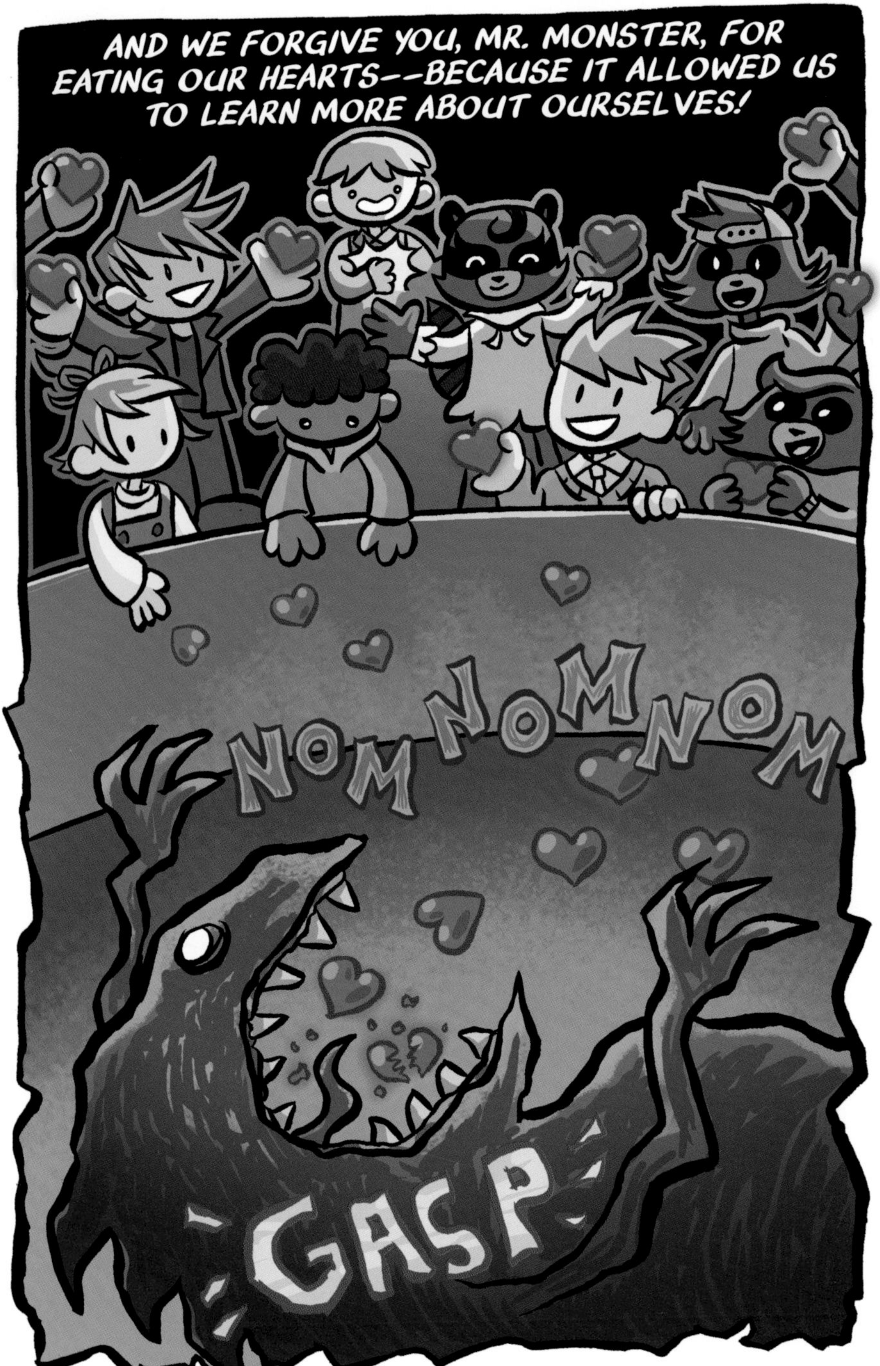
AND WE FORGIVE YOU, MR. MONSTER, FOR EATING OUR HEARTS--BECAUSE IT ALLOWED US TO LEARN MORE ABOUT OURSELVES!
NOM NOM NOM NOM
GASP

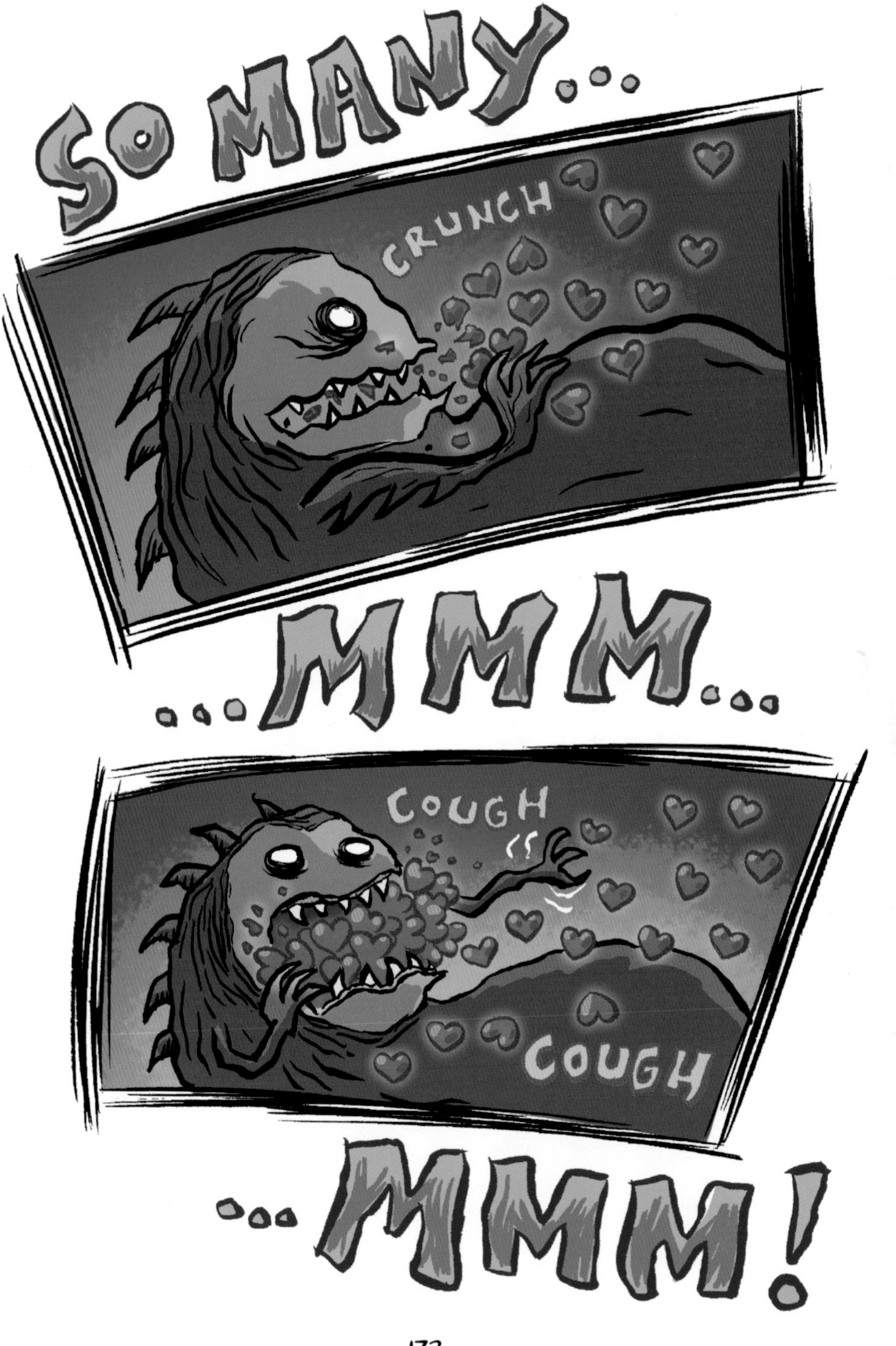
SO MANY...
CRUNCH
...MMM...
COUGH
COUGH
...MMM!

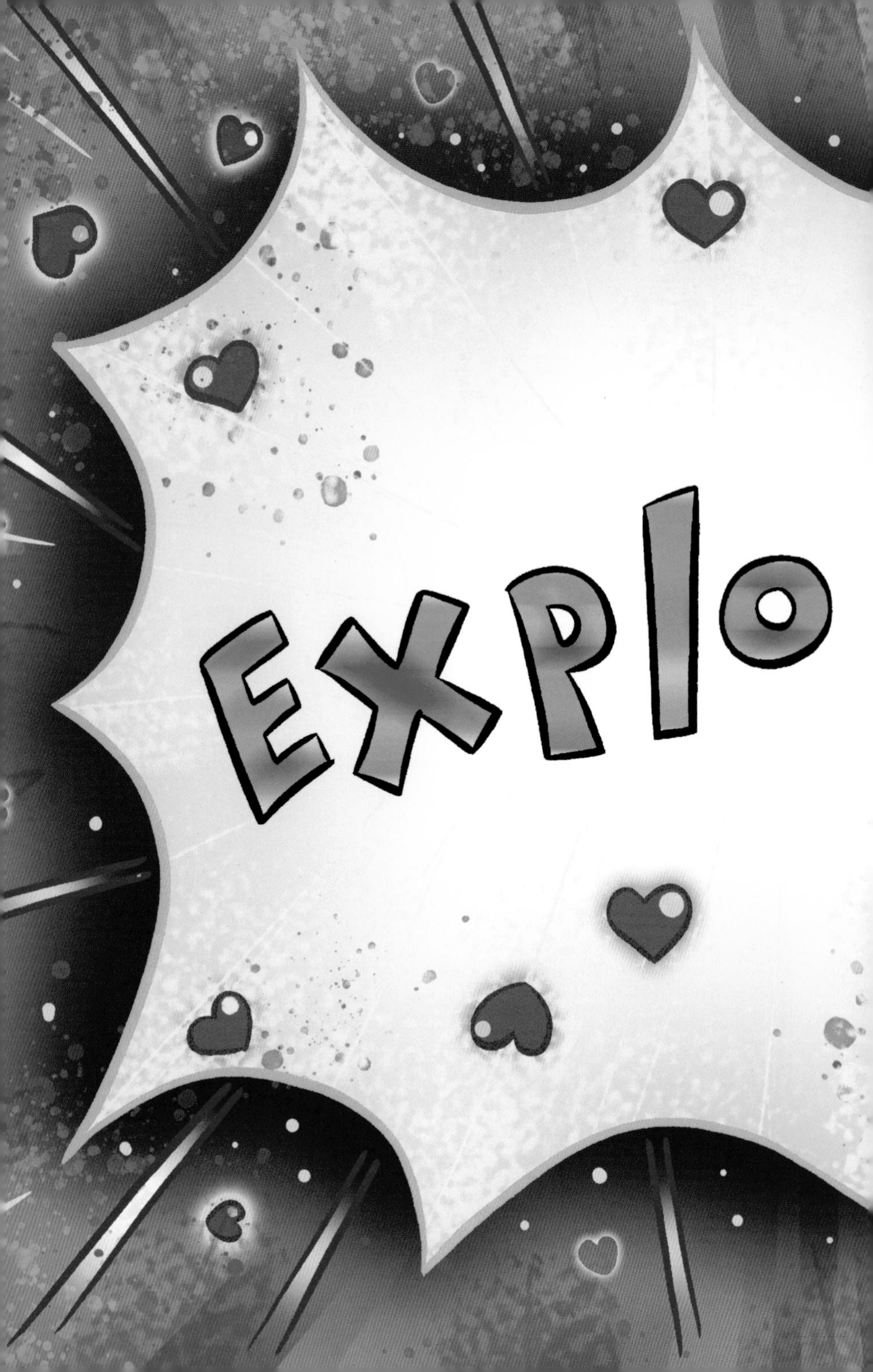
Explo

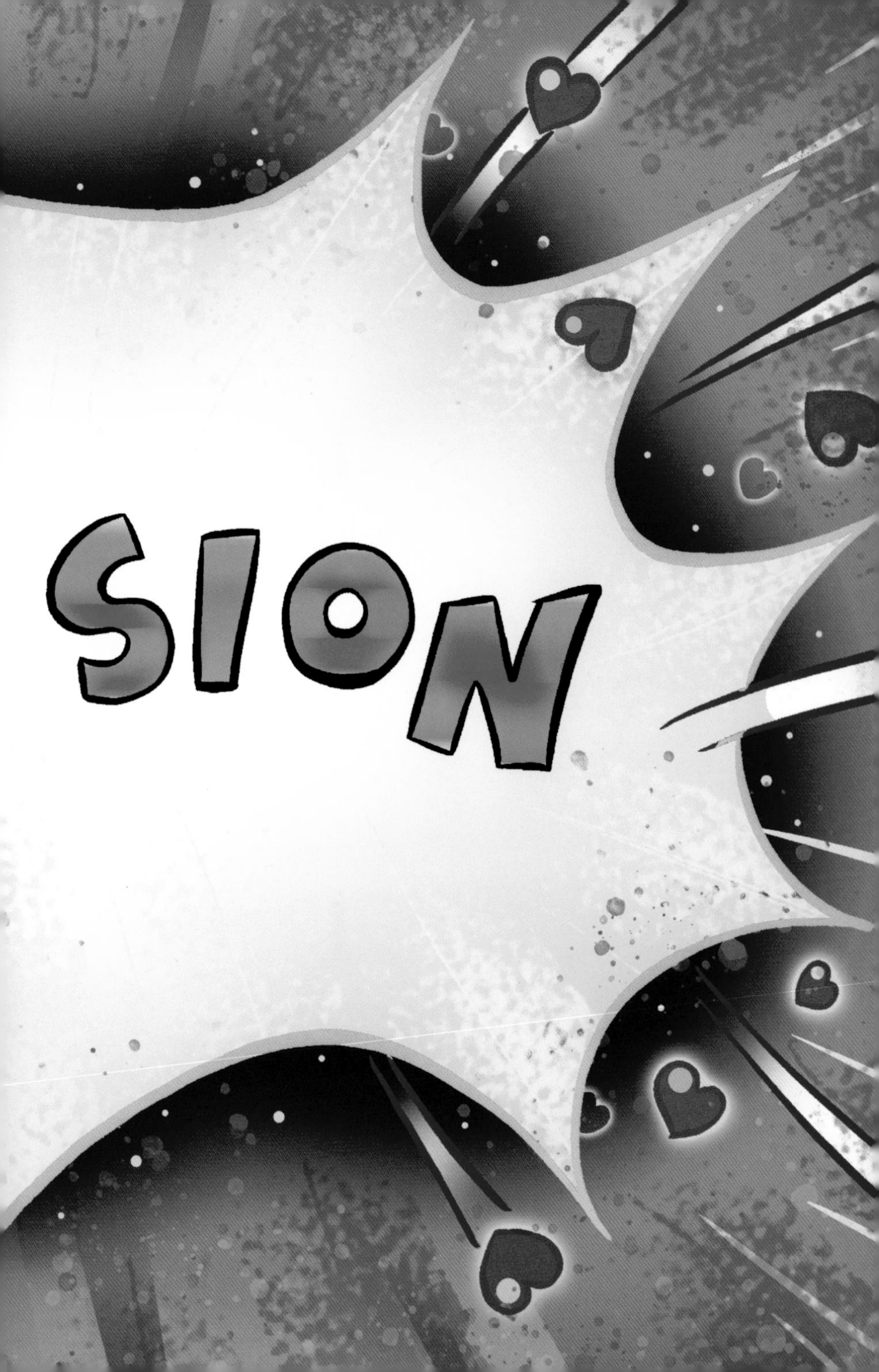
SION

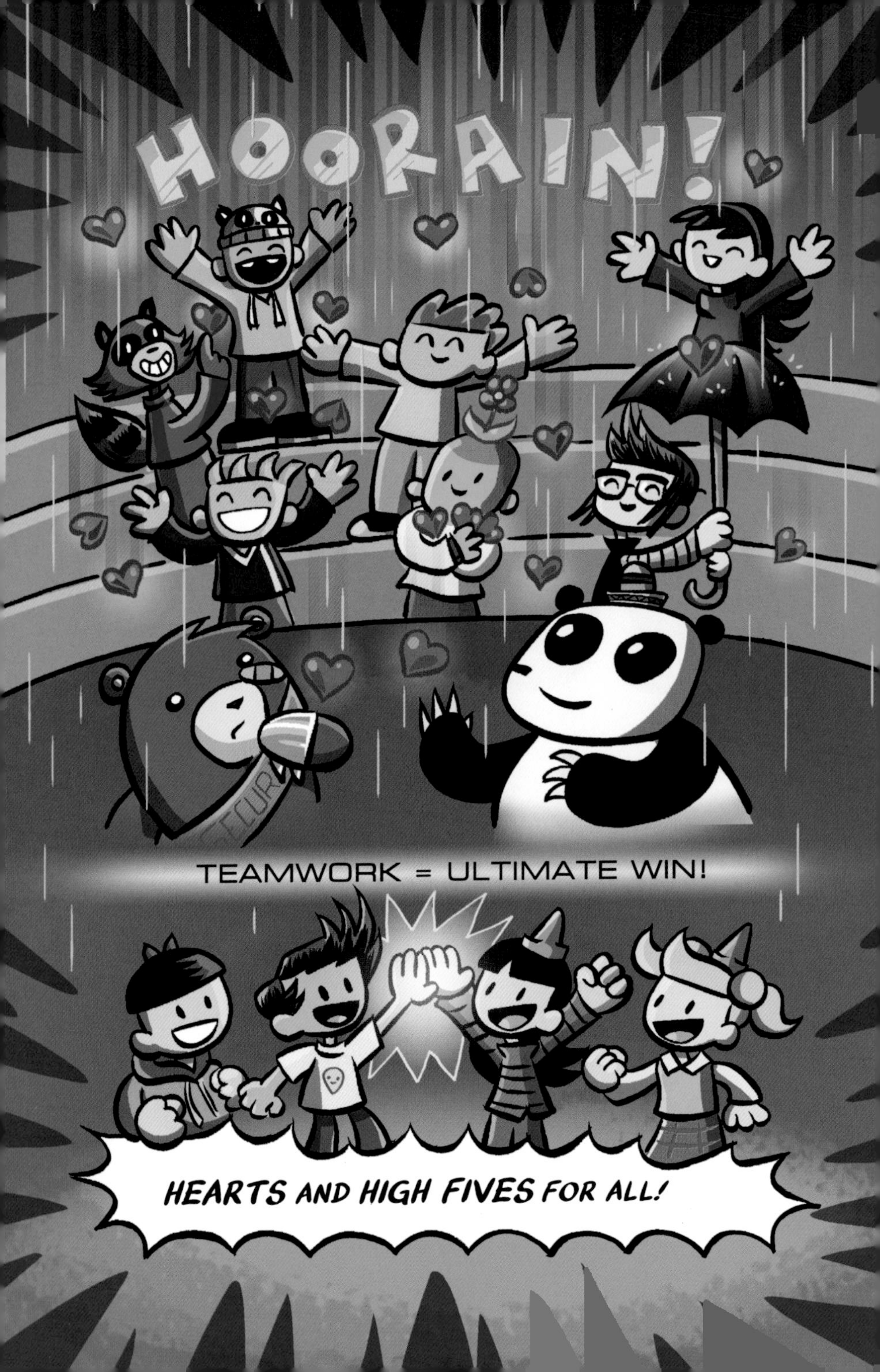
HOORAIN!
TEAMWORK = ULTIMATE WIN!
HEARTS AND HIGH FIVES FOR ALL!

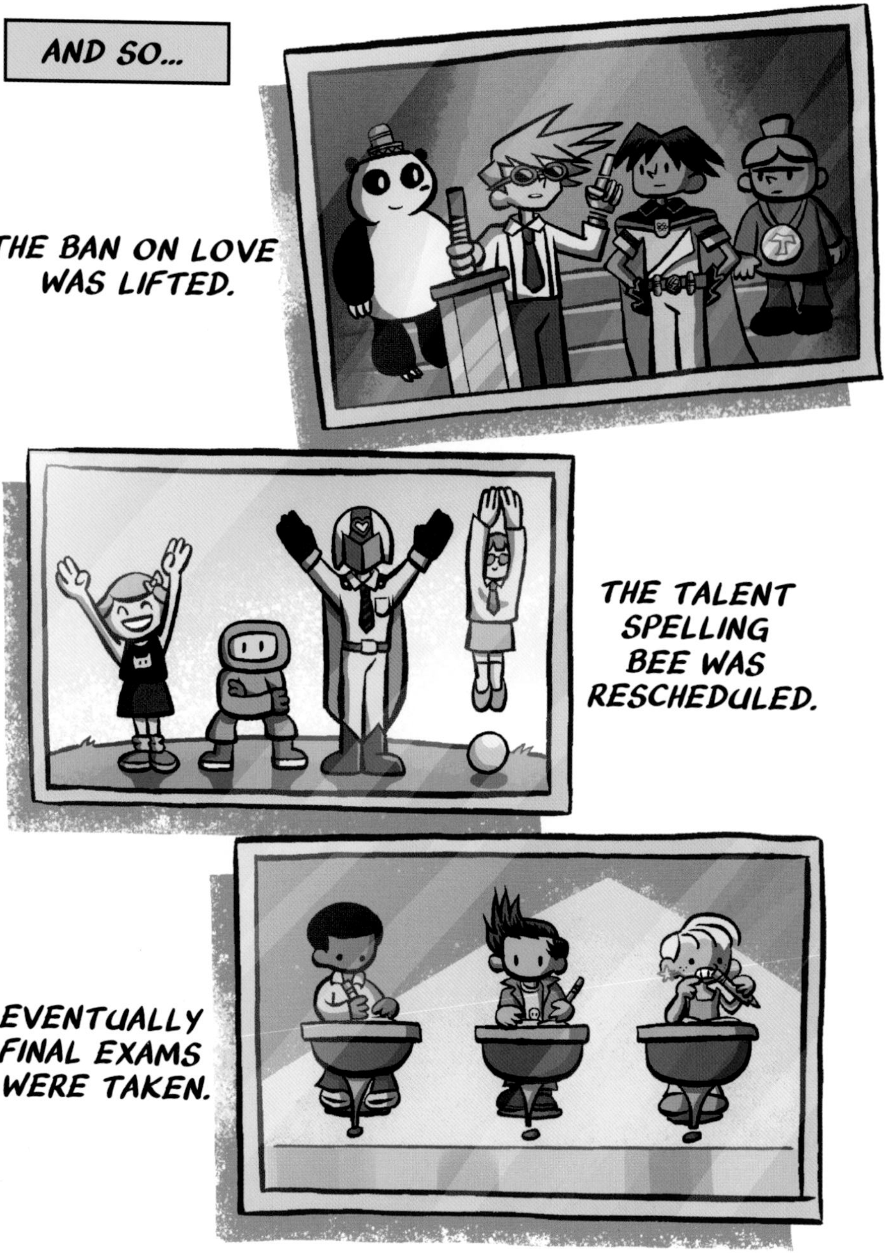
AND SO...
THE BAN ON LOVE WAS LIFTED.
THE TALENT SPELLING BEE WAS RESCHEDULED.
EVENTUALLY FINAL EXAMS WERE TAKEN.

BUT FIRST...
THERE WAS A DANCE PARTY!
(As is customary for the end of dramatic conflicts.)

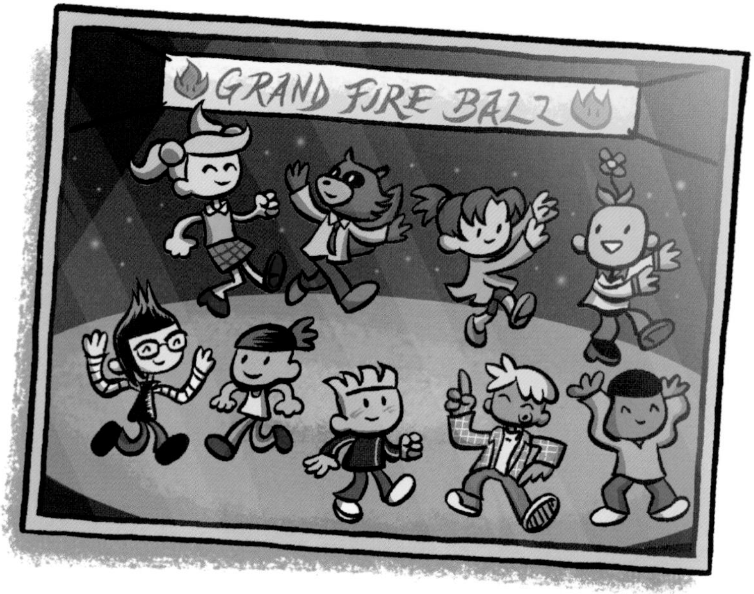
GRAND FIRE BALL

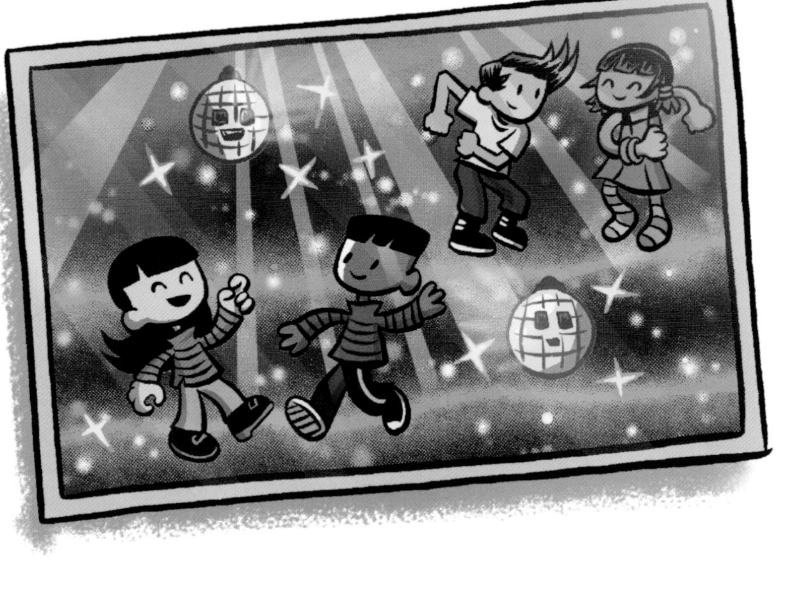

EVEN THOUGH A LOT OF RIVALRIES ENDED...

...NOT EVERYONE WAS READY FOR
FRIEND REQUESTS.

BUT NO ONE KNOWS WHO OR WHAT
THE FUTURE CAN HOLD!

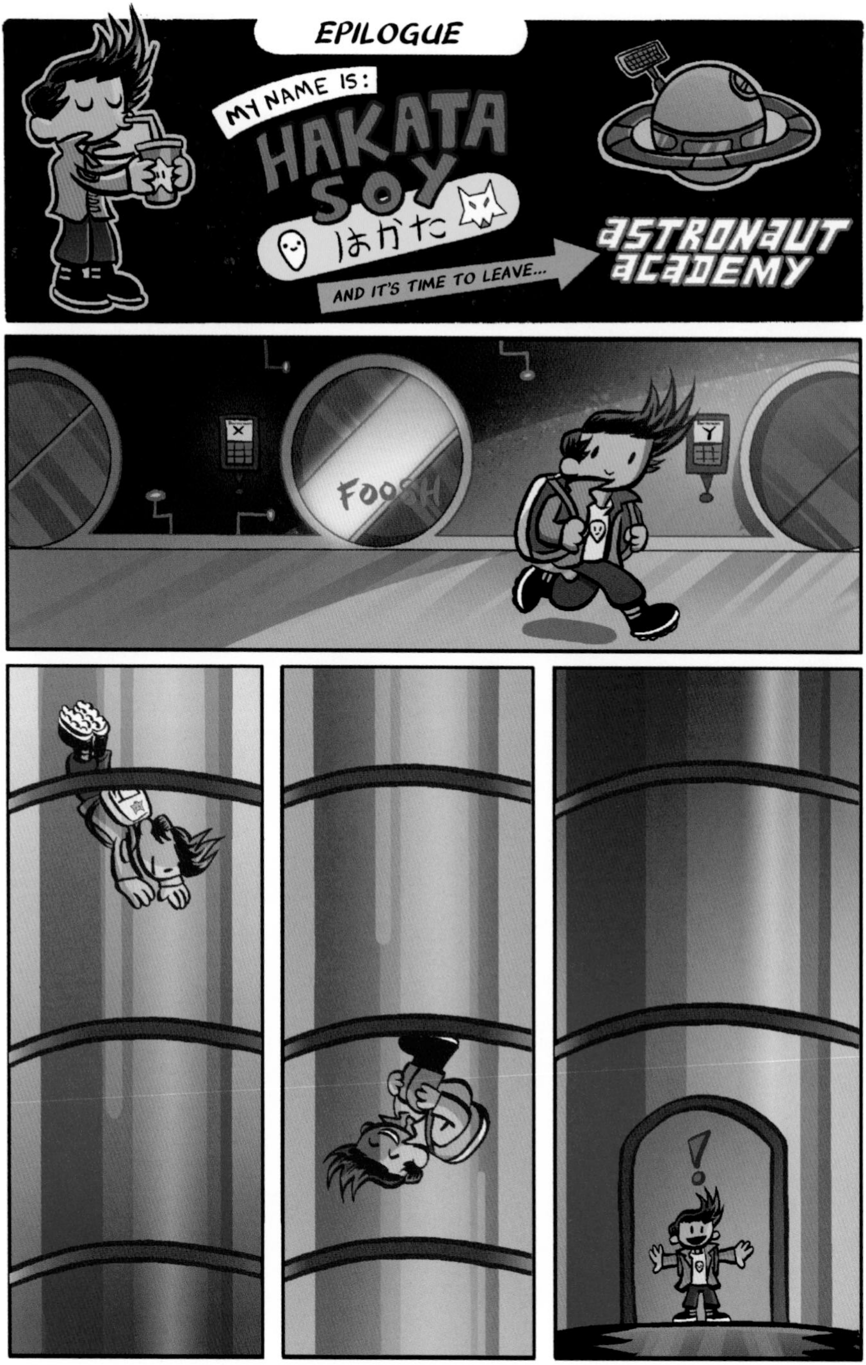
EPILOGUE
MY NAME IS:
HAKATA SOY
はかた
AND IT'S TIME TO LEAVE...
ASTRONAUT ACADEMY
FOOSH
!

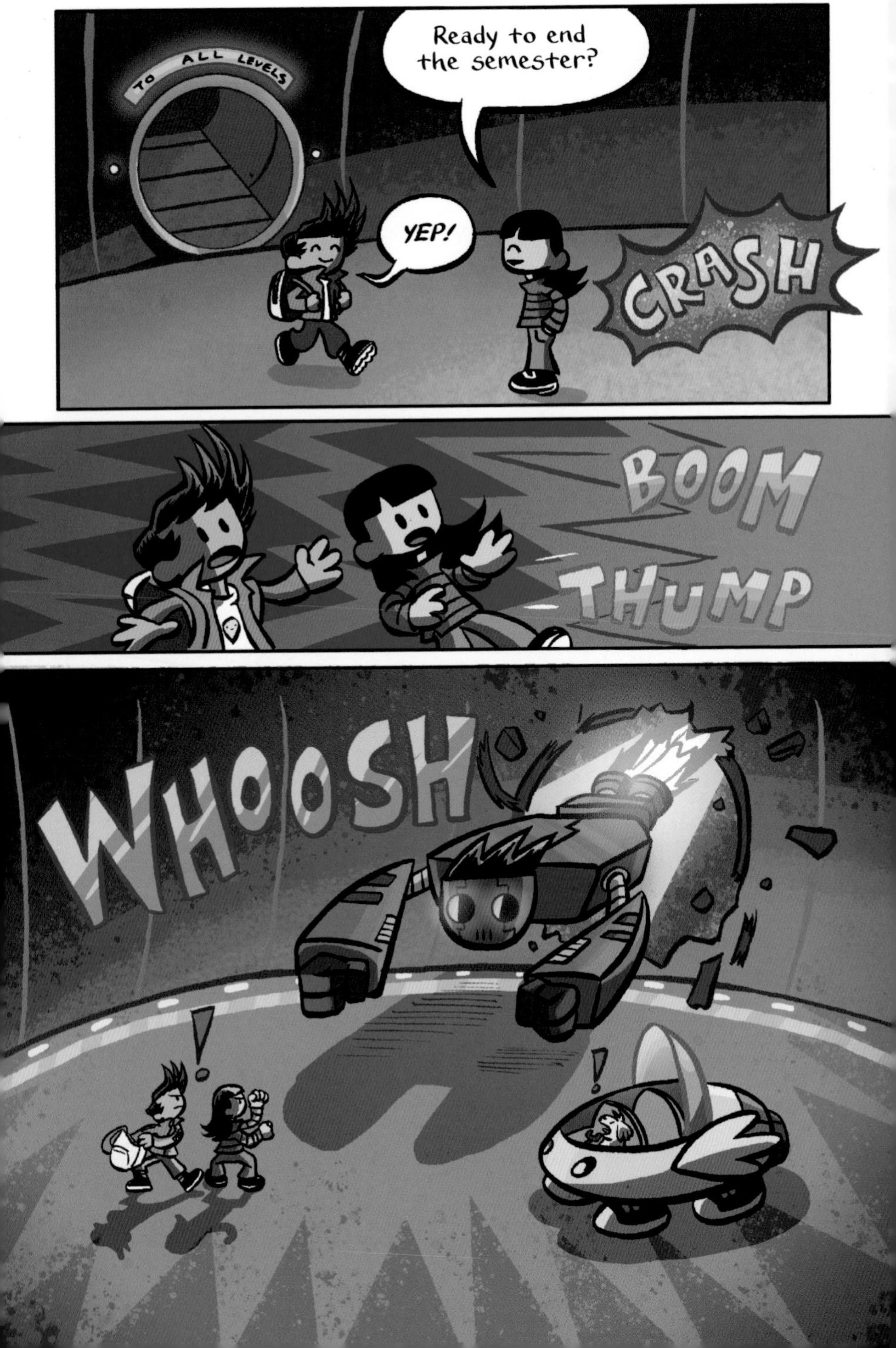
TO ALL LEVELS
Ready to end the semester?
YEP!
CRASH
BOOM
THUMP
WHOOSH
!
!

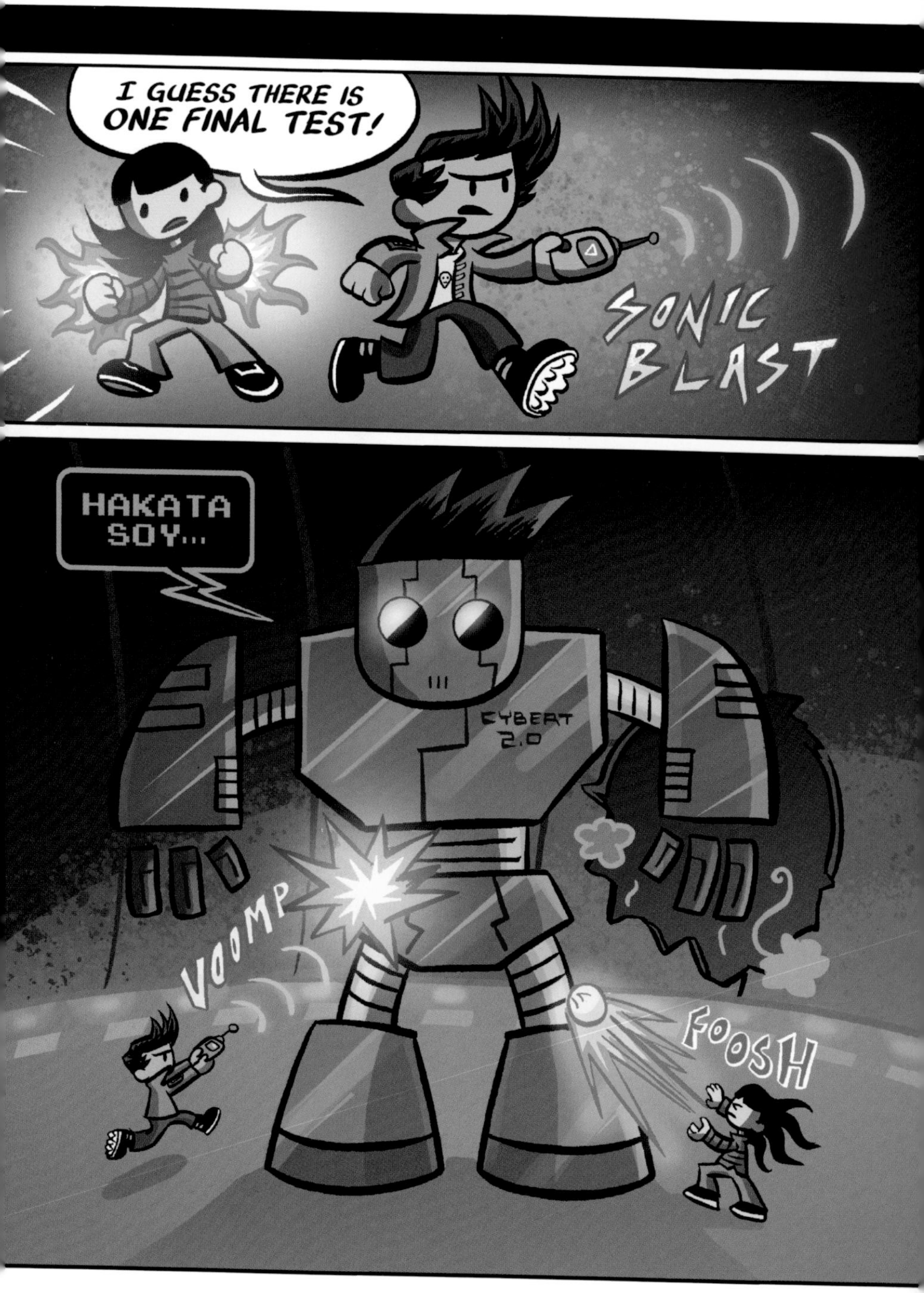
I GUESS THERE IS ONE FINAL TEST!
SONIC BLAST
HAKATA SOY...
CYBERT 2.0
VOOMP
FOOSH

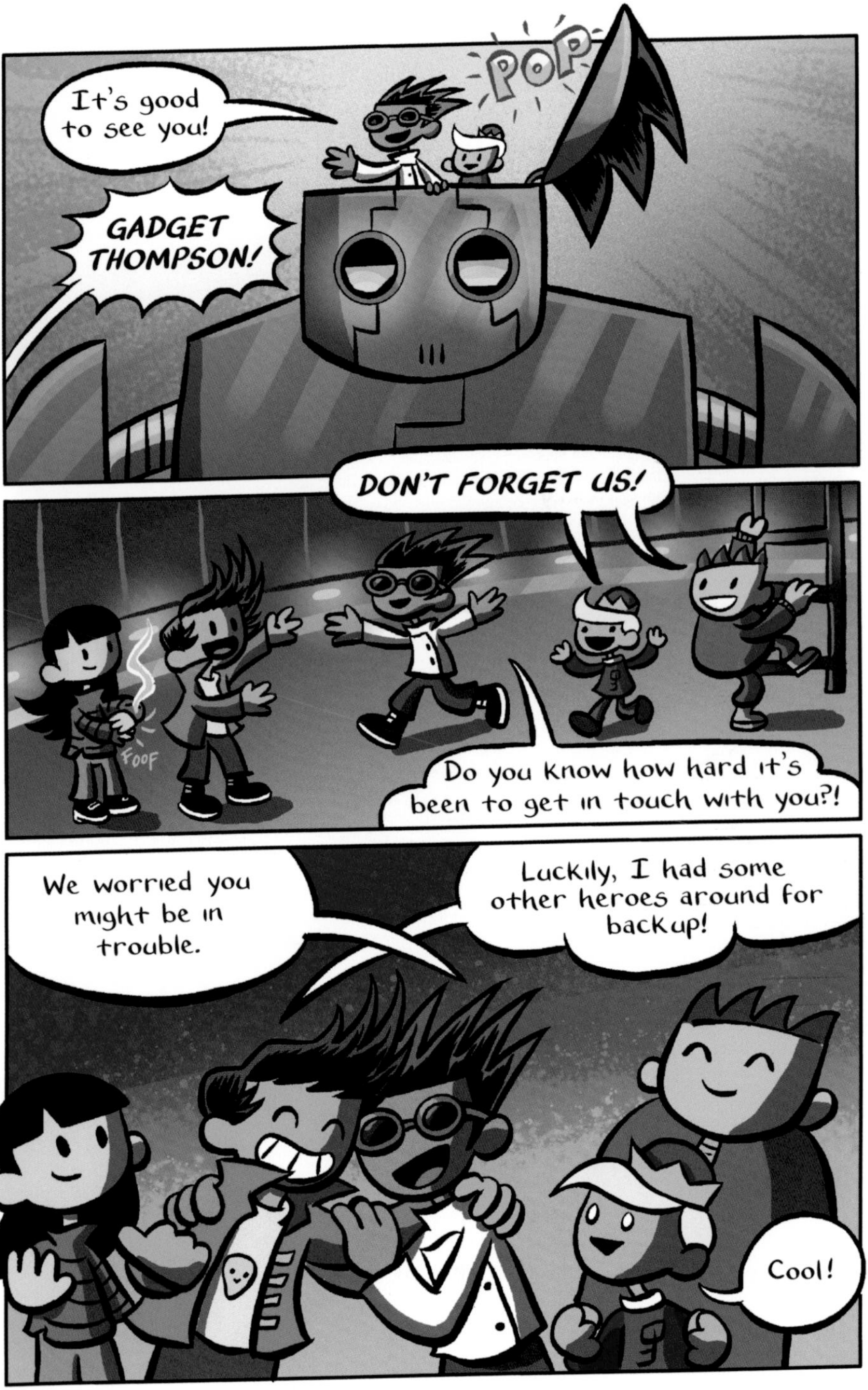
POP
It's good to see you!
GADGET THOMPSON!
DON'T FORGET US!
FOOF
Do you know how hard it's been to get in touch with you?!
We worried you might be in trouble.
Luckily, I had some other heroes around for backup!
Cool!

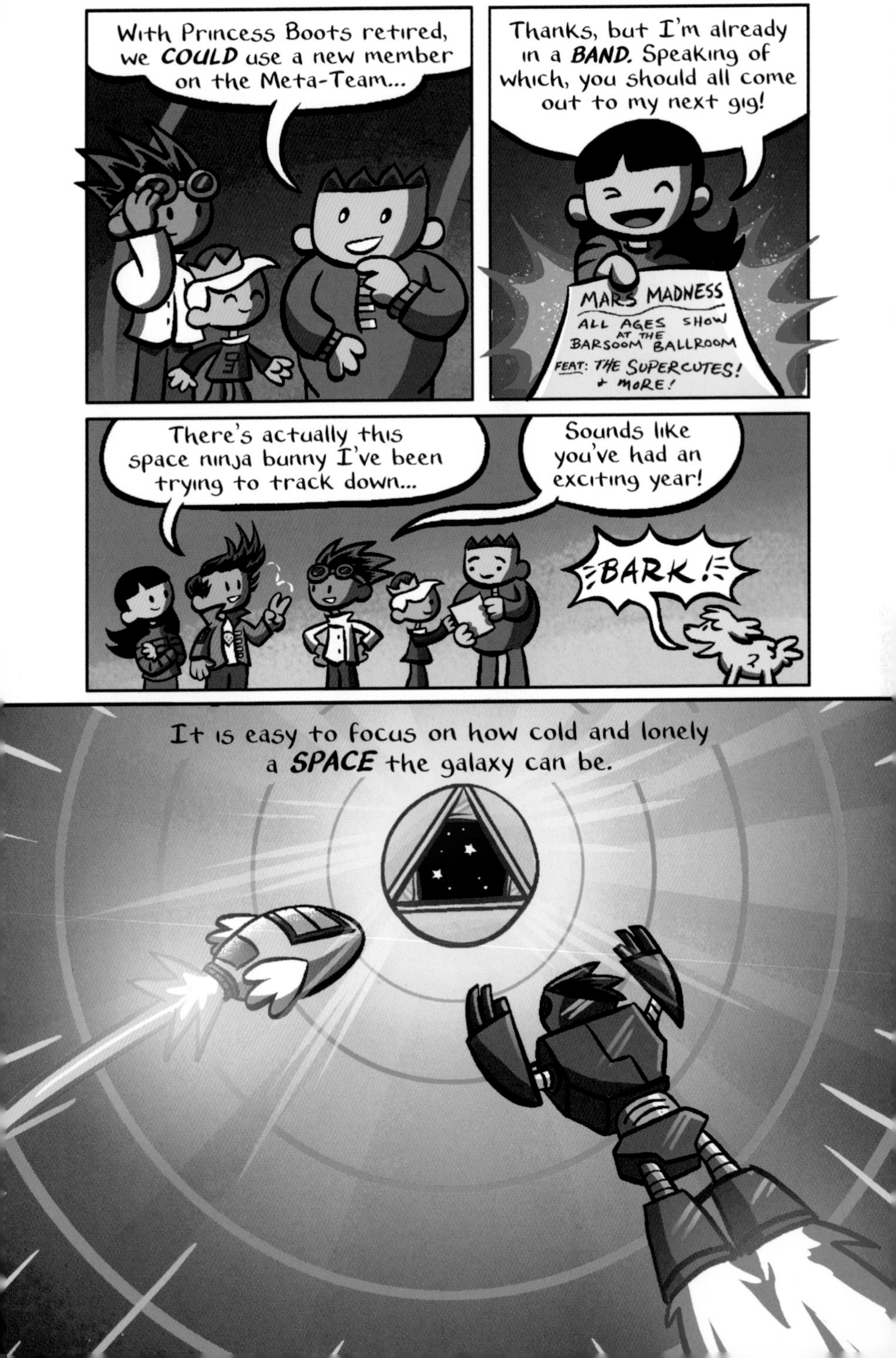
With Princess Boots retired, we COULD use a new member on the Meta-Team...
Thanks, but I'm already in a BAND. Speaking of which, you should all come out to my next gig!
MARS MADNESS
ALL AGES SHOW AT THE BARSOOM BALLROOM
FEAT: THE SUPERCUTES! + MORE!
There's actually this space ninja bunny I've been trying to track down...
Sounds like you've had an exciting year!
BARK!
It is easy to focus on how cold and lonely a SPACE the galaxy can be.

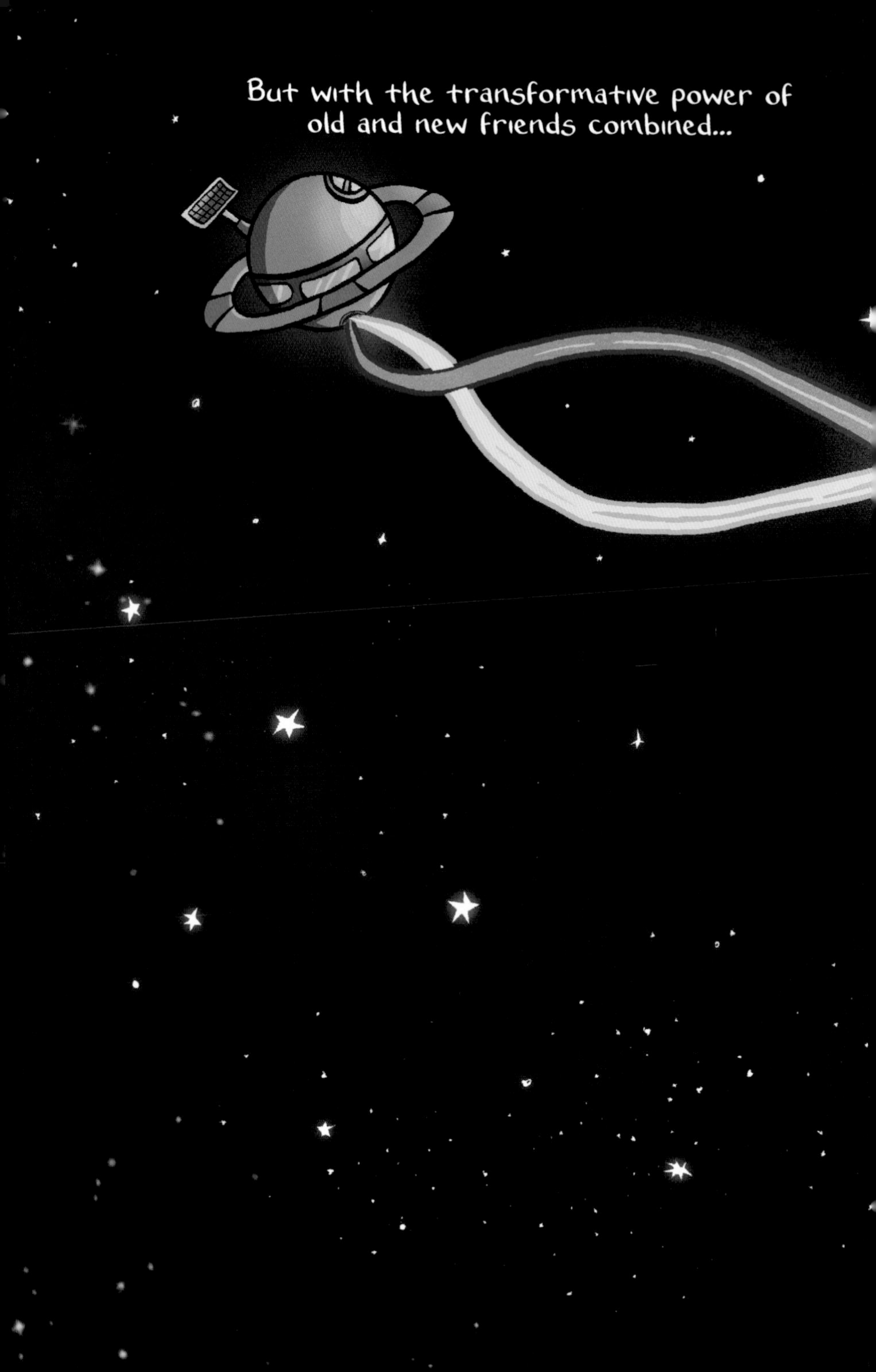
But with the transformative power of old and new friends combined...

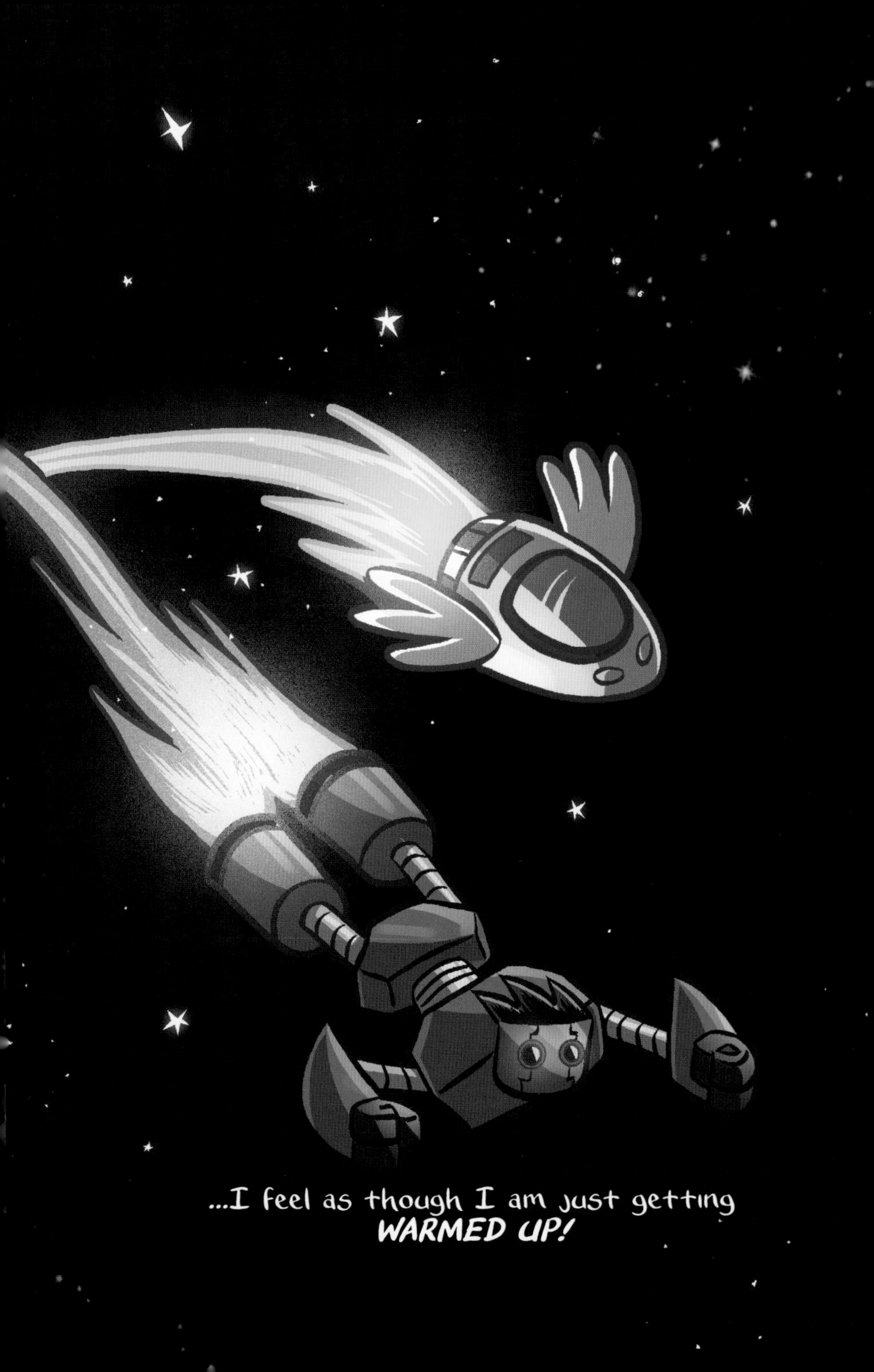
...I feel as though I am just getting
WARMED UP!

making astronaut academy

by dave roman

Ideas can come at any time, so I always keep a sketchbook and pencil close by.

I love designing new characters and imagining how they might interact with each other.

Prelude ??

1) Middle
2) Beginning
3) END!
4) Epilogue   SHOULD THIS GO FIRST?

I organize my various ideas by making lists and a story outline.

I write the "script" as a series of rough layouts called thumbnails.

My editor will read the early draft to give feedback and request revisions before I move on to the final art.

The pencil art is drawn on thick Bristol board, which can handle lots of erasing!

India ink is used to create dark, permanent lines. I apply it with a watercolor brush capable of various line weights.

The inked pages are scanned into a computer for cleaning up and lettering then shared with the colorist so they can create their magic.

The final files are sent to the publisher and we start the process all over again!

First Second
New York

Text and illustrations copyright © 2013 by Dave Roman
Published by First Second
First Second is an imprint of Roaring Brook Press,
a division of Holtzbrinck Publishing Holdings Limited Partnership
120 Broadway, New York, NY 10271

Don't miss your next favorite book from First Second!
For the latest updates go to firstsecondnewsletter.com and
sign up for our enewsletter.

Library of Congress Control Number: 2020911251
Paperback ISBN: 978-1-250-22593-1
Hardcover ISBN: 978-1-250-22594-8

Our books may be purchased in bulk for promotional, educational,
or business use. Please contact your local bookseller or the Macmillan
Corporate and Premium Sales Department at (800) 221-7945,
ext. 5442 or by email at MacmillanSpecialMarkets@macmillan.com.

Edited by Calista Brill and Rachel Stark
2021 cover design by Kirk Benshoff
2021 interior design by Rob Steen
2021 color by Fred C. Stresing
2013 cover design by Colleen AF Venable
2013 interior book design by John Green
2013 production assistants: Gale Williams and Megan Brennan
2013 gray color assists: Ma. Victoria Robado (Shouri),
Charles Eubanks, and Craig Arndt
2013 technical support: John Green
2013 life support: Raina Telgemeier

Printed in China by RR Donnelley Asia Printing Solutions Ltd.,
Dongguan City, Guangdong Province

First edition, 2013
Revised edition, 2021

Drawn with Staedtler graphite pencils on Strathmore 500 series Bristol paper.
Inked with Winsor & Newton Series 7 sable brushes and Speedball India ink.
Lettered with a combination of Speedball Hunt 107 crow quill nib and Yaytime font.
Colored with Photoshop.

Paperback: 10 9 8 7 6 5 4 3 2 1
Hardcover: 10 9 8 7 6 5 4 3 2 1